Believing Your Eyes

A Medieval Romance

The Sword of Glastonbury Series

Book 3

Lisa Shea

First Printing: July 2012

- 10 -

Print ISBN-13 978-0-9798377-1-5
Kindle ASIN: B008RIBYTI

Each night I dream of a world
Where people live with honor,
Where the truth is what matters,
Where it is important to stand up
For what is right.

I hope these books help share my dreams
With those who connect with my visions.

Believing Your Eyes

Chapter 1

England, 11180

"Full wise is he that can himselven knowe."
The Monkes Tale
Geoffrey Chaucer

The forest landscape undulated innocent and pristine beneath the frosted white of a fresh blanket of snow. Sunlight glinted mischievously through bare branches of oak and chestnut. Stephen drew in a lungful of the crisp late-January air, riding with lighthearted ease along the narrow path, keeping just in front of his younger companion.

Ian pulled ahead suddenly, his blonde hair shining in the sun. The wintry air made his breath puff in clouds of glittering lace as he cheerfully shouted out, "A pound says I beat you to the clearing!" He kicked his sleek, alabaster horse into a gallop.

Laughing, Stephen spurred his black mount and raced after him, his horse ploughing up the snowy trail with its hooves. It was only a matter of moments before he had caught and passed his friend.

The woods stretched on in a sea of twisting branches and sparkling icicles. Long streaks of clouds drifted far above, wafting across a pale-blue sky. The steeds flew across fallen logs and narrow streams. The distance between the two horses grew until Ian's horse had fallen far behind. Ian's challenges echoed distantly from the hollow depths of the woods.

The opening drew into view, and Stephen smiled. His younger friend was improving, but it would be a while before Ian could keep up with him through the twists and turns of the wooded path. He slowed the horse – and then as he drew in closer to the clearing he pulled harder, sliding to a stop in the dense snow. Every sense went on high alert as he scanned the area before him. He held up a hand, hearing Ian approach, and his friend was soon cascading to a stop beside him.

The horses snorted softly as they caught their breath. Echoes of the chase faded into silence. The pause lengthened as the men surveyed the woods with alert eyes. The two waited, watching, hearing only the distant sound of snow sloughing off branches.

The forest seemed, suddenly, very quiet.

Ian's voice came in a soft whisper. "What is it, Stephen?" He ran a hand through his short blond hair, then wrapped his brown traveling cloak tightly against a gust of crisp wind. Ahead to his left the sun was streaming through a gap in the trees, and the silence seemed almost palpable.

Ian shivered and looked around again. Gulping, his left hand lowered to the hilt of his sword, loosening the leather clasp on the scabbard with a deft twist of the thumb. "Do you think the Grays are finally turning south? Is that why you recommended we patrol the far north borders?"

Stephen's voice was soft. "Steady, Ian." Stephen motioned for Ian to be patient and listened intently again for a moment. He pointed to himself, and to the west side of the clearing. Then Stephen indicated for Ian to move to the east. Ian nodded, slipped off his horse and tied the reins securely to a nearby birch. He turned to Stephen, but dropped his eyes. Stephen saw in a glance the nervousness that added a tremor to Ian's movements.

Stephen looked with fondness at his friend. Ian had been trained well in the ways of arms, but although he was nearly twenty-five, he'd not been in many actual combat situations. Stephen gave him a nod of encouragement. The lad was long past ready for patrol. He reached out an arm, firmly clasping Ian's forearm, offering a smile. "Courage," he whispered.

Ian stood a moment to regain his composure, glancing over the sturdy, elegantly decorated breastplate and bracers he wore as if to steel himself. Then, taking a deep breath, he drew his sword and approached the clearing from the right.

Stephen watched him for a minute before slipping noiselessly to the left. Ian was Stephen's junior by five years, and Ian's father had routinely shielded his son from danger. Stephen knew the older man was nervous about risking the life of his only child. Still, surely the Lord knew it was critical for Ian to gain practical knowledge of how to defend his lands and home. When Stephen had been tasked with the training of the keep's forces, he had insisted that Ian join the patrols and put in his time on the wall.

The winter sun was bright against the open field of snow; Stephen gave his eyes a moment to adjust from the relative shadows of the forest. The cold seeped in through the leather armor he wore, but he preferred its flexibility and lightness over the heavy bulk that Ian gravitated toward.

Easing carefully through the deep drifts along the edge of the clearing, Stephen's eyes were drawn to a clutter of objects. He froze as their nature became clear. Sharp tension drew across his shoulders, and his grip tightened on his hilt. Ten snow-coated, rough looking men lay sprawled on the ground, their darkened blood marbleizing the pure white around them. To one side, hidden by trees until now, a cairn of ash sent wispy tendrils of smoke upwards, the melted snow around it languidly extinguishing the edges of the low flame.

Stephen's every sense went on high alert, attentive to the slightest movement, the faintest sound. The woods obliviously went on with its raspy sweep of branch on branch, the delicate flutter of snow easing from a passing breeze. At last he gave a calling wave to Ian, and the two moved into the clearing proper.

Stephen's brow creased as he drew close, taking in the gear on the fallen men. "Bandits by the look of it. All long dead. A few survivors ran off north." He glanced at a swath of tracks leading out of the clearing. "Those belong to the fleeing wolves' heads." He took in the signs of their lack of discipline; it was one of the few advantages they held against the bandits. He glanced up past the tracks with concern; a new wave of the storm was darkening the edges of the sky overhead, and a light flurry gently drifted down, slowly swirling into their prints.

Stephen motioned toward the glowing embers. "Whoever took them on, at least one person remained alive," he added quietly, walking toward the low mound of ash and stone. "Grays would leave their dead for the wolves. These bodies have been given a decent sending off." His eyes scanned the dead bandits for a moment, then moved again with curiosity to the cairn of ash. "I wonder who ..."

His voice trailed off as he gazed into the reddish glow. Something within gleamed and caught his eye. He picked up a stick and pushed the object out of the coals with it.

Ian's eyes lit up. "A bronze bracer!" He jumped forward and reached for the glowing object. The metal band was finely worked and glinted brightly as the clouds opened for a moment.

"Wait!" shouted Stephen in alarm, knocking Ian off balance enough that the blond fell sideways into a heavy drift under an oak. Stephen sighed and smiled fondly at his friend. "It is red hot - you would have burned your hand!" He shook his head as Ian ruefully climbed out of the snowbank and brushed himself off. "Still, do look at it," Stephen remarked, kneeling near the bracer to get a better look. "I have not seen lettering like this for years. An old language, but the engraving is new." He sat quietly for several moments, examining the markings.

A far-off horse's whinny snapped Stephen's head up, and he grabbed Ian by the arm. Together they sprinted toward the trees, coming alongside their own mounts to steady them, loosing their ties. A hush fell over the woods again; Stephen concentrated to hear any noise that seemed out of place.

Several full minutes went by without a sound. The light snow continued to fill their prints, melding them with the landscape.

Then, growing in intensity, the distinctive crash of hooves on dead branches approached from the north. Stephen drew back, pulling deeper into the shadows. The noise grew louder until two bearded men with wolfskin capes galloped thunderously into the clearing, broadswords held high. The redheaded man in front trampled through the edge of the cairn as he twisted the reins forcefully to slow his mount. He turned to snarl angrily at the second, who quickly spoke up.

"See, she ain't here," whined the smaller man, a greasy, unkempt redhead in a makeshift uniform. "We killed off her escorts, we did. Just like you ordered. Then Barney, yeah - it was Barney! He tried to wing her horse with an arrow, see, to make sure she didn't get away. But she was near the beast and the arrow got her in the side." His eyes furtively slid from side to side as he related his tale in a quick staccato. "It was poison dipped. It was an accident! He panicked and ran. I came back to tell you what happened. You wanted me to face her alone? Anyway, she didn't get far, it's sure. She's gone to her maker by now. What a tigress she was. Yeah, she put up a fight!" He licked his drooling lips, and his eyes glowed with some obscene thought.

The leader's face glowed crimson with fury at this news. "Your orders were to bring her in alive, fool," stormed the heavyset man. He cuffed the smaller man across the head, sending him tumbling off his horse.

"It was Barney!" pleaded the man, cringing in the snow.

"But you were in charge," shot back the larger man, "and Master was adamant about wanting her alive." A wolfish smile twisted his face. "I'll send *you* in to give him the news. Maybe you'll die more quickly than Barney did." He chuckled to himself. "You'd better hope so," he added with a sneer.

He looked around the clearing for a moment, then up at the sky. His brow furrowed. "With the storm, she won't last long, if she is even alive. We'll come back later to fetch her corpse." He glanced up at the gathering clouds again, then nodded. "That will have to do." Wheeling his shaggy mount, he galloped out of the clearing.

Gulping, the other scrambled onto his horse and spurred it on after his leader.

The hoofbeat echoed, faded, and then was lost in the valleys of the deep forest.

Ian let out a shuddering breath, creating a cloud of frost. "We had better get back to town," he whispered nervously, his hands shaking as he smoothed down his hair. "There could be more of them searching for the woman." He jumped as snow tumbled from a heavy branch.

Stephen retied his horse to a limb and circled the edge of the clearing, examining the ground. "This woman, whoever she is, is obviously wanted for a reason. She could provide valuable information on the Grays' movements. Search around to the west - see if you can pick up her tracks."

Ian made as if to protest, but seeing the set look on Stephen's face, he instead turned and set off hunting for any sign of the wounded woman.

Stephen moved with careful attention, his eyes scanning every drift of snow, every stray bent branch. His gaze moved past a shadow – and then swept back again.

There. Scattered drops of dark crimson – and the faintest of scratches, made by the sweep of a pine branch.

He kept his voice low, but pitched it to carry. "Here, to the east."

Ian ran to join him, and Stephen pointed out the signs. "Whoever she is, she has talent at covering her trail," he murmured as he eased forward. "Get our horses and follow behind me."

Soon they were tracking the tracing path through the wilderness, a light snow falling about their shoulders.

After an hour, they had traversed quite a distance. Many times the trail seemed to disappear in a stream or rocky area, but, with diligence, one of them was able to spot a broken branch or a smear of dried blood clinging to a sapling. Still, as twilight settled a violet cape over the forest, Stephen worried in earnest that they might lose all view of the faint signs under the gently falling snow.

Then, all at once, the way became clear. The pair came over the crest of a hill to find quite distinct footprints heading down the slope and ending under an ancient willow tree by a frozen stream.

Stephen stopped to survey the scene. Beneath the tree lay a roan stallion that turned his head protectively at their approach. Curled up against his flanks was a sleeping woman wrapped in a thick, black cloak, the hood pulled close around her face. She had apparently been there for a while; the snow had covered much of her body with a fine layer of white. The sun was setting behind them, and shadows were stretching across the hollow.

Stephen motioned Ian to stand guard and handed his own horse's reins over. He glanced around the clearing with a sharp eye, then he carefully worked his way down the snowy slope. The horse watched him steadily, but there was no other sound or movement. Stopping for a moment at the foot of the hill, Stephen then slowly moved toward the tree, careful to keep his hands away from his weapons so as not to frighten the woman. He grew concerned when she didn't stir at his approach, and, reaching her, he dropped easily to a knee at her side. He gently brushed off the snow to find a sign of the arrow the Grays spoke of.

In a flash, Stephen felt cold metal at his throat. The woman's eyes flew open; a pair of fever-bright green eyes burned into Stephen's own. He kept his body perfectly still despite the decidedly wicked edge on the dagger pressing into his neck. He looked steadily into that desperate gleam.

"I am here to help," he told her quietly. "We come from the keep at Penrith. We can take you there; you will be safe and cared for." He didn't move a muscle, willing her to trust him.

The woman seemed undecided, but her arm did not waver.

Stephen gently placed his fingers over the hand she held the dagger with. "You must know that you have been poisoned. If you kill me, it will not matter if I am telling the truth or not. You will die here in the snow."

This seemed to penetrate the fog behind her eyes; she nodded her acquiescence and reluctantly allowed him to take the dagger from her hand. He reached behind her and put the dagger in the leather saddlebag on her steed. Stephen then lifted the edge of her cloak to see the damage. Her blue tunic was ripped open and soaked through with blood. The scarlet rash flaring around a jagged wound on her lower ribs showed that some sort of poison - probably dwale - was already working its way into her system.

"We have got to get you back quickly," he explained as he worked. Examining the injury more closely, Stephen swore beneath his breath. The wound in her side was bad enough, but the poison was already taking hold of her. He could see how dilated her eyes were, and her body was trembling, although that could be the cold doing its own harm. Stephen looked back up the hill. "Bring the horses," he called to Ian. "She needs treatment as soon as possible." Ian led the steeds down the hill as Stephen lifted her in his arms. Her horse stood immediately beside them.

"Who are we rescuing? The lost daughter of a nearby Lord?" Ian asked in breathless wonder as he drew near. Stephen could almost see the puff in Ian's chest, the stories spinning in the man's mind with which he would boast to the serving wenches in the local taverns.

Stephen shook his head. Taking care not to jostle her, Stephen gathered the woman securely in his arms. He gently placed her onto his horse sidesaddle, then climbed up behind to steady her. Her roan moved close in, apparently prepared to follow. Ian reached for the horse's tack, but the horse only had a leather saddle and bags - no bridle or reins. He glanced around, shrugged, then mounted and turned his horse to follow Stephen.

Night fell quickly, and soon the winds were swirling the light snow into their faces, stinging their eyes. Stephen guided their horses back through the woods, moving with speed now that they could follow their own trail back. He held the woman tightly against him with one arm and tried to keep her warm despite of the dropping temperatures. Behind them, Stephen could hear Ian following close with the riderless roan.

Blinded by thick falling snow on this moonless night, Stephen struggled to see the path before him. Yet, when they drew near the clearing, the woman straightened against him and turned her face up to his. She tried to speak, but was unable to make any sound.

Understanding her need, Stephen turned the horse to face into the clearing and reined in to a stop. She raised her head and looked evenly out over the bodies, to the now dark cairn. She pulled the left side of her cloak back, revealing a long leather scabbard at her hip. It was made with high quality leather, but was simple in design - meant to last rather than impress. Down the center were stamped the letters 'Lucia'.

The woman took a deep breath, then drew her sword. It matched the scabbard - it was sturdy and well-made without being flashy. The hilt was wrapped with green leather and secured with bronze wire. The sword bore the hundred small marks of frequent use. She solemnly saluted the cairn with her sword, paused for a wordless prayer, then kissed the hilt before resheathing it. Stephen watched the tears slide down her cheeks as she looked up at him and nodded. She was done.

"Thank you," she rasped softly, pulling her cloak around her body. Then she closed her eyes and slumped back against him.

Stephen wrapped her within his own cloak and moved off again at a quicker pace. They were still a half hour at least from the keep, and the temperature was dropping quickly.

Shivers racked her body, and he drew her even closer. His mind sorted through the possibilities as they rode. What woman would be traveling in the winter with the bandit attacks coming so hot and heavy? Where had she trained with a sword? He rode the remaining miles as quickly as he dared, pushing to get her to safety.

It seemed too long a time before the town's outer stone walls and main gate loomed ahead darkly, somber against the storm clouds. Stephen rode hard across the open meadow to the sturdy doors, pulling to a stop beneath the walls.

Ian's voice rang out in order. "Open the gates," he cried. "We've a wounded girl! Open up!"

Torches could be seen moving around in the windows by the stout wooden gate as the soldiers recognized the two men. The logs holding the doors secure made a low grating noise as they slowly slid free. The heavy doors were pulled open, and the three horses galloped inside.

Stephen led the way through the wide dirt streets of the town, galloping past the lights from windows and torches to the main building atop the hill. A few sleepy heads poked out of stone-lined windows to see who was racing through in the dense darkness. The streets were clean and the buildings well-kept; garden plots scattered in open areas were tended and neat.

Soon they had arrived at the main keep's gates, which stood open. Stable boys hurried with torches in hand to take the horses and guide the two companions inside. Stephen put his injured charge over his shoulder and hurried up the main stairs, taking a right in the great hall, down a narrow, twisting flight of steps to the healer's room. He grabbed a torch from the wall as he passed.

"It makes no sense to me why they heal down here in the dark," he muttered, balancing Lucia on his shoulder while carefully lowering the torch toward the bronze oil lamp on the side table. The wick caught, and suddenly the room flickered with light and shadow.

Ian came in behind him and lit the other candles while Stephen placed Lucia on the low central oak table, draping his own cloak over her for warmth. She lay curled up and motionless while Stephen moved to a cluttered bench beneath a tall set of shelves. Stephen reached for a pottery bowl holding a scant amount of yellow powder, a glass vial of water, and a marble mortar and pestle. All four stone walls were lined with shelves full of odd-smelling potions, drying herbs, and musty parchments.

Ian finished with the candles and stood by the wood table, apparently unsure of what to do next. Stephen let him be, carefully mixing the ingredients together, then adding in a pale yellow liquid from another glass vial.

A raspy voice called from the top of the stairs. "I am coming, I am coming." An elderly man in a rusty-brown robe hobbled down the flight, rubbing tired eyes beneath heavily sprouted brows. "I heard from the stable boys ... she has been poisoned?"

Stephen nodded, brow furrowed as he showed his results of his efforts to the tonsured monk.

"I know," sighed the monk. "It has been a long winter, and the Grays have been very active. Our supplies are running out. If only we could find more, and did not need to ration our remaining medicines. I guess this will have to do for her, though."

Lucia lay on the table, motionless now except for the slight trembling of her hands and feet. Her eyes were closed. Stephen gently drew the cloak back. In the light of the many candles, he now saw that she wore a long, blue tunic over a pair of black leggings. He heard Ian's snort of surprise, and smiled to himself. Not so unusual after all. He had met numerous women on his travels who preferred the warmth of pants for winter riding.

Stephen loosened the brown leather belt and gingerly slid the tunic up above her stomach, revealing her waist. The fabric was soaked with blood, and a long slice could be traced from her hip up to her lower ribs. He could also see that a speckled rash was spreading across her skin. He took a folded square of cloth from a shelf and poured some of the mixture into its center.

The monk turned to Ian. "Hold her wrists. She may struggle because of the pain," he warned the blond, gently pressing down on her ankles. "We have got to try and keep her from hurting herself. May the Lord calm her," he added to Stephen.

"Thank you, Matthew. Let us hope we have gotten to it quickly enough this time."

Stephen carefully cleaned the wound with a damp cloth, doing his best not to cause her further harm. She moaned softly while he worked, twisting beneath his hands, her body shivering more violently with every passing moment. As he wiped away the layers of caked blood, he found to his surprise that it was not deep after all; rather, a glancing slide along her ribs that had bled a great deal. Others he had worked on had been poisoned by far deeper wounds. With such a shallow injury, he didn't believe that enough poison could have gotten into her system to cause the spreading rash and bone-deep trembling.

Maybe the Grays were using something new, something even more vicious?

He held back the racing thoughts with practiced effort. For now he had to address the task at hand. Then he could have the luxury of dreading an even greater threat.

He quickly finished cleaning the wound, then put a clean cloth against it to hold back the bleeding. He used another cloth to wrap around her waist and hold the first one in place. A leather thong was tied to hold the bandage in position.

Satisfied that the wound was not mortal, he did a quick survey of the rest of her outfit while Ian looked away in embarrassment. In addition to the tunic and pants she wore high black, well-worn leather boots, which he removed, and simple stockings. He did not find any other indications of a wound beneath any of this, and his gentle examination of her arms and legs found strong muscle, but no obviously broken bones. This arrow wound seemed to be the only serious injury. Still, it should not have caused the rash that he could see on her stomach, nor the trembling that had seized her.

The reactions concerned him. What had happened?

Ian's eyes drew with curiosity over the woman's face. "She does not look familiar," he mused. "Who could she be?"

Stephen did not break his concentration, staring intently at the wound. "I think her name is Lucia," he replied, and glanced at the sword at her side. The Grays had deliberately sought her for some reason. They'd apparently poisoned her by accident, and had wanted her alive. As for the poison - it didn't seem to him like the arrow wound could account for her state. What, then?

He looked up at her face, at her closed eyes, down to the rosy lips. They were dark crimson against the paleness of her cheeks.

Dark crimson?

He looked more closely. There were flecks of blood around her lips. He took one of her trembling hands from Ian, examining it. He could see now that there was ash and blood mixed in with the dirt, and that they were singed, as if by fire.

Suddenly, the answer hit him clearly. She must have tried to clean her wound herself, of course, when her enemy had fled. She had gotten the poison on her fingers. His mind searched the possibilities. While building the cairn for her fallen comrades, she had burned herself. Naturally, she put her fingers in her mouth to soothe them.

The poison wasn't on her body - it was in her stomach.

"Sit her up," ordered Stephen, as he turned to the bench for his bowl of mixture.

Lucia half-opened her eyes as she was raised, and he could see again how dilated her pupils were. She tried to speak, but no words came out, and she gave up in exasperation and weariness. Stephen stood before her for a moment, holding the bowl. He looked across at the exhausted woman.

"You must drink this," he quietly requested, again willing her to believe him. She hesitated, looking up at him. "Please. Trust me," he added softly, holding her gaze.

She looked down at her tended wound, and at the rash that was visible even beyond the bandages. Looking back up at Stephen, she appeared to be weighing something in her mind. Finally, she nodded quietly.

Her hands were shaking too badly for her to hold the bowl herself, so he carefully poured the mixture into her mouth. She drank it down, closing her eyes at the taste of it. Almost immediately, she clutched at her stomach and moaned in pain. Matthew grabbed a nearby pail, and after a few moments, she vomited convulsively, gagging out the contents of her stomach. She continued to retch long after her belly was empty, the shivers wracking her entire body. All the while, Stephen wiped her brow with a cloth, keeping her long, auburn braid to one side. Matthew held her shoulders, and Ian kept her from rolling back.

When she was finally done, she slumped back onto the table, limp and exhausted.

Ian looked with concern at the still figure, but Matthew gave Stephen a pat on the shoulder. "I believe you were on the mark," he asserted. "She must have ingested some. That explains the symptoms." He put the pail to one side. "We have done what we can to get the base of it out – we will need to keep her warm now, and help her to stay awake, at least for a short while."

Stephen glanced around at the room, which, while bright with candlelight, was chill and damp. "It would be best if we could settle her in one of the rooms upstairs."

Matthew nodded in agreement. "With the seriousness of her symptoms, we should arrange a twenty-four hour watch too, for perhaps a week, until the symptoms fully fade." He glanced to the younger man. "Ian, could you arrange that?"

Ian brightened with a task to take charge of. "For my lovely lady, of course!"

An odd twinge ran through Stephen at Ian's possessive language, but he said nothing.

Ian continued, "I shall go wake my father right away. We can arrange for her to have one of the larger bedrooms." He looked over to Stephen, then his smile widened. "She should have great fun spending time with Anna once she recovers," he added with glee. "I need to get things ready!" He grinned with pleasure, then turned and ran up the stone steps.

Matthew turned to Stephen as Ian's footsteps finished echoing off the cold, stone walls. He chuckled, then looked down at Lucia, who lay with her eyes closed. "Aye, she is a pretty lass, though perhaps not the Lady that Ian is hoping for! Whatever she is, she is real enough. Call me a fool if he is not already smitten with her." Matthew smiled to himself at the thought, then gathered a woolen blanket off the shelf to wrap about her.

Stephen turned away from Matthew and gazed down at the exhausted woman. Lying there, she almost seemed to be a child, her arrow wound perhaps a youthful nightmare. He reached absently to her face and eased a stray hair back into the braided weave. She made a small noise, then lapsed back into silence.

Child indeed. Stephen could tell by the firm muscles in her arms that any appearance of helplessness was deceiving. She obviously knew how to wield that sword, and much else besides. Yes, it would be interesting to find out where she was from and where she had been headed.

His brow furrowed. For all he knew, she was the 'companion' of one of the wolves' heads and was being hauled back to pay the piper for some misdeed. Time would tell the truth, though.

Stephen took the blanket from Matthew and wrapped it gently around Lucia's body. He lifted her swaddled form easily, then snagged the handle of the oil lamp and headed toward the stairs. He could already hear muted footsteps and shouted orders as the great hall came to life.

Above it all, Ian's voice gave the commands.

Chapter 2

Lucia blinked her eyes open into a flickering darkness, moaning in pain. Last she knew, she had been in a damp, candlelit room. Her world had consisted of shadowy figures, staggering agony, and a pair of deep brown eyes that dared her to trust them.

Her limbs ached as if she had been lying for a while, and her lips were cracked and parched.

There was a movement at her side. A steady hand was behind her head, raising her up slightly, while a mug was placed at her lips. She drank down the warm mead gratefully. The same dark eyes were there, comforting her, half in shadows from the bronze oil lamp which sat beside him on a small table. A wet cloth was drawn across her forehead.

She tried to speak, but no voice emerged from her tight throat.

"Penrith keep," he rumbled in a low, reassuring voice. "You are safe."

Her hand went to the sharp pain at her side. The area was bandaged, and she groaned. What had she done now?

"It is healing," he offered. "Right now it is the poison we are more worried about. You need to rest."

He offered another drink of mead, and she took it, then fell back, exhausted. Pain seemed to blossom across her entire body, and a wave of chills ran over her. He drew the cloth across her face again, his eyes attentive. "I am here," he murmured.

For some reason this soothed her, and she nodded, closing her eyes and falling back into troubled dreams.

* * *

Bright light streamed against her eyelids. She pried them awake against the sleepy crust. The room seemed to glow in brilliant white, from the embroidered alabaster curtains at the window to the thick ivory fur rug which fronted the blazing fireplace.

A slim girl in burgundy turned, laughing in delight when she saw Lucia's eyes were open. Lucia tried to speak, but no words would come.

The whiteness flared and faded away.

* * *

Darkness again. The deep brown eyes were back, steady at her side, and this time he eased her to half sit, then slowly fed her spoonfuls of chicken broth. She shivered but could not tell if it was with an icy chill or a searing heat. Her side throbbed with pain. She struggled to voice a question.

"How …"

He brushed a tendril of hair back from her eyes. "How long have you been out?"

She nodded weakly, staggered at the exhaustion caused by such a simple effort.

"This is your second night," he informed her, putting the empty bowl on a table beside the oil lamp. "One more night and you should be through the worst of it."

She moved a hand down to her side again, but this time she could not get even a word past her lips.

"You want to know how bad it is?" he asked.

She nodded wearily.

"The wound was shallow; it will heal in a few weeks and leave a minor scar. It was the dwale you ingested which your body is fighting with now."

She looked up at him in confusion. She had been poisoned?

He glanced down at her fingers. "You got it on your hands when you cleaned your wound," he explained gently. "And then, when you were building the cairn, you must have put your singed fingers in your mouth at some point."

The vision hit Lucia clearly. The leaping flame as she had set the pile alight, her instinctive move to soothe the burned fingers. And then she had stood back to watch …

Tears flooded her eyes as it came back to her. Her dear friends had been slain, had fallen at her feet protecting her life with their own. She shuddered with sobs, and suddenly strong arms were holding her, comforting her, wrapping her in their security. She cried against him for long minutes.

Finally, when she had exhausted herself, he lay her back against the pillow. She found she had twined herself around his arm, and he did not withdraw it as she descended into an ebony darkness.

* * *

The whiteness blinded her, and with it came a lively, fast-talking man with blond hair and bright gaiety. He streamed out story after story of dragon-filled battles and beautiful maidens with flaxen hair. The young girl in burgundy brought mugs of ale; he helped Lucia down a mouthful or two before resuming his recital of his tales.

She wanted to know their names, but he seemed not to sense the questions in her eyes. She lay back, drifting.

* * *

The embers of the fire flickered against the darkness, and she turned toward the brown eyes she knew would be at her side. His voice was comfort and familiarity. "There you are," he murmured. "Ready for some soup?"

She nodded weakly, leaning against his sturdy warmth as he eased her to sitting. He smelled of musk and leather and juniper, and she breathed in the aroma as he settled her back against her pillow. She opened her mouth dutifully as he brought the bowl to her lips. The tight burning in her throat had gone, although it still felt raspy from disuse.

"Out of danger?" she ground out between sips, overcome with a fresh fit of shivering.

His eyes shadowed slightly. "Getting there," he murmured. "The wolves' heads must be working with a new mixture, something more potent than we've seen before." He brushed her hair back with a tender move. "But you have a fierce strength within you. A lesser person would not have made it through this far. Just one more day and the fever should break."

Lucia thought back to when she had first seen him. She had been racked with pain, curled up against her horse's flank, all hope lost. And then he had been there by her side, and even when she flashed her dagger to his throat the man had not moved a muscle. He had remained still, willing her to trust in him.

To have that kind of courage ...

Her lips creased into a smile. "Glad I did not kill you," she forced out through a tight throat.

His eyes widened for a moment, and then he chuckled, nodding. "So am I," he agreed.

His look grew serious. "One more night," he urged her. "It will get worse before it gets better. You hang in there."

She nodded, and then her lids fell closed again.

* * *

The brightness of the sun, the whiteness of her room, nearly blinded her, and her body convulsed with endless shivers. The blond man glanced nervously at the maid who waited nearby. "Ellie, maybe you should call Matthew," he muttered.

"But surely Stephen – "

The man gave a sharp shake of the head. "Stephen is exhausted; he barely leaves the room as it is," he countered. "Let the man sleep another few hours."

The room went awash in ivory sparkles, and she was lost.

* * *

Orange and crimson shadows danced on the walls, a steady hand was brushing along her forehead with a damp cloth, and a concerned voice murmured at her ear. "You can do it," he insisted, holding her as another wave of teeth-rattling tremors shook her. "Hang in there. This will be the worst of it."

There was a movement by the fireplace, and she wearily looked up, her eyes creasing in surprise. Her father stood there, his gaze warm and steady on her. He was wearing his leather armor, his sword at his hip, and he nodded in approval at her struggle against the poison.

"Father," she called out weakly, her voice rich with relief. "I thought you were dead." *Thank God*. He had escaped the bandit onslaught after all. She had believed him lost when he held the exit gate, refusing to come as she fled with the final group. How could he have stood against so many?

Stephen's voice was tense with concern at her side. "You hang in there," he repeated, drawing a moist cloth against her forehead again. His eyes glanced to the fireplace, then back to her again.

Another movement, and her brows creased in confusion as Michael, her twin, stepped up next to her father, his eyes shining with pride. "Michael?" she ground out. She forced herself to speak, to rasp out the words against a burning throat. "You should not be here. I love you dearly - but who is watching over our people?"

Stephen's glance grew more focused, and it was a moment before he let out a breath. He turned to take a mug of mead, and then he was holding her in his arms, easing the warm liquid down her throat.

"You need to rest," he insisted, his voice rough. "Let your body fight the poison off. You can get through this. I know you can."

With an effort she dragged her eyes from the wavering vision of her family and back up to his warm gaze. His eyes were rich with worry, and she gave a half smile.

"Thank you," she murmured.

The tension in his forehead eased slightly, and he nodded, then carefully laid her back down against the pillow. Again she curled up against his hand, and again he made no move to pull it free as she drifted into an endless sea of night.

Chapter 3

Lucia gradually became aware of her surroundings, slowly drifting up from a thick cocoon of contentment and quiet. The first sensations to penetrate the dense fog were the gentle comforts of her bed. She felt mild surprise; the last she remembered that seemed real she was curled up next to her horse, huddling for shelter against an icy winter storm. She had been wounded in her side.

Her numb mind refused to admit the events which had driven her to that spot. Her eyes still closed, she stretched her fingers gingerly down to her side, waiting for the pain when she touched the wound.

Her hand instead found soft bandages and a dull, throbbing ache. Her eyes flew open, and she looked around in surprise. She was immediately struck by the ivory glow of the furnishings. The bed she lay on was covered with soft sheets and a fluffy, alabaster tapestry comforter. A diaphanous hanging surrounded the bed and protected her from drafts.

She turned her head to the right. A wooden chair was pulled next to her end of the bed. A table beside it held a bronze oil lamp with a beautiful, spiral handle. She gazed at the lamp for a long time. It was unlike any she had seen before, with an elegant swoop to its body and a row of sturdy raised bosses tracing a line across its middle.

She pushed herself up to a sitting position and gazed around the rest of her room. A comforting fire crackled in the marble fireplace. A door to its right was closed, and near it stood tables and an intricately carved dresser of fine, stained mahogany. To the left two windows, through which the winter sun shone brightly, were curtained with a thick white cloth, tied on each side. In one corner, an old harp sat, polished to a soft sheen.

Lucia felt very out of place. She didn't belong in this pristine setting. But it was more than that. Something was missing ... something important.

Confused, she tried to get up, but as she moved a voice rang out from the second, open doorway to the left.

"Don't you get out of that bed, miss," scolded a young-sounding voice. A girl with straight, waist-length blonde hair and wearing a deep burgundy overdress over a long white linen chemise, walked out of the open door and crossed to the first door, checking that it was locked. She appeared to be no older than thirteen. "I am under strict orders to keep my guest rested, healthy, and clean, and that I am doing. Though it is not easy what with all of your visitors," she added, smiling. "That Ian has looked in on you at least twice this morning already! The other girls are quite jealous."

Lucia tried her voice, and found that she could talk, despite her dreams of raspy muteness. "Good morning," she murmured, and Ellie smiled delightedly. "Your girls have no cause to worry," Lucia added with a wry smile. She wasn't going to be here long enough to cause anyone any jealousy.

She pulled back the covers. Who was Ian? The eyes that watched over her? Was that a dream?

Ellie's young face lit up with insight. "Oh! Do you mean you are already married?" she asked, coming over to the side of the bed and pulling aside the bedcurtains.

Lucia shook her head. "No," she replied quickly, as she pushed up into a sitting position. She found that she was dressed in a long, cream-colored nightgown with delicately embroidered slippers to match. White, white, white!

She was a dirty stain on this room from a fairy tale. This wasn't where she belonged.

She swung her feet around and tried to stand, but a sharp pain shot through her side, and she stumbled. The girl was there in an instant, supporting her by the arm, strong despite her small size.

"Thank you," offered Lucia ruefully. She sat back on the bed and tried to clear her thoughts. "I guess I was 'rescued' by this Ian, then." Her voice began to come to her more easily, and the fog slowly dissipated. "I think I remember someone in the storm. Yes, someone found me ..." She looked over at Ellie. "Did Ian find me in the woods near this place? Where are my belongings?" Lucia was still having trouble with her memory. She looked around the room, but could see none of her possessions amongst the perpetual whiteness of the accommodations. Lucia didn't like this - she felt much better when she was in control of a situation. The annoyance helped her think more clearly.

"It was Ian and Stephen who found you," supplied the girl with a smile. "They brought you here. Matthew, one of our brothers, helped work on your wounds. That was a week ago."

That caught Lucia's attention. A week had passed! Maybe some of her dreams were not quite fantasy after all. She knew this girl's name, after all. She glanced over at the table, at the oil lamp which sat on it. Had the warm eyes been a dream or a reality?

Ellie continued, "Lord Edmund will be holding a council meeting later tonight to go over what they know. They had hoped you would be well enough by then to give them some information. They are still not quite sure what to make of you." She chuckled, but looked sideways at Lucia, her own curiosity clearly evident.

The young girl continued. "Ian's last visit today was to bring the message that, if you felt up to it, his father requested your presence at tonight's meeting." She smiled broadly at the memory. "He really has fallen for you, and has been with you at least a half hour each day, telling you all manner of stories! Just think - if Ian has truly been caught by your beauty ..."

Lucia's frustration flared briefly at the romantic pushes Ellie was giving. She held in her impatience with an effort - the throbbing pain in her side was quickly being overtaken by a pounding headache. It appeared that keeps of all sorts bred silly gossip.

Keeps ... Lucia brightened at the thought. She must have made it to Penrith. If the maps were right, it was the town closest to the front of the Gray's advance. It was where she had been heading when she was attacked.

The maid's giggle brought her back to her current situation. The thought crossed Lucia's mind that she didn't remember being silly when she was young. Maybe she just hadn't had the luxury. It seemed so long ago.

She struggled to her feet. "Not to worry, I am not going after your hero!" She glanced around. "Do you have anywhere to wash up in here? I would like to change into my own clothes, if I may. If they want to meet me, I am prepared to talk to them." She had a million questions she wanted answered, now that her mind was regaining its focus, but she doubted Ellie would have the information she sought.

Ellie paused for a moment, and Lucia flushed. She realized she did not know the customs of this area. "I understand some regions feel bathing is dangerous, especially when you are ill," she commented quietly. "My father was in the Crusades, and he learned something of medicine while in the Holy Land. I know it might seem odd to you, but I think getting this dirt and sweat off of me will help me feel better."

Ellie gave her a soothing pat. "Oh, it was not that. My family comes from the town called Bath. As you might imagine, I am probably as fond of them as you are," effused Ellie with a smile. "You seemed to be regaining yourself, so I took the liberty of drawing a hot bath for you in the next room. It will take off that layer of dirt."

Ellie tucked herself under Lucia's arm to support her, and together they moved to the doorway. Ellie glanced up momentarily at Lucia before continuing.

"I was hesitating because you mentioned your apparel. I have put your clothes on the shelves by the wall." She held her tongue for a moment, but then asked with curiosity, "They look like, well, if you do not mind my saying so, men's clothing. Have you brought any dresses?" Lucia shook her head no. What good would dresses have done her on her journey? Still, in these story-like surroundings, she flushed with embarrassment. She apparently didn't fit the part they expected her to be playing.

Ellie continued, "Well, not to worry. My friends and I are going to fix that. You are taller than I am, but we can make do. No woman as pretty as you should be without a good dress or two."

To Lucia's chagrin, her face deepened to berry red. To hide her confusion she turned, quickly looking down at the floor. She couldn't remember the last time someone complimented her on her looks; she usually didn't brook such talk. True, sometimes the question had come unbidden to her, in the privacy of her room, when another long, lonely night stretched out before her. Was she pretty?

Would a man find her attractive? She shook her head. How long ago had that been, when she'd had the luxury of idle thought? Lucia couldn't remember.

Ellie took Lucia's silence as denial; she stopped and turned to face Lucia. "You are pretty," she repeated firmly. "With the way you had braided your hair and wore those rough outfits it would be tough to tell, but if we get you in the right clothes you could be the prettiest woman here!" She gave a sharp nod of her head to emphasize the point, then smiled and took up Lucia's waist again, careful to avoid her mending wound.

"Anyway," she added brightly, pursuing yet another thought, "the council does want to meet you. After all, we do not know who you are. They just found you half frozen and brought you in here. That is what the meeting is all about. That and the recent Gray attack. There seem to be so many assaults recently, but we are holding strong!"

With such good nature behind it, and the soft lilting sound of Ellie's speech, the prattle became almost soothing, and Lucia's headache eased. "Thank you for your help," she smiled to the young maid, genuinely appreciating the assistance. "And please, call me Lucia."

They finally made it through the doorway, and Lucia was impressed and grateful to see a golden-tiled room with the typical wooden half-barrel tub in the center. A wooden plank laid across one end held a bowl of rose petals, undoubtedly dried the previous summer. Colored glass filtered the sun into a pretty mosaic across the beautiful tile which covered most of the floor. The tub was filled to the brim with steaming, rose-scented water. Lucia slowly slipped off her slippers and nightgown and eased herself into the warm water. She leaned her head back as Ellie gently unwound her braid and lathered her hair.

Lucia realized that it had been an awfully long time since she had had a good bath, and even longer since she had received this kind of treatment.

"You just relax, Lucia," lulled Ellie. "I will take good care of you." Under Ellie's expert fingers, Lucia's rigid muscles gradually loosened and her eyes drooped.

* * *

She was seventeen, out on her first patrol, and Evan was smiling at her, a breeze ruffling his short, blond hair as they settled in the hollow for an afternoon meal. She worked easily at his side as they laid out their cloaks and sat down to their bread and cheese. She had known him for six years, ever since he had arrived at the keep to join the guard. He had proven his worth, soon becoming one of the lead trainers in sword. He had taken her under his wing, helping her and Michael become quite proficient with the blade.

Evan gave a low cough. "Lucia, I need to ask you something."

Lucia had half expected Evan to officially present his suit today, but even so her stomach suddenly fluttered with butterflies.

"Lucia, I have known you for several years now, and you are one of my finest students. You are becoming an adult now, and it is time to consider new responsibilities." Evan bent onto one knee, holding her gaze. She noted absently how the sun's light gleamed off his hair, making it shine. "Marry me, Lucia. Be my wife, and I shall be the one at your side, holding off the wolves' heads. Your father has already blessed our joining."

Lucia took in a deep breath and looked over Evan. She wasn't sure she loved him, exactly. He had been a skilled trainer, tough but fair. The men respected him, and her father approved of him.

Her heart gentled at the thought of her aging father, struggling to hold off the growing onslaughts of the bandits. She knew how important this bond would be to him – to ensure the continuance of the family line. She owed it to him, and to her brother, to do her part. Tying Evan to their family would help add another link in the chain which kept them all safe.

She drew a smile onto her lips. She was sure she would learn to love him over time.

"Yes, Evan, I will marry you."

He drew her forward into a sturdy hug, and she leant against him. It was certainly not that she disliked him, but there was no interest, no spark within her. He had been a good trainer, but she had never thought of him as more than that. She could scarcely believe that soon she was going to be a married woman.

Evan turned his head to hers, drawing her into a deep kiss. She wondered if she should feel some sort of reaction to his lips against hers, his hands moving from her face to her arms, yet none came. She knew her duty as a betrothed woman in this wild corner of the frigid north. She must now demonstrate she was fertile. Most unions did not become officially sealed until the woman showed signs she could produce that all-important next generation.

She would do as her family expected.

She did not resist Evan as his touches became more intimate, as he slid off her tunic.

The mantra recited in her mind. She would strive to be a dutiful wife. She would do her part to protect the family and ensure the family line.

* * *

Lucia fiercely shook herself, sending water splashing onto the decorative tile. Ellie looked up with a start, then smiled. "Guess you dozed off there," explained Ellie apologetically, rising from the carved chair near the door. "I was trying to let you rest; I have added more warm water to keep you comfortable. Do you want to dry off now?"

"Yes, please," replied Lucia. She was more than willing to let Ellie chatter on for hours, as long as she didn't have to think about her dream. She knew what had come after that sunny day in the woods, knew well the harsh betrayal which had followed hard after.

Lucia concentrated on the sounds of the gentle splashing of the water as Ellie used a pewter flagon to rinse the soap from her body. She gingerly climbed out of the tub, looking herself over as she did so. She saw her own well-toned muscles - a soldier's body. It was silly for her to be thinking girlish thoughts about lost loves.

Ellie shrewdly noticed the motion and patted her reassuringly as she began to dry her off. "You will have a husband soon enough, Lady Lucia," she encouraged soothingly. "With a figure like yours, you will have no problem. Why, Ian is everything you could hope for in a man!"

Lucia was exhausted, and the pain of Evan's betrayal swept back on her with full force. She looked down, her shoulders slumping.

Ellie's bright face suddenly became still. "I am sorry," she apologized softly. "I should not keep talking about Ian like that. I do not know anything about your background." She hesitated for a moment. "Many women here have lost loved ones in the bandit attacks." She was quiet as she finished drying Lucia. She laid the towel on the chair, then turned back to Lucia. "I have brought you up some lunch; please try to eat something."

Ellie carefully helped Lucia walk back into the bedroom. Lucia retrieved a nightgown from the shelf and wriggled it down over her shoulders, then sat at the small carved table. She looked over the food laid out for her - a fine white pottery plate held roast lamb, bread, and some vegetables, while a pewter goblet contained a thick red wine. Two beeswax candles added to the fire's light as the winter sun faded from the windows.

Lucia started in on the lamb, closing her eyes in pleasure as she tasted the herbed flavors of the food. "When does that meeting start?" she asked between bites. "I think it is important that I attend."

"That Council meeting is starting in an hour, at five," Ellie replied dutifully, pulling the thick curtains across the windows to keep out the winter's chill. "I can try to prepare you for the council members, at least what I know of them." She took a deep breath, thinking about the group. "Well, there is Ian, whom you have met. He is the only child, but I give him credit. He is not chomping at the bit to take over, as I have seen in other neighboring areas. Instead, he is patient, not eager to have his father step down. He seems content with his ample free time for drinking and wenching."

"I suppose that is better than having an antagonistic relationship," mused Lucia between bites. "How does his father view this?"

Ellie chuckled. "Ian's father, Lord Edmund, is of course the Lord of this town. He takes a very relaxed view toward war, and has supported his son in his lassitude. Both have said they want to avoid fighting if they can. Now that war seems nigh upon us, they are working to defend our lands, as well they should."

The girl tapped a finger to her lips. "Then there is Matthew, who helped you when you arrived here. He is one of our brothers who strive to guide us. He has been praying for a sign to help give us a direction."

"Who controls the soldiers?" asked Lucia as she nibbled on the greens. The vegetables were dry and tasteless, which was understandable because they had undoubtedly been stored since the harvest some three months past. "He will probably be the one I need to speak with most, if I get the chance."

Would they accept her help? Believe what she had to say? Care what a woman thought? Lucia dismissed the questions for now and concentrated on listening for pieces of information that could help her puzzle out her next steps. At least the fog that had plagued her these past days was finally clearing.

"Captain of the Guard? That would be Hector. He is a bear of a man, and a fine warrior. Although for the past few weeks Stephen has been giving him advice. Now there is a man..."

Ellie shivered and smoothed her dress out unconsciously. "Stephen is much different than Ian. Ian is all grace and elegance, where Stephen is a *wanderer*." She said the word almost with distaste.

Lucia glanced back at the chair in the corner, at the oil lamp which sat beside it. She could feel the draw of his eyes, smell the comforting scent of juniper and leather.

"A wanderer?" she asked in confusion, baffled at Ellie's reaction.

The girl nodded. "Stephen's family once owned the lands to the north; the Grays razed the area early on. Stephen has been Lord Edmund's ward for nearly twenty years – but he never really fit in here. You can see it in his clothes, his eyes." She shrugged. "Now Stephen lives in the northern woods with two of his kinsmen, harassing the Grays, only visiting town for a day or two to restock his supplies."

"But he seems to be staying longer for now," mused Lucia.

Ellie nodded. "He is a skilled fighter. Even though Hector has been training all his life, and has fought some border skirmishes, he has not had much real combat experience. Lord Edmund asked Stephen to join us for the winter, to help train up every able man in preparation for the Gray advance."

Lucia thought to the sturdy eyes again, how he had stayed at her side. He was at the council meeting – she needed to be there as well.

She finished her meal and pushed back her chair. "I have got to get ready. Where are my clothes?" She stood up. Her legs wobbled beneath her weight, and she closed her eyes until the vertigo ceased. With ingrained discipline, she ignored the pain and moved toward the shelves.

Ellie hesitated a moment, then spoke up. "There are several other ladies in the keep; would you like me to see if I could borrow a dress or two for you? I am sure they would not mind."

Lucia was pleased to see her tunic and leggings neatly folded on the shelf, and took them down. "Thank you very much, but no," she replied gently. "I really would feel most comfortable in my own things." She shook out the tunic and held it before her.

The blue uniform brought back a wealth of memories of those she loved, of the four she recently rode with who wore similar outfits. Her anger was returning, and it made her feel strong. "These are the trappings of the protector of a people," she told Ellie with pride, looking over the tunic.

"Our soldiers work hard to prove themselves worthy of wearing the colors. Our townsfolk can rely on someone in these clothes with their lives."

She laid the items out on the bed. First she pulled on the tight black leggings, then put her head through the opening of the loose, deep blue tunic. A leather belt went on next, fastened with a bronze buckle shaped like a hawk. She accepted Ellie's help with fastening the lacings and pulling the black cloak over her shoulders.

Ellie gave Lucia's hair a final brushing as Lucia sat on the edge of the bed and pulled on the black leather boots. The young maid asked, "Would you like me to braid any ribbons into your hair?" Ellie's hands moved rhythmically down the full length of the thick, brunette locks, working out the knots. "Perhaps a head covering of some sort?"

Lucia hardly heard the question - she was mentally preparing for the meeting ahead. "I always wear it in a simple braid," she responded absently, stamping her foot soundly into her boot. She took the brush from Ellie and briskly worked the weave, her hands moving automatically from long practice. She fastened the braid at the bottom with a copper pin.

Stephen's warm eyes came to her again, and she put a hand hesitantly to her side, to the wound he had carefully tended. He had seen her at her worst, feverish and delusional. What would he think of her when she was more herself? Would he approve?

"How do I look?" she asked hesitantly.

"Very crisp" commented Ellie, looking her over critically. "Here, let me adjust your brooch." Lucia's mouth quirked as Ellie gave the intricate clasp holding Lucia's cloak a twist - it had been fine, but the gesture touched her. "Oh, you will not need that," Ellie added as

Lucia reached for her sword and scabbard. "There are never any dangers in our halls."

Lucia's response was automatic. "My sword always goes with me." Seeing the confused look in Ellie's eyes, she added more gently, "No fighter should ever be caught without some form of protection, even in a friendly area. What if there was an attack, and I was called on to help defend?"

Ellie nodded uncertainly.

Lucia cinched the belt tight around the scabbard, then nodded to Ellie with a look of the bravado she was trying to muster. "I am off to the council meeting. Try to keep out of trouble until I return."

She smiled at Ellie, turned, and walked slowly, but steadily, out the door.

Chapter 4

Lucia stood for a moment gazing at the stone hallway, marveling at its width and elegance. The building complex she lived in from birth, along with the few she had visited during her life, were narrow and dark with twisting passageways, narrow arrow-slit windows, and stairs steep enough to foil would-be attackers. Her home keep's rooms reeked with the musty smells from people living for weeks, often months, in close quarters. The walls and floors, half-stone, half-dirt, were usually slick with moisture. Even with maids carrying fresh herbs into the rooms every morning, most of the building's occupants tried to find some excuse to venture daily into the fresh winter air.

Apparently this keep had been designed primarily for comfort rather than defense. While the large windows were shuttered, she could imagine a bolt or projectile sailing clear through the decorative thin wood. Peering out through the crack between the panes, she could see the town below was laid out in neat lines, easy for an invading force to move through. The lush forest nearly came up to the outer walls of the town. Her father would have had that cleared out in a wide swath to give the watch an unimpeded view of their territory, and attackers no easy way to breach the walls.

She shook her head and drew her eyes back to the hall. A delicate carpet ran the length of the hallway, adding a splash of burgundy to the light grey of the stones. A breeze blew through the hallway, stirring the orange flames in the polished brass sconces and making the wall tapestries depicting past victories sway.

Lucia looked in both directions down the hallway, then turned right toward the sound of voices. The air grew warmer and more comfortable as she went down a flight of stone steps wide enough to ride a horse up. A polished stone banister graced either side of the steps, and the burgundy carpet which ran down the center of each step was an exquisite work of art. The smell of roast steer wafted through the air, mixed with a myriad of spices. Lucia could hear the deep rumble of men's voices in a heated discussion as she turned the corner and entered the great hall.

Lucia stopped at the bottom stair and looked around. The hall was obviously built for enormous banquets; the room was spectacular. To the right, a great entrance rose a full two stories. Four smaller archways led off to smaller passageways on the left. Each was surmounted by a burgundy banner bearing a rearing white unicorn. A massive, oak table, covered with strewn maps and candelabras, stretched down the center of the room. Numerous smaller pine tables, currently unoccupied and barren, were placed around it.

Five men were standing at the far end of the central table. They were poking at a large parchment map and gesturing to various portions of it. Each seemed to have his own opinion about what to do.

Lucia gazed out at the scene, taking in each detail with careful attention. She had seen this same scenario numerous times in her own home. Ever since her coming of age she had been invited by her father to the many military meetings he held. At first his advisors had balked, but she had proven herself shrewd and quick in spite of her youth, and now they gave her an opportunity to speak when she had a suggestion to offer.

But this was not her home court, where her father ran things and where, she was aware enough to admit, he had smoothed a number of ruffled feathers on her behalf. This was undoubtedly an environment where women had little voice in matters of combat.

She squared her shoulders. Although she had no intentions of stirring up a debate about that, she at least had to convince these men that she had information vitally important to their decisions, and that she could be relied on. She would be as respectful and proper as she could in order to build that trust.

As she had many times before, she gathered her courage and confidence before she strode forward.

The court page, entranced with the proceedings, started in surprise as Lucia came up next to him and spoke softly into his ear. He cleared his throat quickly, and announced, "My Lord, Lady Lucia of the Keilder realm requests permission to join your meeting."

The heads of the five snapped up to survey the newcomer, and when the robed person at the head of the table nodded his head, the page motioned Lucia to enter the room.

Lucia chose a slow, measured step, extremely conscious of the exact image she was trying to project. She willed herself to hide any sign of weakness and took in deep breaths against the pain from her wound. She needed to be strong, if only for the duration of this talk. Her cloak billowed out behind her, even in this slight breeze. She held her head up, meeting the gaze of each man in turn as she approached the table.

She decided the middle-aged man on the end must be Lord Edmund. He wore an immense, emerald-encrusted pendant around his neck on a thick, gold chain. His clothing was exquisitely tailored and made of a lush, burgundy fabric. Despite his advancing age his body was still strong, and the keen, piercing look in his eyes as he assessed her made Lucia believe that this man was not going to willingly give up his rule for some time to come.

Her gaze passed to the young, blond man on Lord Edmund's right. This must be Ian, resplendent in his court clothes. She remembered him now as the teller of fantastic tales in her dream world. Dressed in a bright burgundy tunic and white leggings, his intricately carved belt supported a richly jeweled dagger on his hip.

Ian seemed to be a prince out of a fairy tale, eager to become a heroic king. She reminded herself that he was not that eager – he was quite content to have the appearance with none of the responsibilities.

Ian had fixed Lucia with a stare so intense that it verged on predatory. Lucia quickly moved her gaze to the next person at the table.

Ah, this must be Hector, she thought with a nod. The man wore a gruff beard and grizzled hair, and struck Lucia as a bear just coming from his den after a long winter. He wore two swords and looked quite capable of wielding them both simultaneously. Even in this warm room he wore studded leather armor, and a thick wolf skin was draped over the back of his chair. He seemed to find this intrusion inconsequential and appeared anxious to get back to the task at hand.

The fourth member of the group wore a long, thick brown robe edged with gold thread. From his belt dangled various leather pouches and worn bags of different shapes and sizes. Matthew, the religious brother. His smiling, friendly face seemed quite different from the strict, military priests popular in her land. Her own religion placed faith in the strength of man, and looked to God for peace after dying in battle. She wondered how this brother viewed the role of his God.

The last man at the table stood in the shadows. As her eyes adjusted, she saw he was tall and broad shouldered, with firm muscles tracing down the length of his body. A mane of thick, dark hair reached just to his shoulders. He was dressed in a light leather tunic; a worn brown cloak fastened at his shoulder with a bronze circlet. He wore a long sword, and a bow and quiver rested against the chair next to him.

The man glanced up at her and held her gaze. His eyes - they were charcoal brown, deep, steady. She was caught in their depths. She felt the power of them, felt the draw of their safety.

His eyes dropped to her wound, and he raised an eyebrow in question. She gave a short nod. She certainly could feel the sharp pain with every step she took, but she had dealt with far worse. She would make it through this meeting.

As Lucia reached Lord Edmund, she dutifully dropped on one knee and lowered her eyes. She was not one to enjoy speeches, but she knew and understood the value of the proper protocols.

"My Lord, I humbly thank you for rescuing me from the forest and allowing me to stay in your home," she stated formally. "I am Lucia, from the land of Keilder, daughter of Lord Keilder."

She stood again, respectfully keeping her eyes lowered. "I request shelter until I heal, and then an escort to Harwich." She took in a deep breath. "Last month, our final defenses against the Grays were breached. Those who survived fled to the coast. Once the winter storm season is over, they will head south to meet up with my uncle at his keep."

Lucia reached into a slender bag hanging from her belt. From it she brought out a parchment tied with a gold ribbon and wax-sealed with the deep blue signet of a diving hawk. "I am also here on a diplomatic quest. This is the letter written by Lord Keilder explaining our plight and requesting your assistance." She offered it to Lord Edmund, her eyes downcast, holding her position with patience.

Lord Edmund smiled at her introduction. "Welcome to my city and home," he greeted Lucia formally. As he indifferently handed the scroll to Ian, he continued more congenially, "We will deal with your father's letter later, after you have told your tale. No need to worry you with the technicalities of our plans."

He smiled at her. "You have certainly been through quite a lot, young lady. An arduous trek, indeed. How long were you in transit? You say you were accompanied here - how were you separated from your traveling companions? Were you lost in the snowstorm, fleeing from the battle?" He motioned Lucia to a seat between Stephen and Hector.

Lucia stood her ground, the memory of her dead friends flashing before her eyes. She threw her cloak back, revealing the weapon she wore, and the mark of the wound still scarring her clothing. She had known she might not be taken seriously, but for the letter to be so dismissed, when it had cost so much to bring it this far? It was not to be borne!

A slight movement to the side caught her attention. Stephen's gaze was on her, holding caution, and his eyes flicked to the map at the table. She glanced down, then looked more closely as awareness hit her. There were no words on the map – only symbols. Carved blocks representing various forces lay on top of it.

Lord Edmund, apparently, could not read. She had just shamed him in front of his men.

She took in a deep breath, staring at the map. Half of the blocks were in the wrong place. She stalked around the table to stand at Stephen's side. With a sweep of her arm she roughly pushed the shapes away. She grabbed up a block of a soldier with a shield and put it in the forest to the far north, perhaps thirty miles given the scale.

"This was Keilder," she ground out. "This was my home until the Grays overran it several weeks ago. It is the northern edge of their range of destruction."

She grabbed several blocks holding images of wolves' heads on them. She peppered them across the mountains and high hills of the map's center. "These thirty miles of wasteland are what I just fought through with my five fellow soldiers. We hit raiding party after raiding party as we forced our way south amongst the smoldering ruins of farm and mill. My men were the best there were; we only lost one during that time."

Her eyes drew down to a line, the border of the lands controlled by Lord Edmund. She picked up another wolf block and pressed it into place with a growl. "And here is where we were ambushed by fifteen of them; right on your borders. We had evened the odds when –"

Tears welled in her eyes, and she pushed them away with harsh effort. Stephen moved a hair closer, and his voice eased into the space.

"Lord Edmund, this is where your son and I found her a week ago. Ian can confirm that we saw the ten dead Grays where they had been slain."

Ian spoke up in delight. "I certainly did see them!" he cried. "And I would have taken on the two Grays that returned to finish the job, if they had not fled before the storm."

Lord Edmund eyed Lucia speculatively for a moment, then nodded to Ian. "Please read the scroll, my son."

Ian beamed with pride, breaking the seal and carefully reviewing the contents. When he was done, he put down the scroll and looked with delight at Lucia. "What she says is true," he reported. "She comes from Keilder keep, and is the daughter of the Lord there." He motioned to the map, and indicated to the others as he spoke.

"This area in the north is where Lucia's land lies. Her father writes to say that this whole area," he motioned to a large radius around the northernmost block, "is now overrun by Grays. They will undoubtedly turn south next, toward us."

He nodded his head at the southern regions. "Lord Keilder requests that we gather all of the local lords and leaders and ask them to unite, putting put aside their petty differences as needed to defeat this common enemy. Until now, the Grays had no fortified base to work from. Now that they have taken the keep, it is imperative we undo their advantage."

Lucia leaned over the map, tracing routes with her finger as she spoke. "The Grays advanced here and here to the south of this river, but their main forces hit us through this pass to the east. We were not braced from this direction, and could not divert our forces in time. The onslaught pushed us back into our keep. Despite our best efforts, we were outnumbered there as well." She moved the small figurines appropriately.

Her hand wavered for a moment as Lucia remembered the ferocity of that battle. "When I left my father, he was fighting two Grays with one hand and pushing me out the back exit with the other. With the keep fallen, most of the townsfolk have been sent east to the coast. They are finding ships, then waiting on better weather to sail south."

She glanced up to Lord Edmund. "It was left to me and my men to bring this message to you and to plan the counter-attack."

Ian bent over to whisper something to his father while Hector scowled at the map. Suddenly the ground tilted sharply. Then Stephen was beside her, his arm at her waist. Lucia leant on its sturdy strength with gratitude. It would do no good for the group to think her a weak female prone to fainting. Luckily, the others seemed not to notice.

Lucia took a deep breath and regained her footing. She motioned toward their immediate area, where the forest surrounded the town and a wide stream stretched along the eastern side of the map. "You all think this river is impassable because of its width, and that the Grays would have to travel much farther north or south before they could ford it. Unfortunately, they have already constructed a series of sturdy rafts, in sections, strong enough to hold horses and wagons. As we speak, they are assembling them into a rudimentary bridge in order to cross the river much closer to your defenses."

Hector scoffed at this news. "How could that possibly be true?" he asked, not bothering to hide his disbelief. "We would have seen them. Who told you this wild story?"

Lucia's eyes reflected her weary amusement. "I saw them myself," she stated simply. "I stole into their camp with two of my companions a few nights before you found me. We watched them finish the construction of the floats." She chuckled softly. "I also released a few of their mounts from service while I was there."

Hector blinked in surprise. "So that is where the horses came from," he commented, half to himself. He looked at his lord and Ian uncertainly, then back to Lucia. "If this is true, then we would have to move our defenses quickly," he suggested to Lord Edmund. "I do not see how we could do it before they set upon us, though. First we would have to decide on the precise course of action. Then it would take months to reinforce these walls." He motioned at various sections of the outer walls shown to need repair on the map.

Lucia studied the map, assessing the weaknesses of the town. "No, not that way," she countered.

Her world spun again, and she closed her eyes for a moment, willing it to steady. Not now, she couldn't afford to be weak now. She felt rather than saw Stephen move closer in concern, and she took a deep breath to clear the encroaching fogginess. She pointed out the three areas where the Grays would be pinned close while they crossed tricky terrain. "Do not concentrate on the last defenses - if they get that far, it is probably too late. Get them here, and here, where they are vulnerable from attack on all sides. With proper preparation, you should be able to pick them all off before they get through."

The men looked at her ambush points, and nodded in understanding.

Lucia pressed on, thinking it through. "Especially with the cold, this current move is likely to be a foray to test your strength. If you defeat them soundly, it will give you that much more time before they contemplate attacking in force. Maybe it will be enough to convince them to turn elsewhere. It is winter, and their stores are running low, at least from what we saw. They are raiding for food and shelter, not for land."

Lucia took another deep breath and mentally cursed her weak body. This was no time to feel faint!

Matthew murmured in a deep, rumbling voice, "It is what I have been praying for, a light to guide us through the darkness." Ian and his father nodded to the robed monk in deference.

Hector glanced up in annoyance, then concentrated on the problem for a minute. He moved the pieces representing troops about the map, focusing on the areas mentioned. "If we do take this approach," he explained to Lord Edmund, "when we move here and here, we have them at a strong disadvantage. It could work!"

Ian joined in sliding other pieces toward the newly-discovered threat from the river. "We would have to get started right away, though. Scouts could get confirmation to us before nightfall tomorrow. Once they cross the river, how long do you think it would take them to get here, Stephen?"

Stephen turned to answer, but Lucia's last reserves of strength gave way, and she spiraled down toward the floor. Stephen deftly caught her limp form in his arms.

Lucia's eyes fluttered open at the gentle impact; once again the dream world seemed to have taken over, and the dark eyes were back, looking down at her with concern. "I have got to get back to my father," she pleaded weakly, looking up into those eyes. He nodded, silently assenting. She relaxed then, giving herself fully to Stephen's care. The table was silent for a moment.

Stephen turned to Hector. "I will find out the details for you by tomorrow," he promised. He snugged up Lucia's limp body firmly in his grasp, then nodded his leave of Lord Edmund. He walked quickly around the table and made his way up the stairs.

He knocked briskly and soon Ellie came running. She seemed surprised to find Stephen carrying her lady, but clucked to herself as she led him to the white-canopied bed across the room. "I just knew she should not go out so soon after her ordeal. Now I will likely spend weeks restoring her to good health. That girl should learn to live like me - careful and safe."

Stephen gently lay Lucia on the bed, gazing at her for a long moment. Then Ellie was at his side, bustling him out the door.

"I can handle changing her – you wait outside," the girl insisted. He nodded, pulling the door shut behind him.

Lucia found herself watching the door as Ellie tugged off her boots, removed her pants and then tunic. In short order she was clothed in the white nightgown and tucked back beneath the warm blankets. None of this mattered to Lucia. Her attention was fully on the closed door, on the man who waited behind it.

Ellie pulled the door open, and in a moment she was sliding out into the hallway while Stephen took her place. He eased the door shut, sliding the bolt in place. A tremor ran through Lucia at the motion, and it had nothing to do with fever this time. It was a sense of security, of warmth, that he was in the room with her, there to protect and watch over her. She drew her eyes over his broad shoulders, the muscles of his arm, and a fierce longing ran through her.

He turned suddenly, catching her eyes, and she flushed, dropping her gaze to her hands. He moved with a cat's grace, taking a candle from the mantle and coming to sit beside her. He lit the oil lamp from the flame, then looked down at her.

"You did well at the council meeting tonight," he murmured.

She gave a wry smile. "I barely lasted ten minutes before I collapsed into a puddle of gruel," she reminded him.

He gave a shake of his head. "Few would have been out of bed at all, given what you went through," he countered. "You presented your case well."

She ran a hand through her hair. "I should hope so; I have joined my father's strategic meetings for what, five years now?"

His eyes drew over her face. "So your father and council respect your opinion; I am not surprised."

She gave a soft shrug. "I have been on patrol since I came of age, and the accuracy of my arrows is easily proven. It is an area where my lesser strength does not impede my worth. My sharp eyes and steady hand are all that matter."

He smiled gently. "I am sure you invested practice as well," he commented.

She nodded in agreement. "Three hours a day," she agreed. "If this was to be my way of helping, I would do it as well as I could." She chuckled. "Michael helped, of course. He set up a swinging target on a rope for me, and that added an entirely new level of challenge."

Stephen looked down for a long minute. At last he spoke in a low voice. "Did you want some mead?"

She nodded, and he moved to the larger table by the windows, bringing back a mug. He put it on the side table, then leant forward to wrap his arms around her, to ease her up to a sitting position. The warmth of his chest, the rich smell of juniper and leather embraced her, and she found herself drawing her hands along his side as he stepped back. He handed the mug to her, and she took a long drink.

His voice was rough as he looked down at her. "You spoke of Michael in your fever."

She smiled, thinking fondly of her twin. He could be an imp sometimes, but she loved him dearly.

Stephen's voice was low. "And yet you are not married?"

A wave of pain swept through her at the words. The topic had been off limits at home; the engagement was never brought up, Evan's betrayal never even hinted at. That the man could have sought to destroy everything she had loved most dear ...

Stephen sat back in the chair, his eyes close on her face. "I am sorry; I see this is not an easy topic for you."

She took another long draw on the mead, shaking her head. The near darkness of the room was comforting; Stephen's face was half in shadow. She handed over the mug, and when he took it their fingers overlapped. She was warmed by the touch, could not release the mug, and in a moment he reached over with his other hand, putting the mug down with it, leaving their hands intertwined.

"I was seventeen," she murmured, closing her eyes, the darkness pulling at her. It had been so long that she had allowed even the slightest thought of those events. Why was this place bringing them to light again? "Evan had been with our guard for several years, had trained me, and had proven himself to my father. We were out on our first patrol together when he proposed to me."

Stephen's voice was low. "You loved him?"

She shook her head, iron bands drawing around her. "He was my father's hope for securing our lands," she countered wearily. "The Grays were just reaching our borders at the time. We needed skilled fighters manning the walls. It was a way to ensure he stayed and lent his talents."

His grip was strong on her hand; tears trickled in warm rivulets down her cheeks. "With the engagement, Evan gained full access to the keep. Any question he asked, my father answered. Anywhere he wanted to go, he went. He had rights to everything." Her voice dropped to a whisper, and her hand moved to press against her chest, thinking of the nights he had come to her. "I gave him everything he requested of me, as was his right," she whispered.

Stephen was silent beside her, lending her strength with his presence. Still, it was several long moments before she could go on.

"Then, one night in deep February, the shouts rose from all sides. The walls had been breached. Grays streamed in like waves in an ocean storm, seemingly without end. We roused every person capable of wielding a sword and fell back to the keep proper. We stood there holding our ground, on those steps, for a full ten hours. I went through every arrow we had, and I lost many dear friends. But in the end, thank God, the Grays gave up and fled."

She brushed the tears from her eyes. "I still remember the last time I saw Evan. It was he who sounded the Grays' retreat from the main wall gates. He had not been involved in any of the fighting and had carefully stayed out of arrow range. But as he gave the call, his eyes came up to hold mine. Even as his bandit horde fled past him, those eyes held a bright note of triumph. He drew his gaze proudly across the slain, across the wounded, and I knew without a doubt that he would be back. He would come, and come, until he had taken the keep wholly."

Stephen's voice was low. "Lucia, I am so sorry."

She turned to look up at him, losing herself in his sturdy comfort. "We never speak of it now," she murmured. "We have not seen Evan since that day, but we know it is his cunning and skill behind the attacks. Every wave became more targeted, and it was harder and harder to hold them off." Her eyes welled. "This last wave was simply too much. We were overrun."

He ran a hand along her cheek. "We will win back your keep," he stated. "These wolves' heads will be brought to justice."

She shook her head, and he lifted her chin so she looked at him. "I promise it to you," he vowed, and she could see the strength of it in his eyes.

For a long moment she was lost, all sense of self drifting, and she nodded.

He smoothed her hair back from her face. "You rest now," he murmured, sitting back into his chair.

She lay against the pillow, her eyes on him, and the darkness slowly came.

Chapter 5

Lucia stirred, turning her head, before the ache in her side told her she was truly awake. From the low howling of the wind, plus the relative darkness against her shut eyelids, she guessed it was already mid-afternoon, easing into evening. Her body ached from long rest. She must have slept straight through the night and most of the next day.

She drew her eyes open. Flickering candles brought light and shadow from several corners of the room, and the fireplace danced with a low flame. Ellie stood at once from the table by the window and bustled over with an oaken tray.

"Here, I thought you might enjoy some fresh chicken soup," she offered as she laid the tray across Lucia's legs. "Matthew was by about an hour ago to check you over. He says your wound is healing nicely, and the poison is mostly out of your system. Still, I am sure Stephen will be by shortly, to wait out this last night with you." She gave a light laugh. "I should carve his name in the chair's back and be done with it."

Lucia flushed, looking down as she pushed herself into a sitting position. Of course Stephen would stop coming by once she was fully healed. He was only showing concern for an injured visitor, after all.

Ellie placed the pewter spoon into Lucia's hand. "The soup is warm - you should dig in," she encouraged. "You need to build up your strength if the rumors flying around the castle are true! I can hardly believe it!" She gazed down at Lucia with pride.

"What rumors? I have only been here a week, and most of that time was spent curled up with a fever!" protested Lucia, picking up the spoon and hesitantly tasting the hot broth. How in the world did wild stories spread so quickly? The warmth felt good as it slid down her throat. Encouraged by the rich flavors, she eagerly took in more spoonfuls. She knew the spices were sometimes used to disguise less-than-fresh meat, but at this moment she could not care less. It was warm and delicious.

"Well," explained Ellie, brimming with excitement, "they say that you warned my Lord about an attack coming, and that you told him and his men how to fight it! They say that you may have saved our lives! And that you are going to save your whole land and defeat the Grays!" She eyed Lucia with a mixture of admiration and apprehension. "Are you afraid? I would never be able to do something like that!"

Lucia chuckled, taking in a mouthful of the warm broth. "I am going to do all of that by myself, hmm? I work as part of a large team. And yes, I imagine we all get scared at times." She looked bemusedly at Ellie as she finished her soup. "Do I get a vacation after I save the world, or is there another great feat that I am supposed to accomplish?"

"Well, I do not believe *all* the stories," admitted Ellie cautiously as she gathered up the now-empty bowl and tray. "But you did bring us the information about the Grays, did you not? Things we did not know? The kitchen boy told me our troops are all getting new assignments and everyone certainly feels like we have finally got a plan that can work."

"Yes," agreed Lucia, not wanting to discourage her. "I did bring fresh news. However, much of it was gathered for me by our spies."

Ellie still appeared crestfallen, so she added conspiratorially, "I did have a key role, of course - the tricky part was me bringing it here through enemy lines."

The news cheered Ellie up. "I am very proud of you for doing that. It must have been horrible." Ellie fluffed up the pillow behind Lucia's head and helped her lay back down. "Now, do not think about those things any more. You get some sleep now, so you can heal up quickly. We will take good care of you." She tucked Lucia in, and quietly set about tidying the room. She blew out the beeswax candles on the mantel as she passed, leaving only the embers to glow warmly in the fireplace.

Lucia lay quietly for a while, her eyes half open. Soon there were steady footsteps in the hall, and the door creaked open. Ellie murmured in a low voice, and then the young maid left while someone else entered.

Warmth swept over Lucia. She knew even in the shadows that it was Stephen's sturdy build standing there in the flickering firelight. He looked her over for a moment before he turned to bar the door, eased across the room, and settled into the chair at her side. Leaning forward, he laid his hand gently against her forehead.

Her eyes flew open at the touch, and he gazed at her for a long moment. "How are you feeling?"

"Better," she agreed. "The wound at my stomach is down to a dull throb, and the nausea is mostly passed." She gave a half smile. "Tomorrow I should be back on my feet, and perhaps get some light sparring practice in."

His forehead creased with worry. "Being out of bed for ten minutes at a stretch was too much for you yesterday. You need to take it easy."

She shook her head. "The north is no place for the frail," she recited.

He raised an eyebrow at that. "What?"

Her smile grew. "It was a saying of my father's, any time I tried to pull the covers over my head on a wintry morning. It was his way of reminding me that this land we chose to call home was not an easy place to live."

He nodded at that. "That is true," he agreed. "And yet it has a beauty few other places can touch."

Lucia gazed into the understanding his eyes held. "My father had served in Italy for several years as a young man. He talked about the lush vineyards, the warm sun, and the easy lifestyle with fondness. But he never spoke of going back. He adored our keep, adored every rock and plank." She dropped her eyes. "He died there, defending it to the last, so I could get away safely with my men."

His fingers twined into hers. "He died protecting the ones he loved," he murmured.

She drew in the warmth of his fingers, the strength in his grip. "My men died protecting me as well," she whispered. "We trudged through snowstorms so fierce we could barely see our fingers before us. It seemed every few days we ran into a raiding party of the Grays, small bands to be sure, but fierce fighters. We only lost one man the entire way down to your borders." She closed her eyes. "And then there was that clearing."

"You were outnumbered," Stephen pointed out quietly.

She nodded. "Three to one," she agreed. "But in the end it was my fault. I should not have agreed to take Vic along. He was too young, only twenty, with barely any experience in this kind of rough situation. But he had pleaded, and his sister Marcie was a dear friend of mine, and I thought ..." She shook her head. "I made a decision with my heart, not my head, and we all paid the price."

"What happened?" he asked in a low rumble.

Darkness wrapped around her as she thought back to the ambush. "We were jumped just before dusk, but my men are good, solid fighters, and we held our own. We were whittling them down, one by one, and I thought we had a chance." She shook her head. "And then Vic made a mistake. He turned his back on a small, weaselly-looking man, thinking him not much of a threat. The next thing we knew, the Grays had fallen back, taking Vic hostage. Three of them pulled bows and aimed them at us, warning us not to follow."

She looked down at her hands. "We would have let them go, and followed in the night to free him. It would have been the wise thing to do. The choice with the greatest chance of success. But then that weaselly one began torturing Vic." Her face went still at the memory. "Vic told us to leave. He begged for us to run. And all the while the Gray was slicing long gouges along his arms, across his face and ..." She closed her eyes. "And I could not take it," she admitted softly.

"You ran to his aid," murmured Stephen.

She nodded in misery. "And my two loyal soldiers, men who would follow me into the depths of hell, went right at my side. They fell within a few steps, arrows deep through their chests. For some reason the Grays did not shoot me. They ..." She blinked her eyes against the tears. "The smaller one turned his dagger, raked it across Vic's throat, and he was gone." She swallowed. "Then they just scrambled for their horses. When I raced back for my own, to follow, that is when I was hit."

"They did not mean to hit you," offered Stephen quietly.

Her eyes flicked up to meet his in surprise. "What?"

He nodded to the wound at her hip. "That was an accident. Two of the Grays came back to look for you just after I found the site. They indicated that you were to have been brought to them unharmed. I imagine Vic being taken hostage was a ploy to lure you into their trap."

She shook her head in confusion. "My keep has already fallen," she countered. "Would they hold me captive to ensure my forces gave up on retaking it, and simply stayed with my uncle in Harwich?" She shook her head strongly. "We would never give up in our efforts, no matter how long it took, no matter what the odds. Keilder is our home."

His eyes held hers for a moment, and they shone with admiration. "I know," he stated at last. "I know."

It came to her suddenly that his lands had been lost for twenty long years, and that the burned-out farms she had passed during her journey were the remnants of what he had once held dear. If anyone could understand what she was going through, he could.

"I am sorry for your loss," she offered, her heart going out to him.

The ghost of a smile came to his lips, and his other hand came up to gently stroke the side of her face. "You heal up for now," he advised her. "Everything else will come with time."

She nodded, then settled back against the pillow, her hand still twined in his.

It was a long while before the darkness of sleep drew her down into its embrace.

Chapter 6

Lucia sprang awake, her heart pounding, sweat streaming down her forehead. She could still see the dark visions – Vic screaming in pain, the men thundering on either side of her, and the sharp twang as the arrows flew through the air, finding their targets with deadly precision.

She swept her hand to the side, but the chair was empty. The oil lamp lay cold. Stephen was gone. Darkness furrowed into her heart, threatening to pull her down.

Ellie came running from her connecting room. Sticking her arms through the sleeves of a heavy white robe, she came to a relieved stop as she saw no one in the room. "It must have been a dream, M'Lady. There is no one here," she called out soothingly as she tied the sash around her waist and came around the bed to Lucia's side. "I had only left the room for a minute. It is over now, whatever scared you." She glanced to the windows with a reassuring smile. "Here, look, the sun is just rising. Morning is finally here."

Lucia climbed carefully out of bed and opened the curtains further, watching the rosy glow spread across the landscape as Ellie placed an identical robe around her shoulders. Since her room was at the back, or eastern side, of the town, most of the buildings she could see between her and the outer walls were stables and farm buildings, low-lying structures with flat roofs of thatch and mud. Just beneath her were the main stables, and she could see horses being led out for a morning walk. The sunlight glinted off a snowy hay pile, and the icy layer on the buildings' roofs gleamed in the light.

Then suddenly the sun was in the air, and the rosy shadows fled before the yellow warmth of day.

"It was nothing," assured Lucia as she carefully examined the bandage covering her wound. It was healing nicely, and gave barely a twinge as she flexed. "The injury is mending well. It will not impede me much. I will just have to be careful." She made a few practice swings with her arms, and smiled when she noticed little discomfort. Still, her muscles were sore from the long bed rest, and would need some soothing before she could begin even a gentle workout. "Please heat me up some bath water so I can get going as soon as possible," she asked Ellie.

Ellie looked at her in surprise. "You are not supposed to be doing anything for at least two more weeks," she objected. "Matthew says you are supposed to stay in bed for another week and drink soup. That you should mostly stay in your room. Maybe, after the week, he will think about allowing you to wander around the castle. You cannot go anywhere today!"

Lucia shook her head. "I have to be on my way south to meet my townsmen as soon as I am able. In a few weeks the worst of winter should be past, and they will be able to make the sea voyage safely. I plan on keeping to my schedule, and I have to be in good shape to make it there alive. Part of this includes my exercising every day. So get out I will, and no injury is going to hold me from it."

An hour later, Lucia was strapping herself into her old pants and rough, well-worn tunic. They had been washed and repaired by the castle's seamstress, and seemed fresh and neat. "Do you think you could lead me to where the local guards usually train?" asked Lucia as she buckled her belt and slid the sword into its scabbard. "I figure I can see what kind of shape your troops are in while I test how my body is recuperating."

Muttering about the doctor's orders, Ellie reluctantly agreed and, putting a heavy grey cloak over her long dress, led Lucia down the hallway she had traveled just two days ago to that meeting. Small groups of courtiers stood talking in the central hall, their tone holding upbeat excitement. Lucia ignored them, turning right through the large archway and pushing out through the large wooden front doors.

A tall, lean man with tawny curls was standing on the front steps and looking out over the courtyard. He glanced around when Lucia and Ellie came out, and nodded. "Greetings, Ellie," he called down to the young maid.

"Lucia, this is Marcus," Ellie introduced with a shy grin. "He is one of Stephen's friends, and is helping out with training the troops."

Lucia's eyes perked up. "That is exactly what I was interested in seeing," she explained to Marcus. "Where are they now?"

Marcus motioned with his head toward the back. "They are working on archery, in the rearmost field. You are still weak; it is probably best if we ride there."

Ellie quailed and took a step backwards. "Horses?" she queried in a tremulous tone. "You mean, as in sitting on top of them?"

Lucia chuckled and patted her on the shoulder. "I will be fine on my own," she reassured the maid gently.

Marcus chimed in with a smile. "I will see that she gets there safely, young one," he promised. He waved to a passing stable boy, calling him over. "James, run and fetch our steeds." The page went scampering out the door. A couple of minutes later he returned, leading Lucia's roan stallion and a larger, grey horse.

"Troy!" Lucia cried, running forward with joy. The roan horse whinnied as she ran a hand fondly along his neck. "What a good boy you are," she cajoled. "It looks like they have been feeding you well. Are you ready for some exercise?" The horse tossed his mane as she climbed into the saddle.

James looked up apologetically at Lucia. "I have searched everywhere for his reins and bridle, but could not find them. They must have been lost in the storm. At least your horse got through without an illness or injury." Lucia could see that even at his young age he respected the value of a strong steed.

"That is fine," she consoled him, "I have learned to not use reins on my horse. I steer him through knee pressure. This leaves my hands free for wielding my bow. The bow does require two hands, after all." She laughed at the surprised look on the page's face. "I will show you sometime," she promised. "Right now I am anxious to be up and about doing something!" She kneed the horse lightly, making him dance backwards for a few steps.

Marcus smiled. "Well, follow me, M'Lady," he offered with solicitude, climbing onto his stallion and moving him into a trot. "We have been using the back pastures to train during the winter; with the wolves getting hungrier, we have found it wise to remain within the outer walls. Right this way." He directed his horse around the castle toward the undeveloped back areas in the wall.

Lucia drew in the details of the keep as they moved. While the front areas were made up of tightly packed stone houses, churches, schools, and shops, the pastures they rode over now were only occasionally broken up by small shelters and barns. It seemed most of the shaggy cattle slept under half-a-roof and huddled together for warmth. She tried to concentrate on following the man in light leather armor who rode before her, but found herself looking about at the contained farmland, always protected by the wall.

"Well, here we are," announced Marcus, topping a rise near the far end of the wall. Below them, about a hundred yards away, Lucia could see twenty men sitting in a grassy semi-circle around Ian and Stephen. The troops had their backs to Lucia, and the teachers were too caught up in their lesson to notice her approach. "This is where I take my leave, M'Lady," he added. "I have got to get back to my duties. Will you be all right?"

"I am quite fine. Thank you very much for your assistance."

Marcus smiled in acknowledgment, then pulled his horse back toward the central building, now half hidden by the rolling hills and squat structures. Within a minute he was out of sight.

Lucia turned her attention back to the group below her. There were a few archery targets painted on hay bales behind the pair, and judging by the number of arrows lying around she guessed the students had spent some time firing at them. Stephen appeared to be making the exercise a little more difficult, for he had suspended one of the bales from a nearby oak tree by a rope. He was swinging it slowly and encouraging Ian to shoot it from horseback. Ian held an elaborately decorated bow, inlaid with contrasting wood, and was making a show of setting up to take his shot.

Lucia settled back on her horse to watch. How many times she and Michael had played this game over the years! It was almost funny to watch the same exercise being explained to grown men. She had to remind herself that most of these men had never wielded a weapon against a soldier before, but had come from farming families - only now needing to build skill to ward off the Grays. Still, could they not even have had bow practice, shooting down an encroaching badger?

Ian let loose an arrow and hit the swinging bale in the outer red ring, prompting the troops to call out shouts of encouragement. Ian moved twenty feet back, and let loose another arrow, this one landing a bit closer to center. The roars became louder, and Ian bowed deeply, basking in the attention.

Lucia smiled to herself, feeling mischievous. So they thought those shots were good? Perhaps she could demonstrate her own skill and help build the trust the men had in what she could offer. She lifted her well-worn bow from the back of the saddle where it was strapped, and slid an arrow from the quiver hanging next to her stirrup. She gently nudged Troy sideways to line up her shot.

Troy whinnied softly as he turned, and though the troops did not hear the noise, Stephen looked up quickly with sharp interest. Seeing Lucia on the hilltop, bow drawn, his eyes twinkled. Watching her carefully, he pulled the bale back again, motioning to Ian that he should try a third shot. Ian slowly, with great show, prepared his aim.

Lucia blocked him, and everything else around her, out of her consciousness. She sighted her arrow on the solid dot in the bale's center, took a deep breath, and slowly let it out. When the arrow tip was a finger's height from the target, she gently let the string slip from her fingers. The arrow flew through the air, down the slope, and it almost seemed that the bale swung back into the arrow's path as it descended toward the snow. The arrow came to rest in the middle of the center dot, and buried itself to the last blue band.

Lucia let out her breath with a smile. The men turned in surprise, and let out a rousing cry when they realized it was she who had loosed the arrow. Ian tossed down his bow and slid off his mount. He ran up to meet her, laughing as he approached, "Why, Lucia! That was quite a shot! We should have woken you and brought you down to entertain us, sickbed be damned!"

He gave Troy a possessive pat on the neck, eyeing the steed with bright interest. Then he looked up at Lucia, continuing, "Do come down and join us. We would love to learn of your techniques." Lucia dutifully nudged Troy to follow him down the melting slope.

Stephen was pulling the arrow free from the hay when the pair reached the bottom. "Your arrow, M'Lady," he offered up to her. Lucia reached down for it, and her fingers ran along his as she accepted the offer. She blushed at the contact, turning and sliding the arrow back in her quiver.

Despite her strongest resistance her eyes were drawn back down. Stephen's gaze was steady on her, edged with concern. It reminded her of the depths of an old forest, the comfort of solid trees, a soft moss underfoot. With an effort she looked away to where Ian was standing.

"Do continue with your practice," Lucia prompted Ian, drawing a friendly smile onto her lips. "I will find an area to sit in this lovely meadow and watch you both at work."

Ian's eyes lit up with delight. "An audience! Wonderful!" He moved into action, rousting the men and getting them organized.

Lucia gave her steed a pat, and then swung her leg over the saddle to dismount.

The simple act, one she'd done thousands of times before, suddenly, baffling, disoriented her completely. The landscape around her swirled in a blur of icy whites and dark greens. Her legs became as wobbly as a newborn colt's. She continued to lower herself down, praying she did not collapse in front of all the watchers.

Then there was an arm at her side steadying her. Stephen's voice murmured softly into her ear, "Hold on. It will pass. Wait a moment." He moved into a position between her and the men, shielding her with his body.

Lucia nodded slightly, taking in long, slow, deep breaths. She leant her forehead against her steed's side, inhaling his musky, familiar scent. Slowly the spinning eased and the ground leveled out. She stood up straight again, then tapped Troy on his hindquarters to send him off with the other horses grazing to one side.

Stephen remained close beside her, his back to his men, subtly providing his arm for her to lean against. Reading the weariness in her face, he deftly rearranged her hand into a position of courtly courtesy, and said in a louder tone, "Yes, M'Lady, let me escort you to your seat."

Lucia glanced up in appreciation as with elaborate ceremony he led her over to a blanket and helped her settle in a seated position. The men smiled and nodded, solely seeing in this interaction the generous behavior of a chivalrous host.

Stephen's eyes showed his deeper concern as he asked lightly, "Is everything to your satisfaction?"

Lucia did feel much better, now that she was seated. The wave of nausea had passed, and she felt fresh again, if tired. "Yes, thank you," she replied gently, hoping her eyes showed her gratitude more fully.

Stephen nodded briefly, then turned to the men, waving up a group to begin their swordplay.

Lucia was more tired from the ride than she would have thought possible. It seemed she would have to spend the morning simply stretching her muscles instead of engaging in more strenuous activities. Pushing herself too hard might delay her recovery, something she could ill afford.

The morning eased past her as Ian and Stephen ran the troops through a variety of combat drills. She held the disappointment from her face as the green recruits ineptly clashed wooden swords on shields. These men needed encouragement, she reminded herself sternly. She wondered if she had made a mistake coming to what now seemed a large farming community for assistance. She reminded herself that this was the beginners' troop; surely the experienced fighters were better trained.

As the hours passed, Lucia was struck by the difference between the two teachers. Ian was full of wild, coltish energy. His actions were highly enthusiastic, doing runs by the book but with great show and flourish. By comparison, Stephen conserved his energy, moving quietly without apparent effort. His attacks and blocks often showed the mark of quick improvisation, and every movement reflected purpose and strength.

Finally, with the sun high in the sky and the men lying on the slope panting for breath, Stephen called a halt to the morning exercises. "Well done!" he praised with a smile, running his eyes across the troops. "You have the energy and drive to learn quickly. We will make fighters of you yet - you all show promise. Let us head back to the castle for our lunch. Do not wear yourselves out tending the cattle, though; the next lesson starts tomorrow morning promptly at sunrise."

Amidst groans and laughter he walked to gather up his horse and Lucia's. He walked the two over to where Lucia had gotten to her feet. His eyes were sharp on her, but he said nothing. Lucia gave him a reassuring nod. She did feel much better after the several hours of rest. She was glad to find that mounting was as easy as it had always been for her, although she was grateful for Stephen's presence at her side should she need it.

Once she was settled in her saddle, he smoothly climbed into his own. He then glanced around at the group, and together they gently herded the troops back toward the castle.

Lucia relaxed as she settled into the familiar saddle, her horse ambling through the winter grass which crunched beneath his hooves. Her thoughts drifted. This morning's session was not encouraging. It seemed she had a lot to think about.

Ian galloped up from behind, laughing as her head whirled at the sound. "Want to race to the main building?" he challenged eagerly. "I have to get back in time to start lunch with my father. You could join us at the head table," he added. "You are one of our guests." He wheeled his horse expectantly.

Lucia smiled, but turned him down gently. "I am afraid I am not up to a race quite yet," she admitted reluctantly. "You go on ahead – I will meet you there." Ian grinned and kicked his horse into a gallop, tearing up the slope back to the hall. Lucia shook her head at her state as Stephen remained steadily at her side.

"I am sure your strength will return soon," Stephen commented softly as their horses walked slowly across the melting farmland, the farmhand troops lagging behind. "You are already far stronger than most women I know." His eyes moved down to the bow and quiver which hung laced to her saddle. "Your archery skills are all you said. You would be an asset to any troop."

Lucia smiled at the praise. "I used to practice that same exercise for months on end," she pointed out. She sighed, thinking back over the exhaustion she had felt after such a short effort. "Still, I wish I was in better shape. It is frustrating to tire so easily."

Lucia winced as Troy picked his way over a rocky outcropping. "My side has been hurting, too," she admitted with a grimace. "I suppose Matthew was right – perhaps I should not be out so soon after the battle. It is tough for me to rest." Troy stumbled again, and she let out a low curse at the sharp stab of pain which followed. She pulled to a stop, looking down. If she had pulled the scar open …

"Here, let me get that," offered Stephen. He edged his horse in more closely to hers, and leant over. As he pulled the cloak and tunic away from her side he commented, "After all of my years on the road, I have become a pretty adept field medic. You learn techniques that can make the difference in the woods, although the keep staff usually have a fit when they see what you have done."

His touch was gentle, and Lucia reminded herself that he had done this many times already, undoubtedly, while she was in the grips of the fever. She drew in his scent, and it reminded her of home, of safety. She could feel every motion of his fingers against her flesh.

Stephen glanced up at her for a moment, and strong emotion flickered in his eyes before he looked down again, focusing on the injury. He carefully pulled the white cloth bandage away from the skin, and smiled in relief when he saw the healing scar. "No damage done. Just remember to go easy."

Lucia gave a half grin. "I think those words have a different meaning here," she protested. "For the north, I *am* going easy."

He smiled at that, then carefully relaid the bandage and pulled her tunic and cloak back into place. "Then I propose you find some sort of compromise," he offered.

Her eyes brightened. "I am not good at compromise," she offered with a low laugh. "It is one of my more egregious faults."

"Oh?" he asked with interest. "And what others might there be?"

She gave him a nudge as they set back into motion. "I am sure you saw most of them this past week," she reminded him. "I do not believe any injury or illness has ever taken me on so hard."

His eyes shadowed. "It would have killed a lesser person," he stated with certainty. "You showed strength to make it through. Never doubt it."

She glanced over at him. "It was your tender care which brought me through," she countered. "I would not be here if it were not for you."

He looked away. They rode in silence for a few minutes, their horses' hooves making soft crunching noises in the crisp snow. They were drawing closer to the keep now, and its wide windows made Lucia long again for her own home, safe, secure, nestled into the crags and juniper trees. She had risked her life to come here for help – but what help could Penrith really offer? Could those greenhorns she saw sparring last more than a half second against even the youngest Gray scout?

Stephen glanced over, and his focus sharpened. "What is wrong? Is it the wound again?"

Lucia shook her head no. She glanced around, but Ian had long since vanished ahead of them, and the troops were now far behind. Perhaps this would be her only opportunity to bring up her concerns in private.

"It is the state of the troops here," she admitted softly. "Ellie told me how Lord Edmund called you in to help oversee the training. Certainly your skill is beyond question, but not even a magician could turn these farmers into warriors in a few months."

She looked over at him, and he nodded in understanding. His voice came rough. "You had hoped to regain your keep instantly," he murmured.

"It is still hard to believe it is lost," she pressed. "I thought, somehow, that I would arrive here, a wealth of troops would be sent north, and the Grays would be drowned in a sea of warriors. But now ..."

She looked up toward the north. "During the ride down here, we passed farmhouse after plundered farmhouse. Mill buildings lay in ruins, fields had long since returned to wilderness. And those were your lands." Her eyes drew back to his, taking in the pain which sheltered behind the dark steadiness.

Her voice came out in a whisper, "How do you do it? How do you hang on to hope?"

"Faith, patience, and determination," he responded quietly. "Yes, it has taken a while for some of the local leaders, like Lord Edmund, to look at the Grays as more than passing bandits. But now that the wasteland has grown to reach their doorsteps, action will be taken. They are investing in the training, and working on combining their forces." His eyes held hers with steady regard. "Come spring, between your forces and ours, we will have what is needed to wipe them out for good."

She shook her head, gazing in his eyes. "But twenty long years," she repeated. "Surely it has eaten away at you?"

Stephen looked away, out over the rolling farmland. "When my family was driven out of our lands," he remembered, "the Grays burned everything. We barely escaped with our lives. My father thought, as you did, to retake the lands quickly. He died six months later in a failed raid. My mother, heartbroken, passed away not long after that. Lord Edmund took pity on me, and brought me on as a ward." His eyes shadowed. "But I came to him with nothing. Nothing but the one oil lamp my father had brought with him from his time in the crusades. That one object is all I have left of the family and lands I have lost."

He gave a soft laugh. "It seems such a silly concern, but I have not one stitch of clothing, not even the smallest item with my family crest on it. It is as if we do not even exist any more."

Lucia's heart echoed in pain. They had both lost so much. He had been shouldering his burden for twenty long years, and had been doing everything in his power to work against the Grays. She smiled slightly. Now, at least, she could lend the strength of her family's forces toward that fight.

She looked over at Stephen, and found that he was watching her. "In the end, we shall be the light in the darkness," she vowed. "To give in to despair would provide the Grays with the victory they desire. As long as we stay strong, we will have won, no matter what else happens." She saw recognition in his eyes. The feeling that he understood her, without need for explanation, filled her with a comforting warmth.

The pair rode in easy silence the remainder of the trip, their horses picking their way slowly along the quiet dirt path. As they came around the edge of a larger building, the main doors of the keep came into view. One of the court women was waiting on the massive stone steps.

Lucia studied her with interest. The woman was quite lovely, delicately thin, with waist-length blonde hair done in an elaborate style. She wore an intricately embroidered burgundy gown. Even the finest dress in Lucia's wardrobe back home came nowhere near the fine stitchery of what the blond woman apparently wore as a daily outfit.

The blonde saw them and waved a lace kerchief to them, a wide smile on her lips. "Stephen!" she cried out in glee, running down the steps with her arms outward. "Finished with your morning lessons already? Let me take a look at you."

She laughed joyfully as he easily dismounted and bowed low to her. "Have you worked up a healthy appetite? It would not do for you to waste away to nothing, my betrothed!"

Chapter 7

My betrothed.

Lucia reeled with shock. Suddenly the scene seemed far away from her, a play on a stage that she was watching but had no part in. Stephen straightened up and glanced at her with a shadowed look before replying cordially to the woman. "The training is going well. We should have the men ready in good time," he assured her. "They will be well prepared by the time the Grays reach us."

The woman turned to look at Lucia with unconcealed interest, and he reluctantly turned with her. Lucia found herself being pulled into this tableau that she would just as soon escape. She had to do something, and the first step involved getting down off of Troy.

She could not be weak and cause a scene – not here, not on the main keep steps with this blonde beauty gazing on.

She turned Troy so his body would shield her from the couple. Then, holding firmly on to the saddle, she carefully slid down his side. A wave of dizziness swept over her; she focused on her breathing and on spreading her weight evenly across both feet. In a moment it passed, and James was there at her side, the young boy giving a gentle pull to Troy's mane to head him toward the stables.

Stephen's eyes were shadowed with concern as he came into view again. Lucia pushed down her weakness and confusion, and forced herself to smile brightly at the couple. She stepped forward and looked to Stephen. "I do not believe I have been introduced to your companion?"

Stephen nodded, blinking himself back from wherever his mind had gone to. "Yes, of course. Lucia, I would like you to meet Anastasia. She is first cousin to Ian. She hails from Dacre, a small town to the south of here." There was a long, awkward pause. His eyes, usually so open and readable to her, were now shuttered and distant.

He was engaged to another woman.

Lucia's heart shadowed with pain, and she found herself unable to draw her eyes away from him. He held her gaze for a moment, then turned to look at the woman by his side.

Anastasia jumped blithely into the opening. "Greetings!" she called, moving forward to clasp Lucia gently. "Call me Anna for short," giggled the woman. "I am very happy to meet you at last! The whole palace has been buzzing with the news! I have been dying to talk with you since Ian first brought you in, but of course you were not feeling well, and Stephen said you were badly poisoned by the Grays. He is good with these things, and has been taking fine care of you. There is no one more patient than Stephen when it comes to nursing someone through that kind of thing, Matthew has always said as much. I have done my part, praying for you in the chapel."

Anna barely took in a breath as she exuberantly threw her arms wide. "I am so glad you are better now! I have been talking to all the court members about where you might be from and how you got here ..." Anna merrily prattled on as she put her arms around Lucia in welcome.

A memory flickered in Lucia's mind. Anna had been at the center of one of the groups of courtiers she had passed.

"I am the youngest daughter of one of the local nobles," Anna continued blithely, "and I was sent here for some courtly education. This keep is just such a pretty place to learn! And there is so much to know about before one is married." She smiled over at Stephen. "But I am really here for Stephen," she continued, wrapping her arm around his waist. He patted her hand automatically, but his eyes were now on Lucia's, and there was a distance in them. Anna bubbled onward. "Is he not *so* handsome?"

"It is very nice to meet you, Anna." stated Lucia absently, while her mind rolled over the question with a bit of surprise. Handsome? When she thought of Stephen, it was his eyes that caught her in their power. Eyes that she could trust to be there when her strength gave way, eyes to watch over her at night when the nightmares overtook her.

Lucia glanced involuntarily up at Stephen and found that he was looking at her still. Yes, certainly he was handsome. His dark hair was thick and curled at his neck, drawing her to twine her fingers in it. But to Lucia those were the trappings – the jewels which decorated a sword. Stephen was far more than that. It was the sturdiness to his hand, the skill which drove his strike during swordplay, the steely resolve to finish what he began, the steady courage that blazed from his eyes when she had held the knife at his throat ...

A deep bell sounded from within the castle, starting her guiltily from her thoughts. It had been years since she'd thought about a man in her life. Now, at last, she longed for one with all her heart, and he was betrothed to another.

She shook herself free from the mental image. She had not known he was taken. Now that she knew, she would have to put him out of her mind, whatever it took.

She nodded to Anna, deliberately keeping her gaze from Stephen. "What is that bell for?" she asked, focusing all of her attention on Anna's pale skin and innocent smile.

Anna looked up in the direction of the noise. "How the morning has flown! It is already time for lunch," she answered merrily. "I am so sorry, I have got to go – I am learning about running a kitchen, too! There are so many recipes and protocols!" She gave Stephen a squeeze and scampered up the remaining stairs, pausing at the top to wave to Stephen. He nodded in response and watched as she vanished in the door.

Lucia stood beside him, a dark hollow forming around her, swallowing her in its depths. A week. It had only been one week since she had felt his approach down the snowy hill, had put her knife to his throat, and he had gazed at her with steady trust. One week of her fingers twined in his, of her pouring out emotions which she'd kept locked within for years.

One week which had seemed to last a lifetime.

The stillness stretched on. In the past their silence had been comforting. It had been a gentle warmth which they had shared together. Now the quiet echoed with cold loneliness. At last the pain became too sharp; she searched for something to fill the void.

"Anna is very nice," she ventured, not looking at him. She racked her mind for something noncommittal to add. "You must be very proud to be engaged to her."

Stephen looked at her then; his eyes swirled with a turmoil of emotions. "Yes," he agreed roughly. "Anna is a fine woman and is eager to be a wonderful wife. Any man would be lucky to have her."

He opened his mouth to say more, then compressed his lips into a thin line. He looked at Lucia for another moment, then deliberately turned his eyes back toward the doors. "We should head in; lunch will be served shortly."

They walked up the stairs and in through the main doors. Stephen spoke up again. "If you are up to it, you are welcome to join us in the great hall. I am sure a seat is open for you at the head table."

The large room was thronging with people. Exuberant noise echoed from all sides as diners shouted for drinks and servants called responses. The air was saturated with fragrant aromas of spiced duck, fresh bread, roasted turnips, and other dishes. Stephen nodded to Anna who had already found her seat at the head table. Motioning to Lucia, he pressed a path for them through the mass of people.

As they approached it, Lucia saw Ellie off to one side, and tapped Stephen on his shoulder. "I am fine from here," she stated evenly. "You go on without me."

Stephen nodded, and his eyes seemed to shutter again. "Yes, you will be fine now," he replied, half to himself. He turned and headed up toward Anna. Lucia watched him go for a moment, then made her own way over toward the other end of the table. Ellie was standing behind an empty chair with a mock frown, waving her over, and Lucia took the seat with exhausted relief.

Ellie started in immediately. "Where have you been? I have been looking for you for hours," she accused with worry as she poured Lucia some wine from a wooden pitcher. "I figured you had stayed out a while, once you got there ... against orders I might add. I could get in big trouble! You would not want that to happen, would you?"

"I could say I drugged you and slipped out while you slept," teased Lucia.

Ellie saw her settled in, then gave her a gentle pat. "Do you need anything else?"

Lucia shook her head. "You go get some food for yourself," she suggested. "I imagine you are starving, after all that long worrying."

Ellie winked and headed off at a trot toward the side door. Lucia called after her, "Do not expect me until dark, though!" She sighed in frustration. Was she an untested child promising to be in by curfew? Her shoulders tensed with the state she was in - helpless, not in charge, not in control. She needed to start changing that.

The noise in the room along with the press of the people caused a claustrophobic pressure to build within her. At the same time, despite all reason, she felt utterly alone. To her left was a corpulent noble engrossed with spreading as much butter as possible on his thick loaf of bread. Ian was to her right, but he was deep in discussion with his father, arguing whole-heartedly for the right to take on a key role in the upcoming conflicts.

She looked down to her trencher. The food, at least, was filling and well cooked. The duck was excellent, and she washed it down with rich red wine from a pewter flagon.

From all around, the sound pounded in at her. The voices of men relating their latest combat triumphs struggled to be heard over the babble of women gossiping. Behind Lucia a pair of noblemen were arguing loudly over what type of attack the Grays would launch next.

The minutes ticked by, and Lucia felt more and more like an outsider. How different this was from her own home, where she knew every face and was greeted by each as a friend.

Her keep had been overrun. It was all lost.

Lucia poked at the food on her trencher a few more times, but she just wasn't hungry. She was suddenly homesick beyond all measure.

She folded up two biscuits and some oatmeal bread from the baskets in the center of the table in a cloth napkin, and drew to her feet.

Ian looked over in surprise and put out a hand to hold on to her arm. "I am so sorry. I have been a rude host," he apologized, holding her back. "I should have put my argument with my father off until later." He tugged her down. "Please, sit. I imagine you were bored stiff by our practice this morning; I will be sure to ask Anna to spend time with you going forward."

Lucia forced a smile onto her lips. "I should follow Matthew's advice and get more rest," she demurred. "I am sure I will be feeling better by tomorrow."

"We can spend time together tomorrow, then? When you are feeling better?" pressed Ian, his eyes bright on hers.

"Yes, of course," she agreed in relief. "That sounds lovely."

She stood, turned, and quickly headed out to the main entrance. As her feet were set in motion, she found that she was almost running to the front doors. She stopped only when the doors closed behind her and she was once again in the fresh air.

She stood still for a few moments, breathing in deeply and struggling to regain her sanity.

James, the same young page who helped Lucia in the morning, now ran up to assist her. Lucia wondered from the concern on his face just how pale she looked. He spoke up immediately. "Are you feeling all right? I can get Brother Matthew for you, if you wish." James wore a burgundy tunic with white pants, and a sturdy dagger was looped through his belt. He looked genuinely worried.

Lucia smiled reassuringly at the lad. "I am quite all right; I would simply like to get some air. That dining room is stifling after being out in the sun all morning."

Lucia suddenly realized what she needed. "Could you bring me Troy again?" she asked. "I know it is quite a bother to get him saddled up." She might not be up to real exercise, but a quiet ride in the forest would give her the solitude she needed to think. If she returned to her room, undoubtedly Ian or Ellie would feel it necessary to keep her company.

Or Stephen.

"Oh, no bother for you," replied the page sincerely, turning to run to the stables. Lucia wondered at the gentle atmosphere that had created this easy openness. She was sure to thank the page profusely when he returned in record time with her steed. James blushed crimson under her praise, a shade that nearly matched his tunic. He stammered, a huge grin on his face, then claimed some chore needed to be done as he ran off to the stables.

Lucia nudged the horse into a quiet walk. She wandered down the empty streets of the city, past the closed storefronts and caught glimpses of the families sitting at their tables for lunch. She traveled on, wondering what it was to live and grow without constant fear of attack. The sensation had just come to this town - how would it change?

The richer homes were congregated immediately around the main keep. As she moved farther and farther away from the center, the homes became less ornamental, more basic. Wildflowers took the place of elegant knickknacks in the windows, curling ivy replacing elaborate trim on the shutters. The lack of wealth did not affect the pride of the owners, however. Even at the outskirts, near the protective wall, the most modest homes were still maintained with care.

There was a twenty foot gap between the buildings and the twin guard towers attached to the inner side of the curtain wall. A few chickens pecked in the dirt and sparse grass in this gap. When Lucia crossed the open expanse, she was hailed by the bearded watchman who stood on a platform over the gate.

"Greetings, M'Lady. What brings you to this end of the city? I thought you would stay in the castle until you'd fully healed. Not many approach these gates now that winter has settled in, and the enemies are so close. You came to keep me company, perhaps?" He guffawed at the notion, holding his spear for support. Lucia saw two guards up on the wall half turn, listening in on the conversation without stopping their visual sweep of the woods beyond.

Lucia could smell the fresh green of the forest just beyond the wall, and suddenly she was struck with a powerful longing to give one last farewell to her fallen friends. They deserved that, at least, in their resting place so far from the home they had loved.

She looked up to the watchman. "I would like to go out and say a prayer in the woods for my fallen comrades. I will stay close by." Her mind, as it had been for the past week, tried to veer away from these thoughts, but she held firm. She had the luxury, at least for a while, of giving in to the sorrow. The realization that they were truly gone brought tears to her eyes, which she wiped away quickly. Not yet, not now. She must wait until she was out somewhere alone. She couldn't afford to be lost in it yet.

The gatekeeper nodded somberly, watching her change in mood. "I will send a guard to go with you, then. The woods have been quiet, but one can never be certain."

Lucia shook her head firmly. "I will be fine," she reassured him. "I promise to stay close. This is something I need to do alone."

The man hesitated for a long moment, glancing over his shoulder at the other two, then motioned with his head. The two soldiers came down from the wall. Lucia recognized one of the men as Marcus, the man who had brought her out to archery practice earlier. She exchanged nods with him as he passed.

The two moved to haul the logs from the gate rungs, then pulled one heavy door open for her. She slowly walked her horse through the opening. She only half noticed as Marcus mounted a horse and rode back toward the main buildings.

"Make sure you are back by sunset," called the gatekeeper. "There are wolves out there - and other dangers."

"I will," promised Lucia, then turned her horse northwards, into the shadowed forest.

Lucia breathed a sigh of relief as the oaks closed snugly around her. The only sounds were the crisp, slow but steady rhythm of her horse's hooves in the thin sheet of snow and the rustle of birds in the trees. The sun was high in the sky, but the tree branches filtered out much of the sunlight. The woods remained cool with the snow barely melting in many spots. For a while, she was content to move languidly through the peaceful oaks, feeling more relaxed than she had in many days.

She wondered if she could find the clearing where they had mounted the last battle. Undoubtedly it was safe for now with the local troops actively scouting for any sign of activity. She knew Stephen and Ian had stumbled upon it while riding one of their well-traveled paths. There was only one in front of her currently, so she decided to let Troy do the steering. In the meantime, she sat back and felt her tension easing with each passing minute.

She thought back to the times as a child when, ordered by her father to attend an important banquet, she had instead ridden for miles to some secluded spot to swim or relax. She eventually returned, and always her father had understood her enough not to be upset with her. "Time enough for social graces when you are married," he'd sigh as he rubbed her head.

Her poor father. He was always so sure that she would eventually marry a soldier and give him the grandchildren he so clearly wished for. Even when her engagement had been shown to be a sham, her fiancé disgraced ... tears welled in her eyes and she brusquely wiped them away. She had hardened her heart after that betrayal. She'd poured herself heart and soul into her work.

A wave of guilt washed over her. Perhaps she was being selfish in keeping every man at arm's length. Was she putting her own raw emotions above her duty to her family? She knew in many other lands that it would be her role to flirt with Ian, perhaps to bind his family and troops to her own through marriage. That would help guarantee their cooperation in the upcoming battle.

Shaking her head, she sighed deeply as Troy walked through the open trees. Who was she trying to fool? She had given in to courtship once out of a sense of duty. It had nearly brought total ruin to her lands. She would not make that mistake again.

No, the only man she would trust in her life was her twin brother. She adored Michael, treasured his firm strength and compassionate heart. He would have snowball fights with her in the winter and ride out on hunts at her side in the languorous summer. They would often share patrols, and evenings were spent contentedly in long talks by the glowing embers of a campfire.

She smiled as she thought back to their years together. He had always been there for her. When she played the harp, he would sing along in that marvelous, rich voice of his. When they attended the local festivals, he would dance as her partner, aware of how she maintained a wall against suitors after the painful destruction of Evan's courtship.

Lucia wondered how her brother was doing on the boat. They were undoubtedly tucked into a harbor near Amble for now, waiting for spring's gentler seas. He held the responsibility for the lives of their remaining villagers. Had he formally assumed their father's place? He had always been ready for the responsibility, or so it seemed. Did he now miss her as much as she missed him?

It would be almost two months before she saw him again, so she resolved to put him out of her mind for now - it would only worry her. It seemed the list of subjects to avoid thinking about had grown. It was bad enough that she had trained herself to be tight-lipped ... but to shut out all thought ...

Coming back to her present situation, she realized that Troy had stopped a while ago. There was a small clearing up ahead. She dismounted slowly and approached the area with cautious steps, drawing her sword with practiced ease as she stepped into the open. She knew she wasn't up to a fight, but it did no good to look helpless, just in case.

The area was almost eerily silent, and there was no movement as far as she could see.

Yes, this is where her companions had fallen. The scene looked much as she had left it, or at least as much as she could remember. Dead Grays still littered the ground, while the cairn of ash was long cold and much was scattered by the winds. She walked forward and knelt at the foot of the rocks, sad that her friends would have no proper funeral. She had done the best she could. She put the sword point-down into the ground, and bent her head in prayer, leaning on it for support.

The sobs came slowly at first, but when she gave in and let them take her, they racked her body. All of the feelings she'd be avoiding, hiding from, these past days came washing over her. These men that had died around her weren't just fellow soldiers; they had been her best friends. Out of everyone that had served with her, these men had insisted, had demanded, that they accompany her on this trip. They were the ones she had spent long evenings with in the tavern, playing games and sharing stories. They'd watched over each other on long patrols, guarded each other's backs when bandits ambushed them on the trail. They had been through everything together, and she'd thought their days as a band would stretch into a long history. She never even imagined that they'd be gone, all at once, without a chance to say goodbye.

* * *

From the dark shadow of the woods, Stephen watched quietly as Lucia doubled over crying, sobbing as if her heart would break. He desperately wanted to go to her, to console her, to let her know her pain would ease with time. He wanted to reassure her that, with patience, the guilt and hurt would settle eventually into distant memory.

He harshly silenced that voice. He sternly reminded himself that he was engaged, bound to Anna. He had to keep Lucia at arm's length.

Stephen shook his head as he swept his eyes across the clearing. He had allowed himself to be drawn in by her. He wondered how much she remembered of their long discussions through the nights while she was half-delirious with fever. She had poured out her pain and the struggles of her life. During those talks he had been continually impressed with her strength of character, with her sense of honor. Even now, when most women would be curled up in bed, she had spent the day striving to rebuild her weakened body and to pay homage to those she had lost.

Stephen's hand tightened reflexively on the hilt of his sword. It did not matter how noble Lucia's character was. He could not allow himself the luxury of caring for her. Anna had never questioned all of the time he had spent this past week tending to the newcomer. She deserved a husband worthy of that trust.

Yes, he was here now. It was his duty, after being alerted by Marcus that Lucia had gone out alone, to make sure she got back safely. He would shield her from attack should it be necessary. But as to the rest, she was on her own. It had to be this way.

He took a deep breath and turned away from her, watching the woods with an alert eye.

* * *

Lucia was overwhelmed with darkness; her body-shaking sobs shook loose all sense of time. The shadows drifted, lengthened, and still she wept, unable to find an end to her sorrows. Finally, out of sheer exhaustion her shoulders slumped and her breath raggedly slowed to normal. She was left only with a deep ache that seemed to be part of her very bones.

Lucia knelt motionless, drained, unable to think or move. More time eased past in swirling drifts of snow. At last she dried her eyes and put her forehead down to the hilt of her sword. She vowed revenge for the four who had fallen here, so dear to her heart. Then she kissed the pommel and sheathed the sword.

She saw a glint to one side of the cairn, and retrieved a bronze bracer, somehow separate from the pile. It seemed like an omen to her, and she put it carefully into an inner pocket.

She knew the bracer well, and breathed a deep sigh. It belonged to Vic, the youngest member of their band. He had never complained, never hesitated once on the difficult journey. Even when the Grays had taken him hostage, even when the weaselly one had tortured him, Vic's only thought had been for the safety of the group. And then …

Her eyes went to the pile of rocks, to all that remained of her loyal friends. They had given their lives. It was her duty to protect them from harm, and she was the cause of their deaths! Lucia kicked angrily at a Gray's sword which lay to her left. It was her fault. Frustrated, she turned and strode back to Troy.

Mounting the horse, she urged him into a gallop and headed back the way she came. Anger and rage swept through her. Anger at those who had attacked her homeland and killed innocent people who were simply trying to escape. Anger at the fiend who had tortured Vic for the sheer delight of it. Anger at the complacent keep dwellers who couldn't see the threat even when it was upon their doorstep.

Black thoughts raced wildly through her head, thundering in time to her horse's heavy footfalls. Who was she to bear this responsibility? To have people die to protect her life? Just the second child of a minor lord! If she hadn't been there, no one would have died. She could ride west, to the sea, and escape on a boat across the ocean. She had heard wonderful lands were said to exist beyond the waters.

She didn't even have to go that far. Bandits lived for years in the deep woods, after all. It simply took a bow, a knife, and an understanding of the woodland creatures. She possessed all three. Perhaps she could simply disappear into the forest somewhere.

She reined in Troy, exhaustion settling over her. Disappear? To where? What would she do without her friends and townsfolk? Who would help her brother when he needed someone to talk to? Who would tell Marcie her brother died honorably? Who would make sure her father had not died in vain?

She slowed to a walk. A light seemed to kindle within her, slowly at first, and then with growing strength. She was warmed by the companionship echoing from the guards she had served with over the long years. She was bolstered by the feeling of standing up for what was right and encouraging others to do the same.

She took in a deep breath. There would be deaths, whether or not she was around. Stephen's tragic loss proved that beyond a shadow of a doubt. She could only do her best to minimize the losses. She and her friends had sworn to protect their people, even if it meant their own deaths. The sacrifice was not made unknowingly, nor in vain.

A sobering peace washed over her, taking its place alongside the sorrow. She let it fill her mind.

A small clearing opened up to the left, a quiet stream trickling along its far side. She knew the keep's walls were perhaps five minutes ahead. This was a safe enough place to stop and rest for a while.

She climbed down carefully from Troy's back, hobbling him to graze and drink from the nearby stream while she sat on the banks. This part of the forest was less thickly grown; most of the snow had melted except a few patches on some rocks in the flowing water.

She lay her sword at her side. Surely this area would be safe from attack, but she would take no chances. Then she opened the pouch at her hip, removing the bread. She leant up against a sturdy willow, gazing over at her horse as she nibbled on the edges of the meal.

"Something worth having is worth fighting for," she mused out loud. Troy glanced up, disinterested, then continued nibbling on some clover. She found it helped putting breath behind her thoughts, if only to the brown-eyed steed who had loyally carried her so far.

"I was raised to value my people beyond all else. If valiant soldiers lose their lives while protecting them, it is my duty and honor to accept that. Now it is my responsibility to gather a force to join with Michael, to give our people hope."

She sighed, the heavy burdens exhausting her. Her voice dropped down low. "Sometimes I wish I was a quiet villager. So many people depend on me; rely on my strength."

She lapsed back into silence for a while. A magpie jabbered in a nearby tree, then fell silent. Lucia needed something to raise her flagging spirits; she thought of a song she and her brother used to sing to pass the time on long rides. Hesitantly, she took up the tune herself.

"Gather, camp-mates, list my tale -
Swords of honor did prevail
'gainst foes en masse with weapons steeled
Our fighters' fates were all but sealed.
If not for faithful Keilder.

Spies by night, a sneak attack
betrayed our captains from the back
The soldiers fell and children, too,
evil winds came blowing through.
All turned to faithful Keilder.

A rousing cry – in arms he came
The chant of many raised his name
Spirits mustered, banners flew.
Each passing day the forces grew
Drawn by faithful Keilder.

Lucia's voice faded away into silence. The stirring ballad brought to life her land's history and the struggles her ancestors went through to secure their homeland. The thought that she was exiled from the keep she loved racked her with pain.

She searched her memory for a better tune; after a few minutes one came to mind. It was an older tune, from before her family settled in the rocky crags over the northern forests. This was one she and her brother had hummed while doing the Welcoming Dance in one of the back rooms at the keep. She stood, and slowly did the steps in time with her words.

Welcome the shimmering sun.
Welcome the glistening moon.
Rain cascades from the ebony sky
Water nurtures the suckling ground
Life blossoms.

The gentle rhythms and long, drawn-out phrases relaxed her almost immediately. Questions fled her mind - the dance was all. She closed her eyes and stretched out her arms.

Ah - she could hear her brother's deep baritone voice filling in the harmony. A step to the right, two quick to the left, a gentle spin and a low dip. She smiled at the memory of practicing that move with her brother by firelight. She prayed fervently that he was safe.

Welcome the glittering stars
Scattered by a generous goddess
Their steady light always pointing,
A beacon always trusted,
Guiding all to safe harbor.

The old dances were fluid - nothing like the modern,
formal dances many of the neighboring areas were
adopting. Smooth, gentle, Lucia forgot time and place -
suddenly nothing else was important. She was dancing,
and the two voices twined through the crisp winter air. She
spun in abandon.

Lucia's mind crystallized as she became one with the
trickling water, the crisp breeze, the slick-winged magpie
in the willow. She could hear the recorder join in, as
Marcie had often done on those wintry days when they
were trapped inside by the snow.

Welcome the steady waves of the sea
The salty bringer of life
The never-ending tides,
Holder of secrets, power beyond reckoning,
ever present ... ever present ...

Lucia spun about in bliss, a perfect emptiness which at
the moment felt full to bursting.

A cracking noise sounded sharply in the silence. She
snapped back to the real world and her dangerous
situation. It was like coming fully awake from a powerful
dream.

Where was her sword?

She shook her head, reorienting herself in this strange
forest. Visions of her brother and friend evaporated,

replaced by a trickling stream and swaying willow branches.

Where had the sound come from?

Standing by the bubbling water, patting Troy on the head, was Stephen. He watched her with a tender smile on his lips. After a moment he stepped deliberately back off the small twig at his feet.

Lucia let out a deep breath - she hadn't realized she was holding it in. "Stephen!" she half-sighed in relief, half-cursed in annoyance. She turned away from his watching eyes, walking quickly back to the leaning willow where she had left her sword. She burned with flustered embarrassment, and spoke rapidly to cover her confusion. "I wondered how someone could have gotten this close without Troy alerting me." She reached down to pick up her sword, sliding it smoothly back into the worn scabbard at her waist.

"Your horse is well trained," commented Stephen, giving Troy a gentle pat, "but I have been doing this for years."

Lucia ran her gaze down his lean body. The man, with his small team, had been effectively picking away at the Grays, their only advantage their ability to strike without warning. She had no doubt that he was very good at what he did.

Her mouth went dry, and she turned her head, looking over at the stream.

Stephen let the silence stretch out for a moment, then continued more quietly. "You have a lovely singing voice. I have not heard that song for quite a while - not since my youth in my own homelands." He clucked to his horse, and when it drew near he tied it to the tree.

"Anyway," he stated briskly, coming around Prince and standing in front of Lucia, "We need to talk."

His tone bordered on a command and Lucia grew prickly at it, her gaze sharpening. She moved to a curving willow, settling warily down against it.

Stephen looked down steadily at her, meeting her gaze evenly. "We have a responsibility to keep an eye out for you and ensure your safety. You should know better than to ride into a hostile area alone while you are still injured. You were quite a way from the keep walls ..."

Lucia wondered if she imagined the concern she saw in his eyes. Chastised, she again reminded herself of her responsibility to focus on healing, so she could fulfill her mission. This was really only her first day out of bed, and she had been pushing herself hard. Still, had she been away from the keep for that long? Lucia didn't remember much time passing. Her chin jutted out. Despite her injuries, her pride chafed at the implication that she couldn't care for herself.

"I do not consider myself a prisoner here," she reminded Stephen strongly, her voice coming out a little more sharply than she had intended. "I came to your lands of my own volition, and I am capable of protecting myself. I assure you that the momentary lapse of watchfulness will not occur again."

Stephen's somber face did not change. Lucia wanted to know how long he had been watching her, but bit her tongue. She pressed her main point.

"I am not planning on returning to the castle until dusk. If you want to keep an eye on me, you will just have to sit here until then."

Stephen's eyes flared with surprise, but he held in whatever response he might have made. It was with clear reluctance that he eased himself down against an elderly oak facing Lucia.

Time drifted by, and Lucia found her anger easing as the water rustled gently through the reeds. It had been a while since she had simply sat enjoying nature. She glanced over at Stephen. It seemed that he, too, was relaxing into the quiet, the tight set of his shoulders gentling.

Stephen's voice came softly into her thoughts. "Your dancing was beautiful," he finally complimented her with quiet feeling. "Most people nowadays do not bother to learn the older dances or songs. I always did enjoy them."

She drew her eyes up to meet his, and she was struck by the mixture of pain and strength she found here. Stephen, more than anyone, could understand the challenges she faced. His skill with a sword and experience in the midst of the Grays was exactly what she craved by her side. And his steady eyes …

He dropped his gaze suddenly, and she gave herself a harsh shake. He was engaged to another. If he had come out to follow her, it was only in the role of a guard caring for an honored visitor.

She tilted her head to one side, pondering the situation more closely. Surely one of the regular guards could have come out to babysit, if the keep's staff had felt it necessary to keep an eye on her. Marcus had been right there. He undoubtedly had fewer duties to juggle. Why had Stephen come himself?

As she looked him over, she felt that he belonged here, out in the woods. His worn leather armor blended in with the rough tree bark and mossy ground. His quiet patience fit with the serenity of the water flowing along the rocky stream. She thought back to the morning's sparring practice, when she had watched him in mock combat. His moves had been sure and purposeful. He was a man she could rely on if trouble came. He would be a worthy ally to watch her back …

Lucia shook her head. On one hand she wanted to be alone and think, but on the other, she appreciated having Stephen here in case trouble arose. She had to be honest, to admit that she was not currently up for a fight, even with a lone, inexperienced bandit. She had not been thinking clearly when she approached the gates on her own; right now, being alone in the woods would have been far from wise.

Still, did it have to be Stephen, sitting there, watching over her? She felt so comfortable with him nearby… too comfortable. A hundred different topics of conversation sprang to her lips, and she squelched each one in turn. She was constantly reminded that this man was intended for another woman. She had no right to draw him in more closely to her.

Frustrated, Lucia let the silence stretch on. The sun traveled slowly across the sky; the warmth fading.

The forest was quiet; the two horses were resting, their breath softly blowing clouds of steam into the brisk air. Stephen calmly began whittling a small stick with his knife. The silence drifted on. To Lucia's surprise, sitting quietly with Stephen was even more relaxing than talking with him had been, all those nights. She had never felt this way with another man.

She could not feel this way about this man.

Stephen's presence called to Lucia, throwing her thoughts into an ever-growing turmoil. She felt as if she was pressed against a shop window, staring at something she desperately desired – but could never afford. She had to get away.

Lucia stood up and made a show of stretching. "I do not feel like relaxing out here any more," she bit out in harsh frustration, keeping her eyes away from Stephen. "I am going to head back to civilization." She did not want to leave. She wanted to stay here with him; but she knew she could not. The bitterness of her feelings added an edge to her voice. "If you still want to play baby-sitter, you are welcome to join me on my short ride."

Stephen's eyes flashed, and she saw the effort of will it took him to rein in his emotions. A burst of satisfaction washed through her. Good. He deserved it, after not telling her that he was engaged.

The ludicrous nature of her charge struck her, and she shook her head. Surely the man was not required to warn her that he was unavailable. He had cared for her through a life-threatening illness. He had done all he could to keep her alive. And now she was dismissive of his efforts? All because she had become fond of him – something she heard was quite normal for patients in this situation?

She turned to Troy, preparing him, then struggling to climb up into his saddle. Stephen stood by his own mount, watching her but not stepping forward to help.

Once she was ready, he called to his own steed and mounted easily, glancing once around the clearing. Dusk settled across the forest, swirling shadows and mists filling in the nooks.

After a few minutes, Lucia finally felt ready for the short trip back. She looked up to him, her voice low. "Lead on."

Stephen nodded without comment and kicked his mount into a slow trot. In a moment Lucia's horse was following him. It felt so natural, so peaceful to have Stephen guiding her through the woods. She forced herself to push those feelings aside and to focus on the trail ahead.

The pair rode along the path in silence. Lucia reminded herself that she was going to need help from Stephen when she rejoined her brother. Clearly it was not his fault that he had already found a partner in life. She could not take out her own frustrations on him. She sought to rein in her tormented spirit, and nudged her horse to come alongside his.

"I plan on coming out here every afternoon," she commented in a low voice, "for some rest. Just for an hour or so. It is a practice I used to follow back home." She hesitated for a moment. "I am capable of looking after myself, but," she continued, glancing quickly at Stephen, "if you feel a need to watch over me, I will not object."

Did she imagine it, or did Stephen seem both relieved and upset? The emotions flickered across his face so quickly that it was hard for her to know. He only nodded in response, his eyes focused on the path ahead.

Lucia settled back into her own thoughts, and the two did not speak again until they reached the large wooden gates.

The gatekeeper gave a wave as they approached. "I am glad to see you back," he called. The logs were quickly slid aside and the two rode through the entryway.

Inside, Stephen pulled to a stop, and Lucia reined in alongside him. He gave her a brief nod. "This is where we part," he stated quietly. "You should be fine with the rest of your trip. There is a group of trainees who wanted assistance with their shield work." He sighed, adding half to himself, "They need the practice."

Nodding in farewell, he turned and headed off down a side street.

Lucia sat still for a moment, watched him until he vanished from sight. Giving herself a shake, she nudged Troy into motion, riding the narrow streets back to the castle alone.

The long shadows made the buildings indistinct in the coming dusk; evening always seemed to come more quickly than she expected in the winter. Soon she reached the inner wall and buildings.

James was waiting for her when she rode up, and took her horse with a smile. Lucia was suddenly exhausted. She headed straight for her bedroom.

Ellie's voice came sharp with relief as Lucia stepped into her bedroom. "Where have you been?" she cried. "I have been so worried about you. Ian came by to my table after lunch and asked where you had gone, and then the page said he had saddled your horse for you, and Ian could not find you in the town. I heard that Stephen went out to look for you; I thought you had been attacked again and I am so happy you are safe!" Ellie fussed on while she helped Lucia out of her outfit. "Look at you – you are covered with snow and dirt! Let me get that bath ready and we will have you clean in no time."

Lucia tried to calm her. "I was out relaxing in the forest – do not worry yourself. I know how to defend myself." This reassurance did little to dissuade Ellie from clucking like a mother hen for another ten minutes while the bath was filled.

"I am sure you can fight under normal conditions, but you are hurt! You are still recovering! You must promise me to never go out again without notifying the castle guard so they can keep an eye out for you. I am responsible for you, you know." Ellie looked sternly up at Lucia, her hands on her hips.

Lucia held her hand up and solemnly stated, "I swear that someone will know what time I plan to go out every day." She thought of Stephen - would Ellie think him a proper guardian? She doubted it, but didn't really care. She didn't need a protector, in any case.

Ellie nodded her pert head. "I feel a little better...but what do you want with the forest, anyway? There is nothing interesting out there. Inside is where the excitement is - the troops, the food, the dances, everything!" Ellie continued expounding to herself in the other room while Lucia stood by the window, looking out into the deepening dusk. A quarter-moon was just rising over the stables. The sky was really beautiful here in the forest - it seemed softer somehow. Perhaps it was because it wasn't against the backdrop of sharp, jagged mountains, but gently waving trees.

"The moon, half-hidden by branch and leaf,
More perfect than one unbroken and pure."

The words of an ancient poet seemed appropriate. Lucia thought that the poet was thinking of a night like this. She spoke over her shoulder to the young maid. "I'm afraid I am not up to the main hall's dinner, not tonight. If it could be arranged, I would much rather have dinner in bed," she admitted to Ellie. "Could you ask to have something brought up for me?"

"I will do it right now, M'Lady. You just settle yourself into the tub and leave the rest to me. I am just surprised you are able to move, after being out all day. What if the Brother Matthew found out what you had been up to? He would skin me alive!" She went out the door still talking to herself, gently closing it behind her.

Lucia headed into the next room where the fragrant, warm water was waiting. Rose-petals floated on top, filling the room with their soft scent. Ellie was really something. Lucia smiled at her maid's concern as she lowered herself into the water. Her father had always trusted her implicitly, and she had never had someone cluck after her so much. She barely remembered her own mother, who had died in childbirth. Ellie's attentions were a nice mothering to give in to occasionally, she decided with a smile.

Lucia lay in the tub for a while, her muscles gently loosening and unknotting. She thought of Stephen's presence in the clearing, how secure and safe she had felt with him at her side. She slid her shoulders down, immersing her head in the water for a long moment, driving away the longing. She couldn't afford fondness for a man intended for someone else. She had to find a way to break his hold over her.

When the water began to cool, Lucia got out of the tub and dried herself off, hunting for some comfortable clothes. She eventually put on a fresh nightgown from one of the drawers. She whirled around once, and shook her head. The cloth connecting her legs would make running almost impossible. How could other women wear such ungainly clothing all the time? She held the fabric out to either side.

Ellie came in the room with a tray of food, and smiled at the sight of Lucia examining the gown. "A dress looks good on you! I will have to sew you up some new ones. Of course, we will have to figure out which colors would do you justice, and try different styles, but I am sure we could come up with some you would enjoy. Probably start with some traditional dresses..."

Lucia sighed in exasperation. "If you are going to sew for me, make me some pants!" she exclaimed. "At least I can wear those riding. Wearing something like this during the day would be impossible." Ellie moved as if to protest, but seeing the set look on Lucia's face she nodded and promised to get Lucia some more comfortable clothes, at least for a start.

"What a day – I am famished!" breathed Lucia, settling herself into the bed. Ellie brought over the tray, and while Lucia sat back and nibbled on the drumsticks she'd brought, Ellie brushed out her hair and braided the sides, joining them in one large braid down her back. When she was finished, she motioned for Lucia to look at herself in the window's reflection.

"Not bad, not bad," approved Lucia, turning her head to and fro, finally giving it a couple of shakes. "This looks like it will hold my hair away from my face even when I am riding. Oh, it is very pretty," she added when Ellie turned away forlornly. "Please put my hair in this every morning from now on." Ellie seemed cheered by this, and cleared the plates with a little more spirit.

Lucia played on the harp for a while, her mind absently running through the events of the day. Soon weariness overcame her; she let the strings rest and climbed into bed. Ellie, wishing her a good night, went to the main door and locked it with the thick wooden bar before leaving through the other, smaller door to her connecting room.

Lucia watched her with curiosity. Something was wrong. Then it hit her. Stephen had always come before, to watch over her at night. But she was over the danger of the poison now, and he would not be there.

He would not watch over her.

She knew she should be grateful that the temptation had been removed. Despite all her efforts, it was a black loneliness which stole over her, sucking the light out of her world.

Exhausted, Lucia fell into a deep, troubled sleep.

Chapter 8

Ellie cleared away her breakfast tray, bubbling with enthusiasm for the sunny morning, but Lucia's thoughts were still shadowed in murky grey. When Ellie streamed out of the room, used dishes in hand, Lucia stared at the closed door in bleak despair. He would not be coming to her side any more. His steady eyes, his warm grasp, were gone to her forever. They seemed a feverish dream, as much as her father had been.

He was gone.

Lucia roused herself to move to the chair by the windows, staring out at the distant fields. It was as if she had been drained of all will. The shadows drifted and lengthened, and still she could not bring herself to stir.

A pair of giggling women in elegant burgundy gowns strolled along the path below. They took the grassy walk at a leisurely pace and eventually turned to move into the main building.

A thought flickered at the corner of Lucia's mind. Ian had suggested that she spend time with the court women and engage in their traditional activities. Perhaps it would be well to take his advice.

She found a white chemise and a simple, long burgundy dress in one of the trunks. After a moment's hesitation, she slid them over her head. She spent a while brushing her hair out, convincing herself she was not nervous. Finally she pursed her lips and headed out the door. The gales of high laughter made finding her way toward the sewing room an easy task.

Reaching the open door of the women's apartments, Lucia cautiously peered inside. Ten women, bedecked in wonderfully ornate dresses, were seated in various chairs. Maids hovered around the room fetching wine or adjusting a footstool. Beautiful tapestries hung on a rose-colored wall, and, in deference to the brilliant sunshine, the shutters were thrown open. The chatter sounded gentle and inviting. Encouraged, Lucia gathered her courage and walked in.

Her loneliness was banished immediately by the warm welcome she received from the women. Anna was the first to spot her, and was clearly thrilled.

"Lucia, dear!" she exclaimed happily. "I am so glad you are feeling better! I hear from Ian that your keep is located far north. You must have so many interesting things to tell us! New dances, new dresses, oh the possibilities are endless! Come, come, sit down beside me and tell me all."

Anna quickly made room on the settee for Lucia to join her, and the other women settled themselves comfortably within hearing distance. Needles and thread moved all around her in a soothing rhythm.

Lucia found herself drawn into the conversation, answering Anna's myriad of questions about Keilder regarding the type of food that was served, the arrangement of the kitchens, the organization of the mending groups, and more. Anna was fascinated by every detail of running a household, and Lucia found it soothed her soul to talk about the daily life of her keep as if it would soon once again be whole.

The lunch bell seemed to ring all too soon, and the women walked side by side up to the head table. Anna settled herself in her chair to the left side of the table, and Lucia moved to the right where Ellie was waiting for her. She glanced up at a movement – Stephen and Ian were coming in, side by side, and for a moment Stephen's eyes caught hers. She looked down immediately, then Ian was plunking himself down next to her, Lord Edmund was taking his place in the center, and boisterous sound rose all around them as the meal got underway.

Lucia barely heard the commentary Ian ran at her side. All she could feel was Stephen's presence, three chairs down, and her heart warmed at the thought that in a few hours they would be alone in the clearing with only the gentle trickling of water as a backdrop.

It seemed the blink of an eye before she was climbing down off her horse, hobbling him by his patch of grass, and spreading out a blanket. And only a heartbeat after that when hoofbeat came down the path, and Stephen dismounted, lowering to sit by the elderly oak opposite her.

He offered her a nod. "Anna was impressed with you," he said by way of greeting.

"I liked her very much," answered Lucia truthfully. "She is quite serious about becoming the best keep manager possible, and has thrown herself wholeheartedly into learning everything she can about it."

"She has dedication," he agreed.

His eyes moved down to her hip. "How are you feeling? Any ill effects, now that the fever has run its course?"

She shook her head. "The scar is mending nicely. I imagine in another two weeks or so that I will be ready to start south."

His eyes shadowed. "So soon?"

She turned her head from his deep eyes. "I need to get back to my own people," she murmured.

There was a long pause. "Of course."

* * *

Lucia brushed down her new dusk-blue dress and admired the effort Ellie had put into it. The color reminded her of home, and she appreciated the gentle fall of the fabric. She glanced around the sewing room for a moment. The women were merrily chatting to each other, occasionally taking stitches in their embroidery or mending work.

Lucia looked down again at the simple hem she was working on in a guard's uniform. She knew that her own sewing skills were minimal, but certainly she had handled enough hems in her life to be able to be of some use. She did feel a sense of satisfaction as she finished off the pant leg. The household had welcomed her with open arms, tending to her wounds and lodging her without a word of complaint. The least she could do was be useful during her stay.

Anna returned from her short trip to the garderobe and settled herself next to Lucia. "How are you doing?" she asked Lucia with a smile.

Lucia held up the pants. "Halfway done," she returned. "I will get there eventually."

Anna smiled. "I am glad to see you in a dress," she countered. "You look quite lovely in it."

Lucia blushed. "It would be chilly for riding, though," she pointed out.

Anna's eyes went to the window. "It is winter out there," she returned. "Why you choose to leave our warm fires each afternoon is beyond me. It is not even like you are heading to the hot springs to the south. Just an icy trickle of a stream." Her eyes drew to Lucia's in confusion. "Stephen claims you actually enjoy it out there."

Lucia looked away. Stephen was reporting back to Anna about her time with him? She hardly expected him to keep it a secret – and yet her stomach fluttered at the idea.

"I enjoy being alone," she murmured.

Anna smiled widely. "And that is where you and I are different," she offered merrily. "I hate being alone! It makes me feel so … lonely." She looked around the room to the ladies who reclined on the chairs as they mended and chatted away. "Being here with my women fills me with such warmth. I adore it. It is like being a queen bee in a busy hive." She held up the dress she was working on. "And we are useful at the same time, too!"

Lucia nodded her head. There was something to be said for what Anna felt. Was she being selfish in tucking herself away for hours on end?

"I am sure once I am feeling better – "

"Oh!" cried out Anna in consternation. "I did not mean to chastise you. You are barely out of your sick bed. If your way of healing is to sit alone in the cold, then by all means, I would not stop you. I realize we each have our own ways of doing things."

Lucia winced at the phrasing, but nodded. Anna was trying to understand her, and she appreciated the woman's efforts.

* * *

Stephen watched her from across the clearing, his eyes considering her. At last she could take it no longer.

"What did Anna say now?"

His mouth tweaked into a wry grin, and he nodded. "She is does not understand why you want to come out here," he admitted.

She drew her eyes along the mossy banks. "I wonder how she can find peace in that noisy, endless chatter," she countered, shaking her head.

"You are certainly different women," he agreed.

Lucia found herself smiling. "And yet, Anna is very kind," she murmured. "I could see her becoming a good friend, if I were not leaving soon."

There was a long silence, and when he spoke again his voice was rough. "When I regain my lands, and you retake your keep, there will be but fifteen miles between us. I am sure visits could be arranged."

The thought flushed through her that they would be close, that they could see each other. Her eyes moved up to hold his, and there was a question in his.

She looked away, exhaling slowly. "We shall see."

* * *

Lucia carefully mended the rip in the tunic, smiling with pride at her efforts. This sewing work was really not that bad, once one got the hang of it. She was pleased to think that the staff who helped care for her would have warmer clothing thanks to her efforts.

She held her finished work up to Anna, and the woman laughed in delight. "There, you have got it now," she agreed. "I will certainly miss you once you are gone. It is a shame Keilder is not closer."

Lucia flushed at the thought of Anna and Stephen visiting her as man and wife, but she pushed the discomfort away. "Well, you will only be fifteen miles south of my keep," she pointed out hoarsely. "I admit it is not a short ride, but would be worthwhile for a longer visit. I would be honored to welcome you."

Anna's eyes creased in confusion. "Fifteen miles? But Kendal is at least fifteen miles south of Penrith, and I thought Keilder was another thirty miles north of here. That means forty-five miles total, right?"

Lucia shook her head. "I do not understand. What is Kendal?"

Anna grinned eagerly. "Kendal is a keep under my father's control. It is beautiful, with wide open windows and a meadow of daffodils around it. Just right for elegant masquerades and music-filled picnics."

Lucia looked at her cautiously. "And Kendal is where you and Stephen will live, once you are married?"

She nodded contentedly. "Of course we will. Where else?"

* * *

Stephen's eyes were shadowed, and Lucia's heart billowed with guilt. Had she somehow introduced discord into his relationship with Anna? She drove herself to speak.

"What is it, Stephen?"

He gave his head a shake, bringing himself back from distant thoughts. "Just a minor misunderstanding," he murmured. "There is plenty of time to sort that out before our vows in May."

Anna flushed with heat. It was already mid-February; May seemed only a breath away.

She found her throat was tight. "That is when you will marry?"

He nodded. "Anna has had everything planned out, in great detail, from the moment she laid eyes on me," he mused somberly. His eyes flickered up to meet hers, and then he looked away again. "I will do my part to meet each expectation that I can," he added. "And for those I cannot …"

His gaze followed the stream as it tumbled down past the rocks.

* * *

Lucia carefully repaired the pulled seam on the burgundy dress. It seemed that every woman in the room wore burgundy except her. They laughed and bubbled around her as they took sips of mead and enjoyed the bright sunshine of the late morning.

She glanced over at Anna. Stephen had said that she had been planning their wedding since she first met him. The thought sliced at her heart, but she found a curiosity mingled in there as well. How had Anna caught his love?

Lucia put on a warm smile. "You must be very excited about the upcoming wedding," Lucia prodded, turning to the woman. "I would love to hear all about it. Just when did you first meet Stephen?"

She glanced down at her needlework and found that it served as the perfect shield for any rough emotions she might have while going through this conversation. She simply had to focus.

Stitch, press. Stitch, press.

Anna smiled happily as she thought back. "Oh, I have known him for a good fifteen years, almost since infancy!" She took a bite of dried apple, nodding to herself. "It began about five years after Stephen came to live here with Ian. I came up to visit quite often, first to play, and later to learn about sewing, cooking, and household management. I would also take religious studies from Brother Matthew."

Her eyes sparkled. "Stephen was often out in the courtyard, practicing his sword fighting. That is, when he was not off in the woods on some sort of expedition. Even at fifteen he was handsome – like a prince come to life. Each night I dreamt of him sitting at a table across from me, presiding nobly over our home, taking the lead position at a ball, you know, that sort of thing."

Lucia could imagine that easily, the young girl caught up in romantic fantasies. "You sought a prince. Surely Ian would have suited nicely! He is in line to inherit the keep, after all." She continued to concentrate on her sewing.

Anna laughed merrily. "Ian?" She replied with a smile. "Why, I am sure he is just perfect for many ladies. Maybe he is the one for you!" She chuckled when Lucia flushed crimson. "But not for me," she continued with a pensive look. "He is out too much at the taverns, drinking with friends and listening to musicians. I would hate to be left alone with the young ones." She shrugged. "Many women are rugged enough to keep hearth and home safe, but I know I would be no good at keeping robbers at bay. I need someone who will take care of me, who I can fully rely on. Someone to stay at home, keep me protected, and take care of things. He is the man, after all. I will do the cooking and cleaning, but everything else will rest in his hands."

Anna merrily continued as she sewed her delicate stitches. "Sure, Stephen seems quite rough right now. However, I am sure that will all change once we are married. I will dress him up in elegant tunics. We will host social events that will be the talk of the land. Just you wait and see."

Lucia knew she should keep the conversation going, but her throat closed up. It seemed so clear that Ian was more of what Anna was looking for. Ian adored the pomp and ritual of social events. Stephen would never be content overseeing balls.

She sighed. Maybe this conversation had been a bad idea after all. Her mind searched for a new topic as she mended.

Stitch. Press.

Maybe if she talked more about their relationship, perhaps that would help make sense of the situation. Lucia knew most women loved to talk about the stages of courtship, so with dogged determination she pressed on.

"I am sure your marriage will be exactly as you want it to be. So, tell me more. How did he propose to you?"

Anna sat up proudly at the memory. "Well, as you might expect, the proposal was handled very formally. My father took me aside on my sixteenth birthday. He said I had officially reached the marriageable age, and that it was time to choose someone suitable for our family rank. He asked if anyone had caught my eye or made overtures."

Her eyes sparkled. "There was no doubt in my mind - I immediately brought up Stephen. After all, he is foster son to the Edmunds, certainly a wealthy enough family. For my needs, he is strong and handsome too! My father was quite pleased to countenance a union with the Edmunds in such a way. He set out the next day to speak with Lord Edmund. Lord Edmund then talked with Stephen. In two weeks, Stephen was at our home, and the whole thing was official!"

Lucia's mind whirled. She focused on her mending to give herself time. She knew that she should feel proud of Anna. Where most girls sat around and waited for a man to come propose to them, Anna had grabbed the bull by the horns and clearly stated what she wanted. She had gotten it, too. How many girls could say that about the men their parents chose for them to marry?

Still, Lucia could not shake off the feeling that this relationship was not created for the right reasons. Anna had built a childhood fantasy around her ideal protector, maybe even a new father figure to run her life. She was going to force Stephen to fit into that role, no matter what it took.

Lucia reminded herself that Stephen had agreed to this. He could certainly have refused to go forward with the engagement. Instead he had taken her hand.

* * *

Stephen's eyes were steady on her. A gentle breeze drifted across the clearing, and a robin called from high in a tree.

"Anna says you were asking about how we became engaged," he mused in a low voice.

Lucia blushed and looked away. "I was just curious," she murmured.

A tightness crept into his voice. "Curious how an elegant woman like her ended up with a wanderer like me?"

Her eyes flashed around in surprise. "No!" she called out in shock. Her eyes drank in his strength, his courage, and she realized it was quite the opposite. How could such a man as him be content with …

She blushed, fighting the urge to look away.

His voice remained tight. "I am sure some say she is far better suited to Ian."

Her blush deepened into a dark crimson. She had thought that very thought, herself. It made so much more sense …

His eyes sharpened on her. "No need to be jealous," he bit out. "Anna is not a contender for Ian's side."

Lucia did turn away at that, heat flaring from every corner of her body. That he could think her interested in that prancing, babbling boy ... she took in long breaths, drawing up her walls fully. If she allowed herself to speak further on the issue, she could easily say something that she would regret.

* * *

Lucia focused with careful attention on the seam before her. She was tackling a more challenging project now – creating a new cloak for Lord Edmund. She had ten days left to her stay, and hopefully there would be just enough time for her to finish the outfit. She thought it an appropriate parting gift for the man who had sheltered and fed her.

Anna's eyes were bright on her, and at last Lucia looked up, shaking her head. "All right, what is it," she asked her friend.

"What do you think of Ian?" Anna asked, a smile on her lips.

Lucia flushed. Surely Stephen did not report every aspect of their conversations to her.

Anna's eyes sparkled. "Ian certainly discusses you every chance he can get," she pressed with delight. "After you left lunch yesterday, he spent a full half hour trying to convince Lord Edmund to change his schedule around. He wanted to be the one to keep watch over you on your afternoon rest periods."

Lucia's heart pounded in her chest. Ian would interfere with her quiet afternoons with Stephen? She focused on bringing her breathing back under control.

"What did his father say?"

Anna shook her head. "The poor lad, it just could not be done. He was quite disheartened."

"That is probably just as well," Lucia replied, trying to hold in her relief. "I am sure with Ian around I would not have the serenity I seek."

Anna raised an eyebrow. "Oh?"

Lucia blushed. Anna was a friend of Ian's, and the last thing she wanted to do was insult him. "I enjoy Ian's company," she amended. "His stories are quite engrossing." She looked down at her hem-work. "But when I take my afternoon rests, it is quiet nature that draws me. I am not interested in conversation."

Lucia started stitching again, focusing her eyes on her piecework. She realized suddenly that what she *had* enjoyed about her time with Stephen was the conversation. She had been more honest, more open, with him than with any other person in years.

She blushed, fighting off her confusion. Anna was still gazing at her, and she felt that she had to undo the damage she had done to Ian's reputation.

"Maybe when I am more fully healed, I will be more energetic and able to have long talks with Ian," she offered in a conciliatory tone.

Anna smiled and nodded. "I am sure that is it. Just give it time. Remember, there is someone for everyone, I always say. Somewhere out there is someone for you, whether it is Ian or another man. I suppose you will know when you find him."

They stitched on in silence for a while. Lucia couldn't help but wonder if she already had found the *someone* that was a perfect match for her. Stephen's steady courage, quiet wisdom, and unflagging loyalty were all she could want in a partner.

She sighed at the twists of cruel fate. He was to be married to someone else, and she would be left alone.

The lunch bell rang, and Lucia moved into the great hall with Anna by her side. The men were just coming in from their training, and Stephen and Ian came over toward them.

Stephen's eyes flicked to Lucia before holding out a hand for Anna's, lowering his head to kiss it.

Ian's stride was more exuberant. "Lucia! There you are," he called out with pleasure, wrapping an arm possessively around her waist. "I missed you!" He pulled her close in at his side.

Lucia fought down with effort her impulse to bristle and pull away from this unwanted familiarity. Was this type of touching usual amongst men and women of this region? Despite her resolve, her eyes moved up to glance at Stephen. He was watching her with concern, his body tense.

She willed herself to look away. She forced a smile on her face and moved alongside Ian, settling down with him to Lord Edmund's right.

As she had at every meal, Lucia tried her very best to invest herself in the conversation with Ian. He was, after all, her gracious host. She just could not do it. Ian's sole focus was on himself. He relished the precise details of each jewel which made up his scabbard. He examined at length the symbolism of each item of embroidery on his tunic. He knew six generations in the breeding lines of his horses. He could expound at length on the reputation of his family and the relative power they wielded.

Lucia scanned the room as he talked at length about the precise mixture of oils to achieve the best shine on a dress saddle. To her surprise it seemed that many women were watching her with a mixture of interest and envy. She wondered just how many of these women had an active interest in Ian's romantic life. Certainly the two maids who brought them fresh pitchers of wine made sure to rub up against him at every opportunity.

Lucia wondered that Ellie and Anna had thought this man even remotely a match for her. His appraisal of a sword focused on the jewels in its hilt and the engraving on its blade. Her own judged the sharpness of the edge, correct balance, and sturdiness of construction. He spoke proudly of the gold on his armor, its intricate designs. She was far more content with something proven to protect the body from harm.

When Ian excused himself to talk to a passing blonde woman for a moment, Lucia sat back and shook her head in confusion. She wondered with true curiosity what it was about herself that Ian apparently found so attractive. She knew that she did not dress as well as the other ladies did. Her attire was far from intricate or elegant. She knew she was not *bad* to look at, but neither was she one of the beautifully decorated butterflies that she saw on all sides. Maybe it was simply that she was strange and unknown, another exotic story to add to his collection.

She glanced across the table at Stephen and Anna. Anna was smiling up at her betrothed, prattling along about something. Stephen listened patiently, deftly buttering a roll while she spoke. Lucia gave a quiet sigh at her inability to understand the human heart.

Ian followed her gaze and smiled widely. "They are a wonderful couple," he commented, his eyes running over his cousin in appreciation. "Stephen deserves the best, of course. He is a courageous fighter. She is young, pretty, and from an appropriate family. They belong together!"

He took a long pull on his tankard, then gave a laugh. "Although Stephen did not see that at first, of course.

When my father told him he should marry Anna to bring the houses together, Stephen was quite out of sorts about it. I remember him riding off into the forest for days. After a while I wondered if I would have to go in after him!" Ian laughed and took a swig of wine. "But eventually Stephen saw the wisdom of it. He said he would be proud to do his duty for the family that had taken him in."

Ian nodded at the memory. "My father was so pleased; the heralds went out at once. I remember that afternoon with perfect clarity. I told Stephen, how could he not be happy with such a beautiful woman at his side! I was right, of course. Just look at them together. It is enough to make you believe that you, too, could have such happiness."

Ian put his hand solidly over Lucia's and gave it a firm squeeze.

Lucia blinked in shock, barely feeling Ian's grasp. Suddenly the situation shimmered into perfect focus. No wonder Stephen hadn't talked about his engagement or elaborated when it was brought to light. He was doing what he had to do, what he felt honor-bound to do. He would not disgrace the woman to whom he had become bound.

The engagement had been neither his choice nor his desire.

The thought, though tinged with sadness, inexplicably also filled her with great joy. A smile drew across her face

Ian's eyes were fixed on her, and he brought her hand to his lips, pressing it there for a moment. "Yes," he murmured quietly. "You too might find that same happiness, someday soon."

* * *

Stephen's face was shadowed, and he stared at the stream with fixed attention. At last Lucia could not take the silence any more.

"What is it?"

He gave a shake of his head, not looking over, and it was several minutes before the words ground out of him. "So you like living at Penrith?"

Lucia blinked. "It certainly is nice here," she hesitantly responded. "The food is well-made, and Ellie is wonderful."

Stephen's voice was a growl. "The house of the unicorn," he muttered.

Lucia thought back to the burgundy banners which seemed to flutter on every wall of the keep, of the rearing unicorn which formed the house crest. "Yes, I know," she agreed. He seemed tense, so she sought for something encouraging to say about his foster family's sigil. "A noble beast."

"An *imaginary* creature," he corrected harshly.

He pressed his lips together, falling into silence.

* * *

Anna and Stephen were sitting side by side in the front pew of the chapel as she came down the aisle. They looked so well paired, Anna's golden curls, Stephen's broad shoulders, and her heart caught. Soon they would be married, having children, starting a new life together …

She looked down, easing herself into the row, leaving a space between her and Stephen. There was a movement at her right, and in a moment Ian was sliding in next to her. He came up against her, and she took in a deep breath. It was only for one mass. She could get through this.

She folded her hands in her lap, resisting with all her strength the urge to slide left. She found her eyes glancing down at the polished wood that lay between her and Stephen, the wall it represented, the gulf which could not be crossed.

* * *

Monday was back to the sewing room, and Lucia was much more aware of the burgundy tapestries which decorated the walls, the white unicorns prancing and gamboling within their woven threads. She was suddenly reminded of her ride with Stephen from the archery field, at how he mentioned that he did not retain anything with his own crest on it.

She turned to Anna. "Anna, what is Stephen's crest?" she asked with curiosity.

Anna laughed with bright merriment. She waved a hand around the room. "Surely you are not as blind as that," she teased her friend. "It is the noble unicorn, the creature of classic stories!"

Lucia shook her head, glancing up at the large tapestry over the fireplace. "But that is Lord Edmund's crest," she gently corrected, "And Ian's."

Anna's mouth went into a round O. "I suppose you are right," she conceded. "I always think of Stephen as being part of their family." She scrunched her brow in thought for a moment, then shrugged. "I suppose I do not know," she admitted with a laugh. "I shall have to ask him at lunch."

* * *

Stephen's gaze held her with curiosity. "Anna said you were asking about my crest."

Lucia nodded. "I assumed it must involve burgundy, given the beautiful dresses she has been making in that color. But it seems she might have been mistaken about -"

She looked down, blushing. It was not her place to speak poorly of her friend.

"She was mistaken," agreed Stephen, his voice even. "That is the color of my foster father's banner, not of my own family."

Her eyes sunk into his depths. "And what is your color?"

He smiled wryly, drawing his eyes down the deep, cobalt blue of her dress. "You are wearing it," he murmured.

She blushed deeply, running a hand along the fabric, soaking in the sight. She was embraced by his blue, sheltered by it. That it matched the color of her own family filled her with the greatest of joy.

Her voice was tight when she spoke. "And your sigil?"

His eyes were steady on hers, and his voice was low. "It is by your side it every morning when you wake, and every evening when you ease to sleep."

She thought to her room, to the ivory tapestry curtains, to the alabaster comforter, and she shook her head in confusion. Surely there was nothing in the room that called to her. There had only been his warm eyes at her side, the deep eyes in the shadows, lit by the flickering oil lamp …

Her eyes snapped back to his, and he half smiled, nodding.

His voice was rough. "When my father returned from the holy land, he brought with him that one treasure, given to him by a grateful pilgrim. The King granted him that sigil in gratitude for his service."

Lucia's throat tightened. "A light to shine in the darkness," she whispered.

"I knew you, of all people, would understand," he murmured.

She looked away, her heart pounding. She could feel the connection between them, feel how it strengthened with every passing day. Thank all that was holy that, in another four days, she would be heading on her way south. She did not know if she could withstand this much longer.

* * *

The bubbling laughter of the women grated on her for some reason, and she diligently focused on the hem of Lord Edmund's cloak and gave her all to making the stitches perfect. Three more days. Her stomach scar was all but healed, she had been taking care to rest, and she was sure she would be up to a carefully gentle ride south. She could take her time. But she knew she had to go. She had to be free of the strong pull of Stephen's eyes, and the powerful draw of his honor and strength.

Anna nudged her. "Did I tell you?" Her face glowed with bright mirth. "Stephen told me what his sigil was at lunch yesterday." Her eyes brightened in expectation. "It is a candle!" She fell back against her cushions, giggling.

A tweak of annoyance ran through Lucia. "It is an oil lamp," she corrected, striving to keep her tone gentle.

Anna waved her hand. "Yes, of course, some sort of a lighting item," she agreed. "Something to keep you from stubbing your toe when you go looking for your chamber pot." Her eyes glanced up to the tapestries on the wall, and her eyes sparkled. "Hardly as romantic as a unicorn."

Steel settled into Lucia's spine. "A unicorn is mythical," she replied. "Stephen's crest is about holding out hope when all hope is lost."

She thought of how Stephen braved Gray territory, tracking the enemy, while the keep guards huddled safely by their fires. "He seems the only one interested in taking action against the Grays," she muttered. "He is the only one risking his life to defend our lands."

Anna waved a hand around her. "The entire keep is in training," she pointed out with a smile. "Soon they will simply march north and flatten the rabble into a paste. And life will return to normal."

Lucia wished it would be that easy. Keeping a tight rein on the turmoil that boiled within her, she dropped her eyes to her project.

* * *

Dark clouds swirled overhead, a sharp wind whistled, and Stephen's shoulders were stretched tight with tension as he eased himself down against the oak. "Anna seems to think the fight will be an easy one," he stated harshly. "She does not understand what monsters those men are."

Lucia shook her head, black fogs roiling within her. "Anna has never seen a fight of any kind," she pointed out. "She grew up in a land where she spent her time weaving daisy chains and sprawling on blankets at summer picnics." Her eyes shadowed. "My summers were spent patrolling our borders, watching for any trace of Gray activity. I buried myself in worm-infested mud to crawl, unseen, into their camps. I wove my arrows past hostage's bodies, to drill the shafts deep into wolves' heads' hearts."

Stephen's voice was rough. "*Wolves' heads* is an apt name for them," he agreed. "They should be tracked down and slaughtered at will."

Lucia's jaw tightened. "We do not *slaughter* men indiscriminately," she shot back. "But if they attack us, we absolutely will defend ourselves."

Stephen's eyes became swirls of dark ebony. "We should ring the wasteland with fire," he growled. "We should hunt down and burn every Gray alive."

Lucia's eyes flashed, anger flaring out of her. "Are you insane?" she snapped. "The children too? Is that all you southerners think about down here, wiping each other out completely?"

Stephen's eyes sharpened with anger, and the thought pleased her. Let him be annoyed. Her voice gained an edge. "My family has always sought a truce, a compromise, some way of resolving this without *slaughtering* every man, woman, and child. My father prided himself on finding some way to connect with even the most distant of enemies."

Her soul chilled with disappointment. "What type of person is motivated solely by hatred, by a lust for death?"

Stephen's shoulders rippled; his hand slid to his sword hilt. "A *person* who saw his sister's throat slashed by a foul beast," he snarled. "Love for your family becomes hatred for those who would harm you. My family and my town practiced kindness and charity. We were known for our open arms. In return, that trust was taken advantage of, and my people were slaughtered like cattle." His voice dropped to a low growl. "The Grays need to be stopped. Permanently."

Lucia took in the tense line of Stephen's muscles; clearly his anger was being held on an exceedingly tight rein. She locked her eyes on his. She didn't know what was whipping her to antagonize him like this, but she was driven to push even harder.

He deserves it. After all the pain I have felt …

He blew out a breath, seeming to strain to draw in his emotions. His voice tightened with the effort. "The Grays are a sickness, and their plague has hurt both our families –"

Anger roiled within Lucia, and she stormed to her feet. Stephen matched her movement instinctively, facing her.

Her voice was rough was emotion. "How dare you imply the Grays sprang up from nowhere, as if you were innocent bystanders?" she spat out. "*You* were the ones who drove the Grays to rebellion. It is *your* fault that they exploded. Our keep was assaulted in a war in which we had no part!"

Stephen stared at her. "What?"

Her father's desperation as the Grays had stormed over the keep walls filled her vision, and her fury grew. "The Grays are from *your* area. They are not raiders from across the seas; they are not foreigners out for gold. These people are *locals*. They were driven to their straits by callous misuse and soul-searing famine."

Stephen had gone very still. She saw the warning sign clearly, but heedlessly plowed ahead, her anger pushing her beyond her limits. "The deaths of your family members are grievous - but I have heard plenty about the motivation of this 'enemy'. Perhaps their warrior leader is power hungry, but where does his support come from?" Her eyes flared. "I've heard that many of his best soldiers joined him to take on injustice - to boldly fight against egregious wrongs wreaked by the '*nobles*' in this area."

The horror hit Lucia full force.

Stephen's family's actions had caused her father's death.

She could barely get the words out. "Your people drove them to this. You killed my father. You are responsible, and by God, you will pay!"

Her hand was at her hilt, his own dropped in a mirror image, and every fiber of her body called for her to draw her sword, to attack, to avenge her beloved father.

The pain nearly overwhelmed her, nearly caught her breath in her throat. A long minute passed, and it seemed she balanced on the edge of a cliff, a black abyss stretching out to the horizon.

Then, with a visible effort, Stephen flexed his fingers and exhaled slowly. He released his hand, dropping his arms away from his side. To Lucia it appeared that the stream started to bubble softly again, that the winds picked up their silent song.

Stephen leant back against the tree and was quiet for a moment. He took in a deep breath, then slowly let it out again. The silence stretched on for several minutes. Finally he looked up at Lucia and spoke in a low but clear voice. "I think we both said some things we did not mean. It has been a while since I have talked with a person with enough at stake to say anything besides 'I am sorry for your loss'."

He looked down at his sword for a moment and ran his hand absently over the hilt. "My world has seemed black and white for many years now. If I look at the history objectively, though, I do admit that this situation grew out of faults - on both sides."

Lucia exhaled deeply, draining of emotion, then eased herself back to the ground. A chill ran through her as she realized what she had almost instigated. She was barely up from her fever-bed, and she doubted even at her best that she would be a match for Stephen's sword.

She had been beyond foolish for driving him to such anger. She had been far more harsh than she had any right to be.

"I was wrong to blame you for the faults of an entire region," she murmured, looking away. "You were barely a child when the Gray rebellion took place. And your father was away …"

Stephen nodded. "He was in the holy lands," he agreed in a rough voice.

Lucia sat back against a gnarled stump. She closed her eyes, letting her head tip back against the tree.

Thank all that was Holy that Stephen's self-control ran as deep as a mountain's roots. She had been playing with fire, and could easily have been immolated, had he been a lesser man.

The thought sent a flush through the deepest reaches of her soul.

It was clear to her why she had burned with such heat; her desperate longing to have him by her side was barely being kept in check.

Her throat tightened. Three more days, and she would be gone.

Chapter 9

Stephen cursed under his breath as Lord Edmund and Ian raised their voices even higher, their shouts echoing across the arched ceilings of the great hall. He knew with keen awareness that Lucia was just one room over, engrossed in sewing with Anna and the other women. If the voices were to draw them in …

There was a movement and a swirl of color and she was there, surrounded by the others, but to him it was as if she were the only woman in the room. Her simple, blue dress shone out in the sea of burgundy, and his heart caught as always at the sight of her strength wrapped in his family colors.

His mind swept back to the openness of their conversations, to the raw honesty which he had found with no other person. He thought of her passion, her wisdom, her intelligence, her strength.

Her eyes drew up to his, and for a moment he thought he saw a reflection of the longing, the desperate desire which echoed within his own heart.

Then she looked down, and it was gone.

He shook his head, looking back at the two men standing across from him. This was a difficult enough discussion as it was, but now Ian had an audience. He would be almost impossible to engage with reason in this situation.

Ian rose his voice a full notch and played to the room. "I still say I should get to lead the main attack," he cried, his voice loud with indignant petulance. "This is my first real battle! Should I not be able to finally do something?" He strode with energy away from his father. "We know the plan. It is an ambush along the path. I have walked these woods since I was able to raise myself on my feet. I know those woods better than any man alive. I will give us the best chance for victory!"

Lord Edmund made a placating gesture to his son. "I am not doubting your intentions," he replied soothingly. "It is important to remember that these Grays are mercenaries fighting for food in the middle of winter. This is not a regular battle with just honor and land on the line. These are not men who will call a retreat if things look bad. They have been butchering cattle on the outlying lands for food. They kill nearby women and children for the sheer pleasure of it." He motioned toward Stephen with one hand. "We simply need Stephen's experience to make sure they do not get through our lines."

Stephen knew Ian's ego would flare at this. He spoke up quickly, his tone holding respect. "Ian, while I will be providing overall direction, I will need an absolutely trustworthy captain to make sure each step is done properly." He clasped Ian on the arm. "Your skills will be key to any success. Every soldier here will look to you for instructions."

Ian's face was a mask of displeasure. His voice remained high and truculent. "I have been studying historical battles for years. I have spent hours each day with the sword masters. I am the better man."

His eyes suddenly lit with an idea. "I will prove it to you both. If I best Stephen in a match, here in the hall, will you admit that I am the man most suited to lead?" He stood tall and defiant, daring them to deny him this chance.

Stephen was shocked into silence. He could not imagine a more difficult solution. Around him, he could see the soldiers who had been watching the discussion now looking at each other with curiosity. Ian was serious. There was no hint of levity in his demeanor.

Stephen hesitated for a long moment. He felt torn between the duty to the land that had adopted him and his loyalty to the only brother he'd ever known. He knew he should do all he could to support Ian in his quest to learn the skills necessary to lead. However, Ian simply did not have those talents right now – and Stephen felt in his bones that to let Ian manage the keep's defenses would lead to its ruin.

Stephen could see no right answer, and after contemplation, he felt it was not his choice to make. The question concerned the safety of the entire keep. Stephen took a deep breath, then nodded to Lord Edmund. He would give Lord Edmund the choice, and abide with whatever was decided.

Lord Edmund looked between the two men for a long while, then set his hands on his hips. "Agreed. We will let skill determine this."

Ian dove into the opening before his father could change his mind. "Time is of the essence, if we plan on laying the ambush in the next week. I say we do the challenge tomorrow night! This will give us time to draw a proper audience. I am in fine shape. I hope this will not inconvenience you, Stephen?" He looked over at Stephen with prideful challenge in his eyes.

A dark foreboding washed over Stephen at this latest example of Ian's competitive and impulsive nature. He was deeply unhappy at the thought of drawing blades against his kinsman in a situation where Ian's self-image was involved. Still, to turn down the challenge as meaningless would shame Ian even more.

Stephen nodded silently in agreement, then bowed to the lord and son. He headed out to the walls, to inform his men of what had happened.

* * *

Lucia watched him leave with a heavy heart, understanding fully what this situation would cost him. She looked back to see that Ian was reacting with quite a different emotion. He had broken into a large grin, apparently thrilled at his victory. He kissed his father on the cheek before calling for a round of drinks for the room.

Anna practically dragged Lucia back into their sitting room. "How exciting!" she crowed to the rest of the ladies, who were bubbling over with eager conversation. "A contest! This should be great fun!"

Lucia sat down slowly, considering. She spoke quietly to Anna, her voice almost lost in the excited chatter. "Is this really wise, to have such a match right before we go into a battle? What if bad feelings result from this contest between our own ranks? What if Lord Edmund wants Ian - his only son - to lead, but Stephen beats him easily? What if Stephen holds back, unwilling to disgrace the only brother he has ever known - but we lose the battle due to Ian's inexperience?" Lucia bit her tongue, and did not mention the worse possibilities, that one or both might actually be wounded.

Anna's enthusiasm visibly lessened. "I had not thought of any of that," she admitted slowly. "You are right; this may be more complicated than I would have thought." She smiled, her worries dispersing without much effort. "Still,

I think it will be great fun. Whatever feelings get hurt, they will sort them out, like boys always do."

Lucia thought about the ramifications of the match from every angle as they finished their work for the morning. The happy chatter around her washed over her. The more Lucia thought about it, the more she was sure that the fight was a bad idea. She skipped lunch, having no desire to hear Ian crow on the topic. Instead, she rode out to the stream at a slow pace, her thoughts muddled. She sat by the water's edge, lost in her musings.

Lucia almost didn't notice when Stephen walked into the clearing, leading his own horse. His eyes were dark and troubled. He didn't speak to her, or even look over. Instead, he quietly tied up Prince and sat down by the edge of the river, gazing down its length with a furrowed brow.

Lucia felt an overwhelming desire to talk with him, to share in his concerns, but each time she began to speak, she reminded herself sternly that it was not her place to intrude. Stephen had Anna, and if support were to be given, Anna should be the one to provide it. Lucia instructed herself firmly that if she should be encouraging anyone, it should by rights be Ian.

Frustrated, Lucia leaned back against a stump and closed her eyes. She couldn't bring herself to get up, to leave Stephen and ride away. If she shouldn't speak, then she would remain and be silent. She watched the stream flowing through the clearing, lending him strength with her presence.

The two passed the afternoon within a stone's throw of each other, each staring at the moving water, lost in their own thoughts.

* * *

The next day brought the swirls of a short-lived snowstorm. The castle spent the daylight hours pent up indoors, which caused numerous discussions and side bets to flourish about the evening's festivities. Lucia spent some time in the sewing room, but there was no mending to be done today. It seemed that every conversation that flooded the hallways involved who was better between the two men. Ian had youth and training on his side. Stephen had the knowledge of real battle, and the experience of death. This was only a battle to first touch, though. Would Stephen's need to hold back from injury hinder him?

At first, Lucia enjoyed the conversations. She'd been in enough matches to appreciate the skill involved. But always it came down to Stephen fighting Ian, and she found she could not keep her emotions separate from the contest.

Rather than reveal her concerns, she bowed out of the discussion and retreated to her room. She wanted to go to Stephen and help him talk through the options - but that was not her place. She knew she should go to Ian, but she could not bring herself to do that, either. Instead she stayed alone in her room, eating a simple lunch at the table, then pacing before the fireplace.

It seemed a heartbeat before the hour had arrived.

When Lucia reached the main hall, the room was echoing with loud voices, brightly dressed people, and blazing fires in the hearths. The tables had been cleared away, with the chairs placed against the back walls for the older spectators to rest on. Most people in the hall stood holding crusts of bread or flagons of wine. It appeared the entire town had turned out for the event, looking for an exciting evening with friends.

Lucia soon found herself standing with Anna and the other women at one end of the hall. A goblet of mead was pressed into her hand, but she did not drink. Fighting required the sharpest of senses, and despite the faire-like atmosphere she could not look on this as a frivolity. Even the most casual of bouts held an element of risk. In this case, Ian would be out to prove his worth, and Stephen ... what would Stephen want to prove? That he should lead the forces as he was the best qualified to oversee the protection of the lands? Would he deliberately drop his guard to give Ian the advantage? Playing those sorts of games sometimes got one hurt ... or worse.

Lord Edmund came out with Hector by his side. The two men eased into their chairs in the center of one wall. The crowd's murmuring grew in volume as they sensed the approaching event.

In a few moments a cheer went up as Stephen and Ian entered the room from opposite ends of the hall. Ian wore his finest armor, freshly gleaming from an application of oil. The intricate engraving and metalwork was quite impressive. Stephen's leather armor was simple and well-worn; it appeared quite plain by comparison. The two men approached Lord Edmund and knelt at his feet. Lord Edmund put one hand on each man's head and wished both luck.

To Lucia's shock, both men then turned and walked straight toward her and Anna. In the past, she had been treated as 'one of the soldiers', and the part of a female watcher had never occurred to her.

The men would be looking for favors to carry with them, and she was now the *giver* of such a favor.

She looked over in panic at Anna, who was dramatically drawing a white handkerchief from her sleeve. Lucia reached into her own sleeve and she sagged with relief when she found she also carried such a handkerchief. She would have felt very foolish to be "lacking" in such a customary female item.

Still, her heart caught in her throat as the two men stood before them. Following Anna's lead, she went through the motions of tying her own favor around Ian's upper arm. Despite her best efforts, Lucia was acutely aware of Anna's interactions with Stephen - of Anna's hands moving around Stephen's strong muscles, of Stephen looking down at Anna with the eyes she could still see in her dreams.

When Anna leant forward to give Stephen a kiss on the cheek, it seemed to Lucia to last an eternity. Lucia felt the eyes of the crowd upon her and likewise gave Ian a gentle kiss on the cheek. Although she tried hard to mimic Anna, she found that she felt only sisterly affection for this young man before her. When Lucia drew back, she was surprised by the fierce shine in Ian's eyes and realized quickly that he had a different reaction to the kiss. In her own way, she had just prodded him on to victory in her name.

She mustered a smile to hide her growing confusion. She willed herself not to look at Stephen, not in front of all of these people. Out of the corner of her eye, she saw that he was focusing firmly on Anna and formally bowing to her. She saw the mixed emotions in his face.

It came to her with sudden clarity. He had not decided on a course of action. Even now he had not decided if he should throw the fight or not.

Ian turned to walk to the center of the stage area and raised his hands to wave at the well-wishers and friends that surrounded him. The crowd roared its approval, and all eyes focused on Ian. Several women fluttered their handkerchiefs at him and offered him a second or third favor to carry. Anna became distracted by a passing page who was distributing chalices of wine.

Lucia saw her only chance to speak to Stephen. Without thinking she stepped toward him. She spoke in a rushed whisper to draw as little attention to them as she could. "Our survival must take precedence over one man's ego," she pleaded in a quick breath, pressing his right arm with her fingers as she spoke. Then she continued walking past him as if she was simply moving across the room for a better view of the event.

When she raised her eyes again to look at Stephen, he was standing across from Ian. Both men had their right hands on their hilts, looking to Lord Edmund for a signal. Lucia saw that Stephen now had a firm look of conviction in his eyes. His left hand strayed briefly to touch his right arm where she'd held him. She blushed crimson. She hoped desperately that her impulsive comment to Stephen had not made the situation worse.

Lord Edmund, elegantly resplendent in a richly embroidered outfit of burgundy and gold, stood and waited for the crowd to settle down. "Friends and neighbors," he called out in a booming voice. "We have before us two men we all know well. Ian and Stephen have both proven their worth many times over. Both have an equal right to lead the troops in the coming days."

He took a deep breath to give a dramatic pause, and then continued. "Tonight we shall have a friendly competition between the two. The first man to land three touches on the other will have the honor of leading our troops into battle. There shall be no harm caused here - we need every man for the coming conflicts. Hector will serve as judge." Lord Edmund paused again. "Ian, Stephen, fight with honor."

Lord Edmund waved both hands open, and sat down with a flourish. Hector stood and moved to the edge of the open area, accepting from a servant a staff with which to signal defeats and victories. Ian and Stephen turned to face each other, and Lucia found the differences between the two men to be spellbinding. Ian was cocky, sure of himself, bouncing on the balls of his feet. His bow to Stephen was quick, yet full of flair. He wanted to get going, eager to prove his worth and relish the victory feast.

Lucia's eyes moved to Stephen. He waited with calm awareness. Gone was the uncertainty she had sensed before. He bowed somberly to his younger friend as he prepared for the test of skills.

Hector held the staff between the two men, and both drew their swords with practiced ease. The hiss of metal sounded loudly in the quiet hush of the hall. The men waited, Ian impatiently, Stephen with cool preparedness. Hector glanced at both men one final time, then with a sudden motion he pulled the staff away.

"Begin!"

Lucia's heart thudded with nervous anticipation and she strained forward to watch.

Immediately Ian leapt in for the attack. His moves were swift and sure, apparently with the aim to decide this conflict quickly. Lucia watched the two as she might a chess match, tracking Stephen's slow, steady responses to Ian's impetuous lunges. She saw Ian open his flank when he went for a high strike, and bit her tongue to keep herself from calling out. She wondered in a flash whether she would have shouted to alert Ian of the danger – or to let Stephen know of the opportunity.

Stephen saw the advantage in a glance and swatted Ian's ribs with the flat of his sword while Ian moved past him.

Hector's call carried across the room. "A touch!"

The crowd cheered with excitement, and Ian moved back, surly. Judging by the look on his face, he hadn't even seen the hit coming. Stephen remained focused and calm. The evening had barely begun.

Anna giggled beside her, but nothing existed in Lucia's world except those two men and the swords they held. To Anna, this was a playful joust, a game between boys. Lucia felt much differently - she had seen enough combats go afoul to be on edge. There was danger simply when two friends played at a fight without anything at stake. In this very public contest there was Ian's ego and Stephen's protection of the town. Lucia had no doubt that the Grays were a strong threat - and that it would take Stephen's skill to keep them at bay. She wondered if the people around her drinking and carrying on knew how much was riding on the outcome of this match.

Hector moved in again to draw up his staff, and suddenly the two men were in motion.

Lucia watched their moves, instinctively categorizing each one. Duck. Parry. Swing, block. She had fought for enough years to feel the motion coming before a man swung the sword. Ian's eyes were bright, looking for the sequence he'd been taught by his instructors. Stephen's eyes were deep and steady, watching Ian's hands and eyes, and gauging what Ian would do next. Ian was halfway through an eight-part sequence when Stephen came in under his sword arm and tagged him on the side.

Hector called out loudly. "A hit! Two for Stephen!" The applause of the bystanders echoed around the room.

Ian's eyes flashed with furious anger, and Lucia winced as he almost took a step forward to call out a retort to Stephen. It was clear from his tensely coiled body language that he felt Stephen's interruption of his routine was unfair.

Lucia took in the roiling anger in Ian's eyes and suddenly remembered her own position as favor-giver.

Perhaps she could use her power to some advantage here, to diffuse the situation. "A break," she called out in a voice forced to be merry. She walked with a smile toward Ian, holding out the goblet of wine with both hands. She saw with pleasure that her gambit had worked - Ian momentarily forgot the fight and smiled down at her instead. His hands folded over hers as she handed the goblet to him, and she willed herself not to flinch or draw away. She smiled warmly up at Ian as he drank.

"It does not matter to me who wins this play battle, Ian," she cooed softly, so that none could overhear. "You will always be the hero who saved me in the woods. That is all that matters." To her relief, she saw Ian's eyes widen and a smile overtake him. If she could help Ian salvage his ego, perhaps the match would finish without incident. "Remember," she added gently, whispering in his ear. "It is not he who is up high on the walls that matters in a battle. It is he who does the actual work. Your true colors might shine most brightly from the trenches, rather than hiding on the parapets."

She touched his hand tenderly as he gave the goblet back to her. To her left, she saw Anna giggling up to Stephen, and her resolve hardened. If Ian was going to lose in front of his community, at least he could lose with pride and have other victories to parade. Lucia handed her wine to a nearby page, leant forward and kissed Ian full on the mouth. Ian only hesitated a moment before pulling Lucia hard against him and kissing her passionately in return. A roar went up from the crowd, but as much as Lucia wanted to participate, nothing stirred within her. She rested her hands on his shoulders and waited in the kiss until he released her with a broad grin. She moved back to the edge of the group, maintaining her smiling encouragement at

Ian. *It does not matter*, she tried to tell him silently with her smile. *This bout does not matter.*

She realized that Anna had joined her and was whispering in her ear. "I thought you said you were not fond of him," came the amused comment. Lucia paid her no mind. Her task for the moment was to keep Ian from hurting Stephen, and to ensure that Stephen's victory came without any bad feelings. Outwardly she nodded encouragingly at Ian, while inwardly she hoped for Stephen to finish the match quickly and safely.

Hector brought the men together again, and once again the staff raised up. Ian was in a fine mood now, waving his sword with flourishes and panache. Stephen seemed, if anything, even more somber, his blocks against Ian's sword short and sharp. His face was an impassive mask, no emotion showing. Then Ian closed in, and there was a flurry of sword work.

Lucia had to admit that despite her concern she was drawn into the fine skill being shown. Ian was apparently past his impulse to make a quick hit and had settled into his years of training. His moves were precise and well timed. Stephen, having won two out of two so far, was indulging in giving Ian his moment in the sun. The crowd cried out in delight as the men went back and forth across the hall, all of their skill shining.

Lucia forgot the danger for a moment as she became caught up in the elegance of the movements. She saw Stephen let one easy touch go - and then two. She realized that Stephen was indeed giving Ian his moment to show his worth, to be able to tell later how he had held his own.

Finally, on the third advantage offered by Ian, Stephen stepped forward for the hit, to bring an end to the match. Stephen turned fully sideways to catch the angle, tapping his blade with gentle restraint on Ian's outstretched arm.

Lucia exhaled as she saw Stephen rotate through the final hit, finally releasing her held breath. It was going to end reasonably, she realized with pleasured surprise. Stephen would take the lead, and Ian would have the stories to tell. It actually could end well for both men.

Lucia smiled with relief as she watched Stephen relax as well. His eyes swept the crowd as he turned, seeking out and finding hers. She saw in them the grim resolve of doing what had to be done, and wondered if her own eyes had held that same look for the past hour. To her right, Anna noticed that Stephen was looking in their direction, and raised her jeweled hand in a congratulatory wave.

Suddenly Lucia froze in shock. Behind Stephen, Ian had not felt the tap and was continuing his rolling sword attack. Ian hadn't realized the fight was over. The crowd roared in excitement, oblivious of the danger of the moment.

Lucia drove forward a step, her cheek scraping open against the edges of Anna's rings. The pain was inconsequential to the sharp dagger of fear which pierced her heart. There was no time …

"Down!" she screamed to Stephen, her voice cracking in desperation.

Her voice seemed swallowed in the din, but without hesitation Stephen immediately dropped to one knee. Ian's sword sliced through the air where Stephen's arm had been. Stephen spun underneath the sword and smacked his sword against Ian's leg in a far more obvious manner. Hector called out, "A hit!" and the crowd cheered wildly as the fight came to an end.

Lucia sagged in relief. Apparently none of the watchers but her had caught the first, subtle tag. Her legs trembled as she watched Stephen and Ian shake hands first with each other, and then with Lord Edmund. Stephen's face was a quiet mask of studied calm, while Ian was already triumphing in his brilliant maneuvers.

A fresh barrel of ale was opened, the tables were brought in, and the real festivities began. Lucia was sucked into the whirl of sound and color; soon she was sitting next to Ian. It was almost too loud to hear distinct words, but Ian's voice rang out recounting every detail of the match.

Lucia played the dutiful partner for an hour, but the din and heat became oppressive. She murmured into Ian's ear that she needed to leave the room for a moment, and he expansively waved her on. Two other women filled her place the moment she stood.

Lucia turned and went up the stairs toward her room. The hallway was deserted, lit only by a few flickering candles. She gratefully stopped in the peace of the long hall of windows. She stood at one and opened the shutter slightly, breathing in the fresh air with gratitude. Exhausted, she leant her forehead against the window frame. It was all going to be fine, she reminded herself with a deep sigh. The evening was over. She began shaking with relief.

She felt rather than heard someone come up behind her. She turned in the semi-dark and saw the brown eyes gazing into hers, the ones she had come to trust beyond all measure. Her face flushed, and time staggered to a halt.

* * *

Stephen was captivated by the woman before him. She seemed almost a dream, hidden in the shadows of the deserted hall. There was so much he wished to tell her, and yet so much that could not be said.

Her whispered guidance had been clear and succinct; the best he had received despite a day of discussions with many other experienced soldiers.

Her keen awareness of Ian's ego had been clearly on display with her intervention after the second hit. He could see in her posture and gaze that she was acting for his benefit, not her own.

And then, while all other spectators had paid scant attention to the actual fighting, it had been her perceptive eyes that had saved him from an injury …

There was not time to speak of any of that; he would be missed shortly. There was no time for the many other things he longed to share with her. Instead, he simply held her gaze for a long minute without speaking and hoped she could read his thoughts in his eyes.

She took a step toward him, moving out of the shadows. He drew in a sharp breath when he saw the three cuts which slashed along her cheek bone, dried blood showing up bright against her pale skin. Against his firm resolve, he reached out and gently touched the side of her face with his fingertips in the softest of caresses. Her eyes battled with conflicting emotions before she leant, ever so slightly, into his hand.

His breath came rough and ragged. He knew that he had tempted fate for long enough.

"Thank you … for everything," he rasped quietly, his voice thick with emotion. Then, with a herculean effort, he lowered his hand and retreated back down the stairs toward the celebration.

* * *

Lucia's breath caught. She remained frozen in place and stared at the empty spot where Stephen had stood.

Giving herself a shake, she half walked, half ran back to her room. She bolted her door, wanting to be sure she was left alone.

She stood for a minute at the door, her hand on the bolt, almost unwilling to leave it shut - but she forced herself to turn. She dropped into the chair by the window and stared out at the stars, fighting with every ounce of her strength to remain in place, to keep herself apart from the man she knew she loved.

One more day.

Chapter 10

Lucia finished the stitchery around the cloak's collar, relieved that she had finished the gift in time. Matthew had given her a clean bill of health earlier that morning. Her daily rides had done their work of rebuilding her strength. She would head out first thing tomorrow morning.

One more afternoon with Stephen. And then it would be over.

Around her, the women chattered in low voices, but the chair by her side was empty. As the minutes slipped past, Lucia's brow drew in curiosity. Just where had Anna gone to?

There were light footsteps in the hall, and she smiled. She looked up – but to her surprise Anna's gaze was shadowed with doubt. Lucia put down her sewing as her friend settled into the seat next to her.

"Anna, what is wrong?" she asked with concern.

A maid came over with a goblet of wine, and Anna drank down a sip before answering. "I spent the morning talking with Stephen," she explained in a low voice. "With the Gray conflict coming so close to this keep, I thought we might push up our wedding date, so I could get settled in our household further south, more distant from the danger."

Lucia's heart thundered in her chest, and she focused on her breath. She pushed down the wild flurry of panic which seemed to overtake her. She turned to the small table to her right, took up her own wine, and downed half the glass in one swallow. It was a long moment before she could turn back to the conversation.

"I can understand your wanting to be safe," she offered, hoping her tone was neutral. "What did Stephen say?"

Anna shook her head as if she could still not take in the response. "He said ... he plans ..." She drew her eyes up to stare at her friend. "He is still obsessed with his lands to the north," she finally choked out. "He has no intention of living further south!"

Lucia's heart swelled with respect for Stephen, and it was all she could do to hold her features even, to maintain a tone of commiseration in her voice. "I imagine you want to retreat to the keep further from the conflict."

Anna's voice was bright with exasperation. "Of course I do!" she burst out. "Any sane person would! Why would I want to remain here, with the fighting nigh on our doorstep? What kind of insanity is that?"

She took another long draw of her wine. "It is bad enough that he lives in that ruined wasteland with Marcus and that other friend of his. I admire his rambunctious spirit as a bachelor. But soon he will be married to me! He needs to settle down. Somewhere safe, somewhere far from harm."

She shook her head in bafflement. "I had our future all neatly planned out. What is Stephen thinking? How can we have costume balls and harvest festivals in lands that the Grays are burning to the ground?"

Lucia bit her tongue, took in a long breath, and released it again. She was Anna's friend and should support her in her goals. "Anna, I am sure this will work out somehow. Maybe Stephen will change his mind once he is married. Maybe once he is a husband and not a single man, he will feel the responsibilities involved and want to settle down." She patted Anna tenderly on the arm.

Anna looked doubtful, but she picked up her embroidery, stabbing the needle through the cloth with steady motion.

Lucia turned back to her own sewing, a turmoil of thoughts swirling through her. She doubted that any ring or vow could ever change the character of a person. Stephen was a man of honor. His desire to cleanse his homeland of the Grays would not vanish solely because a wife was at his side. If anything, he would crave a wife who cherished the same goals …

She pushed the thought out of her mind and focused on the cloak beneath her, then the roast goose presented for lunch, then the steady gait of her horse as she rode out toward the clearing.

She settled against the willow tree, gazing down the trickling stream, hollowness swelling in her chest. What would she have done if she had been in his place? Would she have come back from the woods docilely and meekly? Would she have consented to a marriage her father had arranged? Could she let her father down, after all he had done for her, if this is what he truly had asked of her? Would she instead desert her potential husband, and all she loved, in a selfish desire to be free?

The morning's drizzle had faded into a cloudy afternoon, and the cloak beneath her kept the wet grass from soaking her. The swollen stream carried melting snow and leaves downstream, a reminder that spring was fast approaching. She threw a twig into the water and watched as it swirled away out of sight.

Tomorrow she would be departing, vanishing herself.

Part of her prayed that Stephen would become a distant memory. Perhaps distance would ease the intense longing which twined deep within her.

But she knew. With every breath of life within her, with every drop of her blood, she knew that Stephen's voice would always echo within her thoughts. The steadiness of his eyes had become a visceral presence in her soul. He had become her foundation, and her roots had dug too deep to ever be ripped free.

The gentle rhythm of hoofbeat eased into hearing, and soon Stephen had entered the clearing. She nodded her greeting to him and took in the tight draw in his shoulders, the furrows in his brow. She held her tongue while Stephen dismounted and tied Prince alongside her horse. He sat a short distance from her, looking out into the distance in a distracted manner.

Lucia could not stand his silence, not on their last day together. At last she asked, "Is there something bothering you?"

Stephen remained quiet, his gaze shadowed.

"Perhaps I can lend a fresh view," she added, softly. "As a friend of Anna's ..."

Stephen kept his eyes on the forest and hesitated for a long minute. "It is about Anna that I am troubled," he finally stated, his voice low and tense.

Lucia waited, unsure she wanted to hear what was to come. It was hard enough to keep herself apart from Stephen without having to hear his confessions of feelings for another.

Stephen went on, the words rushing out as if they had been a long-dammed torrent. "It is the marriage," he admitted in a growl. "You know Anna; you know her dreams. She has built a fantasy image that I must now fit - to please her, to please my foster father. I have sworn to do the best that I could, to be a good husband to her. She deserves that. She -"

He stopped abruptly, hesitating to say more. Instead he dug up a small rock with one hand and tossed the stone into the river, watching the ripples it created.

After a moment, he tried again, still looking out at the water. "When Anna first met me, it was easy to see she had developed a crush on me. She was young then, not even a teenager, and I admit that I thought it a passing fancy. I had other things on my mind. Later, as she grew older, I suppose that her feelings matured. Truthfully, I did not realize this until Lord Edmund spoke to me, just how far they had grown. By then -"

Stephen went quiet again, lost in thought. Lucia tried to imagine what that scene must have been like, how Stephen must have felt when presented with that request from the man to whom he owed so much.

Stephen spoke softly, looking down at his hands. "In any case, I consented to be her husband. At the time, I thought that having a wife at home would be something I would ... well ... manage." His voice echoed with frustration and confusion. "Now she talks more and more of a passive life, of staying home, holding parties, and arranging dances." His voice rose slightly. "I do not have time for dances. I am scrambling for the hours to train our troops, to build our defenses against the Grays. When we are done here, my sole task will be to wrest my family's lands from the usurpers. Then it will be a constant struggle to defend them!"

Stephen threw another stone at the water, this time more forcefully, where it made a large splash. He took a deep breath, then gazed out across the water, lost in thought.

Lucia found it hard to answer in a way that did not betray her own feelings. She held her tongue, her emotions in turmoil.

Stephen continued under his breath, half to himself, "I was not made for elegant delicacy any more than she was made for passionate causes."

Lucia glanced over at Stephen, surprised by this raw comment. Looking up, Stephen quickly spoke to cover his unintentional words. "Anna is sensitive and caring," he avowed in haste. "She is a wonderful woman."

He took in a deep breath as he slowly shook his head. "Even so, she just does not have the thirst for life, the need for action, that I have." His eyes met Lucia's, and he looked caught, almost lost. The words seemed to slip out.

"That we both have."

Lucia found herself immersed in his stare, ensnared by the depth and open honesty in his eyes. He was only a few feet from her, and she felt as if she could reach out and touch him. Her mind echoed loudly, 'Yes.' The word rolled around in her thoughts, growing louder. 'Yes, Yes, Yes.' The attraction flowed through her as a powerful stream, over washing anything else.

It was suddenly quiet, so quiet, and all that she knew was that Stephen understood her, that she understood him.

An inner voice cried out to her to draw back, and yet she couldn't stop the flowing river of emotion that had swept her up. There was so much they had not yet talked about, so much more she wanted to learn about him.

Stephen's face ached with pain and confusion, and she gave in.

She drew down her walls and finally allowed her eyes to shine with the full depths of her emotions. An answering passion flared into life in his own smoky gaze, and she smiled. The knowledge that he shared her feelings filled her with immense joy. She accepted with resolution that the knowledge alone would have to be enough. She saw this same awareness in the look and posture of the man before her.

Stephen was engaged to Anna. Lucia's feelings for Stephen, and Stephen's for Lucia, although almost overpowering, were secondary to their honor. Lucia let herself be absorbed by the emotion of the moment, knowing that it could never come again. She would leave tomorrow, and she would turn her back on the man that she loved with all her heart.

In the potent silence, the crack of a twig sounded loudly. Stephen and Lucia were on their feet instantly, their swords drawn from their sheaths in one sibilant hiss. They stood side by side, facing the path.

At the edge of the clearing stood six burly Gray mercenaries, chuckling to themselves at the easy prey they had found. Lucia berated herself for not noticing their approach. How could she have let herself get carried away? Where were the horses?

By now the six intruders had sized up their opponents. Lucia could see in their eyes what they thought they had found. A hapless pair of lovers, simple enough to kill for the fine horses they rode and the weapons in their hands.

A husky one winked at his companion. "This should be easy," he commented as they confidently closed in.

Lucia had been in situations like this before, and knew they had to act quickly. Experience taught her that their best hope was to take the Grays by surprise and break their morale. She hoped Stephen felt the same way, but couldn't spare a glance in his direction. She singled out a weak-looking, smaller one, and with a loud yell, swung her sword and went straight for his throat.

A shout by Stephen at the same moment made her grin even as pandemonium broke out about them. The man in her grasp shrieked, terrified, as she brought her sword across his body and quickly dispatched him. There was a strong hand grabbing her sword arm, and she snagged the knife in her boot with her other hand, slashing the attacker in the face. He screamed in pain, and before he could clear his vision he, too, was also dead.

Only a few moments had passed, and she now stood facing one bearded enemy who was far less certain of himself than a few moments earlier. She had kept her back to Stephen, and found that he had done the same with her. Sparing a glance behind her, she saw with grim pleasure that Stephen had also killed two Grays, and was now facing a single opponent. Lucia wondered if there were any more around. Thinking quickly, she relaxed her guard, lowering the sword and knife she now held in each hand. "That was not very hard," she called over to Stephen. "We managed to leave two of them alive. Lucky that they did not get a chance to send a scout back. We can drag these two in for questioning without the Grays being any wiser."

The Gray took the bait. She saw the dismissive look on his face as he looked down at her and leered at her slender form. His chest puffed out with pride and arrogance as he looked over at the second, a sneer on his face. "I told you we should follow protocol," he snarled nastily to his companion. "Lucky for you I agreed to let him go back before we attacked. Now we finish these pups off."

"Damn!" muttered Lucia, rotating her sword's hilt for a better grip. She didn't relish the idea of chasing a Gray scout through the woods. She had no time to ponder her options, though. With a sudden move, her opponent dove at her, swinging his sword down toward her head. He proved to be a better fighter than the previous two, and she deflected the blow with her sword while she tried to find an opening with the knife. She realized quickly that her strength was fading. Her wounds had healed for the most part, but she was still not quite up to full strength. She was grateful to have Stephen behind her, where she could hear him struggling with his opponent. If she'd been caught alone ... at least now she only had one front to deal with.

Lucia's enemy saw her slowing and pressed the attack. Lucia took advantage of this. She feigned an injury in her side and turned suddenly to the left as if in pain. The Gray took the bait and slashed toward her apparent weakness. Recovering quickly, Lucia brought her dagger in sharply, driving it into his chest. The Gray's eyes widened in surprise, and he staggered backwards. He went down heavily and grew still.

The wind huffed out of her; she dropped hard to one knee, breathing deeply. She realized that the clearing was now silent. A worried thought flashed across her brain, but Stephen was beside her in a moment.

His voice was taut with concern. "Are you hurt?"

She glanced up at him, automatically scanning him for wounds. He appeared to have a small cut on his arm, but the blood was not flowing heavily.

Lucia then looked down and examined herself quickly for injuries. Her ribs ached, and her sword arm was throbbing. Beyond a few bruises, she had a shallow, raking gash along her left leg that was bleeding slowly.

She ripped off the hem of her cloak to tie around the wound. "No more than you," she assured him as she finished the binding. Standing, she glanced at the woods. "There is another one out there, though, ready to call for reinforcements," she reminded him.

"I will find the horses," he called, running down toward the edge of the clearing. Lucia wiped her sword off on one of the fallen attacker's clothing, and recalled the argument she'd had with Stephen about the Grays. Could she really consider herself a lover of life, given the death she had just caused?

She quickly justified the situation to herself - this had been self-defense. The mercenaries had brought the fight to them, intending to kill them. These were not men she could have reasoned with, tried to negotiate a peace. It had been her only choice.

Stephen was back beside her in a few moments. "It looks like someone has taken them." He glanced quickly between Lucia and the forest beyond her, his face reflecting his worry. "I have to stop that scout, but I cannot leave you alone. Other mercenaries may be nearby."

Lucia did not hesitate for a second. "I promise I will keep up with you," she vowed with heat, "I will be far safer by your side than alone here."

Stephen held her eyes for a moment, then nodded quickly. "We will have to go on foot for now. Let me warn the town that the enemy is near, though." He pulled a small horn from his belt and blew strongly. A loud blare sounded clearly through the forest and echoed for a few seconds. Stephen looped the horn back on his belt. "That should get us some help."

He glanced again at her wounded leg, then the shadowed path ahead. His voice was tight with concern. "Stay with me."

She slid her sword into her scabbard, then rolled her shoulders. "I swear it." She would run until she dropped, rather than let the scout go free.

A look of respect swept his gaze, and then he turned and headed off at a steady lope through the woods.

Lucia was right on his heels.

It wasn't very difficult to follow the Grays' trail - they had trampled a wide path through the bushes. About a half-mile down, Lucia and Stephen had another stroke of luck; their horses were waiting near a bush. By the marks in the area, it appeared the Gray scout had tried to take one back with him, but had been kicked or thrown. Stephen and Lucia quickly mounted and continued down the trail.

Lucia thrilled with the excitement of the chase, but also found a center of calm swell within her at cantering down the path with Stephen at her side. Her mind coursed back to the closeness they were sharing when the Grays had first found them. She reflexively glanced over at Stephen. He returned her gaze with a look holding both pride and longing. Then he had turned to watch ahead, driving his horse harder through the dense brush.

The pair rode for another two miles, and Lucia became concerned that they had somehow missed a turnoff. Suddenly, Lucia saw a scurrying shape in front of her. Stephen spotted the movement at the same time, and with a cry the two spurred their horses to lunge through the brush after the Gray. The scout darted away from Stephen, to Lucia's side, and she was able to bring Troy alongside him. He turned his face up to hers in defiant anger.

Her heart caught in her throat, and time seemed to stop. She would recognize that face anywhere. It was the weasel-like Gray who had tortured and killed Marcie's brother in the snowstorm battle.

Lucia's previous thoughts of charity were quickly drowned in a tidal wave of hatred and fierce retribution. Bringing her leg over the saddle and drawing her sword in one deft motion, she leapt off the moving horse and landed heavily on the thrashing Gray.

Stephen's cry was sharp with warning. "Lucia!"

Lucia dove headfirst into the fight. The Gray slashed with his short sword, adding a twisting move at the end which flung her own sword into the nearby bushes. In seconds Lucia's dagger was in her right hand and she renewed the attack. All thought of personal safety vanished. This was the man who had ruthlessly tortured Vic and then had slain him.

He would pay for that.

Lucia slashed toward his face with her dagger, and he counter-punched her in the arm. Her arm instantly went numb with the impact. She rolled for another attack and he viciously kneed her in the groin. She almost laughed at how his dirty tactics would not be effective against her. Fury driving her on, she pressed down against him as he wriggled for a new advantage. She flipped the dagger into her other hand and brought it down toward his throat as he closed his own hand around her neck.

There was movement at her peripheral vision. She cried out angrily, "Stay back! He is mine!"

The Gray laughed roughly at this and used the momentary distraction to push off with his heel, flipping Lucia down on her back. The rough landing knocked the wind out of her, and stars cascaded in front of her eyes as he continued to press down against her throat.

She had to concentrate.

She focused on the blade in her hand, on the face that leered above her. His breath reeked like a week-old compost bin, and nausea rolled over her. She strained against him, sweat beading across her face. She needed to get his hand off her neck.

She deliberately rolled to the left, to leave herself open to a disarming move - and he went for it. At the moment his hand left her throat to go for the knife, she slashed with all her might. The Gray's eyes opened wide in shock, and he fell across her heavy and unmoving.

Lucia let her head fall back against the rough ground and stared up at the forest sky as her breath came in heaving gasps. Her dagger dropped from her hand. She couldn't move, both from his weight and her own exhaustion. As the adrenaline drained out of her body, throbbing pain settled into every corner.

Marshaling her last ounces of strength, she gave a heave and pushed the mercenary off her, then lay wearily on her side and looked down her own form. There was a large bloodstain on the front of her tunic, and she touched it with one hand. As she did so, Stephen dropped to one knee beside her, sword still in hand.

Guilt poured over her; she could not look him in the eye.

He sheathed his sword with one smooth movement before reaching down to touch the bloodied area on her chest.

His voice was low and shaking. "Are you all right?"

She wondered if he had been upset at her fighting alone or at what she had done. She nodded and sat up. He offered her a hand, and she unsteadily regained her feet.

The guilt of her actions overwhelmed her. This scout had not threatened them at all - and by all rights would have been an important resource to question. She had no excuse for killing him. Slowly, she turned to face Stephen. She was conscious of the crimson stain on her tunic, of the act she had just performed in cold blood. She couldn't meet Stephen's eyes.

"This is the Gray mercenary that tortured Vic and then killed him," she explained hesitantly. "Vic was so brave, and so young ..."

She shook her head. There was no excuse.

Stephen's hand on her chin gently made her raise her eyes to meet his own. She saw understanding there, and relief. "You did what had to be done," he replied hoarsely. "To stand back while you fought was the hardest thing I have ever done. If I had lost you ..."

Lucia could not hold herself back. She flung herself against Stephen's chest, burying her face in his leather armor. His strong arms immediately wrapped tightly around her body, his cheek pressing down against her brow. The embrace brought her feelings of safety and security that she had not felt in a lifetime. Lucia knew without any question that she wanted to be by his side always.

If only it were possible …

The thunder of galloping hoofbeat broke them apart. Stephen's hand flew to his sword, drawing it in face of this new threat, keeping Lucia next to and behind him. Lucia stood stock still, her own weapons out of reach. The safety she'd felt dissipated like mist on a summer's day, leaving behind only emptiness. The drumming grew louder, and then suddenly Ian burst into the area, followed by five cavalrymen.

Ian took in the dead Gray, Stephen's drawn sword, and Lucia's bloodied tunic in one glance. He leapt off his mount and raced to her side.

"My God, Lucia - are you hurt? Your chest! Your leg!" Lucia realized that the bleeding from her leg wound had worsened, undoubtedly exacerbated by the ride here and the rough fighting. Her strength drained out of her as Ian took her by the arm.

Ian's voice was bright with energy. "Here, lean on me," he offered, supporting her.

Lucia looked up at Ian in confusion. Her thoughts whirled in a jumble of crimson streams and drifting green.

It should be Stephen.

The thought echoed through her mind with stronger and stronger power.

She turned her head to look for him, but then Ian was lifting her into his arms. The sudden whirl brought on a wave of nausea, and she closed her eyes against the sensation, her face tensing in pain. Her leg throbbed and her breath could barely draw into her lungs. She felt heavy, as if Ian was small and insubstantial compared with Stephen's strength.

* * *

Stephen watched, motionless, as Ian lifted Lucia onto his horse. Ian called down to him with real concern, "Are you all right? Can you make it back with the horses?"

Stephen found he could only nod in assent.

Ian breathed a sigh of relief, his face brightening. "I will leave some soldiers with you, just in case," he continued. "I must get Lucia back to Brother Matthew before she loses more blood. Come behind us as soon as you can."

Stephen waved him to go on, and watched silently as Ian galloped toward the castle. An empty hole billowed within him, accompanied by a pain that was wholly unrelated to the injuries of the fight.

There was nothing he could do. Lucia was not his. He himself was sworn to another.

The world around him drained of color, the tranquil blues and shimmering golds shadowing, darkening, until all that remained was the deepest black.

Chapter 11

Lucia's body throbbed with pain. She blinked her eyes open in the morning light. Various parts of her body were bandaged, and her parched throat rasped. She had barely pushed herself into a sitting position when Brother Matthew eased his way into the room, brightening with a smile when he saw that she was awake.

"Good, good," he called out agreeably. "I am glad to see you up. He moved to her side and lifted her wrist for a moment to feel her pulse. "You were fortunate to escape with so little damage; your leg will take several weeks to heal properly." His eyes looked down at hers with tender concern. "You were lucky that Stephen was there to protect you, young lady. This time, when you heal, you might give some thought about staying within the walls."

"Yes, of course," demurred Lucia with docile agreement. It would do no good to get into an argument with the kind brother. She rested quietly while he poked and prodded at her, then he was gone, leaving her in peace.

The day faded in and out. She had a small bowl of soup brought by Ellie, and Anna came to sit by her side for a short while.

Lucia looked up at her friend. "Did they find any other Grays?" she asked wearily. "Ellie seems almost unwilling to talk with me, and nobody else has been by."

Anna's eyes seemed shadowed. "You rest up," she soothed. "Everything is being taken care of." Lucia felt she should press the question, but her eyelids slid down, and she found herself drifting away.

The chair by her side remained resolutely empty.

* * *

Morning had come around again, and the Sunday church bells tolled out clearly in the gentle light. She pushed her covers off with an effort. She had been neglecting mass, but her injuries were not serious enough to hold her back today. Surely she could make it down to the stone chapel and back again. She was half dressed by the time Ellie came into the room.

The young girl saw at once what she was up to. "Are you sure you are ready?" she asked, her voice concerned.

"If I lay here like a slug, I will only become more lethargic," ground out Lucia, pulling her dress down over her chemise.

"If you push yourself too hard, you will relapse and take twice as long to recover," pointed out Ellie quietly.

"I promise, no rides, no swords," agreed Lucia. "Just a quiet walk to the chapel, and then some sitting. I can manage that."

Ellie nodded, helping Lucia brush her hair out. In a short while, the two made their way down to the small stone building.

Anna slid her way down the pew to sit on Lucia's other side, and in a moment the familiar litany slid over her. Lucia lost herself in the music of the words, let her mind be swept up in the serenity of the ritual.

" ... a prayer for the men who are at this moment out bearing arms against a brutal foe ..."

Lucia's eyes sprang up, and she almost stood in alarm. Anna felt her movement and put a hand in restraint on her shoulder.

Lucia's voice was a low growl. "You never said -"

"Shhhh," responded Anna, motioning with her head toward Matthew. "Later," she soothed her friend.

Lucia took another look around her. She had not paid attention before, but she now realized that the chapel was perhaps only half full, and most of those present were women. Stephen, Ian, Marcus, Hector – none were to be seen, nor were any of the other guards. Her body tensed; with practiced effort she forced herself to relax again. It would not do her any good to get riled up now.

Still, the moment the service was over she was standing, drawing Anna out of the stone room and out into the bright sun of the courtyard. The air was frosty and crisp, and her breath came out in bright puffs.

"What is going on?" she bit out in frustration.

"Nothing to worry about," reassured Anna, patting her friend on the arm. "Those scouts which attacked you were in advance of a small raiding party. Stephen figured the Grays would send out a second group to try to figure out why the scouts had not returned, and he laid a trap for them yesterday. They were able to pick off another eight Grays without loss of life."

Her eyes shaded in worry. "The men have an even larger trap put out today. Stephen is testing just how many scouting parties the Grays will send before they give up or return in force."

"I should be there," insisted Lucia, turning to head back toward her room. "I am a good archer. I could easily help with an ambush." She ran a few steps, then winced, drawing to a stop, pressing a hand hard against her leg.

A harsh call came from behind her. "What are you doing out of bed?"

Lucia whirled, nearly dropping to one knee as the pain at her leg throbbed into vicious heat. Stephen took a step forward, then halted as Ellie worked her way around to slip beneath Lucia's shoulder.

Stephen's voice was a growl. "You should be resting," he snapped, drawing his eyes along her injuries.

"I should be out in those woods, that is where I should be," she hotly shot back, her hand moving to press hard against the wound. "You could use an archer if you have laid an ambush!"

"You are hardly in any position to be a help," he pointed out curtly, "and we have ample archers in our ranks. You will do us far more good if you rest back up to full strength."

"What is the status?" Lucia pulled herself up, wincing again at the sharp pain that zagged through her body.

He paused a minute, his eyes drawing over her with worry, before nodding. "There is a lull," he stated, his brow easing slightly. "After that first set of seven you and I took on, there were eight more the second day, and then six today. My guess is that they will stop coming. They will realize we are too well prepared for a casual sortie, and retreat to build up a larger force."

He glanced up at the wall behind her. "They would need some time to organize a larger attack. My guess is it would come several months from now."

"Right, in May, maybe June," agreed Lucia, her mind skipping through the possibilities. "That gives them a few months of warmer weather to build up their reserves, to draw their troops together and raid some early crop farms. Then, when they are well fed, well rested, and the weather is on their side, when they have light to see by and our troops are spread thin watching over our farmers and villages, they will focus the attack."

Anna broke in with exasperation. "What in the world are you two talking about?" she cried. "How can you possibly know what those cretins are thinking?"

The noon bell rang, and Lucia winced at the sound, then moaned as the wound in her leg throbbed into fresh agony. Stephen's eyes went to Ellie. His voice was low and curt. "Get her back to her room. She is to stay there all day tomorrow at the very least."

Ellie glanced sideways at Lucia. "I will try my best."

Lucia's body ached from all sides and she did not resist as Ellie walked her along the stairs back up to her room. Her head touched the pillow, and the world slipped away.

* * *

Heavy footsteps sounded along the corridor, and Lucia sprung to wakefulness, rubbing her eyes against the faint morning light. Stephen was coming to talk with her. It had been so long since he was in her room, by her side …

The door pushed open, and she sunk back down against the bed in disappointment. Ian's eyes looked attentively around the room and brightened when he saw Lucia was awake. He stepped in, closing the door behind him and coming to sit at her side with eager interest.

"We are victorious!" he cried out in delight, taking her hand in his. "We have driven the Grays away!"

"The Grays did send in a main force after all?" asked Lucia in confusion, pushing herself quickly to a sitting position.

Ian shook his head roughly, his eyes bristling slightly. "No, no, but we are victorious all the same," he insisted. "I watched with my group all afternoon long yesterday.

There were no more forays, no more scouting parties sent. They have given up! We are saved!"

Lucia's mouth quirked slightly. She would not have put such a positive spin on the short term respite, but she did not want to dispel Ian's joy. She allowed herself to smile, to relax against the headboard. "That is wonderful news, Ian. I am very happy to hear that."

"Let me tell you exactly how it happened," insisted Ian with delight. He launched into a second by second review of the past few days, starting with when he had heard Stephen's horn blast. By the time he had finished, Ellie had brought over a plate of cheese and bread for them, and Lucia was starting to feel more human. She moved to swing her legs around.

Ellie stepped forward. "Not on your life," she warned, her gaze fierce. "Stephen said you were to remain in bed for another day at least. I take his orders very seriously."

Ian frowned, his eyes moving sharply to Lucia. "Stephen was here?"

Lucia kept her face neutral, seeing the glint of jealousy shine from Ian's gaze. "No, he has not been here," she demurred. "I only ran into him and Anna briefly, at church yesterday.

"Oh, of course," agreed Ian, slightly mollified. "I could not be there – I was on duty at the time. Keeping the lands safe."

Ellie looked between the two. "Lucia really does need her sleep," she commented quietly. "Perhaps you could come back later?"

"Of course," agreed Ian, drawing himself to a standing position. "Until then!" He smiled, then turned and strode out of the room.

It was only a short while later that Brother Matthew came in to check on her. "No infection so far," he smiled with appreciation after a quick but through examination. "If only all of my patients healed as quickly as you do. Of course, most of my patients do not get themselves into nearly as much trouble in the first place."

"I am just lucky, I guess," chuckled Lucia. "Thank you for your time, I know you must be busy."

Matthew shrugged. "Nothing unusual. The soldiers have caught a few scrapes and bruises. I am sure there will be far worse, once we get into the thick of battle."

He nodded to her, then turned and left. She listened as his footsteps faded off into the distance.

She found herself hoping, praying, searching for even the faintest sound of that stride she knew so well, of the soft leather boots moving steadily along the corridor. She desperately wanted to talk with Stephen, to hear his version of the encounters with the Grays, to talk with him about what had gone on between them before the attack. It became an obsession with her, a glowing desire, and she strove to tamp it down. She could not see him, could not open that door. She had vowed not to spend any more time with him.

Tuesday morning dawned with grey mists and a dreary wind whistling outside her window. The lethargy of long bed rest gnawed at her; she willed herself to push off the covers, to climb out of bed. She fought off the hollow in her heart as she prepared to dress and face the world again.

Her emotions twisted in a turmoil that she felt would never heal. Her connection with Stephen had developed because his outlook on life so deeply resonated with her own. She wasn't projecting her fantasies on him and hoping he'd match. They had faced the fire together, and come through stronger.

Lucia sighed. In the end, it mattered little if they were well matched or not. The truth was that Stephen was bound to another. She could not, would not, interfere with that. She resolved, firmly, to let Stephen and Anna work out their problems, unhindered, without any interference from her. If she loved Stephen, well, then, she loved him. Her love would have to go unrequited.

Ian was waiting for Lucia at the foot of the stairs, and she allowed him to escort her over to the head table. His eyes drew down her body. "You are looking so much better," he offered her warmly. "When I first found you, covered with blood, I thought I had lost you for good! Thank goodness it was only spray from Stephen's fighting efforts."

Lucia bit her lip, took her seat, and looked down at the basket of rolls. She felt no desire to correct Ian. She did not want to talk about that afternoon at all, to remember how ably Stephen had stood at her side, the pure joy in having a partner so in sync with her thoughts.

"It is fortunate the Grays came when they did," commented Ian idly as he speared a chicken leg with his dagger. "While we were manning the walls more fully, we have come across several issues which need prompt attention. We will need every man available to take care of these." He took a solid bite of the meat, washing it down with a slug of mead. "I am afraid it will be about three weeks before we can free up a group to escort you down to Harwich." He smiled at her widely. "You would not mind, of course, healing up with me by your side?"

Lucia paled. "Three weeks?"

He glanced at her slyly. "Three, I imagine, should do the trick," he muttered, taking another bite of his chicken.

Lucia sighed, looking down. Her leg wound gave a sharp tweak, and she moved her hand absently down to rub against it. Matthew had said the leg needed time to heal.

She knew better than to risk an infection. As it was, she knew she would spend the rest of the day back in bed.

She sighed. While she did want to get down to Harwich immediately, it would be quite a time before her brother and the rest of her group met up with her there. If she was going to sit and wait somewhere, it might as well be here rather than alone in a strange port town.

"Of course," she agreed quietly. "I am at your leisure. I realize your guards have many other duties to attend to, rather than to escort a lone woman on her travels."

"You will enjoy your time here," promised Ian with a smile. "I will make it my personal mission in life."

Chapter 12

Lucia took a sip of her mead, the women's babble purling around her, becoming a familiar sound. She was working on a chemise now, and to her pleasure the stitchwork was coming out even and neat.

She looked over to Anna. "I think I will try a short ride this afternoon," she told the blonde with a smile. "My leg seems to be healing up well enough."

Anna's brows creased in concern. "Are you sure you are ready for that? What does Matthew say?"

Lucia tweaked her smile into a wry grin. "Matthew says I should trust in my instincts, and go with what feels right."

* * *

Lucia hobbled her steed at the far side of the clearing, looking around in remembrance. Only five days past, she and Stephen were standing here, side by side, facing the enemy. She could still feel the thrill in her body, the intense pride, the heart-warming feeling that everything was just as it should be.

There were hoofbeat and suddenly desire and fear warred side by side within her breast. He could not come to her. She was not ready yet, not prepared for …

A horse rode into the clearing, and she was swept with relief and disappointment. Marcus reined to a stop, a smile on his face, looking around at the surrounding area and then down at her.

"Good afternoon," he greeted warmly.

"Good afternoon, Marcus," she returned, drawing a smile on her face.

"I will be patrolling this area regularly, so there should be no repeat of last week's excitement," he informed her with a grin. "I will be by every twenty minutes or so."

Lucia could not tell if she was warmed or saddened by the news. "I appreciate that," she found herself saying.

He glanced around the clearing again. "Is there anything you would want?"

Lucia could think of *exactly* what she wanted, but she pushed the thought aside with fierce effort. She moved her gaze around, bringing it to her horse, to the bow and quiver tied to his side.

"A hay bale?" she asked.

He nodded at once. "Certainly, I will see that it is here by tomorrow."

She smiled in earnest then. "Thank you Marcus, that would be perfect."

* * *

Lucia tried to concentrate on the hole she was mending in the apron, but Anna's furrowed brow kept calling to her. Finally she looked up, spreading the cloth across her lap.

"Well then, out with it," she prodded.

"Are you sure you are really up to practicing archery?" Anna asked, her eyes going down to Lucia's leg.

Lucia shook her head. She knew exactly where this question was coming from, exactly who had voiced the concern.

"I am quite sure; I will be fine," responded Lucia. So he was going to try to restrict her movements from afar now?

Anna's brow creased in confusion. "But, from what I understand, you need your legs planted firmly in order to shoot a bow well."

Lucia doubted that Anna had ever held a bow, never mind come up with that argument on her own. "I am being careful with my leg," she reassured her friend. "I will be doing my practice mounted for now until my leg has more time to heal."

Anna's brows came together. "Mounted?"

Lucia nodded. "Shooting from horseback is an important skill. So I will simply figure out a way to arrange the hay bale at the height of a man standing. Then I can ride Troy around and practice from various angles – all without bothering my leg in the least. To my leg, it will be as if I am sitting in this chair."

Anna's eyes lit up. "Oh, I understand!"

* * *

Lucia's mouth tweaked up as she rode into the clearing. A platform had been built at the far end, and the hay bale was arranged vertically to represent the torso of a standing man. It was just the right height, and the space around it gave her ample room to practice from various angles and distances.

It was only a few moments before Marcus had joined her. "So, what do you think?"

She nodded in approval. "That will do quite nicely," she agreed. "Thank you."

"It was my pleasure," he returned. "This way you will have something to occupy your time while you are out here."

Lucia dropped her eyes. Before, her time had been occupied with wonderful conversation, with sharing discussions with Stephen like she'd had with few others. And now they would be gone …

Marcus' voice dropped low. "You know, if you are lonely out here, I think I could find a way to help with that."

Lucia's heartbeat quickened. Would he put in a word with Stephen?

"Ian has been asking his father, again, for time off in the afternoon. That way he could come and spend time talking with you while you rested out here."

Lucia blushed fiercely. Why did it seem that everyone was pushing the man at her? Her voice was firm. "No."

Marcus looked at her in curiosity, and she blushed even more deeply. Ian was her host, after all. She did not want to disgrace him in any way. "What I mean," she amended, "is that Ian is a skilled fighter and a talented teacher. With the assault on the Grays coming up so soon, I know it is critical for him to be with his troops at every possible moment."

Marcus nodded. "Of course. It is good for you to make that sacrifice."

If Lucia's face could turn any more crimson, it would have burst into flame.

* * *

Anna's eyes were dancing with delight, and finally Lucia put down the tunic she was repairing and turned to her.

"Yes?"

Anna gave her a nudge. "And here I thought you were not interested in Ian," she smiled.

Lucia sighed, shaking her head.

Anna leant forward, a grin growing on her face. "I know, we could have a double wedding!" she cried out. "Just think, you and me, and Stephan and Ian, all standing on the chapel steps side by side!"

The vision came clearly into Lucia's head, of Stephen beside her, the priest there before them. And then Stephen was turning away, taking another woman's hands into his own ...

Anna's eyes brightened. "Ooooo," she sighed in delight. "I have it. You need to make Ian a gift."

Lucia looked at her friend in confusion. "An engagement gift? I think you are leaping a bit too quickly here."

"No, no," corrected Anna. "A thank you gift. You made that cloak for his father, in thanks for his hospitality. The one you plan on giving him on the day you leave. But you do not have anything for Ian." A smile came to her lips. "After all, he is the one who rescued you."

"He and Stephen," corrected Lucia automatically. Her mind went back to that snowy evening. Stephen had knelt before her, she had put her blade to his neck, and he had not faltered. He had trusted her with his life.

Anna's voice shook her from her memories. "Ah, but it was Ian who challenged Stephen to a race. If he had not, who knows if they would have found you in time!"

Lucia shook her head at the creative logic. Undoubtedly that was exactly how Ian saw the event.

Anna patted her on the arm. "In any case, I know exactly what you should make."

"And that would be?"

"A decorative sword sheath!"

Lucia blinked in uncertainty. "Out of *fabric?*"

Anna nodded enthusiastically. "Exactly. He saw one on a trip to the market last summer and has been talking about it ever since. It looks like a functional scabbard, but it can have the colors and flourishes that only fine fabric offers."

Lucia gave up trying to understand it. "If that is what he wants, then I will do my best."

* * *

Marcus arrived just as she was sending her last arrow into the hay man's chest. He smiled at the tight grouping, then went over to retrieve them, bringing them to her.

"So, I hear that you are making a scabbard for Ian," he said by way of a welcome.

Lucia flushed. "That was supposed to be a surprise," she muttered.

Marcus brought a hand to his chest. "Not to worry, he will hear not a word about it. Only a few people know."

Lucia thought she could name all three people in that chain of communication.

She sighed, struck again by how silly it seemed to make a scabbard for a sword out of fabric. "I do not even know how I will do it," she admitted. "I am more used to thinking in terms of functionality. I am worried that I will waste valuable fabric while I figure out how it should be done."

* * *

Anna plunked an enormous pile of burgundy fabric down alongside Lucia's chair. "You make all the tests you want," she encouraged her friend. "In certain matters, persistence and care are what pay off! And besides, I have more burgundy fabric than I know what to do with."

Lucia drew her eyes across the reams of fabric. "Apparently you do," she agreed. "Well then, let us get started."

* * *

Marcus' face creased into a smile as he stopped in on his patrol. "So, how goes the sheath made of silk?"

Lucia chuckled. "Well, at least I have ample material to practice on. At the rate things are going, I may need it."

* * *

Sunday morning dawned with streaming sunshine and high-floating clouds. Lucia lowered her eyes as she moved into the small chapel, as she slid down the pew to Stephen's side. It was the closest she had been to him in a week, since she had seen him after mass the previous Sunday. A long week of only glimpsing him at meals, of torments and longings.

Ian slid in on her right side, his face glowing. "We will all celebrate this afternoon, with a delicious feast of wild boar," he chortled, nudging her in the side.

"Oh? What is the occasion?"

"Why, it is exactly a month since we found you, and brought you here!" he returned, his eyes bright with delight. "Surely you cannot say you have forgotten. I have been counting every day."

Lucia shook her head in confusion. Surely that could not be true. Had it really been a full month? But reviewing the events, she realized that he was right. It had felt so comfortable, so easy with Stephen's conversations, his steady presence by her side.

And now that he had been taken from her, she felt the absence with every fiber of her body.

* * *

Lucia had finally figured out just the right shape which would mold to the sword and not be cut by its draw. She looked at the pile of scraps she had created, littered at her feet.

"So just why do you have so much fabric?" she asked Anna in curiosity, drawing a portion of it up into her lap.

"For the outfits, of course!" cried Anna in glee. "Everyone in the wedding party will match. I know at most weddings that people simply wear their Sunday finest, but ever since I was a little girl, I had visions of my ideal ceremony. Ribbons of burgundy, flowing across the Penrith courtyard, drifting like summer streams. Like a waving field of wildflowers. My wedding day will be absolutely perfect – just the way I always imagined."

Lucia glanced down at the rich blue of her own dress, the color Stephen had said was his own.

"But I thought Stephen's color was dark blue?"

Anna shrugged. "This is *my* wedding day," she pointed out. "One I have dreamed about for years. Surely he will not be concerned about what color I am clothed in."

* * *

Marcus shook his head as he came into the clearing on his rounds. "I might advise staying clear of Stephen this afternoon," he advised her with a wry grin.

Lucia flushed. With the way Stephen had been actively avoiding her, she would be lucky to lay eyes on him for three seconds at a time.

"Why, what is wrong?"

Marcus shrugged. "Something has gotten him annoyed," he commented. "Stephen tends to hold in his feelings, but I have known the man for years. Something has wriggled under his skin."

* * *

Anna's face lit up in delight as she leant back in her cushioned chair. "It is February 29th," she advised her friend with a grin. "Traditionally, this is when the woman is allowed to propose to the man she desires." Her eyes glanced toward the great hall. "I think I know who you should go talk with!"

Lucia shook her head. "I appreciate the thought, but I am leaving in two weeks," she reminded her friend. "I hardly think rushing things would be appropriate."

"Oh, but you must be back in time for my wedding," pleaded Anna, her face going pale. "I have it all planned out!"

"I am sure I will be," soothed Lucia. "It is only a few weeks travel each way, even at a slow pace. Plus, we want return before the Grays attack in force."

Anna's face darkened. "Those darn Grays. I cannot believe they are interfering with my perfect wedding plans."

It occurred to Lucia that Anna had, indeed, laid out and gotten exactly what she wanted. A thought occurred to her. "Lucia, did you talk to your father on February 29th?"

Peals of laughter burst out of Anna at the idea. "No, you silly," she countered. "I get my way, no matter what the date." She leant forward. "But I am sure Ian would love to hear any plans of yours during lunch!"

* * *

Marcus glanced at Lucia as he pulled the arrows from the target. "Your groups are getting better," he praised her. "The leg is healing up?"

She nodded. "I think I might be ready for practice from the ground tomorrow."

He came up before her, handing over the arrows. "So, how was your lunch with Ian?"

She flushed. This communication chain that had formed was becoming a bit too much. "It was fine," she answered tightly, her face warming with heat. Indeed, Ian had made all manner of hints and prods that he would be open to her requests of any kind. It had been all she could do to get through the meal and escape him.

She dropped her eyes. "Perhaps when I return with my family's forces I will stay with Anna at Kendal, and we can launch our assault from there," she muttered under her breath.

* * *

The sewing-room women were all crowded in excitement around a red-headed lady, and Lucia moved up to Anna's side. "What is going on?"

"Oh, Nicole has been injured," she murmured with bright eyes. "It is all too shocking. She tripped over a root in the gardens, and look at her arm!"

Lucia peered through the crowd. A bandage was carefully wrapped around her right forearm, perhaps two inches in width.

Anna turned to Lucia. "Stephen was called right away, and he wrapped it up," she explained. "Nicole insisted on his help, after seeing how quickly he healed you from the poison."

Nicole's high voice carried over the murmurs of the women. "I hope it does not scar me! I could not live if I were scarred!" The women immediately fluttered around her, soothing her.

Anna sat back in her chair with relaxed contentment. "I am sure it will heal perfectly," she promised. "Stephen is the best at these things."

Lucia looked down. She remembered all too clearly his dark eyes at her side, the way he had tended to her all through that long week. She could still feel the warmth of his hand ...

Anna chuckled. "Although apparently the man is not much for conversation."

Lucia looked up at that in surprise. Stephen's conversations had enveloped her with hope, had filled her long hours with comfort.

"Why do you say that?"

She shrugged. "I ask him what he thinks about my beautiful dresses for the wedding, and he says nothing. I ask him when he plans for us to move south to Kendal, and it is as if he did not hear me. I swear, getting the man to say two words in a row can be a challenge."

A shadow settled over Lucia's heart. He had been so open, so warm, and now ...

"You deserve a man who will be fully honest with you," she muttered. "We all do."

* * *

Marcus nodded in appreciation as she stood a distance from the target and carefully sent her third arrow in between the other two. "You certainly are healing up well," he praised.

She nocked another arrow against the string. "One day at a time," she responded. "I will take it slow and steady. I would not want anything else to delay my departure."

Marcus' mouth tweaked into a grin. "You might miss all the excitement then," he teased.

Lucia sent her arrow flying. It thunked into the hay bale alongside its brothers. "Oh?"

He nodded his head. "It seems someone must have questioned Stephen's honor, and I do not think I have ever seen him so angry. The heat in his eyes, it is something to see." His grin widened. "I sense a fight coming."

The tension in Lucia's chest darkened and roiled. He deserved it. It was time he felt some of the torment she lived with each hour.

"I will have to ask Anna, and see what she has heard," she commented. Her lips twisted in a smile. This little communication chain could be used in both directions. "I hear she appreciates it when people share their honest thoughts with her."

* * *

Anna turned to her with wide eyes. "Can you believe it? Stephen had a long talk with me last night."

"Oh?" asked Lucia, keeping her voice even. She stared down at the elaborate needlework she was finishing on Ian's scabbard. She found it gaudy and bright, but Anna had insisted that it was exactly what he had wanted.

"Yes, on all sorts of topics. For example, he actually would like some blue color in our wedding gathering!"

Lucia kept her eyes lowered. "And what did you say?"

Anna nudged her head toward the window. "The women are dyeing it now, in the courtyard. I said I could certainly compromise, if it was important to him. So each person shall have a blue sash to tie at their waist."

Lucia glanced up at that. It was a small token, but at least Anna was trying. "That was kind of you."

Anna nodded in satisfaction. "I felt it was the least I could do, since I will have my way on living at Kendal."

Shock washed over her. "Stephen agreed to that?"

Anna laughed merrily, her eyes twinkling. "No, he insisted that he wanted to retake his family lands, and to hold them." She leant forward and lowered her voice. "But I know well how this works. It is like my father insisting I cannot have another piece of apple pie. I simply go on with my plans, and eventually he will give in."

Dark shadows swirled through Lucia, and she looked away. She and her brother Michael had never hidden anything from each other; they had always shared every thought, every hope, every dream. She had found that same easy openness with Stephen. And now there was this twisting of truths, a state that pulled at her innards like a hungry wolf tugging at a young lamb.

There was a low, dramatic moan from the doorway, and Nicole walked slowly into the room, holding her arm. "Oh, I could be scarred for life," she groaned, looking around her. "Stephen says I will not be – but how could he know?"

Lucia's mood grew even blacker at the silliness around her. "And how long is the cut?"

Nicole's eyes went wide. "A full inch!"

Lucia hauled up the blue fabric at her leg, revealing the gash on her thigh. "*This* is what causes a scar," she snapped. "Unless, of course, it gets infected, in which case they take the leg off at the knee."

Nicole's eyes rolled back in her head, and she spiraled down toward the floor.

* * *

There was a thundering of hooves as she eased herself off Troy, and she turned with a smile. Marcus was certainly in a hurry today. She wondered what had gotten him riled.

The horse plowed into the clearing, and Lucia staggered back against Troy, her legs going weak.

It was Stephen.

It had been two long weeks since their day in the clearing when they revealed their feelings to each other. Since that day, she had only talked with him that one brief time by the church. Every hour, every minute, her heart longed for him, ached for him.

He dismounted and strode over to her, his eyes hard. "Let me see your leg."

She blinked in bafflement. "What?"

He swept her up in his arms, and the scent of juniper and leather nearly overwhelmed her. She leant against him, and when he eased her down against her willow it was all she could do to draw back, to let him move to kneel beside her.

He slid up the dark blue fabric, lifting it around her wound. He looked at the scar with careful attention, his gaze easing as he gently prodded along its side.

"It is healing well," he growled, his voice tinged with relief.

"Of course it is," she replied. "I have been taking it easy."

He looked pointedly over at the hay bale. "Easy?"

She sighed. "The north is –"

"No place for the frail," he finished for her. "I know."

He stood and paced a few feet toward his horse, then turned again.

"And I *am* a man of honor," he added, as if he had held a long discussion in his head and was now finishing it.

A shadow pulled through her heart. He had stayed away from her for two long weeks; he had cut off all contact with her. His honor was surely beyond all reproach.

"Who has said otherwise?"

His eyes flashed. "If I did not share my feelings with Anna, it was because I did not want to upset her."

Understanding flooded in on Lucia. "Surely Anna deserves someone she can trust completely," she countered.

He took a hard step forward. "She can trust me with her life."

"How can she trust you if you lie to her?"

He gave his head a shake. "I would never lie to Anna."

Lucia crossed her arms. "Where will you live when you are married?"

His answer came back without hesitation. "My lands, to the north."

She raised an eyebrow. "And where does Anna *think* you will live?"

His face shadowed. "She has her heart set on Kendal, but with time -"

She leant forward. "So you are letting her build fantasies and plan for them, because it is easier than helping her understand and prepare for reality?"

His mouth opened ... and then slowly closed again.

Lucia eased back against the tree. "If *I* were going to have that kind of life-altering change happen in a mere two months, *I* would want to know about it."

* * *

Anna's eyes held a baffled confusion, and she made the same stitch four times in a row before putting down her fabric. "I am not sure I understand," she offered at last. "I think he is actually serious."

"He wants to live in his family lands," stated Lucia. "I would agree, he seems set on it."

Anna shook her head. "But surely he is just confused. I have this all planned out."

"Not all plans end up the way one thought they would," suggested Lucia gently. "You could learn to be happy in -"

Anna shook her head, her eyes focusing in determination. "It is a test of some sort," she decided. "I just need to figure out how to get him to change his mind. I always win in the end."

Lucia pursed her lips. "Be honest with him," she advised. "Everything will work out as it should."

Anna shook her head vigorously.

Chapter 13

Lucia stared in confusion around the empty courtyard. James was not there waiting to meet her. She had grown so accustomed to the young page knowing her schedule that she stood there for several minutes wondering where he might be. Finally she headed over to the stables on her own. She was certainly capable of saddling her own horse.

She had just finished cinching up the straps when James burst into the stables, his face red and swollen from crying. Lucia turned in surprise, then ran over to him and took the young man's face between her hands.

"James! My God, what is wrong?"

James shook his head, stubbornly refusing to talk. His face a mask of agony, he looked down at the ground.

Lucia's heart went out to the lad who had so loyally helped her all this time. "Was it bullying from one of the boys in the area? I can have Marcus give him a talking to without revealing that you said anything to me. Was it a fight with a girl you are fond of? Or maybe trouble with one of the castle folk?"

James flinched slightly, but for Lucia it was enough. She dropped to one knee and looked the boy in the face. "I know it can be hard on servants who speak against their masters," she consoled in a soft whisper. "Remember that I do not have ties to this place, nor would I ever reveal anything you told me. Please, just tell me this … is there some way in which I can help?"

James seemed torn, and looked around to ensure there were no others in the stables. Then, finally, he asked in a low, hesitant voice, "Do you know anything about … mending cuts?"

Lucia nodded promptly. "I have been wounded more times than I can count – tending cuts is second nature to me by now," she promised solemnly. "I can do quite well as long as they are not life threatening. Please, let me help, and we will see what we can do."

James didn't need any further encouragement. He grabbed her hand and dragged her behind the stables, past the keep and toward the back of the walled area. After a few minutes they came to one of the small huts which held the cattle in inclement weather. It was an isolated spot, and nobody else was near.

As they approached, Lucia heard a soft sniffling noise. Turning the corner, she found a young girl, perhaps fourteen, lying in a pile of hay. Her clothes were torn, and there were numerous cuts and bruises on her body.

Lucia dropped to her knees besides the girl, aghast. "Who did this to you?"

James' voice was hoarse. "This is my sister, Lily," he grated. "Please, do not ask us anything further. Just help her."

Lucia bit her tongue and nodded. She set her mind to the task at hand. "Fetch me some water and fresh, clean rags," she instructed James. "I am sure the laundry room has some lying on a shelf. Also, get a spare dress from my room."

He was off in a flash. Lucia spent the time calming the girl and removing her remaining clothes. James returned far more quickly than she had imagined possible, and soon she was carefully cleaning the various cuts and bruises. Her mind ran over numerous possibilities as she worked, but she honored James' request and did not ask any further questions of them.

When she was finished she sat back, sighing in relief. "None of your injuries seem serious," she told Lily. "You should heal up without any problem." James gave his sister a tender hug at the news and kissed her on the forehead.

Lucia helped Lily into the dress and, once she had it on, there was barely any sign that the girl had been hurt. There was a small bruise on her forehead, but a re-parting of her hair made that disappear.

Lily took her by the hand, pressing it gently. "My Lady, I do not know how to thank you," she confessed in a soft whisper. "You have been so kind to me."

Lucia blushed and looked at the young woman. "I only wish I could do more," she admitted quietly. "Please know if there is anything else I can do. I am quite willing."

Lucia hesitated a moment, not wanting to pry. Was it an abusive courtier who had unleashed his rage on an innocent maid? Had the cook beat her for dropping a precious tureen? Or was it something more personal? Looking between the two, Lucia had the feeling that the young pair could use a guardian angel. "I am not a part of the family here. I am not involved in the politics or power struggles. If things are this bad, I can take you with me when I leave for Harwich."

Lily quickly shook her head. "I appreciate that, but the situation will be fine now," she promised. "I cannot leave my family. They need me."

Lucia was torn between interfering and allowing the girl her privacy. "Whoever did this to you, he or she could lash out again, and next time -"

Lily gave a short, cynical laugh. "That is not likely," she responded curtly. "He has what he wanted. I am sure I hold no further interest to him." She climbed to her feet and brushed the straw off of her dress.

A cold shaft of fear plunged through Lucia's core. Her mind raced as she worked through the possibilities.

Lily caught her eyes and her face steeled. "You must promise me – promise us both – that you will never speak one word of this," she insisted hotly. "I am fine. There is nothing to be done now. It is critical for us both – and for our family – that this entire incident be forgotten completely."

Lucia hesitated, but Lily took her hands between her own. "Please, you must promise."

Lucia felt guilty at such a bargain, but she reminded herself that she had no place in telling others what to do. She had helped the girl as best she could, and she had made herself available for any other assistance she could render. It could very well be that the girl was right – that her family and future would be best served if this situation was never mentioned again.

"I promise," vowed Lucia solemnly.

* * *

She had just hobbled Troy when Stephen came riding into the clearing. He swung down from Prince, glanced at her, then his eyes sharpened and he came striding over to stand before her.

His voice was tight with concern. "What happened?"

She looked down. There were large spatters of blood on her dress. She flushed, wiping at them with her hand.

He went pale. He took up her left hand and pulled her sleeve back. He carefully ran his fingers along her arm, looking for the source of the blood.

The closeness of his body, the scent of him, it was all she could do not to lean into him. She took a step back, pulling herself free, her breath coming in deep draws.

His eyes scanned her body, and he pressed again, "Where are you hurt?"

She shook her head. "I am fine."

He waved a hand at the blood. "But surely —"

She put her hand over the larger stain, shielding it from view. "I do not want to talk about it."

He took a step forward, staring at her, and she flushed.

His voice dropped lower, gaining a note of confusion. "You refuse to tell me why you are bloody?"

She found she could only nod in answer.

He ran a hand through his hair. "Lucia, I do not understand."

Her throat closed up. They had always been so honest before, so open, but she had given Lily her word.

She looked down. "You will have to trust me."

His eyes sharpened at that. "So you want me to trust you, even though you refuse to share your thoughts with me?"

She flushed hard at that, realizing that this was exactly what she had challenged him with two days ago.

Her voice was barely a whisper.

"Yes."

* * *

Saturday dawned with a deluge of spring rains, sending a fresh, sharp tang through the air. The sewing room was full as all the women took refuge from the storm. Lucia found her quiet sanctuary full of bright, amused chatter, and took a place by Anna with a nod.

Anna looked up at her friend with sparkling eyes. "Oh, Lucia, you have got to hear," she chuckled. "Ian was seen with that redheaded barmaid from the tavern two towns over. What is it called?"

Nicole leant forward, a dense bandage on her wrist. "The Waddling Goose," she chimed in, her eyes glowing with delight. "Abigail swore she was his only one – and then the very next day he had that blonde from the Pickled Herring in his lap!"

Anna grinned. "That is only because Lucia here resists his overtures," she confided to the group. "She could make an honest man of him, if she only tried."

Lucia shook her head. "Surely there are enough women in this keep to entertain him," she objected.

Nicole's mouth set in a pout. "Oh we try, believe me," she commented. "Every woman I talk with says the same thing. He will court you hot and heavy for two months, maybe three. Then – poof – his interest will fade. No matter what you do, he will move on to a new woman. The harder you try to keep him, the more quickly he will run."

Lucia looked back to Anna and shrugged. "See? If he has already worked his way through the keep, and is now taking on nearby villages as well, I doubt I have a chance to tame that wild spirit. I will continue to have lunch with him; he is the son of my host, and I owe a great debt to gratitude to this family for their support. But it seems he is a wild stallion, and wild stallions must run free."

The room burst into giggles at that, and Anna's face was bright with mirth.

* * *

Stephen stared at her with curiosity for a long while, and she made no move to break the silence. Would he try again to pry out of her the mystery of the bloodstains?

At last the words burst out of him. "You are not interested in Ian?"

"What?" she asked in confusion. "Ian?"

He waved a hand back toward the keep. "Anna said you had finally finished that decorative thing you were making for him."

She nodded. "Yes, as a thank you present."

"But then she said that you feel he is too wild for you."

The corners of her mouth tweaked up. "Too wild, too childish, too self-absorbed, too -"

His gaze went still, and she flushed. This was Stephen's best friend she was talking about. Her throat tightened. "Stephen, I am sorry," she amended. "I am sure that for some woman -"

He was shaking his head. "No, it is all right," he murmured, gazing at her with new light. "It is just that I thought, with what had been going on, that his plans were succeeding."

She chuckled at that. "His plans to perfect his monologues?"

A brightness came into his eyes, but his focus was steady on her, and her soul kindled with warmth.

* * *

When Lucia eased down the pew toward Stephen, he turned, his eyes warm and welcoming. Lucia felt it as a heat rising within her heart, easing out through every part of her body, and she smiled in return. She barely noticed as Ian came in on her other side, as he slid until his thigh gently rested against her own.

* * *

Nicole drew off her bandage with a flourish, waving her arm to the room of women. "Look, you cannot even tell that I was tragically wounded!" she sighed in relief. "Stephen truly is a miracle worker."

Lucia shook her head, running a hand along her thigh. "I am just hoping for sturdy strength," she commented to Anna. "I leave in a week, after all."

She smiled. "At least your gift for Ian is all set," she returned. "Whatever will you work on next?"

Lucia's eyes twinkled. She had already picked out her gift for her friend. It was a necklace she had been given years ago, one she never wore due to its bright colors. She had a sense that Anna would adore it, and that it would do far better where it was fully appreciated.

Anna clapped her hands. "Oh, I know!" she cried out with delight. "Stephen was there too, when you were found. He lent Ian a hand with your rescue. Maybe you should give something to him."

Like my respect ... my longing ...

Lucia gave herself a shake, looking down. "What would you suggest?" she asked in a low voice.

"Oh, I will think of something," promised Anna.

* * *

Stephen held her gaze from across the clearing. "You do not need to give me anything," he murmured. "What I did for you, I did without any desire for reward."

"I know," she returned, gazing in his eyes. She was comforted by his presence, and she resisted the instinct to look away.

It was only one more week. Surely she could make it through this last week.

* * *

Anna shrugged her shoulders. "He says he does not want a reward," she told her friend, shaking out the length of blue sash she was working on. "He can certainly be a strange man sometimes."

She glanced up at the unicorn tapestry behind her. "Much different from Ian, that is for sure."

Lucia followed her gaze, and suddenly her eyes took in the tapestry more fully. She remembered clearly, now, when Stephen rode by her side back from the first day of archery practice. He had said he had nothing at all with his sigil on it – no clothing, no banner.

"I think I might have an idea," she murmured. "Do you have a spare length of blue fabric?"

Anna nudged the pile with her toe. "Have at it," she offered with a smile. "We have more than plenty."

Lucia leant forward. "I would like this gift, at least, kept secret from Stephen."

Anna nodded her head merrily. "My lips are sealed!"

* * *

Stephen's voice came suddenly across the quiet of the stream's gentle babble.

"Do you trust me?"

She looked across the clearing at him, surprised. "Yes, completely."

"Anna said she had to order more blue fabric, but she made it very obvious that she was not to tell me why."

Lucia flushed. The woman's ideas about holding in secrets were certainly unique. Undoubtedly Anna had done everything she could to rouse Stephen's suspicions.

His voice became tight. "Clearly the fabric is for you," he pressed.

She looked down. "I do not want to talk about it."

His eyes swept across her dress. "It is obvious that the outfit you wear is stained with blood, and now you need to replace it," he pointed out in a low growl. "Matthew says that you do not have any new injuries that he can find. What happened then? Are you in some sort of danger?"

Lucia looked up in surprise at that. Stephen's eyes were shadowed, haunted, and she could see the concern that lay within them.

"No, not at all," she promised him.

"And yet you will not tell me."

She looked away for a long moment. He had always been completely honest with her, and she saw how much this worried him. But she could not violate Lily's trust.

"Imagine you found Marcus hurt. Would you tend to his wounds?"

"Absolutely," stated Stephen with conviction.

"And if he then made you swear not to reveal those wounds to any other person?"

Stephen opened his mouth, looked at her more closely, then slowly nodded. After a moment he stated, "I am a good medic. I could help, and I would vow secrecy of my own."

The corner of Lucia's mouth tweaked up. "You are an amazing medic," she corrected him gently, "and everything is settled now."

He eased back against the oak, his shoulders relaxing, and for the first time in weeks Lucia saw a gentling of his brow.

* * *

Lucia was just finishing off the hem around the edge of the tapestry when Ian came bounding into the room. He came right over to the two women and pulled up a chair to sit before them.

"I have fantastic news," he greeted them, his mouth wreathed in smiles. "Our Spring Equinox celebration is going to be the greatest Penrith has ever seen!"

Anna's face lit up at the news. "That is fantastic! Can I help in planning?"

His eyes twinkled. "Absolutely. Between you and me, we will create a celebration that will be spoken of for generations."

Anna's brow creased. "That is the Wednesday after next, barely two weeks away. We shall have to work morning, noon, and night!"

She turned to Lucia. "Oh, Lucia, you absolutely must be here for this. You will be the guest of honor!"

Ian nodded, taking her hand in his own. "I agree wholeheartedly. She will be the crown jewel in the day's events."

Impatience drew across Lucia. "But I had planned to leave *next* Wednesday," she reminded them.

They were both shaking their heads even as she spoke. "Just one more week," pleaded Anna, holding onto Lucia's arm. "It will be a perfect farewell party for you, and then you can give your gifts in front of an audience!"

Ian's gaze swiveled to her with bright interest. "Gifts?"

Lucia sighed at their dual assault. She wanted desperately to be heading south toward her brother and friends. Surely he would be in dock by …

She shook her head. Actually, it was unlikely that even if she delayed one more week, that he could beat her there. She would be stuck in a grimy inn in a worn-down harbor town to wait weeks for his arrival.

Her leg gave a twinge and she absently rubbed at it. Besides, healing up further would be the best for all concerned. It would make the ride go more smoothly and ensure she was in better shape for the coming conflict.

"If it means that much to both of you, then of course I shall stay for the event," she agreed, drawing on a smile.

"Thank you!" cried out Anna, pulling her into a warm hug. And then Ian was lowering his head to her fingers and pressing a warm kiss against them.

"You will not be sorry," he vowed.

* * *

Stephen's eyes were shadowed; it seemed a turmoil of emotions swirled behind them. "So you are staying an additional week?"

Lucia sighed. "Anna and Ian were both so insistent, it was hard to resist them."

He gave a low chuckle. "Well do I know." A long moment passed. "Well then, if you will be here for another two weeks, I have an idea."

Lucia flushed. What is it that he had in mind?

He nudged his head toward the hay bale, now in tatters on its wooden platform. "What if I were to get you a fresh bale, and set it up on a swinging rope? You had said you enjoyed more of a challenge."

Lucia's heart brightened with interest. "Oh, absolutely!"

He smiled at that, and she found herself lost in his gaze.

* * *

Lucia carefully stitched at the large golden circle which formed the outer ring of her design. It was centered on the field of blue. She had worried at first that Ian would ask what she was up to, but the man was completely unaware of the project in her lap. Instead he leant forward with eager excitement, laying out his plans for the events to Lucia and Anna.

Anna chimed in enthusiastically with idea and suggestions, and Lucia was happy to let them run wild, calling for servants, ordering supplies, laughing in mirth at a spectacular new vision. It seemed that the celebration would have everything but elephants and tigers.

Ian ran off to consult with the keep carpenter, and Anna whispered in Lucia's ear, her eyes sparkling. "See, this is what the ideal man is like," she murmured in glee. "This is exactly what Stephen will be like, once he settles into married life."

* * *

Stephen pulled back on the hay bale, his eyes sparkling in delight. "Are you ready over there?" he called.

She nodded, and he released the bale, setting it into a slow swing. She took her time, eased her breath, then released the arrow.

THUNK. It caught the left edge of the bale and stuck in firmly.

"Well done!" he praised.

She shook her head. "Barely adequate, but it is a start," she corrected with a grin. "With all my injuries, I will need to be patient with myself."

He leant forward to haul the bale back off to the side. The corner of her mouth tweaked up as she watched him taking on the job usually handled by a stable lad.

"Are you sure you do not mind – "

"I do not mind in the least," he interrupted, smiling. "I am enjoying myself immensely." He released the hay, setting it into motion again.

* * *

Anna burst into delighted laughter at Ian's suggestion, and the two of them were toasting their mugs together in delight. Lucia shook her head, continuing to work on her golden circle. The two of them were certainly enjoying this process immensely. To her, all the talk of apple varieties and styles of mead seemed fairly inconsequential, but they took on the examinations with great gusto.

"Oh, Ian, you are delightful," smiled Anna, relaxing back against her cushions. "I have not had this much fun in years."

She rolled her eyes, glancing at Lucia. "That darn fiancé of mine seems to lack enthusiasm for anything in life. I tell him step by step what we are planning, and not even the glimmer comes to his eyes!"

* * *

Stephen burst into a delighted laugh as Lucia's arrow whistled through the air and embedded itself into the center of the swinging target. "There you go!" he called out. "I knew you could do it."

Lucia smiled in satisfaction. Her days of exercise were paying off; her body was responding in its old ways, was performing as she ordered it to. "Patience, hard work, and dedication," she advised him. "And of course, your diligent help with my recovery."

He gave a low bow. "It has been my honor," he offered with a twinkle in his eye.

* * *

Servants passed around the elegant cups of cyser. Anna's voice rang out over the room. "Now each of these is a combination of honey mead and apple, but the difference comes from the variety of apple and the type of honey. So let us know how you like each one."

Lucia took small sips as she worked, but the differences, if they existed at all, were subtle. She focused her attention on the curving handle of the lamp she was embroidering within the golden circle. She knew its spirals intimately; it was what welcomed her when she woke up every morning, what soothed her soul as she fell asleep each night.

* * *

Lucia eased back against the willow trunk, exhausted and content. Her skill was returning, as was her endurance. Soon she would be back to full strength. She would be an asset to her comrades in the upcoming fight.

Stephen knelt at her side, offering her his ale skin. She took it, drank back the golden brew, and smiled in satisfaction. It was absolutely delicious.

* * *

Lucia gazed down the pew at Stephen, and he returned her look with warmth. She eased herself down the polished wood to rest at his side, and it was comforting, soothing, and all she could want out of life.

If she only had ten more days with Stephen, she would treasure each one.

* * *

Lucia breathed in the warm scent from the gardens, thrilled that the easing March breezes had let them move their sewing outside. The top of the lamp was coming into shape now; its golden peak was vibrant against the dark blue background.

Anna turned to Ian. "Ian, you must have a talk with Stephen," she insisted. "You grew up with him. Make him give up this silly obsession with those homelands of his."

Ian shook his head, taking another drink of his wine. "That is a losing battle," he advised her with a smile. "The man has been obsessed since he was ten years old. The years have only hardened him." He shrugged. "People are the way they are," he mused. "It is that infinite variety that makes life so enjoyable." His eyes caught the sight of Nicole as she walked by, and she flushed, moving more quickly past the trio.

* * *

Stephen's gaze held hers with relaxed contentment. She eased against the tree and soaked in the spring sunshine.

His voice was low when he spoke. "So, what will you do, once you have regained your keep and the Grays are vanquished once and for all?"

She smiled. "It has been so many years that I hardly know," she admitted. "I suppose I would finally go for those swims in our local pond, like I did as a child."

"We do have a hot spring just south of the wall," he teased.

Lucia laughed. "Yes, Anna swore she would never go near it," she agreed. She pitched her voice to hold the appropriate amount of horror. "*Who knows what monsters lurk in its depths!*"

She gave a stretch. "But really, I have no idea. I suppose I would stay at Keilder, take my turn on patrols, man its walls, and life would go on."

His voice became rough. "Stay with Michael?"

She shrugged, thinking of her brother with fondness. Surely someday he would marry. Would his wife enjoy having her authority compromised by her sister-in-law's constant presence?

The thought came to her of Stephen's lands, just a short ride south, and how it would be to be the lady of the land there. She could dedicate herself to protecting the weak, to creating a new community from the burnt out remnants. Her heart warmed.

"Perhaps I would find another home," she murmured.

Stephen's eyes were attentive on hers. "Michael would not mind?"

She shook her head, soaking in the vision. "He would wish me the best of joy," she mused, her voice rich with warmth.

* * *

Anna frowned as Ian headed off to oversee the arrival of two wagonloads of apples. "I am beginning to think Stephen is serious," she ground out. "I have tried everything. He simply will not budge. He will stay on his lands."

Lucia was working on the mouth of the lamp now, where the flame would glow, steady, guiding all who depended on its light. "I would say you are right," she murmured.

"Well, I absolutely will *not* live in that swamp," stated Anna with firm resolution.

Lucia glanced up at that. "But you want to marry him," she pointed out gently.

Anna took in a drink of wine. "I wanted to marry the Stephen of my dreams," she corrected her friend. "This man that I am seeing before me, I am not quite sure who he is. He seems to be less and less what I had planned for."

* * *

Stephen's brow was furrowed, and Lucia let out a long breath. She could not help but feel that she was partially responsible for the unraveling of the relationship before her. If only she had not been ambushed, if instead she had simply arrived, relayed her message, and then headed south. Everything would have gone on just the way Anna had wished.

She shook her head at that. Would it have? It was easy to imagine that alternative stories held a perfect solution. But in reality, the chasm had already existed between Anna's visions and Stephen's reality. That gulf would have yawned between them whether she had arrived or not.

Her voice was low when she finally spoke. "Is there something I can help with?"

He gave his head a shake. "I will do my best – but on some things I just cannot bend."

* * *

Lucia put the finishing touches on her oil lamp banner, and smiled in satisfaction. She was quite proud of the result; she could only hope that Stephen would find it worthy. She folded it carefully and put it to the side.

Anna looked up at Ian with petulance. "Ian, you are enjoying our planning of the celebration, aren't you?"

He beamed at her. "Absolutely! Our praise will be sung for years to come."

She shook her head sullenly. "Why cannot all men be like you?"

He chuckled, giving her a nudge. "Then where would my advantage be?" he pointed out. "This way, I have an area in which I shine!"

* * *

Stephen's gaze was serious. "Are you are sure you will be back by mid-May? I would guess the Grays will launch their final assault at the end of May, or early June at the latest."

She nodded. "With a full sixty men, if all goes right. We will have plenty of time to integrate the troops and make our plans."

He pursed his lips. "Those scouts were barely the tip of what we will face," he mused. His gaze became distant for a moment, and he quoted the old Roman proverb.

*"He who holds a snake by the tail
does not have it under control."*

She glanced down, and there was a beautiful, aquamarine caterpillar ambling its way along her leg.

Vibrant tangerine strips traced along its sides. She marveled at its beauty, and found herself saying,

"Caterpillar one day, butterfly the next.
Who is to say which is more beautiful?
Each is a creature of nature,
perfect in its own way."

Stephen looked up and eyed Lucia with consideration. "Is that a saying of your people? That was nicely put. Not many would see the same beauty in a caterpillar."

Lucia glanced at him, flushing.

"I am afraid I must claim credit for that poor offering," she admitted in a low voice, dropping her eyes. 'It was a ... game ... I would play as a child, with Marcie. Nothing more. Your saying brought it to mind."

Lucia couldn't help herself; she again brought her eyes up to meet Stephen's.

His voice was warm, resonant, and wrapped around her with tenderness. "Well done."

* * *

Anna glanced around her in petulance. "All the other ladies have gone to the hot springs," she grumped. "We are the only three here working on the plans!"

Ian patted her gently on the knee. "All is well in hand," he pointed out. "Let them have their fun. It is us against the world!"

She smiled at that. "At least you understand me," she teased.

* * *

Stephen smiled at her. "It is a shame you will not get to try those hot springs once before you go," he mused. "They really are quite wonderful."

She shrugged, taking a sip from his ale skin, corking it, and tossing it back to him. "Plenty of time for that after the fight is won," she pointed out. "For now, there are more important things to do." She pushed herself back to standing. "Ready for another round with the swinging hay bale?"

"Absolutely," he agreed, and in a moment the target was in motion.

* * *

Lucia ran a hand idly over the pile of dark blue fabric at her side. Should she make a dress for Ellie? The girl seemed to wear burgundy outfits provided by the keep. She was not sure if giving her something else to wear would be appropriate.

At last she turned to Anna. "What should I give to Ellie?"

Anna tapped her fingers in thought. "The girl was interested in bracelets that Lily made," she mused.

"Lily?" asked Lucia in surprise.

"Yes, the sister to James, your stable boy," explained Anna. "She makes delightful bracelets out of seeds; she hand paints designs on them. I know that Ellie has wanted one."

"Oh!" replied Lucia with a smile. "That sounds perfect, then."

Anna nodded. "I will have Lily come by tomorrow morning, and we can arrange that."

Her gaze moved down Lucia's dress. "In the meantime, we really should get something better for you to wear. That dress of yours is all stained."

Lucia blushed, looking down at the residual bloodstains still visible on the front of her dress. She knew Ellie had tried scrubbing them, but they would not fully come out.

She gave a soft shrug. "If you wish; I don't mind wearing this."

"Oh, I insist you have something new," replied Anna, shaking herself out of her shadows. "It will be the crowning glory to our celebration."

* * *

Stephen's eyes held hers. "So I hear Anna is helping you with a new dress for the grand celebration."

Lucia glanced down. "Well, this one is stained, after all," she murmured, a blush tinting her cheeks.

Stephen's eyes flicked down to the blood spatters, and after a moment he nodded. His voice was low and steady. "I do trust you completely, you know."

Her throat went tight, and her voice came out rough. "I know." She drew in a breath, holding his gaze. "And I trust you with my life."

He gave a wry smile, and she was lost.

* * *

Ian glanced up across the gardens, then drew to his feet. "I see you have guests," he murmured, turning. "I will leave you to it."

He passed Lily on his way out, and she moved aside, letting him go, before nervously coming to stand before the women. Her eyes went to Anna's. "You wanted to see me, M'Lady?"

Anna tilted her head toward Lucia. "My friend here would like to buy one of your bracelets. She is planning to give it to her maid, Ellie, as a thank-you present."

Lily's eyes swept to Lucia, and she blushed. Her hand immediately went to her wrist, and she swept off an intricately designed bracelet in white and yellow, with delicate daffodils painted along each bead. "Take this, with my blessings," she offered. "It is my best one, and I know Ellie likes these colors."

Lucia put her hand to the leather pouch at her side, but Lily shook her head immediately. "I insist, it is a gift. I will not accept a coin."

Lucia wanted to argue, but she also did not want to press the girl in front of Anna. Clearly the girl was nervous enough as it was. "As you wish," she agreed. "Thank you very much."

Lily nodded, her eyes full on Lucia for a moment, and Lucia saw the thanks within them. Then the girl was curtsying, turning, and hurrying back toward the keep.

Anna's mouth quirked into a smile. "My, you do have the touch with the servants," she grinned. "I am sure half of them will want to be by your side as you head south, to lend you a hand."

Lucia knew the only person she would want by her side, but she pressed her lips shut, holding back the longing.

* * *

Stephen's voice came out low and gruff. "I am sending Marcus and Shawn with you for your trip south."

She glanced up at that. "Those are your two best men," she pointed out. "Surely you will need them here for training and patrols."

He shook his head, his eyes serious. "Ian and Hector can handle what training remains. The other keep guards need to put their time in on patrols, to build up their abilities in the woods." His voice became hoarse. "It is far more important that you return safely."

She saw the worry in his eyes, and she nodded to him gently. "It is several weeks each way, but the roads are well traveled. I am sure, especially as I near London, that there will be little chance of trouble."

He shook his head. "Quite the contrary – a woman like you, traveling with only a small escort, would attract all sorts of attention from wolves' heads."

She chuckled at that. "Like me? What? Scarred and barely healing from my battle?"

He shook his head again, and passion smoldered within his gaze. "A woman who is filled with courage, who echoes with honor, and who is the most beautiful I have ever seen," he murmured hoarsely.

She flushed, her breath drawing to a stop, her gaze becoming lost in his.

* * *

Lucia slid down the pew to sit alongside him, and every part of her body tingled with awareness, drew in his scent, felt the heat radiating from him. It was all she could do to stop from laying her hand to her left and drawing him in to clasp it as he had done all those long nights while she fought the fever.

Three more nights.

Wednesday would be the Spring Solstice celebration, and then she would be gone, finally free of this torment.

* * *

Anna gazed at the burgundy banners fluttering in the breeze along the length of the keep's outer wall. She ran a hand idly along the rose at her side, its velvety petals bending beneath her fingers.

"You know, unicorns do not exist," she pointed out to Ian sadly. "It is just a fantasy, a dream that could never be true."

He laughed at that, smiling at Anna, while putting an arm around Lucia and pulling her close for a moment. "Ah, but reality is far better than any fantasy," he chided Anna. "When you open your eyes, and believe fully what is right before you, that is when you truly begin to live."

She turned to look at him. "You think so?" she asked with hope.

He nodded, his eyes drawing up to Lucia.

"I absolutely know so."

* * *

Stephen gazed at Lucia. "What is it you dream of?"

She smiled at the question. "Peace."

His voice became hoarse. "And what do you dream of in a man?"

She held his gaze, basking in the warmth it held. "Someone to stand loyally by my side, to ensure that the peace has space to blossom and grow."

Chapter 14

Lucia looked over her assembled supplies with satisfaction. She had spent the day gathering, packing, and checking her gear. The sun had already slipped below the horizon, but she was at last pleased with the results. There would be the celebration tomorrow, and then at long last she would head south to meet her brother.

Lucia knew she should get to sleep early, to strengthen herself for the big day ahead, but she was far too full of energy. What she really needed was a bath – but Ellie was off getting some well-deserved supper. The lass had been at it all day with her, helping organize and arrange the travel gear.

It struck her suddenly – the hot springs south of the wall. Ellie had said they were only a short distance from the walls, and were in a well-patrolled area. Many of the sewing women had been going to them each day as spring came on. It would be the perfect way to ease her tension and end her day.

She made her way down to the stables. James was undoubtedly at his meal as well, but she waved away the lad on duty and saddled Troy herself, running a hand fondly along his neck. In just two days the two of them would be on the road again, enjoying the fresh air, heading down to reunite with Michael. The thought filled her with joy.

There was little motion on the streets as she moved through town, and at the gates the guard smiled in welcome as she approached.

"Not going far, I imagine?"

"Just a last ride," she offered with a smile. "I will stay south, and close to the wall."

"Patrols report our entire borders are completely clear," he agreed. "Still, stay close."

She nodded, the gates were pulled open for her, and she was walking Troy beneath the streaming moonlight.

The woods folded around her, quiet, peaceful, and her heart was soothed. Tomorrow would be a cacophony of noise and people. And then, the day after, she would be gone. She would like to remember Penrith like this, quiet and serene.

There was an opening before her, and she smiled in appreciation. It was all that Ellie had said, and more. A ring of willows circled the hot spring, and gentle spirals of steam drifted from its surface. The moon shone full and luminous; the stars floating in the blackness of night seemed to twinkle as brightly as small candle flames in the sky. Every object stood out in sharp relief.

Lucia dismounted from Troy; in a moment he was munching contentedly alongside a curved sapling. She walked down to the bank and took off her boots and socks. She sat at the edge, splaying her feet in the pond. The water's warmth eased her aching toes. She sat for a while on the bank, splashing in the moonlight. The sensation was delicious.

She glanced around. There was not a sound, not a trace of movement. The water's surface was mirrored by the moon – even if a patrol came by, she would have her privacy beneath its surface. She stripped all of her clothes off and was soon drifting through the warm pool.

Homesickness swept through her. It seemed ages since she had last splashed, carefree, through the pond of her youth. So much had happened since then.

She dove under the surface and twisted, spiraling, moving through the shimmering liquid. Her troubles streamed away, her muscles easing in the warmth.

Suddenly, with great composure and calm, Lucia knew someone else was in the clearing with her.

Lucia wasn't sure how she knew this presence was not a threat, but it seemed to her the most natural thing in the world. She sensed that he was in the trees near her horse, and on her next leisurely glide around the pond she glanced in that direction. Yes - she could see a silhouette next to an elm. His hand ran down Troy's neck, and Troy gave a contented nicker before going back to eating the clover.

Stephen.

Longing spread through her, coursed down her limbs, sending tingling sparks into her fingers and toes. She craved him with every part of her being, with the depths of her soul. Thank all that was holy that she was leaving in two days. Any longer, and the torture would become unbearable.

She submerged fully, swimming underwater for several lengths, hiding from the world. If only things had been different – but they were not. She would head south, reunite with her brother, and immerse herself in the preparations for battle. It would have to be enough.

Stephen took a step into the moonlight, his gaze on her, and then he was striding down to the mossy bank. His shadowed eyes held a hesitance she had not seen before. She felt like a forest nymph, a mystical creature, and if he blinked she would vanish and be forever lost from sight.

She took a deep breath, moving toward him, keeping just her head above the mirrored surface. She drew to a halt when she was ten feet distant.

Her voice was hoarse when she spoke. "Hello, Stephen."

It seemed that Stephen's emotions rested on a knife's edge. His eyes watched her intently, and when he spoke, his voice resonated with raw emotion.

"Anna had a serious talk with me this afternoon." He paused for a long moment, letting out a shuddering breath. "We are no longer engaged."

Lucia's eyes widened in surprise; time staggered to a stop. She had steeled herself so strongly against becoming attached to Stephen, worked so hard to drive those emotions out of her mind. And now, in an instant, her fantasy was becoming a reality.

Pain and regret echoed in Stephen's voice. "I tried to do what I was supposed to do. I tried to be who she wanted me to be. I have failed. I vowed that I could change - but her decision was final."

Stephen looked down for a moment, then he blew out his breath. He looked back up at Lucia and once again she was caught in the depth of his gaze.

"I can finally say now what I have felt for so long. What I have known with every part of my being." His eyes held hers.

"I love you, Lucia."

Lucia's heart blossomed with joy, with relief, with answering emotion. Still, she stayed motionless in the water, her elation tempered by the serious look in his eyes.

What was bothering him so much, to cause him to speak in such a tense manner?

Stephen's face creased; he had the look of a man riding a thin line between joy and despair. "Lucia, I will not lie to you. I am a soldier, not a diplomat. I am a loner, not a socialite. I will not draw you into a relationship that brings you sadness, as I did with Anna. The war is upon us, and life is too short to base choice on fantasies and dreams. I need to know if, as I am, you will take me. Would you be my wife?"

Lucia exhaled a deep breath, never more sure of anything in her life. She stood and walked slowly toward him, her body glistening naked in the moonlight.

"Rather I should ask you that," she countered slowly. "I am not a woman of elegant clothing; I prefer my outfits simple and functional. I am an awful cook. My skill with a bow is not of much use in a wife. I strive for controlled emotions, but I often speak my mind when I should be silent. I race at a foe when I should wait for a better moment."

She glanced down at her body. The scars on her stomach, on her leg, glistened clearly in the moonlight. She ran a hand absently along the one made by the poisoned arrow, thinking back to that long night.

"Rather I should ask you, are you sure you will be happy with both what I can offer, and my many flaws?" She stopped when she stood before him. "This is what I am," she stated simply, feeling as if every corner of herself was open to full scrutiny. "You see me with all my injuries exposed. I am far from perfect. I am far from being the material one would require to make a proper wife." She hesitated, then forced herself to lay her heart on the line. "Even so, if you truly want me, I cannot imagine anyone but you standing beside me through troubled woes and joyous celebrations."

Stephen stared at her as if he could barely believe her meaning. "Is that truly a yes?"

Her smile grew to encompass her whole being. "Yes. Yes, yes, yes. I will absolutely be yours, now and forever."

Stephen groaned with emotion and crossed the space between them in one long stride, gathering her strongly in his arms. Lucia's wet skin molded to his clothing, so tightly were they pressed together. She eagerly ran her hands over his body, wanting to touch every part of him, feeling like they were already cohesive parts of a greater whole.

He was hers.

Stephen's mouth found hers and the kiss penetrated her entire being, at once possessive and gentle. His arms wrapped around her, and they kissed ... kissed ...

Lucia wanted more of him, all of him, and she gently pulled at him. He felt the movement and in a smooth motion he lowered Lucia to the soft ground. Lucia eagerly helped him remove his own clothing. She reveled in his muscular arms, and traced the scars she found with her fingers. She wanted to know every corner of him. Her perusal became too much for his passion, and his hungry mouth again lowered to her own. She willingly opened her full being to his onslaught. She wanted to be with him always and could think of denying him nothing.

Soon they were merging, crying out, and Lucia was laughing, kissing, hoarse, riding at heights she had never dreamt of. She would fall back, exhausted, and then he would be in motion again, and the tidal waves would sweep her back in, drawing her to even greater heights. The night went on forever.

Finally, long hours later, Lucia lay on her back in utter contentment, curling clouds drifting lazily across the star-spattered sky. Stephen rested beside her, head propped up on one arm, gazing down at her with smoky eyes. Lucia's mind was a joyous whirl. Everything had changed so quickly. She was immensely happy, beyond her wildest imaginings. The future stretched out before them, glorious, and this night was a new beginning.

She smiled up at Stephen and swept aside any worry of what might come. She would simply give in to the feelings she was experiencing now. With the war, anything could happen.

Stephen ran his hand tenderly through her hair, and she pulled him back down into her arms, her lips seeking his, wanting him, needing him.

After another long while her exhaustion overwhelmed her. She drifted into sleep, sprawled across his chest, contented beyond measure.

* * *

Lucia awoke at dawn to peaceful silence; she luxuriated in the quiet. The sun shone in a golden stream through the windows, bringing a fresh glow to the room. Eventually she noticed a weight on her stomach. To her surprise, a medley of wildflowers were strewn across her bed.

Her eyes widened - where had they come from? The events of the evening came rushing back into her awareness with a powerful rush. She didn't have any memory of returning here! Had Stephen brought her? Was it all a dream?

Her emotions were so strong that she knew at once this had been no dream. Her life had forever changed with that encounter.

Her mouth quirked in a smile. The wildflowers were real enough. She climbed out of bed and filled a pottery vase with water from the pitcher. She placed the lovely bouquet into the vase and admired it.

Next, Lucia hesitantly examined herself in the mirror. She didn't look any different ... but she certainly felt wonderful. The flowers proved that the night was no fantasy. Lucia smiled to her reflection. She dressed quickly, headed downstairs, and turned the corner into the sewing room.

Anna was standing before the doorway, and Lucia pulled up sharply, her face flushing crimson. It came to her with full force just what position she was now in.

Anna seemed blithely unaware of Lucia's turmoil, and the blonde radiated a joyfulness Lucia had not seen in some time.

Lucia's throat had gone dry. "Good morning, Anna," she finally greeted her friend.

Anna glanced around and then drew Lucia into a side chamber. The two women sat on a bench by a window overlooking the gardens below. Anna played with her hair for a moment before turning to Lucia.

"I have called it off, Lucia," she admitted with quiet joy, her voice rich with pride and satisfaction. "I have told Stephen that I did not think it was a good idea for us to get married." She smiled and watched a pair of magpies fly into a nearby tree. "I know I should be sad, but I feel free and light! I thought for so long that I could make it work, but it was simply frustrating."

Her face beamed with pleasure. "I know we will both be happier this way. Somewhere out there is the man that will truly make me happy the way he is, not the way I hope he might be."

Lucia's shoulders eased. It was clear that Anna was genuinely happy with this decision. She reached over and patted Anna's hand gently. "You took your time and thought this decision through," she reassured her firmly. "I truly think this is the way you will be happiest. It did not seem like what Stephen could offer you was what you wanted."

Anna nodded. "You are quite right, of course. I can see that now. I am glad I was able to realize it before we both made a serious mistake!" She smiled and paused for a moment. "I wanted to tell you, since you are so close to me. However, I would rather the news was not spread around quite yet. It will make the whole evening ball very uncomfortable. I will let people know about the breaking of our engagement after he leaves with your escort to Harwich. I will ensure everybody knows that it was an amicable decision, one we made together. That timing will be easier on everyone."

Lucia spoke without thinking. "Stephen is coming with me to Harwich?" Her heart swelled with immense joy. That she and Stephen would be together for the journey, riding side by side, free to talk, to laugh, to share their intimate thoughts …

She flushed and lowered her eyes. She wished they could leave immediately, so there would be no chance of an accidental slip between now and then. She had no wish to bring any unhappiness to her friend.

Anna smiled gently. "Yes, he told me this morning of his desire to go to Harwich as an escort. He thought having time away would give me the opportunity to let people know of our decision without making things uncomfortable. It was very sweet of him. We just need to get through to tomorrow morning without making a fuss."

Lucia's heart sang. Everyone would be happy. She nodded encouragingly to Anna. "That makes sense. You can count on my discretion."

A wave of guilt swept over her as she acknowledged that her silence would also protect her own actions. Should she tell Anna what had happened the previous night?

After a long moment she shook her head. Anna was feeling content with her decision. Soon Anna would fall in love with someone else, and then she would be able to hear the news of Stephen moving on with greater equanimity. It would be selfish to unburden herself now, right when Anna was still coming to terms with the situation. It was one thing to be fully honest – it was another to properly time the revelations when they could be best handled.

Anna stood and hugged Lucia. "I am so glad to have you as a friend," she enthused cheerfully. "You see everything so clearly." She took a deep breath and smiled. "Well then, I am off to get the kitchen in order for the party, then! You take care." She hurried from the room and down the hallway.

Lucia remained by the open window and gazed out, lost in thought. She was grateful that Stephen and Anna had both come to realize how ill-matched they were, and that nobody had been hurt during the process. Now Stephen was free to be wholly hers. She felt guilty for loving Stephen while he was engaged to another, but it had been Anna's choice to bring that to an end. Lucia had done her best to support Anna in her decisions.

Lucia stood and strode from the room, ready to throw herself into her final preparations for the evening's festivities.

Chapter 15

Lucia's room was flooded with springtime gold. Sunbeams streamed through her window, landing brilliantly on her new cobalt blue dress hanging on the door. What fine work Ellie was able to accomplish in so little time! Lucia was sure this was the most elegant dress she had ever owned.

Ellie turned as she stepped into the room. "There you are," she called cheerfully. "I have your rose bath drawn, so you can smell pretty for this evening. Come on," she prodded Lucia along toward the bath area, "we have got lots of work to do before we send you to the celebration!"

The next few hours were a blur for Lucia. She was powdered, made up, scented, slipped into the dress, and then Ellie spent a long time pulling and curling her hair. When it was all done, Lucia could barely recognize herself in the mirror. Ellie had indeed worked a miracle.

As a final touch, Lucia reached into the bottom of her trunk and withdrew a sapphire necklace with a gold chain and setting. The gemstone was a deep, stunning blue and brilliantly cut. It had been one of the two necklaces she kept safe while fleeing her keep.

Ellie gasped in surprise, then stood back to admire the whole effect.

"Lovely, simply lovely," crowed Ellie.

"Only because of you," responded Lucia with warmth. She drew her eyes fondly over her friend. "I am sure all the young lads will be challenging each other to duels over who is able to dance with you," she teased. Ellie was wearing a delicately embroidered white dress trimmed with yellow buttercups. With her blonde hair cascading over her shoulders, she was the very image of an elegant young woman.

Suddenly the trumpets sounded a triumphant song, and Ellie looked up. "That is our signal," she whispered to Lucia in nervous excitement. "All are gathered, and now they await the arrival of the Guest of Honor."

Lucia turned slowly in place and gave herself one last look. Ellie smiled in satisfaction.

"You radiate contentment," she sighed. "I do not know how you do it. Every man will want to be at your side."

Lucia's heart glowed. There was only one man she wished to have at her side, and soon he would be.

The halls were deserted as Lucia and Ellie headed toward the great hall. Lucia found herself slowing as they went, and Ellie squeezed her hand in support.

They approached the circular staircase above the great hall. Rich aromas of roast turkey and boar wafted up the stairs, setting her mouth watering. A low murmur of excited voices mingled with the clatter of goblets and the shuffling of feet.

Ellie went forward to announce Lucia to the trumpeter. The musician gave two short blasts and a hush fell across the great room.

A deep voice called out into the silence. "And now, the guest of honor for this evening, the Lady Lucia of Keilder."

A chorus of cheers and applause came from around the corner. Lucia took a deep breath and slowly descended the long stairs, her eyes sweeping out across the multitude.

The applause rose in volume, the cheers became more enthusiastic, and her face flushed crimson at the attention she was getting. She kept her eyes focused on the ornate oak table before her, where Lord Edmund, Ian, Stephen, and Anna were waiting for her.

Ian's eyes blazed with heat; a swirling combination of pride and possessiveness. And there was something more, a crafty, focused attention, like a wolf stalking a deer and preparing to make his leap at the tender throat. Lucia resolutely held her smile in place. This was the last night. Tomorrow she would be gone, would be finally free of his unwanted attentions.

Anna was elegance itself, with fine pearls woven into her blonde hair and an intricately embroidered gown of smoky burgundy. Her eyes also shone with pride and satisfaction. Lucia knew that Anna had helped Ellie with Lucia's dress, and she gave her friend a warm smile. Anna's talents were certainly on full display tonight. The hall's decorations were a stunning array of painted banners and curling ribbons, of floral displays and culinary achievements.

Lucia kept walking forward, nearing the table. Finally, when she could hold out no longer, she allowed her eyes to meet Stephen's.

It was all she could do to keep in motion, the force of his gaze was so powerful. Her breath caught at the love and passion which shone in his eyes. She looked away quickly, all too aware of the many watchers which followed her every step. There would be plenty of time for her to lose herself completely in Stephen's warmth over the coming weeks. For tonight, she had to play her part, and honor her final night with her hosts.

Lucia took her seat at Lord Edmund's right, with Ian on her other side. Lord Edmund smiled down at her, then turned to call out to the throngs.

"Let the feasting begin!"

Suddenly the hall was filled with a stream of servants carrying in roast boar, steamed turnips, fragrant loaves of bread, plum-stewed duck, and a myriad of other dishes. Pewter tankards clanged together and peals of laughter rung to the rafters.

Although Lucia only sipped at her wine, Ian's goblet was continually refilled. Soon he was amusing the hall with his jokes and wild tales. The meal lasted three full hours, with many courses and diversions. After the final meats were served, the hall dissolved into a one-uppance contest of daring stories.

Lucia bided her time until there was a lull in the laughter. "Sorry to interrupt," she offered, still smiling at the vision Ian had conjured up of fighting off twenty wolves' heads singlehandedly. "This looks like the perfect moment for me to distribute my presents ... or shall I take them with me?"

"No, no!" replied Ian, feigning mock horror. "By all means, get about your business!" He placed an arm around her shoulder in a hug of encouragement, and Lucia counted to three before standing to gently shake it off. She caught Ellie's eyes, and motioned for her to bring in the packages.

When Ellie returned with them, Lucia took the cloth-wrapped objects and addressed the crowd. "Here I have presents for the five people who have made my life wonderful since my arrival." The room reverberated with enthusiastic shouts and whistles. Lucia waited for them to die down, then lifted the first package. "This is for my helper, Ellie." A squeal of surprise erupted from behind her. "She is always finding pretty things for me, and I felt it was time to return the favor."

Ellie came up and shyly opened the present. The bracelet shimmered in the light, its yellow and white decorations almost gleaming. Ellie's mouth dropped open.

Lucia smiled at the girl. "With your complexion and the dresses you wear, these will look stunning," she assured Ellie. "Oh, please do not cry," she added in embarrassment as tears streamed from Ellie's eyes. "You well deserve these with how loyally you have cared for me."

"Thank you, thank you!" cried Ellie at last. She sat back against the wall again, holding the bracelet tightly.

Lucia looked out over the room. "Secondly, a present for my good friend Anastasia. Anna has been quite kind throughout my stay here." Anna smiled in thanks, then gently pulled open the fabric. Her eyes widened with delight when she saw the elegant gold and bronze necklace tucked within the folds.

"This is exceptional," she sighed in delight, holding the piece high to show it around the room.

Lucia called out over the crowd's cheers. "It was one of the two heirlooms I was able to carry with me from Keilder. The designs bring happiness and good luck," she announced, "both which Anna well deserves."

Anastasia's eyes glowed with pleasure. She brought the piece to her throat, fastening the clasp behind her nape. The crowd roared its approval.

Lucia lifted the next package high in the air, unveiling it for all to see. "For my host, Ian," she called out, "A scabbard fit for a prince!" Toasts rang out on all sides, and Ian was pulling it from her hands before she could turn.

His face beamed with pleasure as he rotated the fabric, examining it from all sides. "You are so in tune with me – this is exactly what I wanted!" He drew her into an enthusiastic hug, and it was several long minutes before Lucia could gently extricate herself from it and redirect his attention to the present. At last he pulled free his belt to slide the scabbard into place.

To her relief, the scabbard did indeed seem to complement his outfit. The gold designs in her present set off the elegant needlework on his tunic.

Lucia now turned to Ian's father, resplendent in his elaborate court wear. "For you, my Lord, a cloak to keep you warm even in the chill of winter." Lord Edmund smiled in thanks, and took the cloak with a bow. After adjusting his shoulders for a few seconds, he leaned back and smiled. "Aaah," he crooned, "This is wonderful. Just wonderful." The hall echoed in cheers.

Finally, Lucia turned to Stephen. For a moment it was as if only he and she were there, and the rest faded into a muted quiet. His eyes held hers; his gaze glowed with strength, love, and contentment. She moved her gaze quickly to the package before her, praying that their connection was not glowing as clearly to all watchers as she felt it within her own heart.

She lay a hand on the fabric square before her, looking out over the gathered crowds.

"Stephen found me in the snowstorm, when I had given up all hope. He brought me back from the brink of death, when the Grays' poison was coursing through my veins. When we were ambushed, it was his skill with the sword which kept me alive."

The hall erupted in loud cheers, and Lucia let them ring out, feeling the echo in the deepest levels of her soul. Finally, an expectant hush descended on the hall, and she looked down, unfolding the outer layer, her heart pounding.

She lifted up the folded banner. "With my most heartfelt thanks and appreciation, I offer to Stephen what he has always dreamed of." She turned to him.

Stephen glanced down at the object in her hands, and then back up to gaze into her eyes. Lucia's cheeks warmed with rich heat, and she could see clearly in his eyes that what he desired with all his heart was not being held in her hands.

She fought with every ounce of her self-control to stay her course. She held the bundle out to him, calling out to the furthest corners of the room. He deserved this praise, this acknowledgment for all he had done.

"For the man I trust in, who I am sure will regain and rebuild his homelands, I give what every leader needs. A sign to call his own."

Stephen's eyes lowered and he quickly unrolled the cloth. The fabric fell open to reveal a dusk blue banner. In its center was a golden ring surrounding an embroidered golden lamp.

Lucia ran her eyes across the banner with a critical eye. She had poured her heart and soul into the efforts, but would it be enough? Her gaze drew hesitantly to Stephen.

Stephen stood staring at the fabric for long moments, and with each beat of her heart Lucia's blood pounded in rising nervous panic. Had she disgraced him before the great hall? Was he ashamed of what she had created?

Stephen finally brought his eyes up and spoke to her, his voice pitched to reach the farthest ends of the hall. "This is the most wonderful thing I have ever received," he announced with a hoarse voice. His eyes glistened with feeling. "Thank you," he added in a softer timbre, his eyes shining with the true depth of his emotions. He then gave the fabric a shake to extend it, then turned with it, displaying it to the room.

The hall erupted into cheering and joy. Lucia took a long drink of wine to cover her blushing cheeks, deliberately keeping her eyes from returning to meet Stephen's.

Only a few more hours. She had to keep their connection hidden until they left the keep's walls. She would do everything in her power to achieve that goal.

She turned to Lord Edmund, offering him a toast and a smile. He nodded, then gave a wave of his hand. The hall burst into music as the minstrels launched into a lively tune. He stood, then, offering a formal bow to Lucia. "The first dance of the night is always my choice. I would like to have the honor of your hand as my partner. Do you accept?"

Lucia put her hand in his. "With great delight! However, I give your fair notice - I have asked the minstrels to play some of my favorite selections, depending on who my partner was."

"I trust your judgment implicitly, my dear. Lead on!"

The two walked around onto the central floor, and cheers erupted from all sides. As they settled into place, the minstrels segued into a more sedate formal dance. Lord Edmund grinned with delight as the strains from his youth filled the hall. In a moment other couples had formed lines on either side of them and the group moved back and forth in time. The dance was simple and elegant, and there was rich applause when the music ended.

Anna welcomed Lucia with a warm smile when she returned to the table. "What a wonderful choice! You dance so beautifully. You have never told me you could dance!"

"We did have some training other than military, after all, at our home," Lucia grinned back at her. Before she could take her seat, Ian, on her other side, wrapped his arm around her waist in a strong embrace.

Lucia turned quickly to see his smiling, flushed face, his eyes eagerly hinting at the dance floor. Lucia nodded and followed him up. Better to go with him now, she thought wryly, than later when he'd had even more to drink.

Lucia shook her head ruefully as the musicians nodded to each other to count out the starting beats. She had requested a fun, fast modern song for her dance with Ian. It was a tune replete with fancy footwork, which she felt he would enjoy showing off. When she had made her list for the evening, she had not accounted for Ian's level of drunkenness!

The minstrels launched into the song, and they were off. Ian did fairly well keeping up with the steps, grinning as Lucia cavorted around him. The floor filled with happy, prancing pairs as the music spun faster and faster, the floor growing crowded with the mob. The song spun on and on, the melody cycling around, pushing the dancers to the very limits of their energy. Finally the musicians brought a triumphant close, and a great cheer went up, with toasts and laughter filling the room.

The couples staggered and collapsed back onto their benches, and the hall became a chorus of calls for ale, mead, and wine.

Lucia helped Ian stumble toward the head table. She chuckled as Ian fell into his chair; he reached out immediately for his tankard. "Drink up!" he called to her. "This is a celebration!"

She shook her head and smiled down at him. It was a wonder the man could stand at all, given the volume he had imbibed.

There was a movement at her shoulder, and she was enveloped by musk and juniper, by a sense of home and comfort.

"You two made quite a pair," commented Stephen in a low voice, his breath whispering along her neck in a caress. "Yet somehow I feel the dance was not quite your style, Lucia." There was a pause, and then his voice became hoarse. "Perhaps you would give me a try?"

Lucia looked up at him and her world staggered to a halt. Stephen's eyes were dark with longing, with barely reined passion. Lucia could scarcely breathe; her heart hammered in her chest. A thin shred of sanity fought against a nearly overwhelming urge to wrap herself in his arms, to lose herself in his embrace.

She could not. She would not disrespect Anna.

She slipped her hand on his arm, her fingers sensing every curve in his muscular build, as he led her out onto the floor. The crowd hushed as she took her place before him, caught in his gaze, waiting for the music.

It seemed that the throngs around them vanished from sight. They were immersed in their own world, separate from all else. Stephen's eyes were full on her, his face steady with love. Her heart glowed to bursting. He was perfectly matched to her. He was everything she needed, she wanted, she longed for with every ounce of her body.

Stephen's eyes sparkled when the music began. It was clear he realized what dance Lucia had chosen for them. It was an ancient melody, one from before time began, a song celebrating love, devotion, and loyalty. For most in the room it would seem simply an old folk tune, wordless, with its meaning lost in the mists of time. But for her, and for Stephen, the dance resonated with a tapestry of emotion.

He took her hands and began the slow movements. Lucia matched his smile as she whirled around him, gently caressing him with the soft fabric of her cobalt dress, almost touching his face on each pass. She could feel the audience becoming part of the tension, the gentle teasing and playing the dance portrayed. As a young girl she had practiced this dance with her brother, but never really understood its significance. Now every motion was clear as Stephen's footsteps paralleled hers in large and small circles around the floor.

She trusted him implicitly; his hand was there, sure, when she leaned away from him; his arm caught hers as she went past. She knew the final pass was coming - where she would spin and fall past him; he would catch her and hold her close, leaning over her. It had been a while since she had done this - what if she was clumsy and fell? She looked into his eyes and lost all doubt. The music swelled, she turned with her back toward him, spun, and let herself fall backwards. She had committed herself and left herself in his hands.

His arms folded gently yet strongly about her body, and she was gazing up into his eyes. The music resounded to a stop, and the hall filled with wild cheering and clapping. To Lucia, the room was suddenly quiet, with just her and Stephen in each other's arms. Stephen's eyes glowed with passion, his face only inches from hers, his hands holding her with easy strength.

Then with an effort of emotion he pulled away and swung Lucia to a standing position. He bowed with her to their audience.

Speaking sideways to her during one bow, Lucia heard his muttered growl. "I almost could not stop myself," he whispered to Lucia. "But I did promise Anna."

Lucia took his hand and gave it a squeeze. "Unusual - a man true to his word," she replied softly with a mischievous grin. The moment had gotten to her as well, and she moved her mouth near his ear. "Perhaps that is why I love you so."

Stephen's head swung around in surprise; passion and longing shone in his eyes. For a moment Lucia nearly gave in to the power of his desire. She nearly took the one step forward, wrapping herself in his embrace, revealing the fullness of their adoration to the crowd of watchers.

Three courtiers were turning her with a laugh, pulling her toward the harp, and she sagged in relief. The moment was gone; she would make it through the night without hurting Anna.

The crowd cheered as she settled herself down onto the stool. She glanced around for Stephen. He was returning to his seat, the passion in his eyes at a smolder she hoped only she could see.

The crowd hushed again, and Lucia let her fingers ripple along the strings. She sang to them of love and hope, of longing and contentment. After each song the crowd called for more, the toasts and applause coming in ocean waves.

The trumpets sounded a blast behind her, and Hector was standing, his face flushed with drink. "Three in the morning, men," he called out with a laugh. "Those of you taking the morning shift, I am sure the men on the wall are eager to come get some of this delicious roast duck before the dogs lick the bones clean!"

There were good-hearted groans and complaints, but soon a portion of the men staggered their way toward the main doors. Marcus came in against the stream, making his way over to Stephen and whispering something in his ear. He pointed back toward the main gates.

Stephen nodded, stood, then looked over to Lucia. He gave her a smile that warmed her through, then a farewell bow. Then the two men joined the stream of soldiers making their way toward the courtyard.

With the departure of many of the soldiers, the servants bustled around cleaning up empty glassware, and many of those present staggered their way toward the garderobe or bed. Lucia accepted the compliments and thanks of half the room as she made her way back to the head table.

Lord Edmund raised his glass in toast to her as she took her seat at his side. "A delightful evening, my dear," he praised her. "I hope you enjoyed yourself?"

She smiled at that. "It was a night I shall never forget," she promised him. "The perfect ending to a delightful stay with you. Your hospitality is staggering, and I hope someday to be able to treat you in kind."

He looked her over, his brow wrinkling slightly in concern. "There is no rush on your departure. Are you sure you are ready for the journey? You have several injuries that are still healing, and the trip is not an easy one."

She smiled, touched by his concern. "I am quite certain I am up to it," she promised. "We will take it slowly. If I become weary, we will simply find the next inn to rest at."

Lord Edmund glanced toward the entrance doors. "I suppose, after all, heading south retreats you further from danger."

A flare of defensiveness spun through Lucia at the thought of retreat. With effort she held back the retort that sprang to her lips. The older man was simply being solicitous and meant no offense.

"A temporary retreat," she offered conciliatorily. "Soon I will return with a host of troops, and together we will take on the Grays once and for all."

He smiled at that. "It will be nice to be done with those wolves' heads, and be back to normal," he agreed. "I will see you in the morning then." He offered her a formal kiss on the cheek, then stood, calling out for his servant. In a moment he was striding off to his own chambers.

The soldiers coming off their watch streamed into the room, eagerly settling down to drink and food. An elderly man with a pot-belly launched into a bawdy song; his lanky companion joined in with off-key harmony.

Anna's voice came, amused, at her side. "Not quite the same as your beautiful harp playing," she teased.

Lucia smiled, turning to embrace her friend. "I am sure they enjoy it just as much," she pointed out. "We all have our different tastes."

Ian's voice piped up on her other side. "They are the howling of dogs, while you have the clarity of an angel of glass," he vowed. "I have never heard anything like your singing. I cannot believe you kept that from us all these weeks."

Lucia's eyes sparkled. While she had hit the notes, she knew her singing was hardly of the angelic category. She wondered what combination of his flirtatious nature and his steady marination had contributed to his high opinion.

"Thank you," she offered gently. "If I had known you would adore it so, I certainly would have offered a song at each lunch."

He wrapped an arm around her shoulder, drawing her in against him. "Well then, the moment you return to us, we can make that our new tradition! We can celebrate festivals every month of the year, with you at the centerpiece of each!"

She let him hold her for a minute before easing away, stepping forward to pick up her glass, turning to toast both of them. "We will see what the future holds," she offered with a smile. "But for now ..." She looked up at the decorations, still shimmering beautifully in the candlelight. "You two deserve the highest praise for what we have right here. The work you and Anna invested in this event will be spoken of for years. It was the most beautiful celebration I have ever seen. Everybody adored it."

Anna blushed under the praise, but Ian barely seemed to see the room around them. His voice took on a hint of petulance.

"So many people around," he muttered, "when I wanted to spend time with you alone." His eyes lit up. "I know, come walk in the gardens with me. The moonlight turns them into an enchanted fairyland of dewdrops and rainbows."

Lucia chuckled. "And unicorns, too, I suppose?"

Ian beamed. "Absolutely, I am sure a unicorn could be found."

A loud yawn escaped from Lucia's lips, and she suddenly realized just how exhausted she was. "You have been an excellent host," she vowed to Ian, patting him on the shoulder. "But I am afraid I am done in for the night. I should head up to bed."

She glanced around, looking for Ellie, but the young girl had completely vanished. She smiled fondly. She wondered if she had gone off with James; the two had seemed quite inseparable as the evening had drifted on.

Ian put his arm out to her, his chest puffing with pride. "It would be my privilege to escort you to your room, as the guest of honor," he offered

A thin tremor of nervousness wound within her, but she shook it off with a laugh. Surely the man could not cause that much trouble on such a short trip. "All right, then," she agreed.

She turned to Anna and drew her into a hug. "Good night, Anna. The party was spectacular. You have truly found your calling in life."

Anna beamed, and offered a wave as Lucia and Ian walked across the hall toward the long stairs.

Ian prattled on about the ethereal flowers in his garden, the beautiful decorations of the party, and his ever-growing praise for her scabbard as they ascended the stairs and made their way down the empty hallways. Finally they drew to a stop before her door, and he turned to face her.

His voice lowered in tone, and his eyes became more serious, more focused on her own. "Lucia, my darling, I can barely believe you are leaving me." Before she knew it he had taken up her hands in his own, and was staring longingly into her eyes. "You know I care for you deeply. I hate the idea of you going off alone without me to protect you, but I cannot desert my home when they need me so desperately." He gave her fingers a squeeze. "Can you promise me you will return as soon as you can? I will be counting the days until I see you again."

Lucia gently withdrew her hands from his. "I promise to return with my troops as soon as possible," she assured him.

"And you will stay?" he pressed her.

She lifted the latch, pushing her door open. "Certainly, as we plan out our assaults on the Grays," she agreed. "And then we will push them north, and up, and finally out of my homelands." Her eyes glowed with relief and joy at the thought.

Ian followed her through the door to her room, his eyes close on hers. His voice came out in a half snarl. "Your homelands, your homelands. Is that all you and Stephen can ever talk about?" he growled.

Lucia's eyes snapped up at Stephen's name, and Ian's eyes widened, then he had slammed his fist into her door, driving it shut. He moved to stand between her and the door, his gaze hardening, his face billowing crimson with fury.

"Is it Stephen, that bastard? Has he come between us? Tell me!"

Lucia shook her head in denial, but he angrily grabbed her shoulders. "I saw the way you danced together. I saw how he looked at you. He stole you from me! You were mine! You should still be mine!"

Lucia cried out in surprise and tried to pull away, but he was strong with fury and passion. Lucia let out a shocked shriek, but the thick door muffled her cries from the rest of the castle. She tried to shake his hands loose from her. This was her friend! She didn't want to hurt him!

Ian's grip dug into her arms, wrenching her backwards. She had to get away, she had to get him to stop - but he wouldn't stop ...

* * *

Stephen looked steadily out toward the forest, wishing for the hundredth time that Lord Edmund would agree to cut it back another fifty feet. The twisty shadows were nearly impossible to see through, and it took every ounce of his effort to distinguish rock from branch.

Shawn ran a hand through his greying hair, looking over at Marcus. "I am sorry to have disturbed you both; it was probably nothing," he admitted to Stephen. "I just thought –"

"You thought right," reassured Stephen. "It is always better to be sure. But I think tonight will be a peaceful one, thank God."

There was a thundering of hooves from behind him, and he turned with surprise, staring down the main road. His heart slammed to a stop. It was Ellie. The girl was deathly afraid of horses, and it showed in her frozen face, in the rough bouncing that nearly threw her off. What could have driven her to this state?

He flew down the steps, Marcus and Shawn hard on his heels. He was at her side in three strides.

"What is it?"

Ellie immediately burst into hysterical sobbing, unable to speak a word.

Stephen vaulted onto the horse behind her, pulling the reins hard, wheeling the steed in place. He launched into a hard gallop back in the direction of the castle.

He put an arm around Ellie to calm her, his voice holding soft steel. "Was it at the party?"

They were passing the richer district. "No," replied Ellie between sobs, "They were just gone ... I asked Anna ... she said ... Ian had walked Lucia upstairs ..." Ellie buried her face against Stephen's arm, shaking uncontrollably. Stephen's grip tightened on the reins, then, regaining control with an effort, he nodded in dawning understanding.

"Go on," he encouraged bitterly. The horse thundered on along the street, the buildings beside them a blur.

Ellie took a shuddering, deep breath. "I followed them, to make sure she was all right," she cried. "I went to the room ... and ... he was in there and..." Ellie burst into racking sobs, unable to continue.

Stephen swore loudly, urging the horse to his fastest possible pace. The town raced by in a montage of stone and wood. Reaching the main steps, he leapt off the steed, with Ellie and his men close behind. He charged up the stairs and through the hall. The castle guards they passed took one look at their set faces and joined in behind. Fury and guilt swept over him as he raced down the hallway toward her door.

Lucia was so happy when he left her, playing the harp before admiring fans. How could this have happened?

Reaching the door, he held up his hand to the others and stopped to listen for a moment, his heart pounding. Maybe, just maybe, Ellie had an overactive imagination.

There was silence for a moment. Then Ian's deep voice reverberated loud and clear through the door. "Had enough, whore?" came the shout, followed by a heavy thud. "You will learn to love me, once you are properly broken. You can count on it."

The guards surrounding the door growled in shock and outrage. Stephen was beyond feeling anything. A single, all-consuming hatred for Ian threatened to overwhelm him. His long-time friend, his foster brother whom he had trusted with his life, was now his enemy.

Stephen yanked at the door, but it was solidly locked. He thumped on it several times, then stood back. His voice a cold flash of steel, he called loudly, "Open this door, Ian, or I swear before God, I will make you pay with your life!"

Muffled curses came from the other side of the door, followed by the sound of glass breaking. Ellie came to her senses at the sound. "This way, through my door," called Ellie in panic. Stephen followed her quickly around through the other two rooms. He motioned for the others to stay back, then swung the door open and stepped into Lucia's room, sword ready.

Chapter 16

Stephen's grip on his sword weakened as he looked around Lucia's normally white and pure room. The window was broken out, a cool breeze swirling the torn curtains into the room. Fabric, clothing, jewelry, and furniture lay scattered like leaves on the floor. Lucia's nude body curled, unmoving, at the center of the bed, bloodstains scattered around her in a dappled spray.

Stephen called over his shoulder. "Ian is gone," he announced tersely. "Marcus. Shawn. I want you to find him, and bring him to me." The pair nodded and raced from the room. Stephen continued, "Ellie, get Brother Matthew." The maid bit back a sob and hurried to obey.

The room settled into silence. Stephen carefully closed the door behind him and eased cautiously over to the bed.

Lucia's body was layered with bruises and cuts. She lay motionless, curled up into a ball in the bed's center, eyes closed. Heart pounding, Stephen knelt on one knee at the side of the bed and shakily brushed a stray hair from her eyes.

Lucia flinched, and Stephen let his breath out with relief. She was conscious, at least. "It is me, Lucia. It is Stephen," he whispered soothingly. "Everything is going to be all right. Matthew is coming. Come on, Lucia, open your eyes. Everything is going to be fine."

Every instinct within Stephen called on him to draw her into his arms, but a sharp trembling tickled along each surface of her body. Surely she was in shock, and had to be handled with the utmost of care.

"Michael, is that you?" she rasped weakly, her eyes resolutely shut.

A flare of jealousy moved through him at that; he pushed it down, carefully sliding his hand into her own.

"It is me, my love. It is Stephen. Open up your eyes, Lucia." He stroked her hair gently with his free hand. "I am here to take care of you. Please, open your eyes."

Her voice was tinged with delirium, an echo of her worst night fighting the poisoning. "Michael, let me go," she pleaded softly.

Stephen let out a breath, holding her hand gently. If she was lost in a hallucination, maybe it was best to wait it out, to let it run its course.

Her voice eased out of her, half whisper. "You remember, Michael. I trusted him." She winced. "He betrayed us all. I swore never …"

Tears slipped from her eyes, and he twined his fingers more tightly into her grasp. The words ground out of him. "Stay with me, Lucia," he pleaded.

"… betrayed …," she repeated, her voice barely audible. "Let me go … please …"

There was a noise behind him, and Brother Matthew stepped into the room, carrying a large leather bag.

"God's Teeth," he swore, drawing in the chaos of the room and Lucia's battered body in one glance. "How badly is she hurt?" He moved forward, and Stephen stepped back to let him near.

Lucia's eyes flew open, and she was sitting, looking around wildly. "Stephen?" she cried out in panic. "Stephen?!"

"I am here," he vowed, dropping back at her side, easing her in against him, and she was sobbing, collapsing into him. He drew his hand shakily down her hair, soothing her, holding her bloodied body close.

He glanced up at Matthew, motioning with his head to the other side of the bed. Gently Stephen lowered her back down on the pillow, and her tremors quieted as she gazed into his eyes. After a minute Matthew was able to begin his careful examination while Stephen twined his hand into hers, stroking her hair in a soothing rhythm.

Ellie moved quietly around the room, gathered up all of the fabric and broken pottery, and ferried the items into her own room. After a while she returned with a mug of mulled wine. Stephen glanced at Matthew, and he nodded somberly, drawing the blanket up over Lucia's body. Stephen eased her to a sitting position, and it was as if time scrolled backward, as if once again she was caught in the agony of the fever, and he was carefully bringing the mug to her lips. She drank with weary movements, and in a moment he was helping her back down again. Her eyes closed, and within minutes her grip had loosened as she faded into sleep.

Stephen brushed the hair gently from her face, gazing at her for a long minute before standing. Matthew followed him into the adjoining room. Ellie was standing before the fireplace, somberly feeding the remains of clothing and fabric into the blaze.

Matthew kept his voice low. "She is not injured seriously," he reported in relief. "Bruised, some shallow cuts, but no broken bones. Given the blood, I would imagine Ian took quite a beating himself."

Stephen's muscles tensed at the image of Ian raising a fist to Lucia, of the valiant woman struggling for her life. He pushed the emotion down with an effort.

Matthew glanced between Ellie and Stephen. "Keep her quiet for tonight. No need to disturb her further right now.

Tomorrow we can wash and bandage her, and see what to do next."

Stephen nodded in agreement, and in a moment the brother had left the room. Stephen glanced back through the doorway to Lucia's bed, but she remained motionless on it, still apparently asleep.

He lowered himself into a chair by the fire, staring into its glowing embers. He spoke to Ellie without turning. "Tell me exactly what happened," he instructed quietly. "Every detail, from the beginning."

Ellie nodded, settling in a slump at his feet, arms wrapped around her knees. She began from the moment Lucia had walked down into the great hall, every eye on her beauty. She reviewed every movement, every action along the way. Stephen hoped for some clue, some indication of what had happened. But when Ellie had finished, he was left with the same simmering rage, the same bafflement at the senselessness of the attack. Ian had simply assaulted Lucia with no provocation.

Stephen stood and paced across the room. If only he'd been here ... His fury grew with each step.

There was a movement by the hallway door, and Marcus stepped into the room, his eyes shadowed.

Stephen's hand fell to his hilt. "Well?"

Marcus shook his head. "I am sorry, Stephen. The gatekeepers let him through moments after he fled the room. The trail goes cold within a few hundred feet. We have the guards roused, but the man grew up here. He knows every rock, every stretch of stream. The chance of tracking him down -"

"I will go myself," snapped Stephen in heat, striding toward the door.

A weak call came from the bedroom. "Stephen?"

Pain seared through his heart to hear her voice so shaken. He looked down, marshaling his emotions. Then he glanced up at Marcus. "Do the best you can."

Marcus nodded grimly, turning and closing the door behind him.

Stephen moved quietly back into Lucia's room. Ellie had done a good job of cleaning it; it looked almost normal, almost as if the chaos had not happened. The alabaster coverlet hid the blood, hid the damage inflicted on Lucia's body.

He lowered himself into the chair at her side, easing a hand along her cheek.

"What is it, my love?"

There was fear now in her eyes, and a wave of anger passed through him. How could Ian have done this to her? He fought it down with effort.

"I wanted to talk with you, Stephen," she muttered uncertainly. "Did you have to go somewhere? I cannot sleep ..." She looked uncertainly into his eyes.

"I will never leave you again, my love," he vowed fiercely. "I will not let anything hurt you." He gently cupped the side of her bruised face with his hand. "It is going to be all right." He wasn't sure who he was reassuring.

"When he pushed me into the room," explained Lucia hesitantly, "I was so afraid ... I was not sure what to do. He was my friend; I did not want to hurt him. I thought I was misreading his intentions. And then he pushed me, and pulled at my dress, and..." Lucia turned her face to Stephen's chest and sobbed quietly. He held her, saying nothing. There was nothing for him to say.

After a few minutes, Lucia slowed her breathing. She took some deep breaths and tried again. "I do not know why I could not fight him," she admitted, her voice thick with emotion. "If it was anyone else, if it was a Gray, or a bandit, I am sure I could have grabbed a weapon from somewhere. A poker from the fireplace, a candlestick from the table. But I just could not think. I could not act. I did not want to hurt him."

She gulped softly and her eyes held the rawest of pain. Her voice was a shadow of a whisper. "Does that mean I somehow ... wanted it?"

Stephen held her face gently with his hand, and raised her chin so she looked directly into his eyes. "Now listen to me," he instructed with firm resolve. "You thought he was a friend, and he betrayed you. His actions were wrong, and they were not, I repeat not, your fault. You are not to blame for this. You are *not* to blame."

She shivered, the tremor running full down her length. He pulled her closer, still looking down at her. "You went to the ball weaponless because you trusted us. You stayed alone with him because he was your friend." His eyes darkened. "He, and he alone, will pay grievously for this crime he has committed." He pulled Lucia close again, holding her as the sobs swelled and overtook her.

* * *

Lucia eased her eyes open against the dense night. The oil lamp glowed from the side table, embers flickered in the fireplace, and Stephen's dark eyes were full on her, shadowed and serious.

Was she still fighting the poison? Her body ached as if a thousand demons had battered her, and she could taste blood in her mouth.

"I am here," he murmured to her, gently brushing the side of her face. "You should rest."

She nodded, blinking, allowing her heavy eyelids to fall shut again.

* * *

A hesitant knocking sounded on the door, and Lucia opened her eyes a slit. It was barely dawn; a cool, grey light streamed in through the window. Stephen glanced down at her, then reluctantly rose, moving over to the door and sliding the bar free. He drew the door open, and Anna eased in, her face pale and frightened.

"Oh, Stephen, is it true?" she whispered, peering around him to look toward the bed.

Lucia remained still, feigning sleep, unwilling to be drawn into conversation. Not now, not when it was all still a jumble of confusion in her head. Anna was Ian's cousin, after all. Lucia was the stranger here, the intruder in their world.

She heard Stephen guide Anna over to the chair by the window, heard them talking in a low tone. It sounded intimate.

A flush of jealousy washed through her. The two had been engaged, after all. And now that Ian had turned her into damaged goods …

Lucia nuzzled down deeper into the blankets, muffling the sounds of the room, blocking the sight of the people in it.

He would no longer want her.

The certainty of it grew within her with every passing breath. She had to get away.

It came to her suddenly that she *was* getting away. Today was the date of her departure to Harwich. A sense of relief flooded over her. She could put everything behind her. She could start with a completely clean slate.

There was a mumble of voices from the other room, and Matthew stepped in. Stephen eased Anna into the adjoining area, and an emptiness slid into Lucia's heart as she watched them go. She turned her focus inward, watching with attention as Matthew carefully cleaned her wounds and bandaged them. The damage was not serious. She would heal. In a short while he was moving back into the other room, closing the door behind him. The murmur of voices grew again.

Lucia could imagine Anna's pale face, envision Stephen's sturdy arm wrapping around the blonde to support her. Her face hardened. Best she leave them both here to get through their grief. She took in a deep breath, then pushed the blankets off her, looking again down at her bandaged body.

The north was no place for the frail.

It was time for her to get into motion.

She pushed herself to her feet, moving to the dresser. She carefully eased on her pants, her tunic, drawing on her traveling gear, falling into the familiar routine. She pulled on her boots, then brushed her hair out, weaving it into a long, simple plait. She turned to fasten the copper pin …

The twisting motion sent a sharp, agonizing pain through her side, and she moaned, staggering back against the bed with a hard thunk.

The connecting door flew open, and Stephen was striding in, his hand on his hilt, glancing around sharply. His mouth opened to speak, and then something in her eyes made him stop. His gaze shadowed.

Lucia pushed herself up from the bed with an effort, turning again to fasten the plait with the pin. Then she brought her gaze around to look over Stephen. His sturdy shoulders, the lean muscles, the dark brown eyes, all called to her with a haunting draw.

She shook her head, looking down at her sword belt. If he still chose to come on the trip with her, it would be as a bodyguard, nothing more.

Lucia focused her effort on keeping her voice absolutely even. "We had plans to leave this afternoon. I intend to depart on schedule. I have nothing to keep me here."

She glanced up to hold him with her gaze. "Lord Edmund promised me six men as an escort. Do I still have them?"

She stood still, waiting for his answer. She knew in her heart that she could not remain within these walls for another night. She would go on with or without his help.

Stephen took a deep breath, then let it out, nodding. "If you are up to the trip, you will have the assistance agreed on," he replied quietly. "When do you want to leave?"

"Immediately."

Every fiber in her body craved to know if he would now remain behind with Anna, if the place at her side would remain empty. A hollowness swelled within her, threatening to overwhelm her.

His gaze sharpened, holding her eyes. His voice was raw. "Lucia?"

Her throat tightened, and her eyes dropped to the hilt at his side, to the sturdy hand which still rested on it. "Will -"

She cut herself off. She would not plead for him to come.

His eyes followed hers, and there was an easing to his tenseness, a gentling to his eyes. "Yes," he answered hoarsely. "I will go with you, and remain at your side."

A flickering of light glimmered in the darkness within her, the most hesitant glow.

Lucia looked over herself. She was ready for the trip. She glanced over at the door – and suddenly she found herself frozen with fear.

He could be waiting on the other side.

He would be laughing at her, trumpeting his victory over her, wondering in a boastful laugh if she were ready for another round.

Her breath caught in her throat, and she could not move.

Stephen gave a low groan, and he took a half step toward her before reining himself in. When he spoke, his voice was a low growl.

"You are safe," he informed her. "Ian has fled. He is long gone. He has not only left this keep, but we cannot find him anywhere within the borders of his father's land."

Lucia breathed a deep sigh of relief.

Ian was not here.

She would not have to face him. She could leave unhindered, and head south, south, until Michael drew her into his arms and told her everything would be all right.

Nodding, she willed her feet into motion, the right, then the left, and pulled open the door.

Chapter 17

Lucia's shoulders eased as Stephen and Marcus led the group beneath the main gates of the keep and turned south toward the main road. The late March weather was warm, with clear skies and a gentle breeze. With luck, even at the slow pace they would keep to nurse her injuries along, they would make it to Harwich within three weeks. And then she would be back with Michael, back with her beloved friends, and everything would return to normal.

Niggling thoughts danced at the corner of her awareness, thoughts of what had happened the previous night, but she resolutely prevented them from coming into view. That was in the past. Her only concern right now was maintaining her seat in Troy's saddle, watching for potholes in the road, and checking on her bandages occasionally to ensure all of her various wounds and injuries were healing properly.

Stephen and Marcus were silent ahead of her, their eyes constantly scanning the road ahead, but behind her the three keep guards kept up a constant, excited chatter. This trip was apparently a novelty for them, and the thrill of it echoed in their every word.

The noise intruded on Lucia's sense of calm, and after a few minutes she nudged Troy into a trot. She moved around Stephen's left side, took the lead, and put enough distance between her and the group that the bubbling voices of the guards faded to a quiet hum. Soon the sounds of her horse's hooves and the birds in the streaming sunlight were all that filled her world.

Just right.

It was easier, now, to keep her mind quiet, to simply become one with nature. Their smaller road joined up with a main path, and they headed nearly straight south, the sun slowly tracing a curve across the sky and toward the horizon. They passed through the occasional village, and stopped every second hour or so to stretch their legs and give the horses a chance to rest. She would not admit it to the others, but she greatly appreciated the breaks. As the day wore on, the aches grew in intensity, and by evening it was all she could do to hold back a groan when sliding off Troy.

Stephen strode over, his eyes on her in concern. "We have pushed quite far enough for the first day," he murmured. "There is an inn another half-mile ahead; we would do well to rest there for the night."

Her brow creased. "What, at an inn?" She looked around the clearing where they had stopped. There was a gentle river running to the east, a good, flat spot of grass, and even a small fire ring left by previous travelers. "Surely this is fine?"

His eyes moved down to the injury at her leg. "Would you not be more comfortable in a bed?"

She gave her head a shake. "Not at all. I prefer it out here. Unless you – "

He gave a half smile, shaking his head as well. "Absolutely not," he agreed. "It is settled then."

The group hobbled the horses and set up camp. Bread and cheese were passed around, and she took a long pull on her ale as the sun finally eased in violets and purples past the edge of the world. The keep guards were curling up in their cloaks in short order, apparently exhausted at the day of riding, as slow as it had been.

Stephen and his two friends sat by the fire and stared into it, immersed in their thoughts.

Lucia's body ached, but she was not sleepy. She stood, stretched, then walked down to the stream. It burbled quietly in the darkening night, the water slipping past mossy rocks and tangled twigs.

The night seemed crystal clear. Every sound, every animal moving around, was a distinct occurrence in the nighttime air. She marveled at her senses. She had noticed during the day how keen her perception seemed, but at night she sensed its sharpness a thousandfold.

She pulled a fresh parchment scroll out of her cloak pocket; the scroll and ink was a parting gift from Anna. She opened it slowly, marveling at the newness of it. The clean, tan surface seemed to invite her thoughts. She sat on a rock overlooking the moving water and gazed about her at the dark green trees, their lines sharp in the moonlight. She enjoyed the stark contrasts. She pulled out her pen and ink, and began.

Stately trunks divide
Dark from dark, and yet
nighttime breathes as one.

Lucia smiled; she had always liked the night. Shadows in the moonlight were crisp, not hiding anything. For some reason she felt in control. She glanced up at the cool, clear sky; the stars twinkled with a pure white light.

Beacon-like gleaming,
Calling strongly, or
Sending down a sign?

She took in a long, deep breath of the night air, the ebony darkness wrapping gently around her. A sparkling thought floated at the edge of her mind that she should lie down and get some rest, but for some reason a tremor of fear accompanied that glistening mote. She pushed it out of her mind. Right now things were quiet and serene. She would remain here, in this moment, and be safe.

Shadowy clouds drifted across the moon, the constellations wheeled in their path, and her mind remained a calm sea without ripples or waves. It seemed but a breath's length when a soft, rosy glow swelled in the east, and a new day approached.

Stephen's eyes were hollow and shadowed as she walked back into the camp.

"You should have gotten some rest," he stated tersely. "Your body needs to heal from the injuries."

Lucia glanced down at her bandages. Part of her knew he was right, but she flared at being told how to manage her own body.

"I am fine," she snapped back, moving to the fire to roust it into life.

His eyes held worry, but he did not speak again as they shook awake the keep guards and passed around breakfast. In short order they had saddled the horses and begun the slow walk south.

When Lucia again nudged her horse forward to take the lead position, Stephen's steed was right at her side. His voice was brusque as they settled into a walk at the front of the group.

"Perhaps you forget that we are escorting you," he pointed out. "You should stay in the center of the party for the greatest safety. We may have left the Gray's range of destruction, but there are other wolves' heads on the road."

A hot temper flared within Lucia. "I am barely ten horse lengths ahead of you!" she shot back. Her hand dropped to the hilt at her side. "And, believe me, if bandits do come, I will be quite capable of wielding my sword. I am no helpless maid."

He moved to say something more, then glanced at her eyes and stopped. After a moment he nodded. With clear reluctance he reined in, allowing her to move ahead, falling in alongside Marcus.

The group quickly fell into a rhythm for the day; the long rides broken by stops for meals and rest was a pattern Lucia knew well from her days on patrol. The pace was far slower than she would have liked, but the growing aches of her body reminded her that she was far from healed.

She was beyond exhausted when they pulled into a small clearing by a pond, dusk easing crimson fingers across the sky. It was all she could do to hobble her horse, to force a few pieces of cheese into her mouth before tumbling down into a small patch of moss at the side of the clearing.

She had barely finished arranging her cloak around her when darkness swept in and overtook her.

Ian's weight had her pinned to the bed, and she stared up at him in unbelieving confusion. Her mind could not wrap itself around what was happening. Surely he would start laughing in a minute, explain this was all a joke of some sort, a rough, drunken joke which had gone horribly wrong.

And then his hand was sweeping down toward her head, and her vision blurred, then staggered into focus again, and she fought ... she fought ...

Her eyes flew open in the dense dark, tears streaming down her face, and Stephen was there kneeling at her side, his gaze rich with concern.

His voice was rough. "It is only a dream," he soothed her. His hand moved shakily out toward her cheek.

She rolled sharply away, turning her back on him, pulling her cloak higher around her shoulders, nestling her head down within its folds. There was stillness behind her for a long minute, and then she heard him rise to his feet and move back toward the campfire.

Dawn was still a long way off, but she steadfastly fought off any thoughts of sleep, waiting for the cold light of dawn.

* * *

It was all Lucia could do to hold herself in the saddle. The sun was only in the midday position, high in the clear, pale-blue sky, but she was beyond exhausted. Her head drooped, and she gave it a shake, willing herself to keep alert. They had a ways to go yet if they were to stay on the schedule she had set.

There was a sound and a movement, and Stephen had come up alongside her. His eyes rich with concern. He held her gaze for a moment, and when he spoke his voice was low.

"We should call it a day," he advised her. "You will do your kinsmen no good if you drive yourself past the brink of health. You need to rest."

Lucia's thin hold on her reserves of strength stretched to its breaking point. She could feel the draw of Stephen's strength, his courage, and it was all she could do to maintain the wall between them, to keep him safely on the other side of her protective shield. Her voice was sharp and harsh.

"What I *need* is to get back to my family," she shot out. "This is my trip. *My* trip." She drilled her eyes straight ahead, focusing with every ounce of her sanity on the path before them. "And if you continue to harass me, you will awaken one morning to find me gone."

Stephen took a long, deep breath. Then, nodding, he pulled to a stop, again allowing her to move forward on her own. When he fell in with Marcus she could hear the low murmur of voices. She had no doubt what the men were discussing. She would be under close watch from this point forward.

A wry smile tweaked at her lips. As if they could stop her, did she truly decide to run. They might have spent years in wilderness raids on the Grays, but she had put in her own years of patrol duty. She knew how to slip through night shadows and remain unseen.

By the time dusk tickled the edges of the horizon, Lucia could barely see the road before them, her vision had become so blurred. She slid her way down Troy's side in agony, and when Stephen came alongside her and began handling the saddle and grooming, she did not voice a protest. She would just take a short nap before supper. The aches in her leg, her side, her back just needed a few minutes to …

Lucia stood on the front steps of her keep, her chest heaving, the moans of the dying spread out before her in the open courtyard. The few remaining Grays were streaming away from her, some carrying wounded comrades, and her eyes were drawn to the main arch of the curtain wall gate.

Evan was standing there, his face bright with triumph, his gaze holding hers with arrogant pride. She could see it with perfect clarity. He would be back, again, and again, until he had driven her keep into submission.

And her father would fall defending it …

Her shoulders were shaking with sobs, her face was wet with tears, and a steady hand was twining into her own, soothing her. His voice was low and rough.

"Lucia …"

She pulled her hand away, turning, curling up, struggling to bring her breathing under control. She waited for him to ease to his feet, to leave her, but he did not. He remained by her side, steadfastly, and after several long minutes her breath was coming in longer draws, her shoulders eased. A tiny glimmer of security warmed her, and she drifted back down into an ebony pool.

* * *

Lucia rode at the head of the group, finally feeling at least a shadow of her former self. The rest had done her some good, and her body was slowly healing. The arrow wound from the snowy ambush was a thin scar which only troubled her when she turned sharply. The slice in her leg from the attack by the stream was still red, but with time that, too should fade.

And the more recent injuries …

She gave her head a shake, pushing them out of her mind. Somehow she would heal.

* * *

A week passed, then two. Each day had her riding alone at the head of the group, her mind deliberately blank and clear, no thought beyond the next hoof-fall of her steed. The dreams still came at night, jarring her awake with their power, but each time Stephen was there at her side. He no longer spoke; simply knelt there, his eyes warm on her. Each time she turned away, but his gentle presence soothed her, allowed her to pass the rest of the night in a dreamless oblivion.

Chapter 18

They had passed Bedford, a week remained of their journey, and the road had more traffic with each passing day. Lucia imagined it was a combination of the warmer weather and the more populated part of the lands which had them passing penitent pilgrims, merchant carts overflowing with goods, and the random detritus which comprised the world.

She ran a hand gently down her leg, smiling as there was no echo of pain at her movement. She was, finally, healing well. Soon she would be by Michael's side. Everything would be back to normal.

A twinge tugged at her. She had the thought, suddenly, that Michael would know she was different – that she was playing a part. She pushed it away with fierce effort. She was the same as she had always been. She was now simply stronger, firmer in her resolve. Nothing had changed.

A lone rider came up over the hill toward them, a rough cloak not quite covering the long sword at his hip. Hoofbeat sounded from behind her, and in a moment Stephen was pulling in at her side, his eyes focused on the man before them. She knew she should feel annoyed at his protectiveness, but instead a sense of warmth stole over her, and for a moment the vision flashed in her mind of the way they had stood side by side at the stream facing down the Grays.

She pushed away the image sharply. That was in the past, and the past was gone to her. She forced herself to concentrate on the man as he came toward them, as he gave a curt nod and rode along past them.

Soon it was only their party on the road, and Lucia waited for Stephen to pull in, to ease back to ride with Marcus, as he had for the past two weeks. But he did not. He remained by her side, not speaking, not looking over. She knew she should speak up, should push him to leave her alone, but she could not put breath behind the words. A deep ache nestled within her heart, and his presence by her side was a soothing balm, easing a tenseness within her.

* * *

All color had drained from the scene. The alabaster curtains billowed into the room, driven by a strong breeze, glowing against the dark shadows. The once pristine ivory sheets beneath her were now speckled with dark sprays of blood. Ian's ebony form sucked the heat from her heart as he violently twisted her back into place, wrenching her wrist as she struggled with all her might.

"I will not yield!" she screamed, flailing against him, pulling open the wound at her leg, pain ripping through her very soul. "I will not yield!"

Stephen's voice was rough but steady at her side. "I know you will not," he vowed.

Her eyes opened; her breath caught. He was there, kneeling beside her, his eyes holding concern and pride. There was no other sound in the dark camp.

A sigh eased out of her, and she knew she should turn, should put her back to this man who so resolutely remained at her side. But she could not bring herself to do it. She gazed up at him, tears wetting her cheeks, her breath easing, and after a long moment there was a new emotion in his eyes, of soft hope.

She closed her eyes, letting the sleep wash over her.

* * *

Lucia reined in at the crest of the hill, a long breath easing out of her. The three weeks had been arduous, but she had made it. Harwich lay spread before her in the growing dusk, torches glittering along its narrow lanes. And beyond it, the sea glistened like a polished jewel, reflecting the rays of the setting sun. A breeze off the water brought a sharp tang, and she pulled her cloak tightly around her.

Her eyes scanned the motley collection of boats anchored in the harbor. Which one was Michael's? She gave her head a soft shake. Even with her delays, she could easily have beaten him here. She would need to go down and find out if he had arrived yet. If not, she would settle into an inn and await him.

She gave her horse a nudge, heading him down the long slope toward the scattering of out-buildings. They wended along narrow streets, moving their way toward the wharf. Seagulls cried out overhead, and there was the steady whoosh of the sea as they drew closer to the waterfront. Piles of aging barrels and half-broken crates lay littered amongst the low buildings.

A large, red-bearded man was climbing up out of a dinghy onto a wharf, and her heart sang with joy.

Charles. The Captain of the guard.

She was off Troy in an instant, running full tilt toward him, and he turned at her approach, putting out his arms, sweeping her up into a powerful bear hug.

"Lucia! Thanks be to God! You are all right!" After a long while they parted, and he stood back to look at her. "We were concerned when you were not here to meet us.

You should have easily been weeks ahead of our arrival. I have to warn you, Michael was fit to be tied."

Stephen had come up alongside them, and his face shadowed. He looked out toward the sea for a moment, his shoulders tight.

Lucia clapped her hand affectionately on the larger man's arm. "I will be sure to personally reassure him I am quite fine, Charles. How was the voyage?"

Charles grimaced at the memory. "The trip was horrendous. There was a great storm, and it was only due to the Captain's skills that no one was hurt badly. I am not sure where the rest are, but Michael is down at the Copper Kettle, asking after horses. I'll warn you, Harwich seems a bit rough ..." He looked over Lucia's well-toned form and chuckled broadly. "Not that that would ever be a problem for you, of course."

He turned and nodded with his head. "The place is right down this street here." He pointed to a dingy alley behind the group. "I will be coming down later, as soon as we get the ship settled. We actually just got in a short while ago. Your timing, as always, is perfect."

* * *

Stephen watched as Lucia fell easily into her role with her fellow soldier. Clearly the man had great respect for her, and Stephen could see the change in her bearing, in her stance. She would slip with ease into the protection of her family and friends, and she would be lost to him.

He wondered for the hundredth time if he should have pushed her harder to face her demons, to break down the walls she had erected. But he knew he could not do it. She needed to heal in her own time. If that meant that he had lost his only chance, that she would return to Michael, and all he offered ...

He turned his head again, looking out at the ocean, willing himself to acceptance.

Lucia gave a final hug to the sturdy warrior before her, then turned to lead her horse up a narrow, shadowed alley. Stephen dismounted and followed close after her, his hand resting on the hilt of his sword. Charles had been right in his description; a number of seedy characters lurked in doorways, watching them with interest as they passed. Lucia's step did not slow, and Stephen stayed steadily behind her.

She drew to a halt. He glanced up; they had reached a dingy inn, and the well-worn sign above them simply depicted a copper pot over an open fire. He handed his reins to Marcus and followed Lucia through the heavy door. The room inside was nearly lost in shadows, lit only by a roaring fireplace and a few wall torches. Night had come on outside, a pitch black weight settling over the small town.

The large main room was packed with twenty sturdy oaken tables mobbed by shadows of boisterous sailors and merchants. The shapes were robust and, to a man, they seemed well armed. The fire roared, dancing an orange edge along the scene.

Stephen's eyes were drawn to a table by the back wall. A well-built man in leather armor sat there, his eyes carefully surveying the room, exuding an aura of strength. Two soldiers sat by his side, conferring with him in low voices. A tremor ran down Stephen's spine. If this room rose into motion against Lucia, he would give his life to hold it back, but he knew it would not be enough.

Suddenly, the room became quiet, and all eyes turned to gaze at the two entering the room. Stephen stepped up alongside Lucia, his hand settling more carefully on the hilt of his sword. A tense moment of silence pulled him to the edge of retreating, of dragging her to safety.

Glancing over at Lucia, Stephen saw her attention was fully on the brown-haired warrior across the room from her.

The breath eased out of her in relief and joy. "Michael."

Stephen followed her gaze. Michael slowly rose, his expression easing from concern to bright thankfulness. Then his arms were stretched wide, Lucia was running, and she flung herself into his arms with laughter. They embraced as if they would never let each other go.

Stephen moved across the room to come up alongside them, taking in the easy way they held each other, the love in Michael's eyes as he stood back and looked her over. "No serious injuries, then?" Michael asked with a smile. "When you were not waiting for us, I began to think the worst. I should have known that nothing on our God's green earth could ever hold you back."

Michael glanced at Stephen for a moment, his eyes dropping to the hand that still rested on the hilt of his sword. Then they swung to look out back across the room. "Where are the others? Stabling the horses?"

Lucia's face clouded, and she dropped her eyes. "We had almost made it to Penrith when we were ambushed," she murmured. "They died defending me. They are all lost."

Michael's eyes shadowed. He put his hand over hers in comfort. "I am sorry they are gone; they were good men. We will see to the proper rites for them." He put a finger gently beneath her chin, raising her face to look at him. "My dearest Lucia, that you are safe ..." He gave a half-smile. "Soldiers die. It is part of what we face. You got the message through, and you returned to us unharmed."

Stephen looked down at that, and Michael glanced at him for a moment before returning to look more closely at Lucia.

Her voice was hoarse when she spoke. "Michael, this is Stephen. His family once owned the lands that the Grays have laid waste. It is he who found me after the ambush. I was near death; it is due to his careful attention that I stand before you today."

Michael offered his hand, and after a moment Stephen took it. Michael's eyes showed the depth of his gratitude. "I appreciate your efforts more than words can say," he offered. "Anything I have that you want, it is yours."

Stephen's eyes flicked to Lucia, but he nodded, saying nothing. A tense pull formed at his shoulders.

Michael turned his head, flagging down a passing barmaid. "Bring along two ales and ..." He glanced at Lucia. "A mead for you?"

"Yes," she answered warmly, giving him a gentle nudge in the side. When he sat, she eased into the chair next to him, twining her fingers into his.

A trio of pottery mugs were plunked down before them in short order, and they clinked them together before downing the warm liquid. Lucia's face eased as she looked over at the man at her side.

"Michael, dear, I have so much to tell you," she sighed. "So much has happened. I am sure you have much to tell me, too." Her gaze drifted to the group sitting around the fireplace. "But first, I need to break the news. I must let Marcie know about her brother, Vic ..."

Lucia broke off, her face shadowing. Then she was standing, turning, moving off into the dark room. Stephen watched as she went, and in a moment she was lost to him.

Stephen looked back to the table and saw that Michael, too, was staring at where Lucia had eased into the shadows. He finally gave a soft shake before turning his gaze to Stephen. A smile eased back on his face.

"Stephen, is it?" He raised his mug high. "Any man who watches over Lucia deserves a toast. She is very special to me, as you might have guessed."

Stephen acknowledged the toast, taking down another drink of his ale. He looked over the man before him. Michael was perhaps twenty-five, wearing high quality leather armor that showed signs of both use and care. A well-worn scabbard was at his side, and the rippling muscles of his arms indicated that he was well able to wield the sword within it.

A jagged tear of jealousy pulled at Stephen's heart. Of course he would have to be a talented swordsman to have captured Lucia's heart so. Michael had been the one she called for in the depths of her fever, and in the trauma after Ian's assault.

A twinkle came to Michael's eye as he carefully watched Stephen's face. "Did my Lucia never mention me?"

Stephen shook his head no. The tremor-induced hallucinations hardly counted as a discussion. He knew he had resisted mentioning Anna to Lucia; had she refused to bring up Michael for similar reasons?

Michael gave a low chuckle. "Lucia and I go back a long time," he confided. "I will have to scold her for not saying anything."

Stephen could not form a response to this. The tightness at his chest grew stronger, and he glanced over to where Lucia had vanished into the crowd. She was beyond sight now; she was lost to him.

Michael's voice took on a serious overtone, and he leant forward. "You will find that I value honesty over all else, Stephen. If you are joining our party, you need to come clean. How do you feel about her?"

Stephen looked up and saw the firmness in Michael's eyes. A hollowness spread within him, and he nodded. Yes, now was not the time for half measures. If this man did have ties to her, then Stephen owed it to Lucia to be truthful, to prepare Michael for the long road which lay ahead. And part of that was revealing his own part in her life until now. It might be the only way Michael would take his revelations seriously.

"Lucia and I became close while she was recuperating from her wounds," he admitted, holding Michael's gaze. "I respect her a great deal; she is an exceptional woman. I believe she felt the same about me. Our conversations together were ... intimate."

Stephen gripped his mug and looked over into the fire. She was gone to him now. He had given her time, and now he had lost her.

Michael's voice came softly across the table, drawing Stephen back from his musings. "With Lucia, the ability to talk honestly rates far above other considerations." As Stephen turned, Michael's gaze sharpened, taking in the pain in his eyes.

"It is clear how much you care for her. Tell me, does she feel as deeply for you as you do for her? Does she love you?"

A tense stillness came over Stephen. It was one thing to admit his own feelings. It was another to cause damage to her relationship with Michael over something which was now in the past.

Michael shook his head, his gaze holding Stephen's steadily. "I say again; my relationship with Lucia is based on complete honesty. In all our years I have never hidden one thing from her, nor her from me." He glanced toward the fire for a moment. "Be certain that whatever happened these past weeks, I will know every detail soon enough. But for now …" His gaze drew back to hold Stephen. "With all she is shouldering, I would spare her the burden of reliving whatever hardships she might have undergone."

Stephen saw the truth of it in Michael's eyes. He would indeed know everything. His respect for Lucia grew further, that she would have this level of relationship, and his heart ached that it was with another man.

He set his mug down carefully, then drew his gaze up to hold Michael's with acceptance. "I love Lucia," he admitted, his heart easing to say it out loud. "And she loves me as well." A tightness came to his throat. "Or, she did," he amended. "Her time at Penrith was not easy. She has put up high walls, and she is sheltering behind them. I was giving her time …"

His voice caught, and he took in another drink of ale.

Michael brow furrowed with concern. "Lucia, needing time? That wild imp of a sister was always the first one to fly into battle, and half the time it was all I could do to stay by her side and keep her safe."

Stephen's mouth fell open, and he blinked, staring at Michael in confusion.

"Sister?" he ground out.

The grin on Michael's face grew wider. "Twin," he agreed.

Stephen could see it now, the similarity in their eyes, the stubborn set to their jaws, and he fell back in his chair, all tension flowing out of him in a long rush. He brought his ale to his mouth, taking down a long swallow before shaking his head.

"God's teeth, you Keilders are something," he muttered at last, a smile easing from him. "Do you normally like to torture your guests as some sort of greeting ritual?"

Michael's eyes sparkled with amusement. "I have had a lot of practice at it," he countered. "Lucia tends to attract enthusiastic admirers. Many times the jealous suitor routine is just what she needs to redirect their energies."

A calm came over him, and he looked at Stephen with fresh appreciation. "It appears, at long last, that in this case it was not warranted." His smile became tender. "I am impressed if she is truly beginning to think in that way again. It has been a long time coming." He gave Stephen a toast, then drank.

Stephen thought back to Lucia's story about Evan, about the betrayal she had experienced at seventeen. Had she pushed away all suitors since that tragic event? He thought to her nightmares, to her solid walls which had blocked him at every turn.

Michael's gaze became serious. "Lucia means the world to me. How did she end up in an ambush? What has happened since her arrival at Penrith?"

Stephen downed another swallow of ale, then began. He told Michael everything he had learned about Lucia's trip down from her homeland, and the battle that ended in the death of her companions. He talked about their time at the keep. The only details he left out were the night at the hot spring, and Ian's assault on Lucia. They were in a public place, and he could not bring himself to describe such intimate situations with others listening.

Michael was sharp, asking many insightful questions about the forces at the keep and the manner of attacks by the Grays. The hours rolled on, stew was brought and taken away, and Stephen found himself relaxing with Lucia's brother.

They had much in common, Stephen realized, these people and his own. Michael could easily become a close friend of his. The group around him at the inn, from the pieces of conversation he overheard, seemed goodhearted and kind. Marcus and Shawn were off in a corner singing with some of the guards, and the keep soldiers had wandered off to bed.

As the room cleared out, he was finally able to spot Lucia again. She was sitting by the fire on a low bench, talking to a young woman about her own age. The woman was blonde, sturdy, and her face was streaked with tears. Lucia was consoling her tenderly. In a lull in the room he could make out what she was saying as he watched her lips.

"Yes, he is gone, Marcie. He died fighting with honor. He would have had it no other way." Marcie nodded and dried her eyes against her dress sleeve. Lucia held her for a while, then eased on to a softer conversation he could not hear. Stephen sat quietly, drawn to Lucia's care and attention for this woman.

Michael's voice at his side brought him back to his present company.

"So Lucia was in an elegant dress, and dancing," commented Michael with a smile, shaking his head. "*That* I would have liked to see."

Stephen nodded and continued to watch Lucia, who had now stood to flag down a barmaid. His mind skipped forward to the painful end of that evening, and his face shadowed.

Michael followed Stephen's gaze to his twin sister. As they looked on, one of the Keilder soldiers staggered over and grabbed her playfully from behind. In a flash Lucia had the knife from her boot and was whirling around, a fierce set to her eyes. Stephen and Michael both had their swords half-drawn with a single hissing motion before Lucia halted mid-attack, suddenly realizing she was in no danger. She made a halfhearted joke to her drunken friend to cover her lapse, and sat down to talk with him. Nobody else in the room seemed to notice the interplay.

Stephen and Michael looked at each other, letting out their held-in breath. They slowly sat back down in their chairs, resheathing their swords. Stephen sighed deeply, then looked over at Michael.

Michael held Stephen's gaze, his eyes hard. "*That* is not the Lucia who left us," he snapped under his breath. "No ambush attack of the Grays did that to her." He looked back over at Lucia, and held his gaze on her for a while, his eyes softening in tender regard. Then his voice became steely. "I demand to know what happened."

Stephen shook his head. "Things are breaking up. Let us wait until the remaining people leave. I assure you I had no part of any harm to your sister."

Michael nodded, his face somber and quiet. The two men drank in silence as the room finished emptying and the remaining people went up to their rooms. Time passed; the logs settled lower as they burnt down, sending forth a shower of sparks. Eventually Lucia came over to the table to say goodnight.

"I am so glad we are together again, Michael," she sighed quietly, holding him tightly for a moment. Releasing him, she turned to Stephen, her smile revealing her weariness. "Stephen. I feel sometimes that I take you for granted. Thank you for bringing me safely here." She paused a moment, looking at him. She seemed as if she might say something further, but she dropped her eyes.

Her voice was a whisper. "Good night."

She headed to the back of the room where Marcie waited quietly for her. The two women headed up the wooden stairs to the sleeping area.

The two men looked after her, then nodded to each other. They picked up their mugs and brought them to the bench by the fire. After making sure the remaining few patrons were fast asleep at their tables, Stephen stood against the mantle and, as evenly as he could, told Michael about the evening of the ball from start to finish. At times Michael would stand up and pace around the room, but he remained quiet during the tale. When Stephen had finished with the main part of the story, he then told Michael about Lucia's behavior during the trip these past few weeks.

"It is as if she has taken the incident as proof that she must stand completely alone. She is locking herself away from everyone." Stephen let out a breath. "Everyone including me, when I would do all that I could to help her through this. It wounds me greatly to see this change, and to wonder if it is a passing change after all."

He paused, uncertain how to continue.

"All of the ... passion ... she used to give to life, she is using to pay more attention to the details of things around her. She watches the road ahead of her feet, and does not look up to see the forest, the hills. What she does see, she sees clinically, but she does not ... feel them."

His shoulders tensed with frustration. "Above all else, she is completely refusing to see anything inside herself. She refuses to look back - to think at all about what has happened, or how she feels ..."

Michael sat down with a heavy sigh, running his fingers through his thick hair. "I do not know what to do," he admitted after a while. "I wish we could help, but I cannot see how. Forcing her to think about that night does not seem like a good idea. Neither does forcing her to think about her pain." He thought for a while, then sighed again. "I think we will just have to let her take this journey herself," he admitted in resignation. "She has got to come to grips with what happened in her own way, on her own time." His face became hard. "Though if I ever get my hands on that bastard..."

Stephen nodded grimly. "Ian deserves to be punished," he agreed with quiet steel in his voice. "It is still very hard for me to accept that my foster brother, who I thought loved me as much as I loved him, could possibly -"

He looked up in surprise as light footsteps came down the stairs. Lucia poked her head around the wall and smiled softly as she saw the two by the fire.

"Am I disturbing something?" she asked quietly, a content look on her face. "I could not sleep." The two men got to their feet and made room for her in the warmth. She sat on the wood bench and snuggled close to Michael. Stephen saw the pain on Michael's face as he gingerly held her close to him. Lucia was barefoot - she must have been ready for bed when she headed down - and she looked quite young with her auburn hair streaming loose down over Michael's lap.

"Sing me a song, Mike," she asked sleepily. "Something nice." She snuggled deeper in his arms.

Michael stroked her hair gently and looked across to Stephen. Stephen could hear his thoughts as clearly as if he had spoken them aloud.

How could someone have wanted to harm her?

Stephen dropped his eyes. It was his fault this had happened to her.

He was responsible.

Michael pressed a soft kiss against her forehead. "I have got just the thing," he whispered.

Slowly the little bird
flies to his nest,
Tucks feathered noggin
on downy, warm chest,

Gets himself ready for
nighttime of rest,
And now, oh my love,
so must you.

Stephen smiled; this was a song he remembered from
his youth. Bittersweet memories of his family flooded
back as the fire flickered and the logs settled into ash.
Quietly, he joined in with Michael as Lucia's eyes eased
closed.

Fish in the pond snuggle
close to the reeds,
Wrap themselves up in
a blanket of weeds,
Nestling on dreams of fresh
cranberry seeds,
And now, oh my love,
so must you.

Stephen waited by the fire as Michael brought his sister
back up to her room. He drew his sword from its leather
scabbard and stared at it for a while before stirring up the
remaining ashes. He didn't look up as Michael's heavy
footsteps sounded on the stairs and he settled himself on
the opposite bench. All he heard was the sound of Ian
hitting Lucia. Its sharp report repeated over and over again
in his memories.

Stephen stood suddenly, his motion knocking over the
heavy bench. "It is not fair!" he growled. He looked
angrily at the sword in his hand. No fancy scrollwork
adorned the weapon. Instead, rough nicks and stains ran
the length of the blade.

"I have spent my life defending others, fighting for
what I thought was right. That night, even, I was on watch,

taking care of the others. Who was taking care of her?" He stared bleakly at the overturned bench. "I trusted him." Stephen stalked over to the window and looked out into the darkness.

He felt a hand on his shoulder. "There was little you could do, my friend," commented Michael quietly. "Lucia is, after all, a fighter in her own right." He chuckled softly. "There were many times in our youth that I tried to shield her, to no avail. Every time she goes through the fire she comes out even stronger. Let us just give her time."

Stephen nodded, but the pain refused to go away. The two took their seats by the fire, lost in thought.

Chapter 19

Lucia awoke to waves of nausea rolling through her stomach. She remembered drinking a fair amount of mead the night before, but somehow little food had managed to pass her lips during that long evening. She staggered over to the chamber pot, knelt over it, and fought to hold in the contents of her stomach. She won the struggle and wiped her forehead off with a nearby cloth. Marcie had already gone down for breakfast, and Lucia dressed quickly to join her.

It seemed that many other people were in the same state; she saw a large number of drooping eyes and long faces amongst her friends that greeted her as she came down the stairs. Even Stephen and Michael, who shared a table at the far end of the room, looked quiet and thoughtful as she sat down to join them. Soon they all dove into a breakfast of fried fish and toast, which, while greasy, was quite filling.

The next week was spent in preparations for the trek northwards. Lucia was glad for the break. The stress of recent events was catching up with her, and she often found it hard to climb out of bed in the morning. The constant diet of greasy food did not seem to be helping her stomach any, either. She took good advantage of the time to sit and rest, although she also looked forward to returning to the trail, if only because the food here disagreed with her so much.

Michael and Stephen kept her well informed of the arrangements that they were making. The villagers had been safely escorted to her uncle's keep nearby, and he had sent thirty men to join their forces. The group could now head north and focus on defeating the Grays' armies.

Michael had not been named Lord yet. He had chosen to wait until this conflict was settled before taking on the title. While some wondered at this, Lucia understood. He wanted to retake the keep first.

The week passed quickly, and by its end Michael and Stephen had garnered horses and supplies for the sixty soldiers that would be accompanying them back to the keep. They would join with the native forces there to help defend that town and push the Grays back over the river. After that, they would continue to push them back steadily to her own area and stage a final battle to regain what was left of the lands she grew up in.

Despite her stomach problems, Lucia was in high spirits. The officers she had grown up with were around her again, laughing, joking. The faces around her knew her, respected her. She fell easily into the old routines. She hadn't realized how homesick she was until now.

* * *

Stephen watched with a heavy heart as Lucia led the party back north up the sunny path, two young men flanking her and telling stories of their recent endeavors in battle. Where was the artist who composed poetry under the stars? The quiet archer who debated politics over a campfire? The woman who had emerged glistening from the lake glowing with desire? At the keep, Lucia had seemed his alone, a jewel in a dark night. Here, she was a star for many, and he realized Michael was not joking when he had said that Lucia had numerous admirers.

Stephen sighed and looked away. It was slow, agonizing torture watching her drift back into her old world. He knew pushing her with his own feelings would be a mistake, and he could not think of a way to have her gently confront what had happened with Ian. He knew her refusal to face that night was the main roadblock in her remembering just how close she had been to him previously.

Lucia needed time - but time was drawing her away from him.

He shook his head in frustration. Watching her slip from his grasp in the meantime was more than he thought he could endure.

Michael rode up alongside Stephen. The two men, along with the original party from Penrith, were guarding the rear of the group. In the spring sunshine it seemed little would threaten them; riding arrangements were quite lax.

Michael was silent for a moment. "She is hurting," he commented softly, seeing the direction of Stephen's gaze. "Be patient. She is starting to relax the walls she put up against the memories. They will come down soon enough. We will make sure we are there when she does come face to face with her pain, and is ready to take it on. She will not avoid it forever."

"It is so difficult," replied Stephen softly, watching how the sunlight sent golden highlights through Lucia's long hair. The waiting was eating away at him. "I am not one to sit on the sidelines and hope for a good outcome," he added.

"*You* are not good at waiting," returned Michael with a grin. "Let me tell you about the time Lucia ..." Soon their laughter rang out down the line of horses.

The weather held up well for the next few days, and the party was in high spirits. They had brought plenty of food from the town, although Lucia was still feeling poorly and tried to avoid the dried fish. Stephen made an effort to supplement those rations with fresh game from the surrounding forest, and it seemed to help her somewhat. The road itself was quiet. The few travelers they met coming down from the north said there was little activity from the Grays. The group fell into an easy pattern that was almost relaxing.

At about the half-way mark of their journey, at the end of one of the warmer days, the group came across a clearing off the side of the road. Stephen took a ride around the border of the clearing, then a second, wider loop. He found that in addition to being easily defensible it had the added attraction of a small pond not too far away. The party, cheered by the good news, made preparations to camp for the night.

Michael was getting a meat stew ready when Stephen returned from a scouting mission. The others had already brought in various game, and the dinner was putting forth a wonderful aroma as Stephen helped Michael skin a deer to add to the pot. Lucia was off to one side, rubbing down the horses and joking with Marcus.

"We are making good time," commented Michael to Stephen, running his knife down one of the stag's leg bones. "We should reach Penrith in another week or so, given your estimations. It is lucky this weather has held up so nicely. It will be much easier to make a stand with troops in good cheer." He looked out at his friends. "That sea voyage was tough. We almost lost a few, and were very lucky to make it through with only a few injuries. It will certainly get worse before we are done."

Stephen handed him a slab of meat and smiled. "Just the fact that they are well trained will help us immensely. Most of this area has never seen fighting. Some seasoned troops will boost morale a great deal."

He thought of the first day Lucia had come out to watch the drill, of her disappointment.

What was she thinking now?

* * *

Lucia felt the weight of Stephen's stare and glanced up briefly, then returned quickly to cleaning Troy's hooves. Marcus continued to joke, and she felt completely at ease. This was the life she loved, being out in the country. Her patrols back home could last for weeks, and the troops got to know one another quite well. Surrounded by her old bunkmates and her new friends, she knew that she trusted each member of her party implicitly.

Then why did she feel uncomfortable? It wasn't just her stomach, which was starting to get over its sickness. There was something else ... not right.

She shook her head. When she took the time to think about it more, she realized that something had been bothering her for a while, perhaps since she left Penrith. She just didn't know what. She was back with her kinsmen. She was where she belonged. Finishing with Troy's hooves, she wiped her hands on her legs and looked down at her clothes. Lord, she was filthy!

Lucia grinned to herself - until recently it wouldn't even have occurred to her to consider her appearance. She realized it had been quite a while since she had taken a bath. That might do her some good.

* * *

Stephen looked up as Lucia strolled over to the cooking area. It seemed weeks since she had really spoken to him. He searched her face for some emotion, some sign, but it was flat, with a mask of simple contentment laid over a base of hard pain. Stephen cut deeper into the meat he was carving, frustrated. What could he do to help?

Her voice was light as she smiled up at her brother. "Michael, I think I will take a bath. I should be back in an hour or so."

Michael nodded, his eyes following her as she stopped to grab her bag and sword before heading out toward the far end of the clearing. Michael watched her go, contemplating something. Then he turned to Stephen.

"I have not asked what exactly passed between you two," he stated. "I know that your feelings were rather strong before ... well, before she was hurt. I would like you to go and keep an eye on her."

He stopped and took a deep breath. Stephen could see that within the strong, powerful man was a caring brother who was uncertain. He easily understood what Michael was going through.

"Do not worry," he promised, his voice solemn. "I would not do anything to hurt her, as much as I want to help move her past this block. I will make sure she comes through this whole, even if it means losing her." His throat grew hoarse as he said this aloud, realizing just how real a possibility that was now.

Michael clapped him on the back, then watched as his friend headed after his sister. Shaking his head, he turned back to their dinner.

* * *

Lucia walked slowly through the dense underbrush, pressing her way through toward the pond. For the first time in many weeks she was truly alone with her thoughts, while at the same time safe with her friends and family near. She took her time, enjoying her surroundings, marveling at the beauty of nature. She took in the budding trees and flowering plants which surrounded her. Everything was so peaceful and different from her home lands. The climate of her youth was much harsher, and vegetation and wildlife that managed to survive was rangy and lean. The forest here, on the other hand, was lush and alive.

Surrounded by the fragrant foliage, her mind open and unguarded, she suddenly, vividly, remembered riding side by side with Vic, having this very conversation. The memory was powerful, overwhelming. She could see Vic's laughing face, hear the merriment in his voice …

Her feet stopped moving of their own accord. She almost felt he stood beside her, his eyes gazing at hers in understanding. Her heart began to pound; she leant on a nearby tree, sorrow sweeping over her. The power of the emotion nearly overwhelmed her. She realized with wonder just how much effort she had put into pushing those memories into the past. She had made compartments in her heart, and had shut things away, finding it easier than accepting the loss and hurt.

She let the tears flow, let the torment come. To her surprise it did not overtake her completely; a cleansing sensation drew through her as she accepted the loss and pain. After a while, strength returning to her, she gave herself a shake and continued slowly down the path.

Cautiously, she allowed herself to consider what she had been doing with her thoughts. She realized that she had not just put away certain emotions and events. Instead, she had refused to think about anything or anyone from her time at Penrith. She had equally blocked out all emotions from her current life. She was riding from day to day, doing what she had to, and leaving considerations of tomorrow to her brother.

She never used to be like this. She knew this was unhealthy, but she hesitated when considering a solution. She focused on the trail ahead of her with deliberation. Her vision narrowed down to the path. Maybe the cleansing bath would do her some good. Perhaps her pinpoint thoughts were just a symptom of the remaining winter doldrums. Spring was here now, and some fresh air and cool water would reawaken her spirit.

She came over a small rise and saw the pond beneath her. Next to her, the stream spilled down over a rocky waterfall to splash gently into the oak and moss-circled pond. The water was clear, and seemed quite deep. It was idyllic. She quickly scrambled down the hill and removed her clothes on the small beach next to the water. Soon she was naked, except for the small knife strapped to her thigh. She knew her security-conscious brother would scold her if she removed that, and she smiled at the thought.

The moon was just rising, waxing over the trees as she eased herself gently into the water. It brought to mind her childhood, her happy days of swimming and playing in the local ponds. At first she stayed near the bag and sword on the beach, but as the moon rose higher she swam the full distance of the pond, enjoying the splashing of the water on the rocks and the sparkle of the moon's reflection. The rocks under her feet were smooth and large. How she loved to swim!

She dove under the surface, relishing the feel of the smooth, cool water running down her side and over her calves. The water felt almost like hands running over her body. She swam strongly, suddenly troubled. Hands? She remembered another night like this, with Stephen, by a pond like this one. She remembered the passion and love. What had happened to it?

She dove under the water again, rushing through the depths. An overwhelming wave of loneliness hit her full force. It enveloped her completely, and she was staggered by its power. She desperately missed Stephen. The pain wrenched at her heart, and she wondered how she had not felt it this entire time. The talks, the closeness. She remembered the dark eyes, so full of caring and concern. Why had she been pushing him away?

Everything swept in on her with a sudden ferocity, and her tears mingled with the water through which she moved. Her rage at Ian, her helplessness under his attack. Her love for Stephen. All of it had been submerged in the same layer of fog, all pushed away with the same smothering movement. She gasped out sobs, realizing how much she had lost. She had to let it all in, the angst and the warmth. She let the pain come as she swam, let it flow over her ... and then she let it pass through her. The pain was worth it, to allow her to refill the hole in her heart with her love for Stephen. She could shoulder the anger she still felt burning for Ian's deed. She could carry that burden. As long as she held the love, she could face anything.

Suddenly a dark shadow was ahead of her. For some reason, it reminded her of Ian, standing in the darkness of her room, laughing down at her. Rage poured through her. He had taken advantage of her friendship, of her unwillingness to act against him. He would not find her so trusting this time. Her hand went to the dagger at her side, and she sprung out of the water at the form ahead of her.

It was Stephen standing at the side of the pool, his body motionless. His face was etched with pain. She realized that he had carried that look since that night. She had not acknowledged it, had not given any thought to what he was feeling. She had hardly spoken to him.

The knowledge startled her. She realized that she had been filtering entire sections of her world. Somehow this had been happening despite her self-congratulations on her keenness in certain areas. She realized she would have to rethink the entire past month, to look at events in a new light. It bothered her that she had been so blind, without realizing it.

Stephen stood still before her, not moving. Lucia could see that his hands were trembling slightly, staying well clear of his sword. His eyes strayed from her face to her hand at her side. Confused, she looked down and saw the knife still clenched in her fist, her body still in a fighting stance. She gazed at the knife for a moment, not really seeing it, then back into his eyes. He had been there for her, even during her darkest times. He had come for her when she needed him; he had stayed by her when she had turned her back.

She was overwhelmed and humbled. To her shock, she realized that in avoiding her pain she had pushed away something far more valuable - her love for this man.

Still, she hesitated. Her feelings felt new, raw, and untested. The rush of emotions - pain, anger, love - would surely overwhelm her. Could she truly come to accept the loss and pain she had gone through, knowing that this action would also let in his love? Could she weather the heartache which pulled her down, knowing he would be there beside her?

His eyes gave her hope with their trust and compassion. Her grip weakened on the knife, and she became lost in his gaze, in the eyes that had stayed beside her for so many long nights. She took a step toward Stephen, who stood still before her, steady, waiting.

A shout of outrage and fury came from down the beach, and she spun. She heard metal sliding on leather behind her, knew peripherally that Stephen had drawn his sword, but this was a mere echo of a sound coming from far off. Nothing registered fully in her consciousness except the movement now before her.

Under the bright moonlight, Ian separated from the shadows of the forest and stepped toward her.

Chapter 20

Ian looked little like the noble son Lucia had known in Anna's company. His elegant dress tunic was ragged and covered with grime. His beard had grown out in shaggy fur. But it was his demeanor which showed the most staggering change. His eyes were cold, small, and burning with hatred. His bearing, far from the cock-sure courtier she had known, was now fierce and aggressive.

A chill coursed through her body; she sank into a combat stance and unconsciously turned her dagger in her hand for a better grip. Her neck arched as she settled into the fighting position. Taking a deep breath, she slowly took two measured steps toward him.

Ian's eyes roamed over her naked body "I knew I would find you eventually, whore," he chuckled hoarsely. A leer crept over his face. "So, you are back to your old ways already. Here I thought after a night of passion with me you would be cured of him."

Lucia heard a deep growl from behind her, but it slid out of her focus. Only Ian stood out sharp and crisp in her thoughts. She took another deliberate step toward Ian. Her previous turmoil was gone. In its place rested the soul of a warrior trained to strength, confidence, and skill.

Her face was set with concentration. She knew how to handle this.

"I do not hide that you hurt me deeply," she called out, her head held high. The pain in her heart dissolved as she put it into words and finally admitted it fully to herself and to the world. The burden on her soul eased, and she continued, her voice gaining in strength. "You violated my trust, a trust I gave to you freely. I had sworn I would not let that happen again. I would not lay trust where it was not deserved. Perhaps that fault rests with me."

Her voice grew steely. "With you still rests the sin of abusing my trust, of twisting it to your own warped desires."

Lucia's eyes flashed proudly. "You have not won. I have survived. I am still a woman, still possessing strength and will. I am still deserving of the love of my troops, my friends, my family." She held her ground. "None of that has changed. I have not changed. Only you have changed. You were not worthy."

She knew in a corner of her mind that Stephen was still behind her, was watching, was ready. To her relief he did not make a move to interfere. A wave of love strengthened her even further.

Ian's face blossomed crimson in anger. "You slut, you should have loved me!" He slashed with his sword to emphasize his point. "How could you possibly refuse me? No other woman dared such a thing. I was the best! You should have been grateful for my attentions! Lily, Abigail and the others all were!"

Lucia went stone still at the mention of Lily's name. Even with what had happened to her, she had never dreamt that Ian would have assaulted that young girl. Her face set with firm resolve.

Ian laughed at her reaction. "You thought you were the only woman in my life? I was the ultimate partner for every woman within riding distance of Penrith." His eyes sharpened. "You made a mistake when you turned me down. I am certainly better than that ... forest vagrant."

His voice dropped down lower, and became harsh. "No, he was not content with the hand of my beautiful cousin, and with the affections of my father," he choked out with fury. "He had to take *my woman* away from me. Well, not today."

His eyes were fierce with blinding rage, and he tossed his head back as if in challenge. "You are mine, Lucia. If I cannot have you, then by God, he certainly will not!"

Lucia braced herself, dropping even lower into her stance. She was ready when Ian suddenly raised his jeweled sword and came at her with a slicing attack that was meant to finish the fight quickly. She side-stepped smoothly, redirecting his back-swing as he tried to take her out on the up-stroke. The two circled each other. Lucia's mind, alert and hyper-aware, flicked quickly through every aspect of watching the mock fight in the Great Hall. This was no playful joust to first touch. Ian's eyes told her that he meant to finish her.

Their weapons rang out another half dozen times, with Lucia carefully dodging out of the way of each blow. Her years of training had taught her to use her agility and speed against a larger opponent's strength and power. She spotted an opening and spun past him, cutting his side as she turned. He flinched slightly but did not seem hurt. Wheeling, she saw out of the corner of her eye that Stephen was balanced at the outer ring of their motion. He stood poised for action, sword in hand, watching every move with an eagle's eye. He was her second, then. Her mind became even calmer, taking on the time-stopping quality that battle brought.

Then Ian launched toward her to attack again.

The pain and rage of her helplessness that night fused with her years of training and combat like the paint and plaster of a wet fresco mural. They became one source of power. She slid under Ian's strokes and took the openings when they were offered her. He was a good fighter, well trained in the basic skills. His fury gave him extra strength, but made his swings wild and without aim. She had the experience of years on the hard trail, and now had her focus and concentration under full control. She was much quicker than he was. Still, his training helped him avoid her strokes, helped him press her back with a flurry of attack. He was stronger than she was, much stronger, and had a longer reach. It was only through sheer determination and her combinations of attacks that she held her ground against him. One exchange left her with a slight wound on her shoulder, but Ian gained two more wounds in return.

The battle began to take a toll on them both, their blades moving slower as they seemed to become heavier. Lucia knew her strength was failing and watched for a chance to draw him in close. She favored her right side, not using the wounded shoulder, and Ian lunged for this advantage. Quickly, she turned and saw an opening. She pressed in hard, twisted her knife and kicked at Ian's forward knee. Ian, not expecting this, went down hard on his back. His sword arm lay outstretched to one side; the sword itself went flying into the pond with a loud splash.

In a flash she knelt over his prone body, her dagger firmly in her hand, and pressed it to his throat. His eyes were full of rage and hatred. Still, looking into them, Lucia remembered how he had helped to rescue her, how he had demanded to be the one to protect his homeland. Her resolve wavered.

Finally, she spoke softly to him and pleaded for reason. "Truly, Ian, I do not want to hurt you. You undoubtedly saw that I travel with my kinsmen. We are here to save your homelands, to end the menace. Give us space while we deal with the Grays, and then we will be gone. Let me find a new home for Lily and James, up in our keep. I will leave it to your father to mete out any further justice, and relinquish all claim myself."

She waited, her heart thumping, hoping he would accept her offer.

Bloody and bruised, Ian snarled up at her. "You expect me to worry about justice? Hah! This is *my* land we are on, *my* life for me to lead any way I wish."

"You are bound by the same laws as anyone else in your lands," Lucia pointed out.

"And as far as you leaving," continued Ian, as if Lucia had not spoken at all, "You belong to me now, or have you forgotten?" He scanned her naked body with a leer. "No, how could you possibly forget that night? I had you first. That makes you mine." He stared up at her with possessive pride.

The last vestiges of the weight released from her heart. "There you are wrong," she replied with a growing calmness, her hand steady. "I was Stephen's long before I was taken by you. No act by you, no matter how violent, could ever sever the bonds that hold us together."

The words echoed in her heart and resonated through every part of her body. To her surprise, she found it was true. Suddenly Ian meant nothing to her. His actions were in the past. They could no longer hurt her.

Her soul soared, released from its heavy chains. She slowly stood. She looked down at him for a long moment, then deliberately turned her back on him and walked away.

It was over. She was free of him.

Ian's howl of anger behind her shattered the forest's quiet, echoing far across the surrounding hills. Lucia watched, as if in a dream, as Stephen ran full tilt toward her. His eyes looked past her as he called out hoarsely, "Down!"

Lucia did not hesitate; she threw herself flat on the mossy ground beneath her. She heard the sharp slicing noise of a blade swinging just over her head, and then Stephen was driving hard past her, and swinging his sword with pinpoint focus. Lucia rolled and turned, all senses alert.

Stephen drew the full length of his blade across Ian's chest. As he did so, he brought his face close to Ian's, and held his eyes.

"Never again, Ian."

He pulled the sword clear with one smooth movement.

Ian gasped once, staggered backwards, then landed heavily onto the moist sand, a wicked looking dagger in his right hand. He was dead.

The forest was silent; Lucia's breathing sounded loud in her ears. She brought herself up to a sitting position, then hesitated before turning to look down at the dead man. Her shoulders slumping, she closed her eyes for a moment in respect for his passing. Ian was a fallen soldier, regardless of what lust and weakness had driven him to do in the end. She felt weary, but also enormously light, as if a great weight had been removed from her.

When a moment had passed, Lucia got to one knee and then stood slowly. She stepped free of Ian's body and turned to face Stephen. His breath was coming in deep heaves, and his face was etched with pain.

* * *

Stephen fought to steady his breathing, his eyes looking over the scene which had almost broken his will to watch. His muscles ached with strain and weariness. He took a step toward Lucia, then stopped. His eyes took in the cuts and bruises on her body, and he thought for the thousandth time how close she had come to …

He shuddered at the thought.

"Lucia, my love, your actions test my very soul," Stephen rasped hoarsely. "I was forced to watch you face danger, knowing that I could lose you if I did not act. Yet if I did act, if I held you from your own resolution, you might never fully heal."

He lowered his sword slowly, letting the tip come to rest on the ground, and his head dropped in exhaustion.

Lucia stood for a moment, then, glistening from the sweat of battle, she walked over to stand before him. He gently touched the cut on her shoulder, and she winced at the pressure. She put her hand over his own and looked up into his eyes. "You mean the world to me," she vowed to him gently. "To know that you were there, watching over me, was all I needed. I did not face him alone. I faced him with your support, your understanding, and your trust in my abilities. That was why we were able to win."

Stephen closed his eyes and wrapped Lucia tenderly into his arms, holding her tightly against him. As he held her, a great calm descended over him. He pressed his lips down against her forehead, holding the kiss for several minutes. He was utterly swept away with love for the woman in his arms. She had stood her ground against the thing which terrified her the most, faced it, and conquered it.

A trampling of running feet came from above them, and Michael came bursting into the area, followed by a group of soldiers. Stephen reached for Lucia's cloak with a deft motion and swirled it around her naked body, pulling her again to him.

Michael took in the scene in one quick glance. He spun to look at the soldiers.

"Scout the area. See if there are any more."

The men were off in a flash, spreading out in all directions.

Michael strode down to join them, sparing a glance for the dead body. "How are you both?" he asked with concern, his eyes scanning each from head to toe. "Any serious injuries?"

"We are fine," Lucia answered her brother with a reassuring nod. "I believe all danger should be past." She motioned toward the corpse. "The man you see there is Ian. He is dead. I do not believe he traveled with any others."

Her face shadowed. "A rider will have to be sent to let his father know," she added with a troubled frown. "I worry how Anna -"

Stephen's voice was rough. "Anna and Lord Edmund will be lucky to have him back in one piece," he snapped, raw anger flaring in his voice. "After what he did to you? Apparently to other women as well? After what he almost did here, now? If he had come upon you unarmed, it would have been you lying there dead, with him gloating over you ..."

Lucia turned and touched Stephen tenderly on his arm. She looked up into his eyes, giving his face a gentle caress. "I know," she soothed softly. "You saved my life, and Ian brought on his own death." She paused, then looked over at the corpse. "Still, he is his father's son, his cousin's childhood friend. They deserve to be able to say goodbye to their memories of him, even if his later deeds became ... twisted."

"He should be left to the wolves," growled Stephen.

Lucia glanced between Stephen and Michael, pulling the cloak more tightly around her body.

A small corner of Stephen's mind understood what she was saying, but it could not overcome the sea of anger which still roiled within him. Ian had been like a brother to him. They had grown up together, played side by side. Countless times Stephen had protected Ian, watched over him, sheltered him from harm.

And this is how he had been repaid.

Michael looked between the two with somber eyes. "Let us head back to camp, and get some food and ale into us. Then we can discuss what to do."

The fire had sunk to glowing embers as they walked into the clearing; Marcus stood up with concern, then walked forward quickly with confusion as he saw the faces of his friends. "What was the shouting?" he asked quickly. "I stayed behind to guard the camp. Are you all right? What has happened?"

Stephen took in a deep breath, marshaling his tension. "Our injuries are minor, nothing serious." He paused, and then went on. They would know soon enough anyway. "Ian tracked us down, and was waiting for us while Lucia bathed. He attacked Lucia there by the lake." He gazed with pride at the woman beside him. "She chose to face him alone, and I stood ready, as her second. In a fair battle, she defended herself from his attack."

His face hardened, but he hesitated, not quite willing to spread the story of Ian's final cowardly action. Maybe he could spare Lord Edmund that much. He instead stated simply but tersely, "I gave the final blow. Ian is dead."

Marcus and the other soldiers in the camp looked surprised, then grew quiet for a few moments. Michael came forward, looking from Stephen's distant stare to Lucia's quiet stance. He exhaled slowly. "What is done is done," he stated at last. "As the slaying was in self-defense, none can speak against it. Perhaps of any person here, Lucia had the most right to face him for what was done. I wonder if that was not better than dragging him, dragging us all, through the wheels of justice."

Stephen felt torn, as if by wild horses quartering him. The woman he cared for had been in mortal danger. The brother he had loved was now dead. A rapist had been brought to justice. But all had happened because he had failed to keep his charge out of harm. Lucia had been his responsibility to protect. If only he had been there, that fateful night ... there were so many 'if onlys'.

He realized Michael was looking at him keenly, and nodded. "It is just as well it is done with," he replied.

Lucia stirred beside him. Her voice was low, but certain. "Michael, we should send a rider to tell Lord Edmund. They should have the option of bringing him back for a burial." Her eyes flicked momentarily to Stephen. "Whatever else has gone on, he deserves to be brought home to his family."

Michael looked to Stephen, but when he did not say anything, Michael nodded and called over to one of the Penrith soldiers. He took the guard aside and whispered quietly to the man for a few moments. The guard listened with his face set, then nodded quickly. When Michael was done giving instructions, the guard saddled his horse with great speed and rode forward down the path at a gallop.

Lucia looked to where the fire crackled in the ring of stones. Her voice was hesitant, and her eyes flicked to Stephen for a moment. "Come sit with me a while?"

Stephen looked up, dragged back from his distant thoughts, a warmth coming over him. She had returned to him. After all the pain, agony, and long waiting, she was back by his side again.

He nodded, putting out a hand, and her gentle touch eased a thousand pains from his heart. Together they walked toward the warm orange glow.

Chapter 21

Lucia awoke to streaming sunshine. How long had she slept? She sat up to find most of the camp had been packed; she realized that the men were all off washing up or gathering supplies for the remainder of the trip. She turned to get up, and saw with surprise that another had also not yet awoken. Stephen must have been sitting up for quite a while even after she had drifted off - he was now sound asleep next to her. In sleep the lines of worry were gone from his forehead; she was struck by how peaceful and serene he looked. She reached over and tenderly eased the hair away from his face, wishing that life could be easier on him, on them all.

Stephen came awake quickly at her touch, reached for his sword, then relaxed with a half-smile when he saw her face. He put his own hand over hers. She found herself lowering down to him, pressing her lips to his, and he was soft, gentle, intoxicating. His arms came up around her, and he was drawing her against him …

Deep laughter came from above them, rich with warmth.

"We do need to get going sometime this morning," grinned Michael with hearty cheerfulness. Lucia smiled, sprang up from the ground, and gave her brother a gentle hug. She felt fresh and renewed as he hugged her tightly in return.

His voice lowered. "Feeling better?"

She nodded with calm assurance. "Yes, much better. Thank you," she replied. Stephen stood up next to her and she saw that he, too, seemed to have a fresh outlook with the spring dawn.

Lucia glanced between the two men. She was glad Michael liked Stephen. She wondered just how much Michael had guessed about how close she and Stephen had been at Penrith. She hadn't spoken much of it herself; hadn't thought of it, really until the past two days.

She watched Michael turn to Stephen, and the two walked off to discuss something by the horses. Lucia bent down to pack. The thought tumbled around in her mind that until now, her time with Stephen had consisted solely of stolen moments. What would their future hold? There was only the one night that they had both been swept away. At the time she had been content to let it stand on its own, a tender memory in a rough-hewn world. Now that they had time, and the other wounds in their lives were starting to mend, would a real relationship work out between them? Would Stephen be interested in seeing that it did?

Regardless of what the future held for them, Lucia did not regret that evening together. She had given herself willingly to him. She would not trade that night for anything. There was little enough love in the world, she felt, to be anything but grateful when it truly swept one away. Even if the bloom faded in the chaos to come, she would have those memories.

She gave Troy's saddle cinch one last tug. Well, she wasn't going to worry about future plans in long-hoped-for times of peace. She had never given much thought to marriage, at least not after Evan ran off. With all of the fighting and trouble coming up, she was going to be happy she had Stephen for now. To have him as a friend, a trusted ally, that was more than many had in the world. If a richer relationship eventually came to them, she would count herself blessed. This was the time to enjoy the present without fretting about the future. Tomorrow would come soon enough.

Pushing some supplies into her bag, Lucia came across her parchment scroll. She stopped her packing, instead sitting on the ground and reading through the poems. She saw immediately how they reflected her pain and her blocked emotions. In the fresh light of morning she could now see where she had been holding back her feelings. She rolled up the scroll tightly, and vowed not to hide things from herself in the future, even if they were painful. Better to live fully and honestly than to submerge emotions in a fog of deception.

The next four days passed more and more easily, like a wheel once gummed with mud that had eased itself free. Stephen and Lucia spent their days in friendly conversation and their evenings in long discussions by the campfire. It seemed that they talked more freely and eloquently now than they ever had in the past. Lucia almost wished they did not need to reach their destination. She longed to prolong this 'space between worlds' that brought her so much pleasure. Before, her relationship with Stephen had been balancing on a knife's edge, caught between conflicting needs. Now it was becoming open, joyous, with their pleasure in each other's company free and expansive. Still, she feared that the coming conflicts, and the return to Penrith, would harm the love she was trying to nurture. She savored the time they spent together.

* * *

Lucia was riding at the front of the group when she heard the riders approaching. The noon sun was just reaching its zenith in a cloudless sky. She raised her hand to bring the group to a halt; they came into a close formation and watched the road ahead with caution. Stephen was especially tense, and she wondered if he was more worried that it was the Grays or that it was not.

As the horses drew close, it became clear that it was only a few riders, and they came fast and hard. When the men came into close range, Lucia realized that they wore the burgundy colors of Lord Edmund's guard. Their faces were somber. Stephen pulled his horse before the others and sat alone to wait.

The riders pulled up a few feet before the party, and the leader hailed Stephen solemnly. "Stephen, we are glad to find you well. We bring greetings from Lord Edmund," he stated formally, then nodded to the rest of the group. "The road is clear for you to Penrith." He paused for a moment, but Stephen said nothing. The soldier continued. "We have been sent to fetch back the body of Ian."

There was a further silence, and this one stretched on. Lucia looked down, but Stephen stared at the soldiers with a set jaw, almost daring them to say anything further. Realizing he had nothing to add, the soldier nodded his understanding. "Fare well, Stephen," he offered, pulling his mount to the side. "We will see you again at the hall." The group rode on down the road in the direction of the pond.

Stephen turned to look after them, anger clear on his face. "Ian does not deserve a soldier's funeral," he growled bitterly. "He deserves to be dragged home in an old cart, drawn by mules." The look of anger became mixed with one of sorrow, and he turned his head. He turned his mount with a sharp movement and started forward on the road again.

Lucia let him go, waiting to follow behind the group. She knew she should feel angry as well, that she should wish awful punishments even on the memory of Ian. She couldn't bring herself to have those feelings, if only because she knew the pain that Anna and Lord Edmund must be going through. They had loved Ian so much, had so many hopes for him, of spending countless years with him ...

It struck her that she concerned herself so much with Anna's feelings because Anna wore them on her sleeve. Should she not feel the same, even more strongly, for Stephen's loss? If Anna cared so much for Ian, how much more would Stephen have felt his death, with Ian being his foster brother for so many years? Stephen had no family of his own, and Ian had been his playmate, his fellow traveler. She remembered how Stephen and Ian rode with each other, how they worked as a team. She had been primarily thinking of Stephen as overwrought because of the harm done her, but how much worse must it be that he had lost his best friend because of her?

Lucia looked forward to where Stephen rode alone at the head of the group. She knew that feeling, of wanting to be independent, to take care of herself. Stephen was trying to cope with the feeling of being betrayed by Ian, and maybe, in a way, of her betraying him by bringing harm to one he cared so much about.

And, despite Stephen's objections, surely she had some small responsibility for setting the course for Ian's assault on her? She had kissed Ian in front of his entire keep. She had publicly led him on. If she had not chosen to take advantage of Ian in that way, perhaps Ian would not have thought of her as "his". Perhaps he never would have built up the emotions which led to his attack.

Lucia began to grow more concerned about the homecoming and what it would bring.

With each dawn the mornings grew warmer, but Lucia's thoughts began to drag her to lag behind. Still, on the final day of their journey, they woke early, before dawn. The sun was just rising over the trees as they headed up the trail not far below Penrith. The group was quiet. Lucia knew their destination was close at hand, and she both welcomed the return to Anna and feared the reaction they might receive. She stayed behind, letting the others pass her, until she was near the tail of the group.

Stephen and Michael soon let their horses trail back to flank her. She had heard them deep in conversation during this morning's ride, and stayed away to give them time to talk. Stephen had been much quieter since Lord Edmund's riders had passed, and she wanted to give him time to think, to come back to her on his own. She wondered what the two had been in such close discussion about. Maybe Stephen had revealed something to Michael. She waited until the two men were beside her, and then put on a smile. "Is what you are discussing open to a third ear?" she asked lightly.

Michael's eyes were shadowed. "I think, in fact, that your reply is needed here," he replied, looking at Lucia with a mixture of confusion and pensiveness.

Lucia suddenly wondered just what the topic of conversation had been, and regretted her entry into the discussion.

Her brother continued on with a tone that Lucia immediately found deceptively neutral. "Stephen and I have been discussing the Grays, and how this whole war came to be. Of course, something like that could be debated for hours without anyone being the wiser at the end. Still, he had some new views that I found to be interesting. Apparently, my sister, so do you."

Michael paused for a moment, seeming to carefully choose his words. At last he put breath behind them. "Stephen tells me that you accused his family of heinous misdeeds, which launched the Grays on their murderous spree."

Lucia's mind reeled with confusion. "What?"

"Well, maybe not those exact words," Michael amended, "but that was your meaning." He looked at her with a concerned eye. "Lucia, did you say that to him?"

Lucia swam with bewilderment. What could Michael be referring to? She looked to Stephen, but he was silent, looking attentively between brother and sister.

She went back in her mind, searching her memory for when that conversation might have come up. Stephen watched her with distant eyes, and it seemed suddenly that a shadowy gulf stretched between them.

Her resolve focused. She had to show them that they were mistaken. She concentrated on tracking down the incident.

It came back to her suddenly. Stephen must have been referring to the time they were arguing about the Grays by the clearing, near Penrith.

"First, we were angry, and words were spoken that were better left unsaid by both of us," she explained to Michael. "My point was not to accuse Stephen's family, but the nobles of this area in general." She took a deep breath and continued. "In any case, I said that the Grays were much like us, people with wives and children. They were poor farmers and tradesmen starved out by richer landowners. They had been driven to extremes by rough usage. On that, I do stand by my feelings."

Michael looked sternly at Lucia, a flush of anger coming to his face. "Where in the world did you hear such tales? I have seen every bit of information you have over the past few years. I have certainly never come across any basis for such a story." He shook his head in disbelief. "Was this something new you found on your travels to Penrith? We have been in this conflict for years. The vast majority of Grays we have encountered have been hired mercenaries, working for the money and the pleasure. They rape and plunder for the fun of it and leave behind a trail of desolation. Very few, if any, have any real cause to campaign." He looked again at his sister. "Just where did you hear this from?"

Lucia was piqued by her brother's harsh reaction, and shot back without thinking. "Evan told me all about it," she retorted hotly. She ignored the shocked look on Michael's face and steamed on. "It was on one of our patrols, just before he left to -"

Lucia suddenly realized what she had been saying.

Her brother drew away from her, shuttering his eyes. She felt the distance as a cold wind whistling down from a high mountain pass.

She dropped her voice lower, her throat tightening. "I always felt that was part of why he betrayed us," she explained. "He truly believed in their cause."

Michael's voice was hoarse with fury. "You are not to mention his name in my presence again," he ordered. "That goes for his nonsensical ramblings, too. Perhaps *you* do not remember what happened to our town because of his ... beliefs. *I* do."

Before Lucia could speak, Michael wheeled with a sharp movement and galloped toward the front of the group.

* * *

Stephen looked over at Lucia in surprise at what had happened. When his conversation with Michael had reminded him of Lucia's comments, he'd been troubled enough to mention them to Michael. He had not expected to renew a family feud.

After riding some time in silence, Stephen felt he should speak. "Lucia, I am sorry," he apologized contritely, moving his horse more closely alongside hers. "It just came out, when we were talking." He glanced forward to where Michael had vanished, then back to Lucia. "I know that Evan is a difficult topic for you."

Lucia dropped her eyes and shook her head. "I have vowed to stop closing out the past," she murmured. "This is as good as any a place to prove it."

Stephen's heart warmed, that she would trust him with such a deeply lodged, painful memory. He nodded quietly for her to continue.

"Evan, you might recall, was one of our captains," she explained. "He came from the Gray territory, back when some of the factions were still peaceful neighbors of ours. When I accepted his engagement, he told me countless stories about his past and the rough conditions of his home village. I never questioned them."

She looked down. "Even when he betrayed us, I still clung to the hope that there was a reason behind it; that he had been driven to it by circumstances."

Stephen nodded in understanding. "You wanted to believe that your trust in him had not been completely unwarranted."

She gave a wry smile. "I suppose so. I suppose I also felt some guilt that I had never truly loved him. I only accepted his suit because I thought it would make my father happy. I imagined that it would ... make sense, given what my role in life was supposed to be. I did what I thought any dutiful daughter would do, I said yes to what I thought was the right path."

Stephen's face shadowed. "Like me and Anna," he commented softly.

Lucia realized that in a way, that was true. Her father hadn't told her to marry Evan, but he'd always made it clear that Evan was a great choice for 'all the right reasons.' She had hoped that she could learn to love him.

Stephen brought her hand to his lips and kissed it tenderly. She looked back over, her eyes glistening. "Never blame yourself for trusting," he admonished gently, and it looked like advice he had been giving himself recently by the way he said it. "Just make sure, the next time, that you find someone worthy of your trust. When you have, do not let go." He gave her hand a gentle squeeze, and then held it in his own as they continued down the road.

The two rode hand in hand in silence through the dappled light, drawing ever nearer to Penrith and all it held for both of them.

Chapter 22

Lucia marveled at the differences in Penrith as her group rode through the open gates, the summer morning sunshine streaming across the cobblestones. It seemed like hardly any time had passed since she last ridden through the streets, yet the atmosphere was completely different - the city was bustling with energy. The forest as they had approached was full of patrols; Lucia was sure there were more that they had passed unknowingly. The trees had been taken down for a full hundred feet from the walls, and the gates were reinforced. The citizens they saw walking in the streets were full of purpose and looked around sharply as the group made its way to the keep.

Lucia relaxed and patted Troy. She had been worried, she admitted to herself, about Penrith's readiness for the upcoming conflict. It seemed she needn't have been concerned. Stephen had been correct - the various armies of the area had banded together against the common threat. Everything looked as if it was coming together nicely. She glanced behind her and saw the same confidence on her fellows' faces.

Stephen pulled up alongside her, his face calm and resolved. She appreciated him being by her side. While it was one thing for the soldiers to band together against the Grays, she still did not know how she would be accepted in Ian's home.

The group arrived at the main steps of the keep, where Marcus led the main force around to the stables. Lucia,

Stephen, and Michael dismounted and let their horses be led away in the group.

A slim figure in burgundy flew down the stairs, calling Lucia's name.

"Ellie!" Lucia called out in pleasure as she recognized her young friend. The two embraced strongly.

"I am glad you are all right," sighed Ellie, her eyes both concerned and warm.

Another face came up alongside Ellie – Lily, her cuts and bruises healed. She gave Lucia a tender hug, then held her hands in her own. "It will be all right," she promised Lucia in a low, but clear voice. "Abigail, I, and the others have made sure of that."

Stephen and Michael came up alongside the trio, and Lucia cut short her reply, unwilling to ask for more details in front of the two men. Stephen glanced down at her, then looked past her up to the main door. Lucia turned to follow their gaze and found herself looking into Lord Edmund's eyes. They were much heavier, much darker than she remembered. She involuntarily took a step backward, and Stephen's hand reassuringly rested against her lower back. Taking a deep breath, she stood her ground and waited for Lord Edmund to join them.

With his cape draped over his shoulders, Lord Edmund stood silent for a full moment before he spoke. "Many things have happened in our past," he called out in a voice which was quiet, yet carried to all in the courtyard. "Many of these events have been difficult. We do face, however, an extraordinary battle. I would like all of us to put any past differences behind us and join together to face this common enemy. I offer welcome - a warm welcome - to Lucia and her friends who have come to assist us."

Lucia walked up and took Lord Edmund's proffered hand. "Thank you," she responded warmly. She held it a moment, then turned to her brother. "I would like to introduce you to my brother, Lord Michael of Keilder. He is in charge of the forces we brought with us, sixty men strong." Michael approached and grasped the other's hand firmly. Lord Edmund nodded his greeting, then turned to lead the group into the great hall.

The hall was set for lunch, and soon the room was ringing with the voices of soldiers. Lucia stood to one side, watching as Stephen and Michael sat at the head table to discuss strategy with Lord Edmund. Anna was nowhere in sight. She waited for five minutes, then ten … but to her concern Anna did not appear. Excusing herself, she went to the sewing room to see if Anna was there.

She entered the quiet room and suddenly drew to a halt, feeling very out of place. She still wore her boots and traveling clothes, and was tracking mud into the elegant room of embroidered dresses. The women of the room all looked up in shock, and Lucia's eyes found those of Anna to one side. Anna's eyes were red with crying, and before she realized what she was doing, Lucia had flung herself on her knees by Anna's side.

"I am so sorry," was all Lucia could find to say, holding Anna's hands in her own. "If there had been any other way …" Lucia dropped her forehead to Anna's hand and wished there was something else she could do. She felt the enormity of her actions – she had caused Ian's death, and had fallen in love with Stephen. Would Anna ever forgive her?

Lucia heard the rustling as the other women left the room so that she and Anna could be alone. "Please, sit by me," requested Anna quietly. Lucia rose and took the proffered seat as she looked at her friend with pity and remorse.

"I know it was not your fault," began Anna slowly. "Still, it seems such a tragedy. If only he could have made different decisions. If only he had been more strong. Now it is left to us to bury him. We will be having a service for him tomorrow just after midday, in the chapel."

Anna took a deep breath and turned to look out the window. "Lucia, I know this will sound unfair, but it might be best if you did not attend. Yes, Stephen is the one who killed Ian in the end, but it was in essence an honor duel over you. There are still so many raw wounds ..."

Lucia nodded somberly. "Of course," she replied quickly. "Whatever makes it easier for you, I would gladly do. If you want me to leave town ..."

It was Anna's turn to speak up hastily. "Please, no. We already have enough disruption caused by what is going on. Stay, and help against the Grays. Perhaps that will be the best way to heal the wounds, for us all to work together for a common cause."

Lucia nodded her agreement, and Anna maintained her gaze out the window to the landscape beyond. After a few moments, Lucia gave her friend's hand a gentle squeeze. She rose quietly and left the room. Her feet automatically turned in the direction of her bedchambers.

And stopped.

Ellie stood before her, a concerned look on her young face. "We have other rooms in the keep that can be made ready in a heartbeat. After what you endured in that room ... I wasn't sure ..."

Lucia paused at that, looking in the direction of the room. Yes, Ian had taken advantage of her trust. His drunken mind had assumed that she would give herself to him, perhaps with some strong-armed encouragement, just as every other woman in his life had.

That dark night would always be a part of her past.

She drew in a deep breath, her soul lifting. Ian had tainted one night – but there had been so many other stronger memories forged in that room. Memories of Stephen watching loyally at her side while she faced the deepest wraths of the poison. Of his hand twined in hers as she struggled through the pain, desperate to stay alive. Of his eyes – his deep, brown eyes – believing in her, when she had lost all hope.

A soft smile came to her lips. That room was a sign of all she had overcome. The golden lamp beside her bed reminded her that, in the darkness, strength must shine out. There would always be challenges. There would always be hardship. And yet, with Stephen by her side, she knew that together they would find what they had always sought.

Peace.

She nodded to Lucia, determination firing her soul. "Lead on. I would not sleep in any other place."

* * *

Ellie carefully poured more steaming water into the bath as Lucia lay back against the edge of the tub. The late afternoon sun streamed through the stained glass windows. It seemed like ages since she had taken a warm bath - her clothes had all been sent to the laundry already, and a clean, new outfit was laid out by the window.

Ellie set the empty bucket down next to the fireplace, then turned to sit on a wooden stool near the bathtub. Judging by Ellie's cheerful demeanor, she had not been overly upset at the news of Ian's death. The girl had been forceful in turning away visitors since Lucia had returned to the room, protecting her mistress from distraction.

Ellie's eyes shone with warmth. "I am glad that you are back; I really missed you," she enthused. "You appear to finally have a man by your side truly worthy of your affection. I saw the way you and Stephen looked at each other as you rode through the courtyard."

Lucia swirled her hand through the water. "I do care deeply for him," she admitted, relishing the rush of pleasure that came with the words. "I enjoy talking to him about issues, about my feelings, about anything that comes to mind. At other times I simply enjoy being with him."

She smiled for a moment, then sighed. "Still, it is not the time now for thoughts like that. I will be lucky to share five words with him before this is all over. Stephen, Michael, Hector, and I are going to lead four separate sets of forces in a short period of time. We will be deployed along the route by which the attackers are apparently going to approach. It looks like the Grays are planning for their assault to occur within the next few weeks."

"That is what we have heard," nodded Ellie in agreement. "Everyone is holding their breath, waiting for the strike. We are very glad you arrived before their main foray." She sat for a while, then stood. "I will give you some time alone. I imagine you need a rest after so many days on the trail." At Lucia's answering nod she left, closing the door gently behind her.

Lucia lay back in the water and admired the gold and ivory trimmings in the room. Penrith continually impressed her with the attention to detail shown in every corner. Even this, a changing and bath room, was elegantly decorated with tile and marble. Ellie had told her this used to be the lady of the castle's chambers; the lady had sadly died in childbirth when Ian was quite young. Although the rooms were not used until recently, they were always kept in good shape.

Lucia wondered idly how life would change after the Grays were defeated. There would be no more war - they could all settle down to peaceful lives. Perhaps all homes would have decorative touches on the ceilings and on the floors. There would be time to spare for such frivolities.

She chuckled softly at the thought - for so long the war had *been* her life. It was hard to think what peace would hold for her. She would love to stay with Stephen - but would he want her? Would the situation with Ian become a wedge between them? Lucia shook her head. Only time would tell.

Lucia climbed out of the tub and dried herself with a nearby towel. She stood by the window a moment and looked at the calm of the surrounding countryside. This area, at least, was as yet untouched by the fighting. She hoped it wouldn't see much battle scarring before the wars were over. She turned and donned the clothes on the sill.

Looking down, she saw to her surprise that Anna was walking below her, accompanied by Stephen and Michael. The three were deep in conversation, and she found herself wondering what they were talking about. Their voices were low and did not carry up to her room. Lucia found that she'd suddenly lost her appetite, and did not want to join them at dinner, with the memorial service being held tomorrow.

She moved to the bedroom. The golden lamp, as it always did, drew her eyes. It filled her with a sense of strength. This was the room where Stephen had held her to this world, despite all odds. It was where she had hallucinated her father and brother, in the depths of her fever. It had been where she poured out her deepest secrets to the man who she had now pledged her life to.

Her eyes flickered to the window where Ian had leapt. The glass had been repaired, but Ian had paid dearly for his actions. He had lost his life over it. He had destroyed his family's name and ended their line. All that could be taken from him had.

A sense of calm came over her. The past was gone. It was time to focus on the future – on the challenges to come.

She moved to the bed, climbed beneath its covers, and turned her head to the side.

The lamp was there, the row of raised bosses steady along its length. She focused on it, on all it represented, and closed her eyes.

Chapter 23

The day of the service dawned grey and bleak. A turmoil of emotions swirled within Lucia, and she found herself unwilling to even stir from the bed. She glanced at the oil lamp in the corner, then turned her back, pulling the covers deeper over her head.

When Ellie came in, she immediately sensed Lucia's mood. "Shall I just bring food up to you for the day?"

Lucia nodded her agreement, burrowing further into the mattress. She didn't know how she should feel. Guilty for having caused Ian's death? Guilty for having kissed and led him on in order to help protect Stephen? Perhaps guilty for not fighting off Ian well enough when he attacked? The complex feelings seemed to stack up until it was unbearable.

There was a firm knocking on the door, and Michael's voice called through. "Lucia?"

Ellie was by it in a second, opening it a crack, murmuring softly with him. To Lucia's relief, after a minute Michael's footsteps eased down the hall. She did not want to talk with him. Not this morning, when she could barely make sense of her own mind.

Ellie slipped out after him, and in short minutes she had returned with a bowl of gruel and a mug of mead. She sat in the chair by the bed while Lucia ate her breakfast. Lucia knew the girl meant well, but all she could think of was how Stephen had sat in that very spot, how he had trusted her, and in the end she had forced him to drive a sword through the heart of his best friend.

A low knock came at the door, and Stephen's voice eased through it, concern rich in its tone. "Lucia?"

Lucia flushed and turned away, and again Ellie was by the door in a heartbeat. He must have pressed her harder than Michael; her tone became more insistent. But at last, again, the footsteps faded, and Ellie returned to her side.

Lucia knew the sun was drifting higher in the sky, and yet it seemed the shadows grew, that darkness settled into the corners. At last even Ellie's presence pressed in on her. She turned to the girl with a weary smile.

"You have done a world of good this morning, and I thank you. I think I would like to be alone for a while now. I hope you understand."

Ellie's face softened. "Of course," she murmured. She took up the bowl, and with a last gentle look, she eased through the door.

The keep eased into an echoing silence. Lucia puzzled at it, and then the reason why drove into her core. It *was* empty. It was time for the funeral mass.

Guilt and regret swept through her, and then steel shimmered into her soul. She would not upset the keep in any way – but she should show her respect for the man Ian had once been. She should show her repentance for her part in what had happened.

She climbed from bed, drawing a robe around her, and then carefully eased her door open. There was not a person in sight. She stole quietly down the abandoned hallways to a small sitting room at the front of the building. From here she had a clear view of the main courtyard and entrance to the chapel. She had no wish to disturb the mourners with her presence - but she wanted to let Ian know in her own way that she was trying to forgive him.

It seemed that every member of the region was streaming into the building to honor a man that she had caused to die. Lucia felt the tears come, unbidden, and let them flow. She watched as Lord Edmund walked toward the chapel gates. Behind him came Anna, and Lucia saw that Stephen and Michael were on either side of her, helping to support her. Lucia bowed her head in shame. That should have been her position, to lend strength to her friend. Instead, she was the one asked to remain away.

Why was she being treated as the guilty one here? Yes, she had kissed Ian. Did that mean he then had the right to do with her as he pleased? Would they have treated her like this if she had refused his touch, and any contact, from the first day? And, if she had in fact not kissed him during that duel, how would her stay at the keep have ended up?

Lucia knew it was silly to even pursue this line of thought. There was no way to know what other paths would have led to. She only had the path before her to follow as best she could.

The doors closed behind the last of the group. Lucia knelt by the window and looked down on the now quiet courtyard. She poured out her sorrow and grief, and wished there was some way she could undo the tragedies. She hoped that the coming battles would resolve the Gray conflict for good, and that peace could finally come to this land.

It seemed an eternity, then the chapel bell tolled, and the doors opened again. A group of soldiers emerged somberly carrying the coffin. Behind it walked Lord Edmund, his shoulders bowed. Then came Anna, supported by Michael and Stephen. A stream of villagers and townsfolk followed as the group moved around toward the cemetery.

Lucia watched until the last of them had left her vision, and then returned slowly to her room. She climbed into bed and fell into a troubled sleep.

* * *

Lucia awoke to a dull grey morning and realized that she had slept through the day and night again. Ellie was moving around the room, and brought over a mug of warm mead once she realized that Lucia was awake. Lucia pushed herself up to sitting, and gratefully drank down the liquid, her throat parched.

A knocking sounded on the door, and Ellie ran to intercept it. "I am sorry, but Lucia is –"

Michael pushed his way past Ellie, ignoring her protests, and came over to the side of the bed. He sat down in the chair by her side, holding her gaze steadily with his own.

Lucia nodded at her brother, then turned to the maid.

"It is all right, Ellie," she soothed. "Please leave us alone."

Ellie's brow creased, but she nodded in agreement, pressing the main door closed before slipping quietly into the other room.

Michael looked Lucia over with a sharp eye. "I know why you stayed in yesterday, and that is now over with." He took a deep breath and pressed on. "Lucia, I know you react better to logic than to sentiment, so here it goes. We only have a few weeks, if that, to arrange our final defenses. You and the archers are a critical piece in this. You are the best person I have to lead that group, but if you tell me you are not ready, I can find someone else."

He took her hand up in his own, and concern creased his eyes. "I'm here, Lucia, Tell me what to do."

Lucia gave a half-smile, squeezing his hand. They had been through so much together, and she would not let him down now. "I will be fine," she promised. "You are right, the worst is over. Now we must focus on the battle ahead."

Michael patted her arm tenderly, relief visible in his eyes. "I think it will do you good to be with your friends, to be busy with training and preparation."

Lucia took a sip of mead and focused her mind on the task ahead. "So bring me up to speed. What are the current plans?"

Michael sat back in the chair, his shoulders easing. "Each group will practice basic skills every morning until lunch," he explained. "Then we will do run-throughs of battle scenarios for the afternoon. We have scouts out so we should have a full day's notice before the actual strike comes. That will give us time to get into position. Each group will eat in the field between stages, so I am afraid there will not be many meals in the hall."

Lucia nodded, not overly upset at this news. With her archers, she would be safe, amongst friends. She had little wish to be around the main hall and local courtiers so soon after the service for Ian.

Michael talked with her for a while about general strategic issues. Finally, sensing she wished to get up and dressed, he gave her a kiss on the forehead, then left.

Lucia climbed out of bed and donned her gear quickly, heading out to the archery fields. Marcus and Shawn were there, guiding the group of forty or so men through their paces. Soon Lucia was in the thick of things. She helped the men refine their aim and practice timed volleys. Some of the women from the castle brought out ale, cheese, and bread for lunch, and they ate it under the trees of the back field. Then it was time for more practice and exercise.

Lucia found she was quite tired by dinnertime, and looked in on the main hall as the group staggered in. Lord Edmund was at the head table with Stephen, Michael, and Anna sitting alongside him.

Lucia shook her head. She just wasn't ready to join them yet. She went past the archway and on to her room.

Lucia remained with her archers for the rest of the week and shunned all other contact. She drove herself hard, forcing away her longing for Stephen with long hours of intense focus and work. By the end of each evening she was utterly exhausted and collapsed into bed. To her relief, she fell asleep immediately.

As the days ran into each other, Lucia found it was easier than she'd thought to be away from Stephen. All of the forces were out practicing, keeping their separate routines. She never saw Michael or the others; the archers were her sole world for now. Soon Lucia's group settled into a cohesive unit that moved with precision timing. Lucia felt quite pleased with the progress they'd made.

Still, she worried about how Anna was recovering. When a full week had elapsed since the service, she decided it might be time to go down and at least speak with Anna again to express her regrets and see if the friendship could be renewed. She left her room earlier than usual one morning; she planned on stopping by the sewing room on her way out to the archery range.

To her surprise, Lucia heard Stephen's quiet voice coming from the sewing room, and it was followed by a melodic answer in Anna's gentle speech. Lucia's heart stopped at hearing Stephen's tone; longing hit her as powerfully as a pounding waterfall.

God's blood, she missed him.

Lucia couldn't help herself; she drew close to the door to listen to the conversation. The hallway was empty, so she tucked herself in against a tapestry.

"You should at least think about it," Stephen was saying to Anna, a note of encouragement in his voice. "I am not saying you need to answer today, or even next week. Please, just keep the offer in mind."

"I do not know," replied Anna hesitantly. "I will give it thought. I promise."

There was a pause, and Lucia wondered what was going on. She bit her lip to fight the temptation of poking around the corner to look. In another moment, Anna's voice spoke up again. Her voice was quieter now. "Stephen, Lord Edmund wanted you to have this. These are Ian's bracers ..."

The change in Stephen's voice could not have been more striking. Where before it had been quiet, almost placating, it was now tight with controlled fury. "I have told you at dinner more than once," he responded shortly, "I refuse to have *anything* that has to do with Ian. I do not want any reminder of him around me. I ask you to respect that."

It sounded to Lucia like he might storm out of the room, so she quickly left her listening post and darted down the front stairs. She didn't look back as she headed out to the archery fields and her own troops.

Lucia wondered about the conversation all day. What was it that Stephen had wanted of Anna? What offer was she considering? She turned idea after idea over in her head as the men practiced their aim. When the sun finally descended below the horizon, she found herself almost heading into the hall when dinnertime came. However, once again she saw the groups of courtiers, Lord Edmund at the table, along with Stephen, Michael, and Anna. The group looked happy as they laughed together.

Lucia felt as if she was gazing at a picture, one she was no longer a part of. She turned quietly and went up to her room. Once there, she moved to stare out the window.

It was time to put aside thoughts of talking to Anna and Stephen for now. Her presence would only cause them pain and remind them of their recent loss. She would wait until after the fight, no matter how lonely she became.

* * *

Another week passed with Lucia diligently remaining focused on her routine and training. She threw herself into every activity; she wore herself to exhaustion to fend off the longings and the sadness.

She was putting on her boots for the morning exercises when a pounding came on her door. Ellie ran to it and was almost mowed down by Michael, who stormed angrily into the room. He strode over to Lucia and began without any preamble. "You have been skipping dinners on purpose?" he cried out in anger. "Here I thought you and your troops were out on evening exercises this entire time, and that you were eating with them. I have just found out that you have been coming to your room and avoiding all of us."

Lucia sighed and nodded. She wondered why her brother was so upset by this news. "Can you really wonder why?" she asked, looking him in the eye. "Everyone there still blames me for Ian's death. Maybe it will be different after we get through this conflict, when my archers and I have done our part in saving Penrith. Right now I do not want to stir up any bad feelings. It just seemed easier this way."

Michael shook his head and sat heavily on the bed. After a few minutes he looked up. "What about Anna and Stephen?" he asked. "They are your friends, and they miss you. Heck, *I* miss you. I had not seen you in months, and now you have vanished on me again."

Lucia sat down beside him and gave him a hug. "The battle will be over soon enough. Once it is, there will be plenty of time for us to talk on the road back home. In the meantime, give the people here time to heal, to accept their loss."

She turned to look out the window for a long moment, then met her brother's eyes. "The attack is sure to come soon. Let us not argue about how much I socialize in these few weeks. There are so many more important things to focus on."

Michael, concerned, looked into Lucia's eyes. "If you are sure ..." At her nod, he took her hand and gave it a squeeze. "We would be happy to eat up here with you, you know," he added as he gave the situation some thought.

Lucia spoke up quickly. "No, I suspect that would make things even worse," she pointed out. "You three need to support Lord Edmund and to keep the spirits up. It is best this way, really." She saw Michael still considering ideas and leapt in. "No coming up after dinner, either," she added preemptively. "I need lots of sleep to optimize my energy and focus. Please - just give me my time for now."

"As you wish," acquiesced Michael, still seeming a bit unsure. "Well then, I am off," he added. "Stephen's already been out with his crew for two full hours. He is quite the early riser." Michael smiled fondly at his sister, then turned and left.

Lucia watched him go, a pang of loneliness sweeping over her. She did worry about Anna, and her longings for Stephen had become a constant ache.

She hardened her heart. A heated battle was fast approaching. That conflict demanded all of her attention. There would be plenty of time once the attack was over to renew those bonds.

Lucia did find that an extra-large meal was waiting for her in her room that evening, with a few flowers on the tray. She wondered if those had come from Michael or Stephen, and decided that it didn't matter. She gorged herself on the delicious food, and fell into a contented sleep.

* * *

The next morning, Lucia found that she was paying the price for her previous evening's feast. Her pants, a close-fitting style that she had grown accustomed to wearing around the castle, were now rather snug on her. She adjusted the belt to no avail, and shook her head in disbelief. This was just too much. She'd noticed that they'd been growing tighter, but today they simply would not close. Had she gained that much weight while she went to fetch her brother?

She shook out the pants to see if the laundry had made a mistake. The clothes certainly seemed like her standard wear. She hadn't eaten lavish meals while on the road, and, in fact, she remembered being nauseous much of the time.

A thought hit her suddenly, and she sank onto the cushion on the sill. It was almost three months since the night of the party. Almost three months since Ian had raped her. She thought back. She had missed her monthly flow, true, but that happened sometimes with the heavy level of activity, never mind the stress she had been under. She hadn't given it a second thought.

Could she be with child?

Lucia cut the tight waistband with her knife and pulled on her clothes. She went back into her room and sat on the edge of her bed. No matter how she thought about it, she came back to that same conclusion. Summer was coming on in full force - she could hear the birds singing outside. It was a glorious morning. With everything else she had to deal with, she was most likely expecting.

A new thought staggered her.

It might not be Ian's.

The night before the party, she had gone to the pool, and Stephen had been there. She laughed wryly at the thought that for a woman who went so long without even one male to be close to, she now had two to name as the potential father of her child.

Could she tell Stephen about the child, knowing it might not be his?

Could she keep the information from him, knowing it might?

She rubbed her stomach gently and was suddenly overwhelmed with the amazing idea of life within her. A new child. A little boy or girl whom she could sing songs to, teach dances to, and pass along her hopes and dreams.

Lucia patted her abdomen, considering how within those walls a small child innocently grew. She smiled and sighed. It did not matter who the father was. The child was her child. Regardless of the identity of the child's father, she would love her baby and care for it.

Her thoughts turned to Stephen, and she considered her situation. She would never pressure Stephen to honor his offer to marry her. Not after what had happened. She wanted him to stay with her because he loved her, not because he felt he had to. There had to be enough time available to properly rekindle their love before introducing the complexity of a child who might or might not be his.

Lucia stood up and walked back to the window. She could modify the rest of her clothes easily enough - the shirts were already loose, while the pants needed little work. The ones she had worn during the trip must have been stretched slowly, and she doubted she was showing much at all anyway. Tomorrow she would go talk to the leatherworker. He was making a tunic for her with her current measurements, so she would simply ask him to leave the sides loose. She would gain the same protection, but it would last her a while.

She leaned against the side of the window, and stroked the soft, white curtain which was tied back against the side. A child - her child. She would stay to clear this area, then when Penrith was safe, she would accompany the troops north to liberate her own lands. If all went well, Lucia's homelands should be swept free of trouble within two months, and she would still be able to hide her condition. That should give Stephen plenty of time to reveal his true feelings.

If he had not shown her by then that he wanted to stay with her, then she would withdraw her attentions and not cause trouble for him. She knew how to take care of herself. She would stay with her brother in their keep. Keilder was a fair distance from Stephen's lands, and their paths would not have to cross again.

Chapter 24

The next week went by quickly as each day brought the tension of imminent attack to a higher level. Lucia saw little of Stephen, Michael, or Anna. Where before she had considered this absence to be a blessing, now she worried about the growing chasm during every waking hour. She needed to spend time with Stephen, if only in casual conversation. She needed to hear his voice, to look into his eyes, and to sense how he felt.

Her mind settled, the next morning Lucia awoke much earlier than usual, determined to catch Stephen before he left for the day. She dressed quickly, buoyed up by the thought of spending time with him, even if only for a short while.

She had barely entered the crowded main hall when a trio of scouts raced into the packed room, calling for attention. The room went quiet in an instant, all eyes turning as one.

"The Grays are on our borders!" called out the taller scout, breathing in hard. In an instant the room became a hive of activity, and Lucia stood on a table, calling out for her archers to attend to her.

Hurried activity swept around her as she laid out her orders. Her men immediately ran to gather up their supplies. As they returned Lucia made sure to talk personally with each man, ensuring he knew his place in the battle and was prepared. Around her, servants labored at a myriad of tasks and soldiers ferried weapons and armor.

Finally she went up to her own room to make final preparations to head out. She sat down on the bed to remove and reseat her boots, her pack ready on the bed beside her. She paused for a moment, one boot in her hand, and took a deep breath. It seemed since she realized she was pregnant that tasks had become more difficult to do. It was probably her mind playing tricks on her. She was only a few months along at the most - did babies grow that fast? She was doing her best to eat well...

She shook her head and put the other boot on. She was probably just imagining things. She wished that somehow there had been time for her to talk with Stephen, if only briefly. She would feel better if she knew what his feelings were. Had they cooled since their time together on the road? Was he just distracted by the preparations for defense?

Lucia stood and put the pack over one shoulder. She reached to where her sword stood next to the fireplace, and ran her hand over the runes engraved on the blade. Her mind felt as if it was a raging river, reflecting the noise and shouting that sounded around her from the castle's household.

How did Stephen feel? She would like to believe he loved her as deeply as she loved him; that for some reason he was holding back. It seemed strange to her that he had not found *some* time to spend with her - to stop by in the morning, to visit in the evening. But was that fair? She realized that she herself had been avoiding doing these things. She certainly had not gone by his room, or made the effort to walk into the dining hall. Could she blame him when she was just as guilty? Perhaps he felt as awkward as she did at publicly displaying a relationship so soon after Ian's death and his breakup with Anna.

Her emotions see-sawed from hope to despair. She couldn't wager something as important as her child's life on a flickering dream. Stephen could have his reasons for staying away, true, but she couldn't wait a lifetime for him to reveal them to her.

She gave her blade a sweep through the air, her face set in determination. More than likely he had decided, now that he was back in court and with nobility, that she wasn't right for him. It didn't matter if it was her past, her personality, or the things she had done. All that mattered was that her child should not grow up with anything less than full love and acceptance.

She slid the blade firmly into the scabbard and took one last look around the room. Deliberately, she forced her tumbling emotions to calm, to soothe the wild feelings which swept around her. Now was not the time for snap decisions. Stephen still had plenty of time to make his feelings known. She wanted to find some ember of that love, some hint that he would want to stay with her and the child, not out of honor, but because he truly wanted to. She was willing to fan any spark into a fire. Barely a few months along - she had plenty of time. They were in the middle of a battle, with far more important things to worry about.

Decided, she strode from the room and headed down to the main gallery.

The hall downstairs was jammed full of soldiers receiving last minute instructions. She moved quickly to join her group of archers, looking over the men with pride. They had proven themselves to be some of the best in the land, and their teamwork had become exemplary.

Lord Edmund stood at attention at the head table, and all eyes turned to him, the room settling into quiet. He cleared his voice, then spoke in ringing tones.

"My friends, the time has come. We all know the plan. Stephen and his scouts will be stationed closest to our enemy's approach. Hopefully the enemy will move right past them without realizing it. The Grays will then continue forward into Michael's soldiers.

"I will be on the castle walls, monitoring the Grays' approach. Once they reach the point of no return, Stephen will close in from the back. Our remaining keep forces will prevent the Grays from pressing into the city. Hector here will rain fury in from either side."

His eyes looked out over the sea of faces, connecting with Lucia's. He nodded quietly at her. "Finally, Lucia's archers will line the forest escape. This guarantees that any remnants of the army cannot reform to harm us again.

"My fellow soldiers, I wish you all luck. To victory!"

The cheers rang out, filling the hall with their noise and thunder. Then the groups began to break up, moving out at a fast pace toward their destinations.

Lucia's heart leapt, and she looked around quickly through the throng. She pushed her way through the crowd to Michael, and embraced him strongly. Michael returned the hug, kissing her on the forehead. In spite of their determination, battle plans could always go awry, and the Grays could somehow overrun their forces. Michael smiled down at her, then clasped her firmly on the shoulder. "Good luck, Lucia," he wished her gently, then turned sharply and headed out the door with his officers. Hector and his forces were the next to leave, to take their positions.

Lucia looked over the emptying hall. Only her own archers and Stephen's forest men remained. She realized that Stephen was staring at her from across the room, and she moved through the crowd to get to him. As she approached him, powerful feelings washed completely through her, almost overwhelming her.

She loved him. By God, she loved him completely. He was everything that she wanted in a partner. She knew it as a certainty; she wanted to be with him forever.

Lucia took a deep breath, and wished with all her heart that he would return her feelings.

Stephen's eyes softened for a moment, then were somber. He took her hand in his, drawing her into a more quiet corner of the room. As he did, a scout ran into the room, heading right for Stephen. The scout was out of breath, but gasped, "They are almost here, Stephen. The Grays are moving more quickly than we anticipated. We have got to get out there."

Stephen swore softly, but nodded to the scout. He then turned to Lucia, and touched her face gently. "There is not time," he murmured half to himself. He slipped something in her hand. "I would like you to have this ring," he offered, folding it into her fingers. He hesitated for a moment, then with a final look he called out to his men. Immediately the group ran out the archway toward their waiting horses.

Lucia stood still for a moment, watching the room empty. What was the importance of the ring? What would he have said, if the scout hadn't sounded the alert? She looked at the ring he'd pressed into her hand. It seemed a simple design, with a blue stone in its center. Was this a ring he had made for her, as a gift? Was it one of his own rings? She seemed to recall a similar one he had worn, but she couldn't be sure.

Lucia shook her head. She would know well enough after the conflict, when she finally had some time to talk with him. She turned to address her group.

"You know well what is expected of you. We are the element of surprise - men in battle will take risks expecting you to cover them. You are the best, and our side will win. To battle!"

The cry was taken up by the others, and they went out at a run to their waiting steeds.

* * *

Stephen soon caught up with Michael's group, and pulled his horse alongside Michael's at a canter, their troops temporarily mingling. "They are about twenty minutes out," called out Stephen, his voice low and urgent. "You need to get yourself in place so that the Grays do not stop too soon. We need them all to enter into the ambush zone in order for this to work."

"I will be there," vowed Michael with conviction. "You can count on our forces to hold the line, no matter what the cost."

"We must draw our net tightly," insisted Stephen, his eyes worried. "Every man that gets past us …"

"… goes in Lucia's direction," finished Michael, nodding in agreement. "It will be done."

Stephen turned to pull his horse away, but Michael reached out a hand. "Wait," he called out, and Stephen edged his horse closer in, the two still riding at high speed down the lane.

"Did you finally get a chance to talk with Lucia?" asked Michael, concern ringing in his voice.

Stephen shook his head, reigning in his horse slightly to make it easier to talk. "The alert came too quickly, there was not enough time."

He took a deep breath, then looked over at Michael. "I love your sister. I hope she knows that by now. Still, to ask more of her would be unfair before she got to know me better. We have barely talked for the past two weeks. I want to renew that trust with her, to show her that I can be depended on."

He paused for a long moment, his face reflective. "I did give her my ring, just in case. She should have that much, in case something happens to me in battle."

Michael sighed in exasperation. "You should have said something to her," he repeated. "Because this *is* a battle. It is best to have a clear mind when going into this kind of situation." He shook his head. "There is nothing to be done about it now; it will have to wait until after the fight is over."

The two men nodded in farewell, then thundered off to their respective positions.

* * *

On the other side of the ridge, Lucia was demarking a line along a main trail with her archers. She motioned the others into their positions and took up her own behind a large, gnarled oak. She focused her mind on the task at hand, mentally calculating where each of her soldiers were, what angle shot they would have on anyone moving against them. She determined which would be able to see the enemy first, and which would have the clearest line of sight.

An hour passed, and they heard the sounds of fighting from far off. The battle had begun. Lucia moved amongst her troops, keeping them settled. It was not their place to rush in to help. Their job was to prevent a retreat. Time passed, punctuated by noise, held by long periods of silence.

Despite her years of training, Lucia's focus began to slip, and a welling of emotions bubbled up within her. What was she going to do about her child, this innocent new life within her? She shook her head, driving herself to concentrate on the task at hand, but it was as if her mind had two masters now. Her eyes teared of their own accord, her breath came in long draws. She bit her lip, focusing on the pain, willing herself to push aside the cascade of feelings, to stamp down the irrational fears and longings which seeped into her consciousness. Now was not the time for this. She knew better, she was better than this. She would do her job.

She brushed her hair from her eyes, focusing her gaze back down the trail, but there was no motion at all there. Things were quiet. Thank the Lord for that at least. She prayed Stephen was doing well in his battles, that the quiet did not intimate a victory by the bandits. Her heart seized with pain at the thought of Stephen being overrun, overwhelmed. What if he was slain? Her heart began to thunder, panic edging every thought. What if her child grew up never knowing how kind Stephen could be, how full of strength, how caring ...

Suddenly a loud snap sounded above her. She looked up and froze as she saw a muscular, scarred man leering over her. There was a vicious glint in his eyes as he grinned down at her. In one hand he held a dagger pointed toward her belly; his other hand raised to his lips. "Shhh, now, my pretty," he soothed in a crackling voice. "There is no need for anyone to know I am here ..."

Lucia moved her hand slowly toward her knife, but at the same time her gaze was transfixed by the dagger pointing at her child ... her child ...

The Gray gasped in surprise and shock, and as he toppled over, Lucia could see the protruding shafts of a pair of arrows that had embedded themselves into his back. She sat back in shock at the suddenness of it all. Marcus and Shawn ran over to her, low and silent, their eyes showing concern.

Marcus's voice was rich with concern. "Are you all right?"

Lucia shook her head, furious with herself "If I had been paying attention that never would have happened," she berated herself in a harsh whisper. "I cannot believe I let that man get so close to me. What was I thinking ...?"

Shawn patted her on the shoulder and chuckled softly. "Do not worry about it, Lucia. Everyone has that happen every once in a while. We will get back to our positions." They ran back to cover, and Lucia, her face burning with shame, determinedly faced the road to watch for more soldiers.

* * *

In another hour, the fighting groups moved nearer as the Grays' retreat was pushed backwards. The archers spotted troops coming through in greater and greater numbers. Often Lucia's archers could only watch as the two forces fought along the path, but sometimes they had a clear shot and could take out one of the Grays without endangering their own soldiers. The day wore on, the strain and noise of battle taking its toll on the fighters involved. Eventually, the fighting in their area slowed, and the remaining Grays retreated the way they had come with soldiers in strong pursuit of them.

As nightfall swept across the forest, the sounds of battle had long since died off. Lucia sighed wearily. The day's melee was over, and she was completely exhausted. Two of her men had been injured, and had already been escorted back to the chapel. She sat heavily against the tree which had served so well as her protection, and laid the bow next to her in the grass. So close - she had come inches from being injured or killed by that rogue scout.

It was no use. She had to face the fact that she would be unable to remain as a useful fighter while she was pregnant. Her lapses in attention could easily cause others to be killed. She could not allow her concern for her unborn child to jeopardize her men.

She felt a hand on her shoulder, and looked up. It was Shawn, his weathered face creased with lines, smiling at her with concern. "It was a good fight," he complimented, straightening up and resting his hand on the hilt of his sword. "You were an excellent leader. We could not have asked for better."

Lucia picked up a small rock, glanced at it for a moment, and absently tossed it at a nearby tree. "You could have asked for someone who was not daydreaming when the battle was first joined," she grumbled, still quite upset with herself.

Shawn grinned. "Now, come on," he rejoined easily. "Everyone has a moment like that at least once in a while. Besides, it could hardly be helped for someone in your condition. Why, I was just telling Marcus -"

Lucia leapt to her feet, glowering.

"What do you know of my condition," she hissed under her breath. "Nobody was supposed to -"

She stopped and took a deep breath. This was not going well at all. Her emotions were a pack of hunting dogs in a flock of partridge, and she struggled to draw them into order.

Her voice was tight with the effort when she spoke again. "What condition do you speak of?"

Shawn took a step back, his eyes creasing as he reevaluated the situation. "We have not said anything to anyone," he promised. "We just guessed, between the way you have been eating, your previous sickness, and, well ..."

He motioned at her waistline.

Lucia looked down. Her cloak was flung back, and the modifications to her tunic, while not yet being taken advantage of by a bulge, were still quite visible.

Shawn gave an expressive shrug. "But if you do not want it known, you can trust us not to be the ones to speak of it," he vowed. "We will not tell a soul what we have seen."

Lucia's shoulders slumped. There was no cause for her to take out her frustrations on her loyal companion. "I am sorry," she sighed. "I am just on edge from the fighting. I would appreciate it if you kept this to yourself, at least for now."

Shawn nodded, his eyes somber. He slipped back into the woods, and Lucia winced as he bent his head to Marcus and spoke to him in low murmurs.

This is how it would begin.

She sighed as she leaned over to retrieve her bow and quiver. If the two men had noticed, others would not be far behind. Soon the whole castle would be whispering about her. About her and Ian's bastard she carried within her.

She remembered the fury in Stephen's eyes when the soldiers had come to retrieve Ian's body. How would he look on her, when he realized that Ian's son now grew within her womb?

She wrapped her arms defensively around her abdomen. *She had to get away.*

She strode over to where Troy was tied, and quickly mounted him. She urged him into a canter, and soon they were traveling the road she had come by only this morning. She occasionally passed discarded weapons and injured men, but already the way was clear and the women tending to the hurt.

Jubilation was all around her; the fight had been won. Only one key battle now remained - that of her own lands back north. With the southern areas clear of danger, a full force would be able to be gathered for that attack. Yes, she imagined the battle could be difficult, but she was sure her side would prevail.

They had no need for one extra woman.

Especially a woman who might not be ready when she was needed. A woman whose inattention could lead to a disastrous rout.

Exhaustion swept over her. It was nearly impossible to think. She needed time to evaluate her choices, to figure out what she should do. She could not stay in Penrith; that was not an option. She had no home to return to, either.

There must be another way.

She thought of her times out on patrol, how much she had enjoyed the peaceful serenity of the forest. Her mind latched onto this solution. She would simply go on her own for a month or two. She would be out of the way of the battle, and have the peace she needed to work on a solution.

She planned out the idea as she rode. Once she got word that her home was regained, she would move back to Michael's side, quietly, to be with him for her final months of pregnancy. But could she stay there, an unmarried mother, once the child was born? Surely it would prove a hard life for the young child ...

Her eyes lit up. She would talk with her brother about living in one of the more remote, northern outposts. The villagers there would accept her without question. Enough families had been shattered by the bandits to make that easy. She would be able to raise her child in peace and quiet, without shame.

Lucia fingered the smooth ring which rested in her pocket. Perhaps Stephen *did* care ... but he had stayed away from her since their return to Penrith.

She shook her head, her thoughts a flock of blackbirds scattering at a sudden noise. Who had stayed away from whom? Nothing seemed to make sense to her any more.

Had she stayed away from him? She hadn't really given him any chance to spend time with her. Had she wanted him to take extraordinary steps to reach her, like a princess in a tower?

Lucia took in a deep breath, then let it out. She supposed it didn't matter at this point. She no longer had the luxury of waiting to see. To stay with the forces would put them into more danger; she could not do that. With time running out, Lucia couldn't trust that Stephen would admit his love, freely, before she felt obligated to leave. She would never pressure him into making this decision.

She rode a while longer, lost in thought. The more she considered it, the more correct her action seemed. She would get clear of the fighting, get clear of Penrith. If nothing else, having time on her own would let her figure out what to do with her life.

After some time, she approached a larger group of soldiers. She saw Michael off to one side, and sighed at the thought of being separated from him for another few months. It would be easier not to tell him, she decided. If he knew of her plans, he would talk her into remaining behind at Penrith while the forces went ahead to Keilder. That was the *last* thing she wanted to do. Her only other alternative was to go with the forces, where she knew she would be in the way.

Lucia tried to smile as he spotted her, rode up to her, and embraced her heartily.

Michael's voice was rich with satisfaction. "The day was a success," he assured her. "All of our plans came together with precision, and we had a minimum of losses. We are going to push on toward Keilder first thing tomorrow morning, to maintain our momentum. Stephen is back at the keep already, spreading the news."

Michael nudged Lucia with his arm, his high energy shining in his eyes. "I hear he is also going to make an announcement, one that you'll be quite interested in. Something special. Come on, we are heading out there ourselves." He kicked his horse, wheeled it around, and headed down the road toward the keep. The soldiers thundered with him

Lucia looked after him with her mouth open in surprise. Her whole being flooded with joy and anticipation. Wonderful news? Perhaps her days of worrying had been for nothing! Of course Stephen hadn't wanted to interrupt the mourning period with a new relationship. It would have been disrespectful for him to court her openly so soon after having broken the engagement with Anna. No wonder Stephen had stayed away from her. He was acting with the utmost of honor while they were still at Penrith.

Her heart sang. Now that the battle was over, and the mourning period for Ian was over, she and Stephen could renew their bonds. They would leave Penrith tomorrow and be side by side on the road again, just as before. Soon they would be back in her homelands. Stephen would be free to spend time with her as often as he chose.

She had been childish to want him to hurt Anna's reputation and the sensibilities of Ian's family. It would have been selfish for them to openly demonstrate their love during the past few weeks.

Lucia was in the courtyard before she realized it. Troy's hooves clattered on the cobblestones as she dismounted and ran up the stairs. She paused in the archway leading into the main hall. Her eyes quickly took in the clamor of servants busily preparing a victory feast. To one side she saw Stephen and Michael talking with Lord Edmund. She paused for a moment and gazed at him with happiness, wondering how she could have been so disturbed over a mere few weeks of separation. Stephen felt her attention, and turned with a wide smile on his face.

"Lucia! We have won! We have won!" he called triumphantly, and then suddenly he strode over to hold her against him, resting his head on top of hers. Lucia embraced him tightly in return, almost crying in relief. It seemed like years since they had ridden together, spoken together. She sighed contentedly in his arms, the stress of the weeks' efforts melting away.

After a moment, he broke the embrace and held her out from him. "The dinner will be in a few hours, and there will be a wonderful announcement. I hope you will be happy with -"

He took in the weary lines in her face, and his brow drew close in concern. He brushed the hair gently from her cheek. "I am being selfish; there will be enough time for talk later. You need to go up and rest."

Michael's voice rang out in the hall. "Stephen, over here!" Stephen glanced up at once, then gave Lucia a tender hug. "Go now, rest," he insisted, then turned to trot quickly in Michael's direction.

Lucia's heart sank as he left her so brusquely. She shook the feeling off with deliberate effort. The battle had barely been finished; there were still important loose ends for him to finalize. He was right – her part was at last complete. She should rest and clean off the dirt of battle.

She moved up the stairs, and down the hallway to push open her door.

It was as if Ian's presence was there with her, his breath hot on her neck, his arms reaching for her, and waves of panic drove her to her knees. She drew in long, shaky breaths, desperately drawing herself together.

What was going on?

After several long moments the feeling passed, and she was able to stand, to push her door shut, and look around the room again. It was as it had always been. The white curtains fluttered at the window. The lamp sat, dark, on the table by her bed.

She ran a trembling hand through her hair. She was struggling on an emotional see-saw, with feelings barely within her control. Maybe the baby being inside her was affecting her?

She made herself breathe more slowly and struggled to rein in her racing thoughts. She had always prided herself on her logic, on maintaining a close rein on her fiery temper. It seemed to her that her grip on her emotions was now tenuous at best.

She thought again of Stephen waiting for her below, and she focused on that with all her might. As long as Stephen was there beside her, she could get through anything.

Determined, she moved into the adjacent room. The bathwater was waiting, but Ellie was nowhere in sight. She stripped off her clothes and eased into the scented water. After the chaos of the morning, it was nice to see the gentle, evening light spilling over the tiles, and to watch the fire crackle under the mantelpiece. She drifted in and out of sleep, dreaming of her future with Stephen and their child.

After a while Lucia shook herself awake, and dried herself off. She donned a loose dress of white muslin and lace, with gold trimming draped from her waist and around her neckline.

There was a sound at the door, and Ellie peered around its edge, smiling in delight as she took in the sight before her.

"Why Lucia, you are positively glowing!" she cried happily.

Lucia simply nodded in response, and sat by the window, slowing brushing her hair until it gleamed. She had worn it braided throughout the long travel to and from the coast. It had been braided each day as she engaged in her archery work.

Tonight she would leave it loose.

Soon it was time for dinner. Lucia stomach roiled with nervous energy. She wondered just what would be announced in front of the group. Would Stephen tell his foster family that he was planning on staying with the Keilders even after the battle was through? Would he go a step further, and let them know how he felt about Lucia? She thought back through her life, and it seemed that every twist and turn had somehow brought her to this point. The heartache and suffering was worth it, if it led to her and Stephen being together. That was all that really mattered. She could not believe how happy she was.

Lucia entered the dining hall with uncertainty. She had not been in the room for a meal for several weeks, and she worried at the reception she might receive. It appeared that time had healed their wounds, however. Courtiers looked at her with a smile, and several approached her to offer thanks for the role she had played in the victory. Even Lord Edmund made a special effort to greet her, and guide her back to sit by his side.

Lucia smiled in relief. Her weeks of longing and patience had at last paid off. Her absence for the mourning period had allowed the family to get through their grief and enabled them to accept her back in their lives once again.

Michael came and sat on Lucia's other side, and between Lord Edmund and Michael she learned many of the details about the day's battle. Stephen was on Lord Edmund's other side, and she could hear that he was also answering numerous questions about the battle. The food was excellent, the early summer harvest providing flavors and colors that had been long missed. Even so, Lucia scarcely noticed the aromatic dishes in her anticipation of the announcement.

Finally, the moment came. When Stephen stood to speak, her whole body tensed. She turned to look at him, and he smiled over at her fondly before addressing the hall.

"Friends and countrymen, we have triumphed against a common evil. Our victory over the Grays today was nearly total. The Grays have now been driven from your country, and soon we will end their rampage with an assault on their sole remaining fortification. The land will soon be safe for peace and prosperity once again!"

Cheers echoed through the hall, and Stephen waited for the room to quiet.

Lucia looked out at the room - the proud banners fluttered in the light breeze, the tables were brimming with food and surrounded by happy warriors and ladies. Dogs, full on a meal of scraps, lounged in the center of the hall. A new spirit had come over the castle - the taste of victory. She would always remember this day.

"Now," announced Stephen into the quieted room, "I have an announcement I would like to make." Lucia took a deep breath, and tried to calm her shaking hands. "Her presence is so warm, we could not think of being without her for long. I am glad to announce that Anna, with her parents' permission, will be following us to Keilder in a few weeks, as soon as the final victories are assured."

Lucia looked up in surprise to see that Michael had joined Stephen, and was standing on Anna's other side.

"Yes," Michael added, taking Anna's hand, "and we hope she decides to stay for a long time."

The hall filled with shouts, and Anna beamed her pleasure at the group of revelers.

The fires crackled, but suddenly Lucia was intensely cold. The sounds rang out, hurting her ears with their sharpness. The lights of the torches and candles flared against her eyes. Lucia was hollow, as if no emotions could reside within the thin, crackling shell of her body. The voices bouncing off of the cavernous ceilings might as well be reverberating inside her empty heart.

Then, suddenly, Lucia was swathed in a ball of wool. Sounds were muffled. The room seemed to dim, with only shifting shadows surrounding her. Her chest constricted inwards and she could barely breathe.

She saw Stephen's smile echoed on Michael's face. She remembered quietly congratulating Anna, who was glowing with pleasure. Somehow she made it out of the crush of people, and found her way up the stairs. Soon she was back in her room, curled up in the window seat. Her mind was a jumbled whirl which refused to settle down into coherent thought.

Lucia groaned in distracted agony as she traced the window pane with her finger. Her thoughts seemed like shards of glass, scattered into a million pieces, reflecting each other, not making any sense.

Tears streamed down her face, but she made no motion to wipe them away. Her sense of loss was too complete to negate it.

Stephen wanted Anna by his side.

She chuckled wryly to herself, struggling to remain strong. Michael's warmth about the relationship made perfect sense. After all, when had she ever talked with Michael about her love for Stephen? In the past she had shared everything with her twin, every slight thought, but she had never mentioned Stephen, not once. For all Michael knew, Stephen was merely a bodyguard who had accompanied her on her trip.

And Stephen …

Lucia forced herself to think about the past few weeks with a logical mind. Stephen's distance could simply have been a sign of his growing re-attachment to Anna. She had found the two together numerous times. All the pieces began to fit neatly into place.

Lucia reached into the bag at her side, withdrawing the ring, turning it slowly in her fingers.

The ring was a parting gift.

Her heart sank into a shadowy morass. It was a final thank-you for their time together before he went off to start his glorious new life with Anna by his side. With the Grays defeated, he could give her all she wanted – a safe home, a secure land to raise their children.

The luminous full moon was just rising over the forest, illuminating the fields in a silvery glow. Summer planting was fully underway, and the young crops shimmered in the gentle light. The city walls, fortified in her absence, loomed strong and protective beyond, and a few cows slept in their shadow. Such a peaceful scene, and yet she felt so alone and desolate.

She gazed out at the moon. So many important turning points had occurred under that large moon. Maybe this was a sign that a new fork in the path lay before her.

She shook off the feeling of hopelessness. The problem was not with the situation. The problem was with her endless vacillations and assumptions. She had allowed herself to get wrapped up in this delusion, and was surprised when the bubble burst.

It was time for her to sort through her options in a cold, logical manner.

She sat up, thinking carefully.

Clearly, Penrith would be an uncomfortable place to remain. Her growing size would be a constant reminder to the folk here of all they had lost.

Keilder was not yet retaken. It would be too dangerous to head north.

She could hardly ride the long distance south to her uncle's keep alone. And no soldiers could be spared during this critical juncture.

That only left being on her own.

She nodded in fierce resolution, her hand dropping to her abdomen. She could do it. She *had* to do it.

Just as she had avoided making waves for the past few weeks, she would find somewhere to remain hidden during these critical days ahead while Keilder was made safe. When the conflict was finally over, there would be ample time to determine her future path.

Lucia stood up and gathered her clothes, packing the ones she would need into a large leather bag. She left the dresses - they would be of little use - but packed the loose shirts and pants. Her belongings easily fit into the bag.

She arranged the room properly, stopping to look at each item in it. It had almost grown to be a home, this room of white. Despite the one night of pain it had held, she would miss it.

She came to the golden oil lamp resting on the table at the side of her bed. Her resolve nearly failed her as she ran a hand along its bossed surface. Stephen had meant so much to her. His sturdy hand had kept her safe when death had advanced against her. His steadfast concern had watched over her. She loved him with every fiber of her being; with every last breath in her body.

She dropped her eyes, looking away. Sometimes life simply did not give a person what they desired most.

She moved back toward the door, then hesitated. She wanted Michael to know she left willingly. There was no use in him mounting a search party for her when she did not want to be found. She fingered the Keilder brooch on her shoulder, and unclasped it. She laid it in the middle of her bed. There, she had finished this chapter of her life. She was leaving this past behind her, and setting out on her own. She was choosing a new path - one that was best for her and her child. Nothing else mattered.

Lucia again fingered the ring in her pocket. Stephen had given that to her, and not to Anna. It was a token of their time together. She would keep it for the child.

Lucia found, to her surprise, that it was easy enough to get out of the keep without questions. As a leader of the victorious archers, she was congratulated and hailed instead of being stopped. Soon she was through the main gate and heading north on the road she had traveled so often when she had first arrived at Penrith.

She doubted she would ever return to that town, and turned for a moment as Troy rode along. She watched as the walls slowly faded from sight.

Sighing, she resolutely fixed her eyes on the trail ahead and did not look back again.

Chapter 25

Michael stretched back in his chair as the enthusiastic babble of the hall washed over him, and smiled tenderly at Anna. He was overjoyed she was going to join them in Keilder when the fighting was over. With any luck, she would agree to stay there with him. They had only known each other for a few weeks, but the connection between them had been immediate. Time would tell if their fondness grew into something stronger.

Shawn and Marcus had joined Stephen, and the three were exchanging tales with increasing laughter. Michael turned to talk to Lucia, but was surprised when he found her seat vacant. He looked around - how long had she been gone? It was unlike her to leave a party so soon, especially when she had seemed so excited earlier. Had she been wounded, and not told the others? He stood, waving Stephen to stay seated when he also began to rise. Turning, he walked across the hall and headed up the stairs.

'It would be just like her not to get her wounds treated,' he thought wryly as he took the stairs two at a time. He realized with a pang he had hardly spoken with her since their arrival at Penrith. All of the preparations and planning had taken precedence, and she had seemed so desirous of solitude. He and the others had assumed that it was hard on her to live in the place that brought her such bad memories, so they had given her the space to be alone.

Michael knocked softly on her door, and got no response. Waiting a moment, he heard soft sobbing coming from within. He opened the door gently and looked inside. "Lucia," he called with concern, "are you all right?"

Ellie was spread out on the bed, holding something, and crying. In a moment Michael was at her side. "What is it," he demanded. "What has happened?"

Ellie sniffed and sat up. Michael saw that she held Lucia's brooch, and took it from her. "She is gone," blurted out Ellie. "She took her clothing, and her things, and Troy, and she has gone. I have asked everywhere. She was seen heading north. Look at this room, she does not intend on returning. I know she was going to be gone tomorrow anyway, but for her to run off in the night ..." She bit her lip and buried her face in her hands as her breath came in long sobs.

Michael stood, confused, and strode to the window. Why had she left a night early? Why hadn't she told anyone that she was leaving? Did she want to scout out some route before the main force headed out? He had no worry for her safety, and the weather was certainly fine. Her motivations simply didn't make any sense, though.

Michael thought back to the last time he'd seen her. She was at the dinner ... and then the speech ...

Michael turned to Ellie, baffled. "Do you have any idea what made her go now, without letting us know?" he asked, bewildered. "She seemed fine before the announcement; she was sitting right beside me. Was it the news about Anna coming to join us? Does she not like Anna? I thought they were great friends."

"Oh, they are," replied Ellie shakily, sitting up and frowning in concentration. She thought for a while, tapping a finger on her lip. "I did not see her before dinner, so I do not know what kind of a mood she was in. Nobody remembers seeing her with anybody else between dinner and her leaving, so I do not think she was harassed by someone here." She sighed and shook her head.

Ellie ran a distracted hand through her hair. "It does not make any sense. She had already been here for three weeks. Staying one more night should not have been a problem, if her intention had been to leave with your forces in the morning. So I wonder if she does not plan on going with you - and had no desire to remain behind ..." She shook her head again and wiped her eyes on her sleeve.

Michael swore and headed back toward the hall. Ellie was right. Obviously she wouldn't have wanted to stay at Penrith, and her actions seemed to indicate that she did not want to stay with the forces either. Where was she going, then? It was almost midnight, and the forces had to be on the move at daybreak to maintain their advantage. There was just no time to figure this out or to find Lucia to ask her.

Michael had worked with his sister in just about every combat situation he could imagine. She had always been there. He just couldn't imagine Lucia leaving halfway through their a fight against the Grays, especially as they moved to clear their own homelands.

It all seemed to hinge on Stephen and his announcement. Could it be Stephen had said something to upset her, and she had left in order to stay clear of him?

His face set, he turned to the stairs.

* * *

Stephen leant back in his chair, relaxation finally easing his shoulders. The few remaining partygoers were stumbling to their quarters while servants moved from table to table, cleaning up dishes and throwing scraps to the few dogs still awake. Marcus and Shawn talked quietly amongst themselves to one side.

Strong footsteps rang out, and he looked up in surprise. Michael was striding toward him, with Ellie scurrying along behind. Her face was streaked with tears.

Cold fear stabbed through Stephen's heart, and he leapt to his feet. "What is it?"

Michael's voice growled with anger. "Lucia has gone, and for good, it seems," he snapped. "She left after the announcement at dinner. Is there anything you would like to tell me?"

Stephen's face paled with concern and shock. "I have stayed away from her these past three weeks, you know that," he answered quickly. "Lucia asked repeatedly to be left on her own while we were here, and I respected her wishes. I knew, once we left these walls, that we would be free of all constraints from the past."

He shook his head, his throat going tight. "I even gave her my ring, before the battle began. We were one day away from being together. *One day.*"

Michael's voice grew louder in frustration. "If she was happy after the battle, and happy before the announcement, then what made her leave? Ellie says that nobody else spoke with Lucia after the announcement. She simply got up and left."

Stephen froze. His mind suddenly focused on that announcement, on Lucia's dazed look. A thought dawned on him, and he let out a soft groan. When he looked up at Michael, his face was haggard.

"Perhaps she thought that announcement meant I wanted Anna for myself again. I was the one who made the statement; I was the one giving her such praise."

Michael's face showed his disbelief. "That is preposterous," he snapped. "How in the world would she get that idea? Anyone who had seen us together for the past three weeks would know that I was actively courting her. You have been busy talking with Lord Edmund and your own troops. You have hardly been *near* Anna."

Shawn stood up at this, a bit unsteady from wine, holding his drink in one hand. He stepped in to distract his two friends. "Come now, gentlemen," he put in appeasingly, "it is pretty easy to see how she could have gotten a little confused. Heck, you know how women are in that condition. Their emotions run wild! Furious one minute, tender the next, and then -"

Stephen and Michael turned as one to stare at Shawn. Marcus stood quickly and stepped in front of Shawn, hushing his friend with a sharp sound. "I am afraid Shawn has had too much to drink," he interjected hastily. "He does not know what he is saying."

Michael's voice was cool and steely, and his eyes flashed. "Oh, I think he does. Explain yourself, Shawn," he ordered.

Shawn and Marcus loyally kept their mouths closed. The silence stretched on. Stephen stepped in, his voice tense but holding a more placating tone. "I know you want to protect Lucia," he reassured them. "Remember, we are in the middle of a war here, and she is now out on her own. We need to know the situation."

Marcus finally nodded and sat back on the table's edge. "It was the nausea, her other symptoms, and then her tunic alterations that we noticed," he explained. "She is apparently with child, maybe three months now, given when the symptoms began." He glanced involuntarily at the seat that Ian had usually occupied, and then back at the men before him. "Considering the circumstances, it would have been awkward for her to remain here."

He paused for a long moment, then continued in a quieter tone. "I did not wish to say anything about the battle, but she was distracted; more so than I have ever seen her before. She was wracked with guilt over her lapse. She probably felt that, because of her emotions, she should avoid the upcoming fighting. So, between wanting to leave here, but not wanting to join our forces, I imagine that left her little choice, in her own mind at least."

Michael slammed his hand into his fist. "She is carrying the child of the person she hates. No wonder she ran, afraid to stay here in Ian's home, or to go with us into battle. To think this whole time I left her alone, figuring she would appreciate the quiet." He sat heavily, his face brooding. "I figured she would be thrilled to have Anna with her, but she had other things on her mind. Ian's child..."

Stephen looked up, and took a deep breath. "It could be my child," he admitted quietly. "The night before Ian's assault, we were together."

The others glanced around in surprise, but Stephen barely registered it. His face shadowed with pain as he thought of Lucia facing this issue alone.

Regret laced through him. "If I had known she was pregnant, there is no question I would have spent time with her, no matter her concerns for Anna or Lord Edmund's feelings." He groaned. "To think she has been shouldering this alone …"

Michael shook his head, running a hand through his hair. "My poor sister, not knowing whether to rejoice or despair at the news."

Ellie blushed deep crimson, then spoke up hesitantly. "Actually, it could not have been Ian's child."

Four pairs of eyes swiveled to look at her in surprise. Stephen's voice was hoarse. "What do you mean?" he grated out. "You saw the room ... saw her ..."

Ellie shook her head. "No, that is not what I meant," she elaborated. "I mean Lily ... Abigail ... the others." Her face was tight, but she forced herself to continue. "Once news came that Ian was dead, suddenly the stories began to be told. Ian was obsessed. He seduced any woman he could. He took several by force. The number of women he was with is staggering – but no woman ever got pregnant." She flushed. "He began to accuse them of losing the children deliberately. He became desperate; he chased after even more women to prove he could father a child." She shook her head again, looking down now. "But he never did. Not even once, in all that time."

Stephen let out his breath in relief. "Did Lucia know that?"

Ellie shook her head no. "We never discussed Ian at all, after she returned. There was no reason for me to think it would matter to her."

Michael pondered the news. "Now this all makes sense, but what are we to do? If we stop the battle now, we lose everything. The Grays will move and reinforce elsewhere. You and I *must* be on the road with our forces tomorrow. If we do not act quickly, we risk having Grays loose and active in the very area she is heading toward."

Stephen stood. "Then time is of the essence. Can I count on your help?"

The other three nodded their assent, and soon the quartet was heading north, spreading out, intent on searching every square mile possible in the short time they had.

* * *

The next morning at daybreak, with heavy hearts, the four led the troops from the keep. Michael rode alongside Stephen, the two men lost in their own thoughts.

Michael's voice was hoarse. "I did not really expect to find her," he admitted quietly. "She has been trained too well for that. In another month she will undoubtedly rejoin us, once the conflict has been resolved. I know my sister. It is the logical thing for her to do."

He paused for a moment. "If Lucia was not going to stay at Penrith, then perhaps she is actually safest on her own for now, hiding out far from the conflict. The best thing we can do is finish off the Grays as quickly as possible."

Stephen nodded, his eyes somber. Every beat of his heart sent a prayer out to Lucia, for her to stay hidden, stay safe, until he could make his way to her side.

Chapter 26

Lucia tested a piece of the rabbit that roasted over her fire. Not quite done, she decided, and went back to washing her clothes in the pond. The sun was up, and it was quite warm. After a month of settling into the routine, she was quite comfortable in this clearing she had discovered for herself.

She hung the last shirt on a tree branch and looked around her domain. She had initially settled on the spot because it was hard to find and easily defensible, but as the weeks went on, she had truly fallen in love with her little home. The trees and pond were quite lovely, and, perhaps most importantly, it was quiet and peaceful. The cave was warm and snug, and kept out the rain and wind. The pond attracted all sorts of forest creatures. Troy had plenty of grass to eat, and she had not gone hungry either.

She picked up her parchment scroll and read through the last entry, but put it down again without adding anything new. She wondered what had befallen Michael and Stephen. She assumed that in the past month they had reached Keilder and cleared out the Grays. Lucia knew the plans by heart - they had discussed them frequently on the trip back from Harwich.

Were they successful? At what cost? Even the best planned fights had, by their nature, many events that could not be anticipated.

She sighed and stood. She ran her hand over the soft rounding of her belly, and she grinned in delight. With no one to guide her, every new occurrence in this child's growth was exciting. She was almost four months along, and starting to show quite clearly. She knew enough to eat well, and to keep in shape. She rubbed her stomach, and took the rabbit off the fire. She ate the meal slowly, and afterwards settled down by the pond to sleep.

That evening clouds rolled in, and by the next day heavy rains pummeled the soft earth. There had been a number of rainstorms recently, and in boredom Lucia had taken to composing long letters to her unborn child. It seemed it was time for another one.

'This interminable rain has given me ample time to think,' she wrote, her pen making soft scratching noises in counterpoint to the thrumming of the rain outside. 'I look forward to returning home, to seeing Michael again. I find that I can even feel happy for Stephen and Anna, that they have worked out their differences. I worry that your presence will upset them, but perhaps they will come to love you as I do. I will wait another month, to be sure the conflict has been resolved before I venture back north again.'

Lucia sighed, and looked out at the curtain of rain which fell across the face of the cave. Troy nickered from the shelter of the trees where he made his home. She looked back to the worn scroll, lit by the small fire she kept going near the cave entrance. 'I must admit, if only in the solitude of these few words, how much I miss Stephen. I do not think I realized how much I enjoyed his constant presence during our trip to fetch my countrymen until I spent time alone here. During the intense turmoil which preceded the battle at Penrith it was easy to push off any loneliness. Here it is not quite so simple to find distraction. I see his eyes when I wake up in the morning. I hear his voice when I'm swimming in the pond. And at night ...'

She again paused, her pen hovering over the surface of the parchment.

'I do not want to impose myself on him, but to be near him would be enough. Maybe he would welcome me back simply as a friend. In a month I shall head up to Keilder. I will be with Michael, I will be near Stephen, or at least find out that he is unhurt. That will have to satisfy me.'

Troy whinnied, and Lucia quickly rolled up the parchment. Perhaps this feeling of unease was more than longing. She tucked her scroll into a niche next to the fire and, wrapping her cloak tightly about herself, walked out into the rain.

A single horseman stood in the rain next to her pool, looking about. Lucia's heart leapt.

Stephen! He had come looking for her!

Filling with joy, she ran quickly down the ledge around to the horse.

The rider turned at the sound, and Lucia pulled back in alarm. The man on the horse wasn't Stephen - he was a Gray! The Gray appeared surprised and pleased to see her. In shock, Lucia stumbled backwards. He was probably a scout, although she couldn't imagine what they were doing this far south. She turned to run, but more horsemen rode from the forest, cutting off her route back to the cave. A good-sized group of riders came into the clearing; there were about thirty in all. They looked tired and some were injured.

Lucia's mind raced over the possibilities as she quickly considered her options. They were injured. This must be the retreating force from Keilder. That battle was over, after all, and the Grays did not look victorious in the least. Lucia gasped quietly to herself. These were the defeated remnants of the army, on the run. Lucia took a step backwards. That would mean they were desperate.

The leader rode up beside her. He was a quiet, somber man of about thirty with a scar on one cheek. "Who might you be," he called down in a low voice, attempting to be soothing. "You might in fact be the one everyone is looking for."

A cry of triumph came from within the cave, and one of the soldiers emerged holding Lucia's sword and scabbard. "It is her, John," shouted the man enthusiastically, "We have got our hostage!"

A weary cheer went up amongst the men. "Search the cave," John ordered to two of his men. He then looked back down at Lucia, who stood in the middle of the group of men, watching for an opportunity to escape.

"My men are tired, but we will be pushing on to our camp," he informed her civilly. "I will be taking you with me. Things will go much easier for you if you don't fight. And in your condition..." he nodded suggestively at her stomach.

Lucia put her hands protectively over the small child growing within her. Apparently her state was common knowledge now. The soldiers tied a rope around Troy's neck, and she mounted him without a struggle.

The men returned from the cave with her extra clothes and blankets, but not, she noticed with satisfaction, her notes. Hopefully someone would discover them in the cave and realize what had happened.

Lucia was not so sure of herself when they left the clearing a little while later. The Grays had apparently learned some things since they first attacked, or maybe this group was different from the others she'd been encountering. To her surprise, the clearing was practically the way she found it by the time the Grays prepared to leave the area. She would have been lucky herself to find their tracks; she doubted anyone who was pursuing the group would be able to follow them, or, if they did, that they would stop to explore the cave along the way.

She sighed, riding on, allowing Troy to be led with the rest as they worked their way eastward through the forest. From what she heard from the conversation around her, the Grays had been all but wiped out in that final battle. The men around her, with twenty at the base camp a little ways ahead, were all that remained. It seemed they intended to negotiate a peace treaty, and to claim a small, remote section of land as their own. Lucia's own appearance had been fortuitous for them - now they had a hostage to trade.

To Lucia's surprise, John was quite solicitous to her, asking after her health and needs. They stopped frequently, with soldiers posted as guards around each location. While Lucia remained silent at their first stop, by the second, her curiosity got the better of her. "You are not what I expected," she commented quietly, looking over at John from where they sat.

John chuckled. "Maybe it is because our group is all that remains of the true cause," he replied bitterly. "As if anyone now remembers how this all began."

Lucia was intrigued. "Please, I am interested," she offered encouragingly. "How did this conflict really start?"

John shrugged. "I do not suppose it does any harm to discuss it at this point. There was a small village, Gosforth, where I lived with my parents and three older brothers. One night we were attacked, our village burned, our animals slaughtered. My oldest brother was killed. It looked like the work of bandits, but we found tokens in the ruins from the local noble family. The nobles of course tried to deny they had done it, but a well known soldier came in and convinced us otherwise."

He sighed and looked off into the distance. "My two remaining brothers went off with him, as did many of the other men. The ranks were swelled by hundreds of mercenaries, looking to take advantage of the looting opportunities. Each foray seemed to take the group further and further from home. Years passed with no resolution. Finally, those of us who remained defending our homelands - those you see around you here - banded together to see how the conflict was going. We arrived in camp a month ago to find all of our kin long since dead, and the mercenaries ..." John's face twisted into a grimace. "Let us just say that the original cause had been long since forgotten."

Lucia knew that she was the prisoner here, but she couldn't help but ask. "So why do you stay, then?"

John chuckled wryly. "Those mercenaries can be pretty persuasive," he responded shortly. "The conflict is almost over, and they are now promising us our fair share of the settlement. Given all we have lost, we felt another few weeks in order to see this come to an end was worth our time." He paused, and then added wryly, "Also, deserters have this nasty habit of showing up dead, not far from camp."

Lucia was silent, and was lost in her own thoughts for the rest of the day as they rode through the thick woods. As night approached, the forward scout gave a soft call, and Lucia saw they were approaching the encampment. They moved past a rough wood stake wall posted with fierce looking men every twenty feet. Within the wall lay perhaps sixty rough shacks in various states of disarray.

Once the group was inside the perimeter of guards, John helped Lucia down from her horse. "It is time for you to meet our leader," he remarked quietly. He looked as if he would say more, but sealed his mouth in a thin line. He escorted her toward a large building in the center of the compound. It was far better built and larger than any of the shacks around it. John motioned her inside, while he remained outside the door.

Lucia pushed aside the hanging skin which served as a door, and stood a moment inside as her eyes adjusted to the light. Her mouth dropped open in shock. Standing before her was the man who had betrayed her in her youth, who had turned against them and joined the enemy.

Evan.

His blond hair and striking good looks had only become more handsome as he had matured. His body was strong and toned. He wore a luxurious robe of rich red ermine over a long burgundy tunic.

"Ah, Lucia," greeted Evan evenly, smiling with cool superiority. "I heard we had managed to capture you. What a stroke of luck! They do not dare touch us while you are in our camp." He chuckled softly. "Come, have a seat next to me. You might as well make yourself comfortable; you will be here quite a while."

He gestured to a large, intricately cushioned chair which sat next to an ornately carved table. Lucia looked around the room - the furnishings were quite grand, nothing like the other shanties constructed around the area.

Evan nodded self-importantly at her gaze. "Only the best for the leader of the Grays," he asserted with pride. He turned to snarl at one of the rough-worn women cowering to the side. "Bring us some food, wench!" She scurried off, and Evan again smiled to Lucia, offering her a chair by his side.

Lucia eyed Evan warily. For all the years she had known him, she had never sensed this side of his personality. She wondered if he had always been like this, or if the intervening years had corrupted him. Evan's look turned sour as she did not obey his bidding quickly enough, and realizing that she should choose her battles wisely, she moved to comply. She sat slowly by his side, saying nothing. She remained motionless, her eyes searching his face, looking for any hint of the Evan she had known.

Evan also seemed lost in thought for a moment, and looked over Lucia with an unreadable expression. Then he gave a short laugh. "I heard you were with child," he snapped curtly, a sharp edge to his voice. "You did not pine away for me, then?" He barked with amusement and glanced around. "Well, no matter. I found everything I could want right here." The rag-wearing woman returned with two trenchers of food and placed them hesitantly on the table. Before she could leave again, Evan pulled her onto his lap and groped her chest. He laughed as she struggled, then threw her to the floor. She pulled her shirt together and ran out of the tent.

Evan laughed in delight at the shocked look on Lucia's face. "Too much for a mother-to-be?" he asked, grabbing a chicken leg off the table and gnawing at the bone. "You would not believe the life I am living here. I am a king! I am not just second fiddle like I would have been back in Keilder. To think your father offered me such a meager position, with the plans I had already made."

Lucia was shaken. Slowly an idea formed, and she paled. "You are the one who convinced the villagers to fight," she gasped, looking at Evan in growing horror. "You found a perfect excuse to attack the nobles in the area, to build your mercenary army. Then you wormed your way into my household to help plan your future expansions ..."

Evan's voice boomed as he gloated. "Of course!" he crowed, triumphantly. "All that time you were the upper class girl, deigning to be with a lowly boy like me. All that time, and I was preparing a conquest that would take you down. To think your family thought I would be happy joining you."

He leant forward, sneering at her. "In the end, your father begged me for peace. He pleaded for me to leave Keilder intact." He laughed. "I took off his head with one blow." He waved his hands expansively. "Now that I have you, your remaining family will come groveling to meet my demands."

Lucia's face was a mask of shock. Evan grinned widely and continued. "Who do you think planted those tokens in the village in the first place? Who do you think began the first fires? It has all been a carefully laid out plan, and it is finally coming to fruition. I am just so glad that you could be here, Lucia dear, to join me in my hour of triumph. It makes everything complete."

Lucia found herself standing before she realized she had moved. Her voice was the chill rasp of steel being drawn. Her body felt as taut as a drawn bow as she faced Evan. "I would rather die than help further your plans," she grated, her voice ice cold.

Evan sneered at her. "I know better than that," he snarled with sarcasm, dismissing her threats with a wave of his hand. "Would you kill your unborn child, too?" He shrugged, drawing his eyes down her body. "Who knows, maybe you would. You are carrying a bastard child of someone who obviously did not even care enough to give you a roof over your head. An unloved child of an honorless father."

Lucia's fury was barely held under the tightest of control. "I gave myself with love to my child's father," she vowed through clenched teeth. "I wonder if any woman who has been with you can say the same thing."

Lucia didn't even see the blow coming. One minute she was standing before Evan, his face contorting from shock to crimson fury. Then she was thrown through the air, landing hard on the table's edge with a horrifying crunch. Gasping, she rolled off to collapse in a heap on the floor.

Her abdomen billowed with jagged shards of pain.

Chapter 27

Evan was screaming, charging at Lucia, and all thought fled. She burst through the skin flap door and sprinted into the woods, the startled shouts of soldiers fading behind her. The harsh sound of metal on metal told her that at least one fight had begun. Maybe Evan's attack on her had been the final straw for his disgruntled men. She ran on, her blood pounding in her ears, her only thought on getting her and her child to safety. The trees streamed by in a tangle of shadow.

Suddenly a dark chasm yawned before her, and she tumbled to her knees, breathing in desperate gasps. She was at stone outcropping high over a turbulent river. There was perhaps a twenty-foot drop into the rapids, and the river coursed downstream at a fast pace. The full moonlight cast an eerie glow on the scene.

Shouts rang from far behind her, and she knew she did not have long.

Lucia dug into her bag and pulled out Stephen's ring. At least if someone found that, they would know she had been here. She pushed hard to regain her feet, then hung the ring on a small branch where it caught the light.

Then, taking one last look below her to find a spot that seemed clear of rocks, she jumped.

The impact of the water burst her breath from her lungs, and she frantically clawed her way toward the shimmering surface, high above her. Finally she breached to air and drew in a long, desperate breath. The river spun and twisted around her, and it was several seconds before she could gain her bearings. She strove to move further from the bank, to lessen the risk of hitting a rock or log.

Shouts became lost in the distance behind her. The bright moon lit her path. She concentrated on staying in the center of the rolling waters.

* * *

Stephen held his sword steadily at Evan's throat, Marcus and Shawn holding the man on either side. His voice was a low growl. "Where is she?"

A Gray ran into the room, his face tight with panic. His eyes swept, not to Evan, but to Stephen. "She's jumped into the river, trying to escape! I couldn't get to her in time!" His eyes flashed to Evan, and hot fury lit his eyes. "That monster betrayed us all. And then he threw Lucia into the table!"

Stephen turned back to Evan in a rage. "You bastard! I swear, if she or her child is injured -"

Evan's eyes widened, awareness flooding his face.

"You are her man?"

Evan snarled in fury, snatched the dagger from his hip, and dove toward Stephen's sword-arm. Stephen twisted to avoid the blow, and pressed his own sword forward.

Evan took the sword through his chest and fell back in shock. His body collapsed against the wall. He shook once, then was still.

The Gray barely spared a glance for his fallen leader. "Follow me!"

Stephen pulled his sword free and raced at his side toward the woods. His heart pounded in his chest with every foot-fall.

She could not be hurt. Not when he was so close.

A dark chasm loomed ahead, and he skidded to a stop. There was a glint of metal to the right, and he blinked in surprise. He knew that shape, knew every curve and facet. He grabbed the ring, slipped it on his finger, then turned back to the water.

He scanned the banks, hoping against hope that she was already to safety. Not seeing her on shore, he did not hesitate one moment more – he jumped from the rocks feet-first, plunging into the inky black water.

Stephen surfaced with a kick and immediately set off downstream with steady, sure strokes. He could barely see amongst the shadows and frothy mist.

What if she had slipped under already?

He shook his head in resolution. Not Lucia. She was hanging on somewhere. She was waiting for him – he could not fail her now. He lengthened his strokes, straining to look amongst the glistening rocks and twisting branches for a glimpse of her.

Long moments passed, and Stephen's heart pounded in desperation, his eyes scanning every inch of both banks as he went. The Gray had said the incident had only just happened. She could not have gotten far.

What if she had gone under?

He pushed the thought away with an angry shake. Lucia was a strong swimmer. She was in good health. She was a fighter. She was out there. He just had to find her.

His breath caught for a moment. There – downstream! He could make out a tree caught up in some rocks, with Lucia hanging on one end. His arms renewed their strokes, with every last ounce of strength propelling him forward.

* * *

A wet, misty, chaotic world surrounded Lucia. Her only thoughts involved her struggle to stay above the tugging water. She realized that her arm was bleeding. She wasn't sure if the injury came from her fight with Evan or as a result of her swimming. She tried to keep the arm out of the water, to lessen the loss of blood. Lucia clung to the fallen tree with all her might. The rough bark felt reassuring beneath her clammy hands.

She glanced around slowly - the spray from the rushing water reduced her vision to a hazy gray. Large branches prevented her from moving to shore, and she was afraid to let go, in case other branches would trap her beneath the tree. She hoped that by resting she would gain the strength to climb up out of the water and onto the ancient log.

A calm washed over her as she hung there, the minutes flowing by in smooth succession. Strangely, she wasn't cold any more. The ridges where she clung no longer hurt her fingers. The world faded, and her eyes seemed leaden. She flinched as another wave crashed noisily over her head. By comparison, the water beneath her seemed quiet, inviting.

She felt her hands slip, and involuntarily tightened them. She couldn't let go of the log - it was her only hope of staying above it all. But did she wish to remain afloat? The water and flotsam jumbled dangerously around her.

Her log shuddered as something heavy struck it, and her grip shifted yet again. Her cry and the other noises of the stream mingled into a single, wordless wail. Her fingers were slipping. Her world spun around her. Something tugged at her, and her focus shimmered away.

The gray waters faded to black.

Chapter 28

Lucia drifted into consciousness, her body a mass of sore muscles and throbbing aches. She stretched beneath the heavy, pungent-smelling blankets that covered her. Thoughts trickled slowly into focus.

Her baby.

Panic infused her. She moved a hand down to feel her belly. It was rounded as she had remembered it. Her arm was wrapped in a bandage, and she felt another bandage around her leg.

Lucia remembered the tug of the river, of her final yielding to its chill. She had obviously been pulled from the water ... but by whom? Where was she now? In another hideout of the Grays?

The room smelled musty but familiar. It seemed to be dimly lit. She opened her eyes cautiously, keeping her breathing even in case she was being guarded. The light from a single oil lamp on a table next to the bed illuminated the room, but kept most of it in shadows.

Her eyes swept the room, all other thought fleeing as relief swept over her, embracing her.

She was home.

Lucia closed her eyes again, tears welling within them. She hadn't realized how much she had missed this place, missed the friends and family it also held. She wanted to find Michael, to learn what had happened these past few months. To ask ...

She took a deep breath. She needed to know about Stephen, to learn the truth, whatever it might be. Lucia wiped her eyes on her blanket and took another deep breath. She did not want to wait a minute more to find out what was going on. She had to know now.

She reached to pull her covers off, then stifled a cry of pain. Her muscles were more sore than she could have thought possible. How long had she been lying here?

A well-worn chair sat next to her bed, with remnants of bread on a wooden platter. Someone had been keeping a vigil. A wooden recorder lay beside it, next to her journal. She smiled weakly - someone had found the scroll, after all. She remembered, as in a dream, the voices and songs in the darkness. She remembered straining toward them as the darkness tried to envelop her.

A noise outside her closed door made her turn. A young girl's voice - Ellie's, she thought with quiet pleasure - was talking to someone. "I know she has been unconscious for two weeks, but I would like to watch her, just in case..."

A muffled murmur answered her. Was that James? Ellie replied hesitantly, "All right ... but only for a little while. I would like to see the ceremony too." Two pairs of footsteps moved down the corridor and faded into silence.

Ceremony?

Was Michael being made Lord? Was ... she hesitated for a moment, then forced herself to think about it. Was Stephen marrying Anna? She wanted to know the truth, whatever it was. Misperceptions had caused enough problems in her past. She would rather face the reality, and go forward with her life. Her child was depending on her.

With determination, gritting her teeth against the pain, she sat up and pushed the covers off. In addition to the two bandaged areas, she saw she had bruises peppering her body. Her entire body ached. She was dressed in a long shirt and loose pants - her old sleepwear.

She crawled to the end of the bed and, leaning over, opened the wooden trunk at its foot. Her clothes were neatly folded within it. She pulled out a cobalt-blue dress from her time with Stephen. She glanced briefly at the blue uniform beneath it - and shook her head. She would show Stephen that she was here for him - if he would have her. If he had chosen another, then she would move on with her own life, and cherish her memories.

With a sense of strong determination driving her on, Lucia pulled on her clothes. Then she reached deep into the chest and warily took out the well-worn mirror that had been her mother's. She sat on the edge of the bed and brushed her hair out. She instinctively began to braid it, but then stopped to leave it loose, nodding as she did so.

Even if Stephen would not have her, she had been granted countless blessings. She was alive. She was home. Her child was safe.

She would treasure each gift.

Lucia was prepared for the weakness when she stood, and she gripped the edge of the bed, willing herself to remain upright. After a few moments the vertigo faded. The strength of finally being able to do something about her feelings sustained her where she might have fallen. She glanced around and pulled on the boots she found nearby. There was nothing else in the room she needed for now. Another wave of nausea hit her, and she staggered. She leaned against the frame of the door for a moment, then straightened.

Lucia pushed her door open and looked down the meandering corridor. It was deserted. Strange, no noise filtered down from the other rooms. Making her way slowly up the hallways, she found only flickering torches and empty rooms. Finally, she reached the small side entrance she had been aiming for, and poked her head outside into the courtyard, leaning on the wall for support.

The fortress entrance, built into the mountain, overlooked a large, enclosed, straw-strewn area which was surrounded by the town, and walls, of Keilder. The area was currently filled to the brim with people, animals, banners, and soldiers of all types. Lucia could make out most of Keilder's troops, many of Penrith's and other surrounding kingdoms. With shock and a fair amount of pleasure, she realized that even the villagers she had been captured by were well represented.

On a wooden platform in the center of the courtyard was a large table, with Michael, Stephen, Lord Edmund, and John standing behind it. John was putting his mark on a large piece of paper, and a cheer went up in the crowd. Michael let it go on for some time, then raised both his hands. The courtyard went quiet as he spoke.

"At last, we have peace. Not the peace of conqueror and defeated, but the peace of friendship and understanding, with the potential to last many lifetimes. It is time to put aside old grudges and wounds and embrace each other. To work together and grow to live and love together."

Michael let the cheer echo off the walls and mountains for a while. When the crowd settled again, he smiled broadly. "To begin this new era, and with her father's permission, I formally now ask Anna to be my wife and Lady." He offered his hand to Anna, and pulled her onto the platform amidst much cheering. Anna stood beside him, smiling and waving to the crowd.

Lucia sagged back against the frame, her mind whirling. It was Michael that had wanted to be with Anna? Is that what the announcement back at the great hall had meant? Her world spun as everything she had remembered about that time took on new meaning. She berated herself for being so unaware of what was going on, of jumping to such wrong conclusions. How could she have wound herself into such a state?

Slowly, turning those memories over in her mind, she smiled in understanding, and breathed deeply. How foolish she had been. To think that she had assumed so quickly, without any reason, that Stephen had turned away from her. If only she had waited, if only she had asked, if only she had given them more time.

Lucia pushed aside her regrets; that was in the past. It was time to think about the future. Anna would certainly be busy converting Keilder from a war fortress to the center of a new peace and culture. Lucia almost envied Anna's position - it seemed she now had everything she had ever dreamed of.

Michael gave Anna a tender kiss, then waved for the crowd to quiet. "Let us not forget," he added in a booming voice, "the many people who worked to make this peace possible. Stephen, my good friend, was instrumental in making this happen. We all owe him a large measure of thanks." He turned and clasped Stephen's arm in a firm hold.

The courtyard became quiet, but to Lucia it was as if all of the inhabitants faded away into shadows. Her attention became transfixed on Stephen's face as he moved to the front of the platform. She felt as if there were only her and Stephen, separated by a short distance in a large audience hall. Although he stood straight, his eyes were heavy with sadness, his forehead etched with lines of worry. She wanted to run to him and hold him, but her old doubts, nurtured for so long, clung to her tenaciously. She couldn't quite allow herself, after all this time, to believe her dreams might come true. What if, after all, he simply did not want her? What if, when she pledged herself to him, he refused her love? The conflicting emotions tore at her. She wanted to be with him, but she feared facing the rejection of all she'd hoped for. She forced herself to simply stay by the door, to listen to his words.

Stephen looked slowly across the assembly, and when he spoke his voice was rich with suffering. "Like many of you here, I have paid a high toll for living through this war. The woman most dear to me is near death. The life of our child, our tiny son or daughter, hangs by a thread." He paused for a moment, head lowered, and Lucia's eyes brimmed with tears, absorbing the fact that Stephen knew about the baby.

He found out I was pregnant - and he does not feel shame. The thought was almost overwhelming, and the relief that swept over her left her weak but happy. She wiped her tears away absently with her sleeve.

Stephen looked out again at the crowd, regaining his control. "The one woman I love, your Lady, lies grievously hurt in the fortress beyond. If I can have one thing, if there is indeed a debt owed me for the work I have done, I wish to have her returned to my side." He paused for a moment, and continued more softly, "For I know not what I will do without her."

Lucia caught her breath as the words rolled across the silent courtyard. Stephen's eyes, so dark and full of pain, filled her vision. That face she loved was wracked with suffering.

The emotion hit her with full force.

Stephen loved her.

She pulled herself up and walked unsteadily out onto the stone steps before her. Her voice rang out clearly into the silence that had settled over the gathering.

"I was never one to follow commands, my love." Lucia paused as Stephen's eyes raced to find her in the crowd, and she smiled tenderly. "This one I shall obey - with all my heart."

The crowd turned in murmuring excitement to look at the speaker, but Lucia saw only the brightening of Stephen's eyes, the look of surprise and joy on his face. A way parted easily in front of her as she went to the platform. Hands helped her climb the few steps, and then she was standing before him, still finding it hard to believe this was all real. Stephen took the few steps that separated them. His arms enfolded her in a tender embrace, pressing her tightly to him.

She closed her eyes, face against his chest.

She would never let him go.

Stephen's voice caught as he murmured, "Oh Lucia, Lucia - never doubt that I love you. Never." He looked down at her, his gaze glowing with pride.

Lucia gazed back up at him, feeling that this was almost too much to hope for. Tears filled her eyes. "I thought I had lost you."

Stephen gently kissed her on the forehead. "I will not risk having you torn from me again." He looked up, and glanced at Michael. Michael nodded, his gaze rich with joy.

Stephen turned and faced the crowd again, holding Lucia gently in his arms. "I have a question to ask afresh, in front of this whole assembly. With Michael's permission, will you marry me, Lucia of Keilder?"

He looked back down into her eyes, waiting for an answer.

The world fell away, and it was just his brown eyes watching over her, rich with love and fierce protectiveness.

All doubt fled, and she gave him a soft smile.

"I was yours when you nursed me through the fever, holding with determination onto the thin thread which was my life. I was yours when you held your anger, despite me driving you past all rational limits. I was yours when you stayed by my side, watching me slip away, willing to give me up if it meant I might heal."

His eyes shone, and he brought his hands before him. He eased the ring off his finger, and she held her hand out to his. The circle was warm from his body heat, and flame coursed through her as he settled it onto her finger.

She looked at it for a long moment, then brought her gaze back to meet his. Her voice rose, to carry across to the furthest reaches of the keep.

"I adore you with all my heart, my beloved, and I shall never leave your side again."

The courtyard echoed with cheers, reverberating up to the dark blue skies, skies the color of his gold-embroidered banner which fluttered proudly in the breeze. His eyes were warm on her, and then he drew her in, his heart-achingly tender kiss sending golden tendrils through every corner of her soul.

At long last, she knew what it was to be utterly whole.

Chapter 29

Three years later

Lucia looked around the courtyard with pride at the wealth of merchants who had come to participate in the first annual harvest festival. It seemed the entire region had poured in to support their efforts. She had seen weavers from Keswick, tinsmiths from Hartlepool, and were those fine bracelets really all the way from London?

Her heart swelled with joy. It was hard to believe that a scant three years ago the ground she stood on had contained only burnt-out husks of decaying buildings. Now a tall, proud keep stood at her back, those who had scattered were returning to their farmlands, and even the mill's wheel had been rebuilt.

Life was returning to the land.

A joyful laugh filled her ears, and she crouched down, swooping up young Naida in her arms. The girl's flowing hair was ringed with flowers, and Lucia smiled at Stephen. "I see Anna's been spoiling her again."

Stephen pressed a fond kiss to her cheek. "Anna and little Daisy both. The three have been nigh-inseparable since your brother's family came down to visit."

A clattering of hooves came through the main gates, and Stephen chuckled. "Our keep will be bursting at the seams if this continues. Anna will be thrilled. She loves to entertain."

Lucia gave his hand a squeeze. "I am just glad to have us all together. When the festival is over, and we settle in for the winter, I will be just as glad to enjoy the quiet again. You, me, and little Naida, curled up by the fire together. Safe in our home."

His eyes shone, and there was no need for words.

Naida stretched her arms to her father. "More sweets?"

He chuckled, drawing her in. "You want those lemon drops from that merchant from Bath, don't you."

She eagerly nodded.

He tweaked her chin. "Well, maybe just one more. It is a special festival, after all."

Lucia made a sweeping motion with her hand. "Go, have fun. I'll welcome our newest guests."

She walked over to the couple as they reined in their horses at the center of the courtyard. The young woman was tall, slender, with auburn hair to her waist. She was perhaps seventeen, if Lucia had to guess. The man was in leather armor and was a few years older, well muscled with short blond hair. Both wore swords at their hips.

The man dismounted and moved beneath the woman. There was something rich in the tenderness with which he took her hand; in the attentiveness as he helped her down from her steed. The emotion made Lucia glow with warmth.

She smiled as she drew up to them. "Welcome to my home. My name is Lucia. Let me guess. Newlyweds?"

The girl's face blazed into a rich blush, and she looked down. "No, no," she murmured. "Gabriel is my bodyguard. He keeps me safe and trains me in use of my sword." Her eyes rose to meet Lucia's. "My name is Constance."

Lucia chuckled. "I recognize that accent. The eastern coastline, am I right?" She looked again at the way Gabriel stood by Constance's side. The way his gaze took in all around them – and the way it softened when it came back to Constance.

An impetuous emotion nudged Lucia, and she added, "You know, having a husband who is talented with a sword can be a handy thing, along that coast. After all, with pirates –"

Constance nodded, her eyes coming up to meet Lucia's. Suddenly Lucia saw a strength within Constance – one which belied her young age.

Constance's voice was steady. "Those dangers are exactly why my father has betrothed me to a strong, older neighbor. A man with substantial forces at his call. When I come of age, in two years, we will be joined together. It is what must be done to secure the borders of our land. To keep our people safe."

A dark shadow moved past Gabriel's face and then was gone.

Lucia looked between them in growing understanding.

There was a soft buzzing at her hip, and she glanced down at the sword.

Suddenly it came back to her clearly, how she had been gifted that sword. It had seemed a lifetime ago that she had met Elizabeth and Richard in their columbine-adorned keep. What was it that Elizabeth had said?

Do not become too fond of Andetnes. When you have at last found contentment, there will be another whose fate balances on the point of a pin. You will know when it is right. And the sword will have a new mistress.

Lucia looked around her. At the homeland her beloved husband had risked his life to reclaim. At the sturdy keep which now kept them safe. She thought of the joy which her daughter, brother, and all the rest brought her.

Resolution filled her, and she smiled at her two guests.

"Constance and Gabriel, welcome to our home. Come inside and let me pour you some mead. I would like to hear all about your travels – and I believe I have something which now belongs to you."

The Sword of Glastonbury series continues with Book 4, *A Sense of Duty* –

http://www.amazon.com/Sense-Duty-Medieval-Romance-ebook/dp/B006M6Y9OO/

If you enjoyed *Believing Your Eyes*, please leave feedback on Amazon, Goodreads, and any other systems you use. Together we can help make a difference!

https://www.amazon.com/review/create-review?ie=UTF8&asin=B008RIBYTI#

Be sure to sign up for my free newsletter! You'll get alerts of free books, discounts, and new releases. I run my own newsletter server – nobody else will ever see your email address. I promise!

http://www.lisashea.com/lisabase/subscribe.html

Join my online groups to get news of free giveaways, upcoming stories, and fascinating trivia!

Facebook
https://www.facebook.com/LisaSheaAuthor

Twitter
https://twitter.com/LisaSheaAuthor

Google+
https://plus.google.com/+LisaSheaAuthor/posts

GoodReads
https://www.goodreads.com/lisashea/

Blog
http://www.lisashea.com/lisabase/blog/

Be sure to download all of my FREE books! Each of these is completely free and available on Kindle.

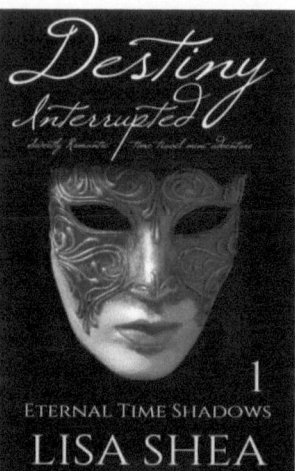

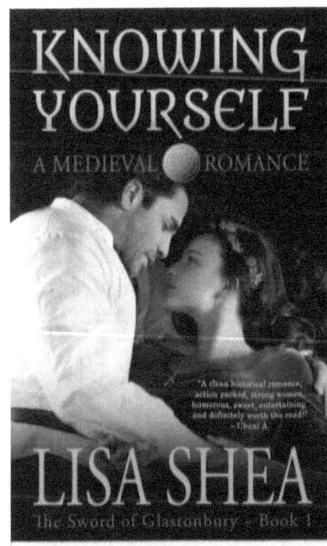

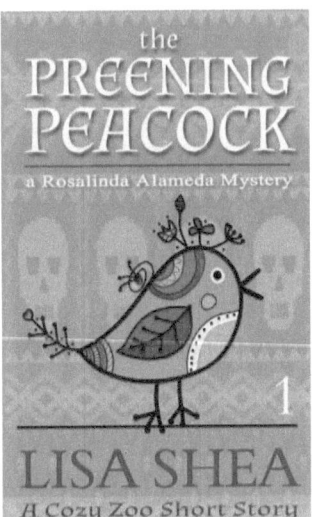

Medieval Dialogue

I've been fascinated by medieval languages since I was quite young. I grew up studying Spanish, English, and Latin, and loved the sound of reading Beowulf and the Canterbury Tales in their original languages. I adore the richness of medieval languages. How did medieval English people speak?

There are three aspects to this. The first is the difference between written records and spoken language. The second is the rich, multi-cultural aspect of medieval life. And the third is how to convey this to a modern-language audience.

Let's take the first. Sometimes modern people equate the way medieval folk would talk, hanging around a rustic tavern, with the way Chaucer wrote his famous *Canterbury Tales*. Something along the lines of this (note this is a modern translation, not the original Middle English version):

> *"Of weeping and wailing, care and other sorrow*
> *I know enough, at eventide and morrow,"*
> *The merchant said, "and so do many more*
> *Of married folk, I think, who this deplore,*
> *For well I know that it is so with me.*
> *I have a wife, the worst one that can be;*
> *For though the foul Fiend to her wedded were,*
> *She'd overmatch him, this I dare to swear."*

Sure, it seems elegant and rich. But did worn-down farmers sitting around a fireplace with mugs of ale really talk like this?

Do we think the London street-dwellers in the 1600s skulked down the dark alleys emoting like Shakespeare –

Two households, both alike in dignity

In fair Verona, where we lay our scene
From ancient grudge break to new mutiny
Where civil blood makes civil hands unclean.

And, in the 1920s in Vermont, did farmers really wander down their snowy lanes murmuring to their farming friends, a la Robert Frost:

Whose woods these are I think I know.
His house is in the village though;
He will not see me stopping here
To watch his woods fill up with snow.

As someone who lives in New England, I can pretty resolutely say "no" to that last one. And, given my research, I'm equally content saying "no" to the previous two. There is a big difference between poetry written with deliberate effort and the way "normal people" talked, flirted, cajoled, and laughed day in and day out. People simply did not talk in iambic pentameter. I'm a poet and even I don't talk in iambic pentameter :).

Modern people sometimes think of the medieval period in terms of the plays we see. We imagine actors on a stage, speaking in formal, stilted language, carefully moving from scene to scene. But medieval life wasn't like that. It was a rich cacophony of people struggling hard to survive amongst plagues and crusades, with strong pagan influences and the church trying to instill order. People fought off robbers and drove away wolves. They laughed and loved in multi-generational homes. It was a time of great flux.

England - A Melting Pot
England wasn't an isolated, walled-off island. It was continually experiencing influxes of new words and sounds. The Romans came and went. The Vikings came and went. The French invaded. Nearly all of the English men headed off to the Crusades, leaving behind women to gain strength and position. The men returned with even more languages. Pilgrims went to

Jerusalem. Merchants arrived from all over. This was a true melting pot.

So, in part because of this, Middle English was a rich, fascinating language. People in this time period had a wealth of contractions, nicknames, abbreviations, and combinations of words they used. Often people could speak multiple languages - their old English, the incoming Norman language, Latin from church, and random other words from tinkers, merchants, and pilgrims they encountered. Medieval people had all sorts of words for drinking, for fighting, for prostitutes, you name it. They had slang and shortcuts just like any other language does. After all, these are the people who turned "forecastle" (on a ship) to "foc's'le" and who pronounce the word "Worcester" as "Woostah."

But, here's the trick. With the medieval language being so rich, varied, intricate, and full of fascinating words, how can we bring that to life for a modern audience?

Centuries of Change

Let's start with a basic issue - most modern readers simply cannot understand authentic medieval dialogue. They don't have the grounding in Middle English, French, and Latin that would be required. Even the fairly straightforward, basic Chaucer works look like this:

And Saluces this noble contree highte.

Modern readers generally wouldn't know that "highte" meant "was called" as in "And Saluces this noble country was called."

This happens over and over again. Words change meaning. In the Middle Ages, if you *abandoned* your wife it means you subjugated her. You got her under your thumb. It didn't mean you left her - quite the opposite. Awful meant *awe-ful* - as in stunning and wonderful. It had a positive connotation. Fantastic wasn't great - it was a fantasy; something that didn't exist.

Nervous didn't mean worried or agitated - it meant strong and full of energy. Nice meant silly, and so on.

If a book was written with proper medieval words and meanings, first, even if the words are reasonably close to what we use now, modern readers would have to struggle with the spelling -

By that the Maunciple hadde his tale al ended,
The sonne fro the south lyne was descended
So lowe, that he nas nat to my sighte
Degrees nyne and twenty as in highte.

But, again, that is just the tip of the issue with medieval language. The word "bracelet" didn't exist until the 1400s. Necklace wasn't a word until 1590. The word "hug" wasn't around until the mid-1500s. We also didn't have the words tragedy, crisis, area, explain, fact, illicit, rogue, or even disagree! Shakespeare invented the words "baseless" and "dwindle" in the 1600s. Staircase is from 1620. A story written solely with words that existed in the year 1200 - and that still retain their modern meaning so modern readers could understand them - would be fairly basic.

(Speaking of which, the word "basic" didn't exist until the mid 1800s.)

Conversely, some words we might think of as thoroughly modern, like "puke", were also used in Shakespeare's time. "Booze" traces back to the 1500s. And these are just the proofs we have. While "shiner" for a black eye can be traced definitively to the 1700s, it could easily have been used for centuries before then and we just don't happen to have a letter or newspaper article which mentions it.

It's fair to say that people in medieval days did get black eyes and had a wealth of interesting terms for that situation. After all, it could be a rough life back then. Was one of the terms used "shiner"? Maybe, maybe not. Out of the ten fun phrases they used, probably nine of them would make zero sense to a modern reading audience. So authors strive to find phrases that provide meaning to a modern audience without being too *l33t* and techno-speak. It doesn't make sense to completely avoid the word "bracelet" simply because it technically didn't exist in the 1200s. Surely people in the 1200s had several words for "bracelet" and we are simply using the word modern readers understand. Similarly, people in medieval times hugged! They just called that action something else.

Medieval people loved playing with words. They called their kids "dillydowns" and "mitings" (little mites). They called sweethearts "my sweeting" and "my honey. They loved snapping out insults, from "dunce" to "idiot" to "pig filth" and "maggot pie." And, again, these are just the ones that happened to get recorded.

Medieval people loved contractions. There's a phrase "ne woot," meaning *knows not*. They'd simply say "noot". They did this with all sorts of words.

So writing in modern English should have this same sort of loose, fun sense to the writing. It's important to remember that even the kings, in this era, were rough fighters. They were out with soldiers, crossing multiple countries, and experiencing a range of languages. They weren't necessarily concerned about speaking in iambic pentameter. They were more concerned about breaking down their enemy's walls to plunder what lay within and then drinking themselves under the table to celebrate.

So, certainly, treasure the poetry and prose of the time. As a poet, I appreciate that immensely. But also keep in mind that people did not talk in poetry. They did not speak in fantasy-speak of *Lord of the Rings* or *Game of Thrones*. They talked and laughed, flirted and cursed, gossiped and cajoled in a rich, multi-lingual, contraction-filled, sobriquet-laden dialogue which mirrors how we talk in modern times.

About Medieval Life

When many of us think of medieval times, we bring to mind a drab reality-documentary image. We imagine people scrounging around in the mud, eating dirt. The people were under five feet tall and barely survived to age thirty. These poor, unfortunate souls had rotted teeth and never bathed.

Then you have the opposite, Hollywood Technicolor extreme. In the romantic version of medieval times, men were always strong and chivalrous. Women were dainty and sat around staring out the window all day, waiting for their knight to come riding in. Everybody wore purple robes or green tights.

The truth, of course, lies somewhere in the middle.

Living in Medieval Times

The years in the early medieval ages held a warm, pleasant climate. Crops grew exceedingly well, and there was plenty of food. As a result, their average height was on par with modern times. It's amazing how much nutrition influences our health!

The abundance of food also had an effect on the longevity of people. Chaucer (born 1340) lived to be 60. Petrarch (born 1304) died a day shy of 70. Eleanor of Aquitaine (born 1122) was 82 when she died. People could and did lead long lives. The average age of someone who survived childhood was 65.

What about their living conditions? The Romans adored baths and set up many in Britain. When they left, the natives could not keep them going, and it is true they then bathed less. However, by the Middle Ages, with the crusades and interaction with the Muslims, there was a renewed interest both in hygiene and medicine. Returning soldiers and those who took pilgrimages brought back with them an interest in regular bathing and cleanliness. This spread across the culture.

While people during other periods of English history ate poorly, often due to war conditions or climatic changes, the middle ages were a time of relative bounty. Villagers would grow fresh fruit and vegetables behind their homes, and had an

array of herbs for seasoning. The local baker would bake bread
for the village - most homes did not hold an oven, only an open
fire. Villagers had easy access to fish, chicken, geese, and eggs.
Pork was enjoyed at special meals like Easter.

Upper classes of course had a much wider range of foods -
all game animals (rabbits, deer, and so on) belonged to them.
The wealthy ate peacocks, veal, lamb, and even bear. Meals for
all classes could be flavorful and well enjoyed.

Medieval Relationships

Some movies present a skewed version of life in the Middle
Ages. They make it seem that women were meek, mild, and
obediently did whatever their father or husband commanded.

This was *far* from the truth!

Medieval times were times of immense change. Men were
off at the Crusades, leaving the women to run things.
Christianity was trying to get a foothold, but many areas of
Britain were still primarily pagan, with all the Goddess worship
and female empowerment which had been tradition for
centuries. The vast majority of brewers were female. Most
innkeepers were female. Women's knowledge about herbs,
health, and food was respected. Healthy women were treasured
as the key to a child-rich partnership.

Medieval life was heavily focused on fertility. Farm animals
had to be fertile in order to create meat to feed the family.
Women had to be fertile to create helpers for the farm and
household. Celebration after celebration in medieval times
focused on fertility. These people weren't shy about the topic.
They watched their horses, cows, and dogs continually engage
in these activities. Their festivals focused on the topic with
bawdy delight. Their songs lusted about it.

The church tried, again and again, to squelch this behavior
so that all aspects of relationships could be regulated by the
church. However, half of all medieval couples were together
outside of a church marriage and, for those sanctified by the
church, a large proportion were "sealing the deal" for a couple
already pregnant.

This was the way the medieval people looked at it: they needed to know their partner could create children. This was a key consideration for a relationship.

The Medieval period was far from an era of Victorian prudity. Quite the opposite. People of this era celebrated fertility, felt it was wholly natural, and even felt it was unhealthy for a man or woman to go for too long without sex. The celibacy would block critical flows of the body.

It was considered natural that a male noble might take on mistresses and that unmarried couples might seek out partners. It was the same as someone needing food if they were hungry. It was a bodily function which had to be tended to for the health of the person.

So where does marriage fit in with this mindset?

Medieval Marriage

In medieval times, marriage was primarily about inheritance. It was almost separate from sexuality. Sexuality was an important part of bodily health, like eating well and getting enough exercise. Marriage, on the other hand, was about ensuring one's lands and chattel were cared for from generation to generation. Sex, within a marriage, was focused on creating family-line children to then tend to that wealth.

For this reason, wealthy families would put immense energy into arranging optimal marriages for their children. This was about the transfer of land far more than a love match. Parents wanted to ensure their land went to a family worthy of ownership - one with the resources to defend it from attack. It was not only their own family members they were concerned with. Each block of land had on it both free men and serfs. These people all depended on the nobles – with their skill, connections, and soldiers – to keep them safe from bandits and harm.

That being said, both the woman and man would be consulted about the match. Their input was a critical aspect of the decision. Choices were often made with intricate selection processes. Keep in mind that the woman and her suitors would have been raised from birth to think of this process as natural. They would participate in that choice-making with an eye as to how it would secure the stability of their future family.

Yes, villagers sometimes married for love. Even a few nobles would run off and follow their hearts. Even so, they would have first seriously considered the potentially catastrophic risks which could result from their actions.

Here is a modern example. Imagine you took over the family business which employed a hundred loyal workers. Those workers depend on your careful guidance of the company to ensure the income for their families. You might dream about running off to Bermuda and drinking martinis. But would you just sell your company to any random investor who came along? Would you risk all of those peoples' lives, people who had served you loyally for decades, to satisfy a whim of pleasure? It is more likely that you would research your options, map out a plan, and made a choice with suited both you and your responsibilities.

Medieval Women

In pagan days women held many rights and responsibilities. During the crusades, especially, with many men off at war, women ran the taverns, made the ale, and ran the government. In later years, as men returned home and Christianity rose in power, women were relegated to a more subservient role.

Still, women in medieval times were not meek and mild. That stereotype came in with the Victorian era, many centuries later. Back in medieval days, women had to be hearty and hard working. There were fields to tend, homes to maintain, and children to raise!

Women strove to be as healthy as they could because they faced a serious threat - a fifth of all women died during or just after childbirth. The church said that childbirth was the "pain of Eve" and instructed women to bear it without medicine or follow-up care. Of course, midwives did their best to skirt these rules, but childbirth still took an immense toll.

Childhood was rough in the Middle Ages – only forty percent of children survived the gauntlet of illnesses to adulthood. A woman who reached her marriageable years was a sturdy woman indeed.

You can see why fertility was so important to medieval people!

To summarize, in medieval days a woman could live a long, happy life, even into her eighties – as long as she was of the sturdy stock that made it through the challenges of childhood. She would be expected to be fertile and to have multiple children, which again weeded out the weaker ones. This was very much a time of 'survival of the fittest.' Medieval life quickly separated out the weak and frail. Those women who ran that gauntlet and survived were respected for that strength and for their wisdom in many areas of life.

So medieval women were strong - very strong. They had to be. They were respected. Still, would they fight?

Women and Weapons
Queen Boudicia, from Norwalk, was born around AD60. She personally – and successfully - led her troops against the Roman Empire. She had been flogged - and her daughters raped - spurring her to revenge. She was extremely intelligent and quite strategic. Her daughters rode in her chariot at her side.

Eleanor of Aquitaine, born in 1122, was brilliant and married first to a King of France and then to a King of England. She went on the Second Crusades as the leader of her troops - reportedly riding bare-breasted as an Amazon. At times she marched with her troops far ahead of her husband. When she divorced the King of France, she immediately married Henry II, who she passionately adored. He was eleven years her junior. When things went sour, Eleanor separated from him and actively led revolts against him.

Many historical accounts talk of women taking up arms to defend their villages and towns. Women would not passively let their children be slain or their homes burned. They were able and strong bodied from their daily work. They were well skilled with farm implements and knives, and used them with great talent against invaders.

Many of these defenses were successful, and the victories were celebrated as brave and proper, rather than dismissed as an unusual act for a woman. A mother was expected to defend her brood and to keep her home safe, just as a wolf mother protects her cubs.

Numerous women took their martial skills to a higher level. In 1301 a group of Italian women joined up to fight the crusade against the Turks. In 1348 at a tournament there were at least thirty women who participated, dressed as men.

This is not as unusual as you might think. In medieval times, all adults carried a knife at their belt for daily use in eating, chores, and defense. All knew how to use it. Being strong and safe was a necessary part of daily life.

Here is an interesting comparison. In modern times most women know how to drive, but few choose to invest themselves in the time and training to become race car drivers. In medieval times, most women knew how to defend themselves with a weapon. They had to. Few, though, actively sought the training to be swordswomen. Still, these women did exist, and did thrive as valued members of their communities.

So women in medieval times were far from shrinking violets. They were not mud-encrusted wretches huddling in straw huts. They were not pale damsels locked away in towers. They were strong, sturdy, and well versed in the use of knives. Many ran taverns, and most handled the brewing of ale. Those who made it through childhood and childbirth could expect to enjoy long, rich lives.

I hope you enjoy my tales of authentic, inspiring heroines!

Glossary

Ale - A style of beer which is made from barley and does not use hops. Ale was the common drink in medieval days. In the 1300s, 92% of brewers were female, and the women were known as "alewives". It was common for a tavern to be run by a widow and her children.

Blade - The metal slicing part of the sword.

Chemise - In medieval days, most people had only a few outfits. They would not want to wash their heavy main dress every time they wore it, just as in modern times we don't wash our jackets after each wearing. In order to keep the sweaty skin away from the dress, women wore a light, white under-dress which could then be washed more regularly. This was often slept in as well.

Drinking - In general, medieval sanitation was not great. People who drank milk had to drink it "raw" - pasteurization was not well known before the 1700s. Water was often unsafe to drink. For these reasons, all ages of medieval folk drank liquid with alcohol in it. The alcohol served as a natural sanitizer. This was even true as recently as colonial American times.

God's Teeth / God's Blood – Common oaths in the middle ages.

Grip - The part of the sword one holds, usually wrapped in leather or another substance to keep it firmly in the wielder's hand.

Guard - The crossed top of the sword's hilt which keeps the enemy's sword from sliding down and chopping off the wielder's fingers.

Hilt - The entire handle part of the sword; everything that is not blade.

Mead - A fermented beverage made from honey. Mead has been enjoyed for thousands of years and is mentioned in Beowulf.

Pommel - The bottom end of the sword, where the hilt ends.

Tip - The very end of the sword

Wolf's Head – a term for a bandit. The Latin legal term *caput gerat lupinum* meant they could be hunted and killed as legally as any dangerous wolf or wild animal that threatened the area.

Parts of a Sword

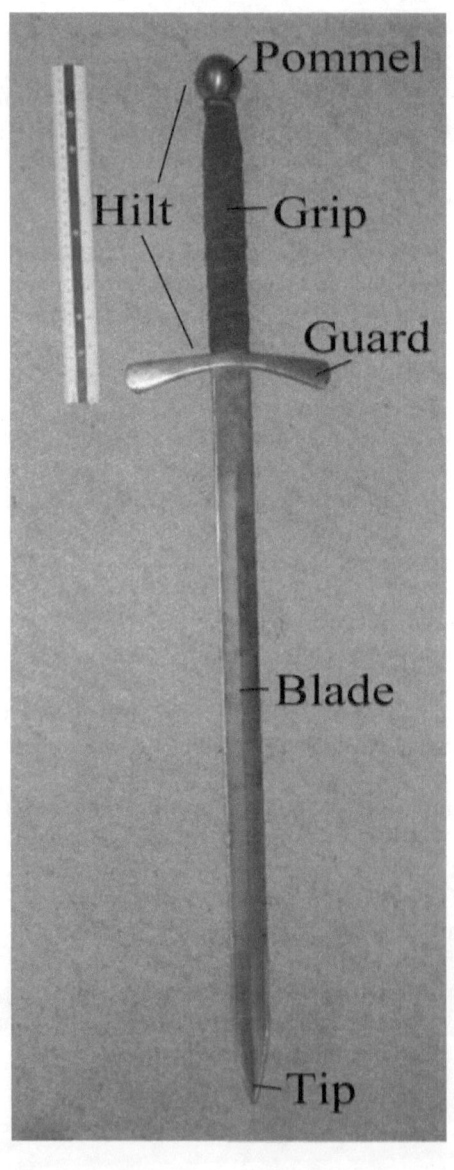

Medieval Clothing

Medieval people - despite modern stereotypes - did have noses and did like to stay clean. Public baths were popular, and people liked to swim as well. However, they did not have the luxury of bathing daily. Also, in medieval times people were often cold. Castles were damp and drafty. Fireplaces were not kept blazingly hot all night long. There is a reason that people wore many heavy layers including cloaks. That way they could add or remove layers as necessary to keep warm.

The basic under-layer was a chemise. This thin nightgown would be worn at night as well as during the day. Because it was against the body it kept the actual clothes clean from sweat. That way you could wash the chemise regularly and not have to wash your actual dress every day. Think of it like when you wear a turtleneck and a wool sweater. At the end of the day you would wash the turtleneck, but you would not wash the wool sweater after every wearing. If you wear a t-shirt under a jacket, you would toss the t-shirt into the washing machine but just hang the jacket on a hook again. The same is true for medieval outfits. The inner layer would be washed, while the other layer would be reused multiple days before it had to be washed.

The chemise was generally not meant to be seen, especially in colder months. It was underwear. There would always be an over-dress with a floor-length hem on top of that. Perhaps a glimpse of the chemise would show at the neckline or at the end-of-sleeve area. In hotter months the chemise might be more visible as the outer dress had short sleeves or no sleeves.

Men would typically wear a tunic over leggings. Men working in summer heat would sometimes wear simple linen "shorts" without anything else. Their chest and lower legs would be bare. This is a stark difference from how covered up women would be.

Both sexes would wear boots or shoes. There was no "left" or "right" - both halves would be made in the same oval shape.

Cloaks would be worn when going out into poor weather, to help keep you warm. These cloaks could be quite heavy if they were full circle cloaks, and incredibly warm.

Monks would wear similar clothing to non-religious men, but the monk's hair would be cut short and have a "tonsure" - or bald spot - shaved out of its center. The tonsure was a sign of their humility.

This illuminated image is from a 12th century manuscript at the library at Cambridge University.

Women's Clothing

A number of readers had specific questions about women's medieval clothing so I created this page with those specific details. To illustrate it, I have included a drawing done by Andreas Muller, a famous German artist known for his work restoring ancient paintings. This drawing was published back in 1861, so it's now out of copyright. As you might expect the drawing shows German people, not English, but the fashions are from the 1200s and are quite similar in style.

So, the basics. Women wore at least two layers of long dress. The bottom layer, or "chemise," was often plain white but could be fancier with nobles. This was what was against the skin, got sweaty, and would be washed. The chemise was often slept in, again especially if the person was poor.

The outer layer, what we would call the "dress," was the prettier layer. This would have the nicer stitching and designs. It could have embroidery or different fabrics stitched together to create designs. The outer dress could have long sleeves, short sleeves, or no sleeves, depending on how hot the weather was. In general, though, a woman's arms and legs were covered by the inner chemise and perhaps also by the outer dress as well. Women in medieval times did not tend to show skin from those parts of the body.

You might see images on the web with medieval women wearing long "trumpet" sleeves which made housework impractical. These were sometimes worn by French nobles who were showing off that they did not have to do menial labor. They were not a normal fashion in England or most other areas.

By the same token, women who had to work hard would wear shorter dresses - ending above the ankle rather than dragging on the floor. That was so their dresses did not catch or drag while they went about their work. Noblewomen who had a quiet day planned or a formal event would wear longer, floor-dragging dresses. These subtle differences helped to show off their status.

If it got even colder women would wear cloaks. These range from light, like the woman in the middle is wearing here, to heavy and full-circle, which could be amazingly warm. I have one of those.

Here is an illuminated image done between 1285 and 1292 which shows the famous poet Marie de France. Marie primarily wrote between 1160 to 1190 and was well known by nobility in France and England. Again, you can see how her outer long dress goes to the floor and the inner dress is visible at the arms. This copyright-free image comes via the National Library of France.

Women had an immense array of colorful dyes to choose from, some more expensive, some less expensive. So clothing could be quite bright and cheery. Just as in modern times, practicality had an aspect here. If someone was going to work in the pig pen all day long they'd probably wear something brown and old. If they were going to church they'd wear their best outfit they had.

In modern times we can sometimes think of dresses as "fancy" items we wear to "dress up" that are hard to move in. In medieval times, a dress was normal and natural! These were the outfits they wore every single day. Women made their dresses so they could do all their normal activities in them. To them a dress was like our modern t-shirt and sweatpants. So they're no question about "could they do chores in a dress" or "could they ride a horse in a dress." Of course they could - that's what the clothing was made for. Medieval women didn't generally hide out in tower rooms. Noblewomen would do archery and horseback riding for fun. Working women would scythe hay, ride to the market, and do a myriad of other chores in their dresses. It was what one wore. So those outfits absolutely were made to easily let them do those tasks. Dresses were loose to allow all of that. Women didn't ride side-saddle in medieval days - they simply put their legs on either side for stability. And their clothing was made for that. To ride, a woman could either tuck the skirt beneath her, like when one sits on a chair, or let it flow behind her. Either way works!

In terms of underclothes, most medieval women did not wear a bra. Their simple, straight dresses were meant to keep the body hidden rather than emphasized. A large breasted woman might wear a "binder" to keep the breasts from jiggling around while they tried to work. Current thought is that women didn't wear "underwear" (underpants) either. With their long multi-layer dresses it would be a challenge for underwear-wearing women to go to the bathroom. Instead, they would just move to a section of the field, fluff out their dresses, and go. Then they could get back to work. The same in the outhouses.

Even during the time of their periods, many researchers feel that the philosophy of the time was that binding or constricting a woman's flow would damage her fertility. So she simply bled into her underdress and that was washed. This free-flow practice continued long after medieval times. It was mentioned in doctors' journals in the 1800s. Even as recent as the 1900s there were cotton mills in the United States that had straw-strewn floors to absorb female workers' blood, so again this was not a short-term trend. And given that tampons can cause toxic shock syndrome, maybe those medieval women knew what they were doing :).

Let me know if you have any other questions about medieval women's clothing! I have a library of books here to help with research.

Dedication

To my mom, dad, siblings, and family members who encouraged me to indulge myself in medieval fantasies. I spent many long car rides creating epic tales of sword-wielding heroines and the strong men who stood by their sides. Jenn, Uncle Blake, and Dad were awesome proofers.

To Peter and Elizabeth May, who patiently toured me around England, Scotland, and France on three separate occasions. Elizabeth offered valuable tips on creating authentic scenes. Visiting the Berkhamsted motte and bailey was priceless.

To Jody, Leslie, Liz, Sarah, and Jenny, my friends who enjoy my eclectic ways and provide great suggestions. Becky was my first ever web-fan and her enthusiasm kept me going!

To the editors at BellaOnline, who inspire me daily to reach for my dreams and to aim for the stars. Lisa, Cheryll, Jeanne, Lizzie, Moe, Terrie, Ian, and Jilly provided insightful feedback to help my polishing efforts.

To the Massachusetts Mensa Writing Group for their feedback and enthusiastic support. Lynn, Tom, Ruth, Carmen, Al, and Dean all offered detailed, helpful advice!

To the Geek Girls, with their unflagging support for my expanding list of projects and enterprises. Debi's design talents are amazing. I simply adore the covers she created for me.

To the Academy of Knightly Arts for several years of in-depth training and combat experience with medieval swords and knives. I loved sparring with Nikki and Jo-Ann!

To B&R Stables who renewed my love of horseback riding and quiet forest trails.

To my son, James, whose insights into psychology help ground my characters in authentic behavior.

To Bob See, my partner in love for over 19 years and counting. He enthusiastically supports all of my new projects.

About the Author

Lisa Shea is a fervent fan of honor, loyalty, and chivalry. She brings to life worlds where men and women stand shoulder to shoulder, steady in their desire to make the world a better place for all. While her medieval heroines often wield a sword, they equally value the skilled use of their intelligence, wisdom, courage, and compassion.

Lisa has studied the Middle Ages since she was quite young. She has trained in medieval swordfighting for several years. She studied medieval dance and music with the SCA. She has been to England numerous times and loves exploring old castles and churches.

Please visit Lisa at LisaShea.com to learn more about her background and interests. Feedback is always appreciated!

As a special treat, as a warm thank-you for reading this book and supporting the cause of battered women, here's a sneak peek at the first chapter of *A Sense of Duty*.

A Sense of Duty Chapter 1

England, 1185

I wish I had been the wife of a better man,
someone alive to outrage the withering scorn of men.
-- Helen in the Iliad by Homer

Constance stood motionless on the rocky beach, gazing out at the rolling ocean waves with slowly growing acceptance. Today had been the most joyful day of her life ... now it would become the most painful. She spared one last glance for the parchment scroll held in her hand, then deftly rolled it up and tucked it into a small leather bag at her belt. A seabird soared far above, wingtips outstretched, drifting easily on the wind currents, but otherwise she was alone. She had walked a distance from town before reading the missive from her parents. She'd had a foreboding of what the note would say; she had wanted time to absorb the message alone, unwatched.

Footsteps sounded on the gravel, and her heart leapt with welcome recognition. Gabriel, her personal guard for the past five years, strode steadily down the beach toward her. His short blond hair, chiseled face, and muscular, lean build were all as familiar to her as the sharp tang of salt in the brisk air. She had seen those dark blue eyes sparkle with laughter at a shared joke, had watched them narrow with displeasure at any perceived slight to his lady.

Constance had grown up around guards, spent her childhood with swords and shields a part of her daily life. Even so, when Gabriel had been hired by her protective parents, her world had changed instantly. Where others had treated her as a porcelain vase, working to keep her safe from all dangers, Gabriel had insisted she learn how to face and conquer threats. She had gone from a cautious girl of fourteen to a self-assured, confident adult. She knew she owed much of that transformation to his diligent efforts.

Gabriel smiled as he came up behind her, drawing his long, woolen, full-circle cloak around her snugly to shield her from the brisk autumn wind. An absolute sense of peace and calm filled her as the folds enveloped her. She was in the most beautiful place on earth. The man she loved cradled her in a protective embrace. If only she could stop time, preserving this moment for an eternity.

A tear slipped down her cheek, and she turned her head to nestle against his chest. The wind blew her long, tawny hair across her face in waves, and he gently lowered a hand to brush them aside. Glancing more closely, he cupped his fingers beneath her chin, raising her eyes to his.

"My darling, what is it?" he asked quietly.

Constance smiled wryly. She would not spoil this moment for the world. "I am just so happy," she replied, admitting only half the truth.

His arms wrapped more tightly around her, and she sighed as he lowered his head, pressing his lips gently to her forehead. The cloak sheltered them there for over an hour, the waves on the beach flowing and ebbing in quiet harmony.

Finally the setting sun caused the sky to redden and mist. Reluctantly, Constance slipped free from Gabriel's cocoon and walked alongside him back toward the village, her protector's hand resting lightly on his sword's hilt. They climbed a short, grassy hill, then moved across a heather-thatched meadow. There was no need for words;

over the years they had become comfortable with silence, with simply being together. He took her hand in his as she passed over a stile in the fence, and the touch was familiar, natural. Even so, every time her fingers met his it sent a new thrill through her body.

She shook the grass and sand from the bottom of her sea-blue dress as they moved on to the packed dirt roads of the village proper, heading toward the small tavern at the town's edge. The building was well kept and neat, with a wooden sign shaped like a copper kettle hanging above the entrance. Gabriel pushed the sturdy door open for her, standing aside to let her in before following behind.

"Gabe! Constance! Welcome back!" called out the portly innkeeper with delight, coming over to clasp Gabriel's hand firmly.

"Pete, always a pleasure," greeted Gabriel with a grin.

"Here, let me bring you to your table." The owner led the pair through the half-empty room over to a small oak round, tucked in a back corner, flanked by a pair of simple wooden chairs. He gave the table a once-over with the cloth from his waist, then went to fetch a pair of tankards of ale for the couple. Pete was back in moments with the fare, then moved on to help another patron.

Constance chuckled as she sipped the proffered drink, looking at the back of the friendly owner. "I swear, you must know every tavern keeper from London to Portsmouth," she offered with a shake of the head. "However do you do it?"

Gabriel gave her a wry smile. "You know I do not reveal my secrets," he rebuffed her with a wink. "Still, keep it in mind if you are ever in trouble. Just leave word at the nearest pub and the news will get to me in a flash."

Constance did laugh at this. "Good to know," she agreed with a toast in his direction. "I will make sure to remember that."

Gabriel took another sip, scanning the room briefly with a sharp eye, nodding to a pair of men who sat by the fire in matching yellow on white tunics. Satisfied with what he saw, he leant forward and lowered his voice. "So, was there anything interesting in that letter from your parents? I take it they want you to come back home from visiting your aunt, since they sent those two with the note and not simply one of the messengers. You have been out here only two weeks – I thought you meant to stay for longer?"

Constance looked down at the worn table. She evaded the answer deliberately, wondering how long she could delay the revelation. With an effort, she kept the tone of her voice light and playful. "I know being here is a welcome vacation for us both - but also difficult for you since I spend all day with Silvia at the nunnery. Few men are allowed within those walls." Her mouth quirked into a smile. "Still, I do enjoy staying with her, assisting her with her daily tasks. She has always been so good to me, and I am immensely curious about her way of life."

Gabriel chuckled softly. "Maybe your parents thought you were becoming *too* curious, and that is why they are bringing you back," he agreed with a grin.

Constance continued to gaze down at the table, taking one of his hands within her own. She ran a finger over the bronze ring he wore on his little finger. The band's face held an engraved cross. She knew Gabriel had been given this ring in the holy land by his mentor, Sir Templeton, the man who had raised him after his parents had died.

Constance wondered again just what atrocities Gabriel had witnessed during his years of service in the Crusades.

There were times she caught him at an unguarded moment, when his look was shadowed and lost. She wished there was a way to keep this fresh pain from him.

She took in a long, deep breath, and then let it out in a smooth rush. She could not dodge the issue any longer. Her voice came out low and flat, lifeless.

"I am to marry Barnard in one week."

There was complete silence, and after a moment Constance glanced up. Gabriel sat in shocked surprise, his drink halfway to his mouth. Slowly, carefully, he lowered his mug to the table.

"You cannot be serious. Your wedding will not be held for another year at least. Barnard had agreed to wait until you turned twenty-one." His eyes searched hers, the color draining from his face. "We have another year ..."

Constance shook her head slowly. "You know what the fighting has been like with the bandits. My father needs Barnard's troops to man the Beadnell lands." Her voice fell into the rhythm of a catechism long recited. "However, to let Barnard's forces move in without legal protection of my family's rights would be suicide. Father needs the marriage to guarantee that our family has some control over that land – through me." Her voice dropped to a whisper. "Through my children."

Gabriel let out a low growl. "The man is twenty years older than you are," he shot out. "He is a coward, a weakling. How could you go to him?"

Constance lowered her eyes. They had gone over this ground countless times over the years, argued about it, talked about it, and it was a situation they had never found agreement on.

"Barnard has waited these ten years for me, since the engagement was first made," she pointed out quietly. "He has been more than patient. The need is upon us, and I will do what I must to keep our people safe."

"You do not have to do what your father orders!" bit out Gabriel, his voice a plea. "There are other options!"

Constance sat back in her chair. "You know full well that I agree with this marriage," she sighed. "Not for me personally, but for all those innocents in the Beadnell area. As a noble I have a responsibility to keep the people on our holdings safe. It is the legacy I will pass down to future generations." Her eyes grew fierce. "I will not neglect that duty due to cowardice or personal selfishness."

Gabriel's voice was hoarse. "And so you would go to that sickly, grey-haired neighbor of yours …" His knuckles went white on the mug still in his grasp. "Constance, you will wither in that home. I cannot sit back and …"

Constance felt the fear grow within her at the prospect of decades of loneliness. She fought it off with familiar effort. "I can handle any personal pain for the sake of those families and children who are at the bandits' mercy."

Gabriel leant forward. "Yes, of course," he agreed tightly, "it is about safeguarding the innocents. If your aim is to protect the defenseless villagers, surely there is another way. One that does not involve you selling your soul …"

Her gaze did not waver. "You know there is not. Could you protect that large area of land on your own? Even my father's forces cannot manage that. No, we need Barnard and the trained soldiers he has at the ready. This is the path I must take, and I am set on it."

Gabriel's eyes became distant, and long moments passed.

"I am lost," he finally stated. "I shall never love another. I shall wait for you to come to your senses, or for him to leave you a widow."

Constance wavered as all color drained from her world. It was one thing for her to consign herself to a loveless, lifeless marriage. She had long since reconciled herself to that fate, and was determined to make the best of it. Her long talks with Silvia had given her guidance on how to find comfort in quiet routine. After all, many girls and women deliberately entered the far more restrictive walls of the nunnery in order to escape life's troubles.

Still, could she doom Gabriel to a miserable existence? Not Gabriel, not the man whose strong arms had protected her for so long, whose sharp eyes could spot danger from a mile away. Not the man who shared walks along the beach during golden-hued afternoons and held her close when ink-black storms hammered the keep's walls. This man deserved to love, to live, to glory in his strengths. Somewhere out there was a woman free to give him the comforts and consolations she could not. He was only twenty-five. His entire life stretched out before him, full of potential, open to all possibilities.

She loved him far too much to deny him that life.

She began to speak, but her throat closed up. She took in a long, deep breath, then let it out again slowly. A second try, and she still could not say a word.

Finally, she took up her tankard and swallowed the ale down in one long draw, pulling strength from the rich brew. When she was done, she put the empty mug solidly down on the table and looked up at the man she loved. She spewed the words out in a rush, knowing if she stopped she would never get through it.

"I will never go to you, Gabriel. You are my guard, and it has been an amusing few years. Now it is time for me to marry, and I must have a real noble as a husband. I need a title for my children, and a fine house to raise them in. Surely you knew this."

Gabriel stared at her for a long moment, stunned. Constance struggled to keep her face still, to keep even the slightest hint of emotion from her demeanor. She nearly broke from the effort, but she held firm.

Then he was standing, his gaze cold, distant. He straightened, turned, and walked toward the door. He did not look back as he strode through the archway and out of her life.

Here's where to read Constance's full story!

http://www.amazon.com/Sense-Duty-Medieval-Romance-ebook/dp/B006M6Y9OO/

* 9 7 8 0 9 7 9 8 3 7 7 1 5 *